Mary Ellen & Dub
Very special friends

# WARRING

## EDWARD WOMACK



COLD RIVER STUDIO
NASHVILLE, TENNESSEE

*Published by Cold River Studio, Nashville, Tennessee*



*First Edition: 2012*



*Printed in the United States of America*
*ISBN 978-0-9848044-5-0*

*To Tish, my rock.*

# Table of Contents

**PART 3:** *Attack*

# WARRING

# PREFACE

*To Frank and Mary Warring*
*1702 Highland Avenue*
*Knoxville, Tennessee*

*Thursday December 4, 1941*

*Dear Mom and Dad,*

*Let me try and bring you up to date from my last phone call on the Friday after Thanksgiving, the 28th I think it was. After Ellen died in the hospital on Friday she was taken to the Norris Funeral Home in Frankfort where I had to go the next day and pick out a casket. Eloise Kostigan went with me to help and I don't think I could have gotten through it without her. You may remember Eloise lives with her family around the corner on the Georgetown road. Eloise and her family kept Teddy during those last days when Ellen developed the infection while she was still here at the house.*

*When Eloise and I got to the funeral home the thought of Ellen in a casket in the cold, wet ground was almost too much for me to bear. I was in a state of shock, I am sure. But Eloise helped and I did make a selection and then I called Everett in Carrolton and he was very composed considering the circumstances. Since Ellen was Everett and Thelma's only daughter her sudden loss must have hurt him to the core, but he soldiered on and made arrangements for Ellen's service at the Presbyterian Church on Tuesday, December 2 and the cemetery burial immediately after. As Eloise and I left the funeral home it started to rain and turned colder. By nightfall it was sleeting with ice covering everything. Then sometime during the night it started to snow hard on top of the ice, it was just one of those freak early winter storms. I was able to get a call through to Everett about noon on Sunday and he said he had borrowed a truck with chains on the tires and despite the snow he was coming for his little girl. That's when he broke down on the phone and cried like a baby. I could hear Thelma in the background crying like her heart was broken. So sad for everybody.*

*It turns out that the snow stopped about the time he left Carrolton early Monday morning and he drove on down to Frankfort about 45 miles. Teddy and I managed to get a ride into town in the Vaughn's truck and we met Everett at the funeral home and they loaded the casket onto the truck and Everett, Teddy and I rode in the truck and started driving back north on Highway 355 along the Kentucky River. The chains worked well and the snow acted as a cushion on top of the ice that kept us on the pavement except for a couple of times we went in the ditch but we always got out. It was a very strange drive, very quiet and it was like the snow had laid down a thick carpet of pure white for Ellen, almost like the heavens had wept for her and covered the ground in white to honor her passing.*

*I can't tell you how sorry I am that both of you couldn't drive up because of the weather. Teddy and I really, really needed you, but I know it was only the weather that kept us apart. Even without the bad weather it's a day-long trip from Knoxville to Frankfort but with the snow it was absolutely impossible.*

*We had the service on Tuesday at 10:00 and many people in Carrolton walked through the deep snow to get to the church. Teddy did well except when we sang the words to Amazing Grace and he cried and I held him tightly and I could not sing either. It was so sad, so sad. Everyone was very nice after the service, but since I did not know them I began to feel very numb and could not respond, what could I say, how could I say good bye to my love of eleven years? How could I tell these strangers how I felt? I couldn't.*

*Despite the snow, the Reed's house was loaded with food as neighbors all remembered Ellen growing up and they knew how Thelma and Everett were grieving so they brought food. On Wednesday Thelma said she wanted to keep Teddy and care for him, but despite the fact she was an emotional wreck and could not care for him, I just could not entertain the thought of leaving him there. She was trying to help and to hold onto whatever she could of Ellen, but I couldn't leave Teddy.*

*Everett drove us home in the same truck Wednesday afternoon and we went in the ditch again as the snow was starting to melt. We needed a farm tractor this time to get us out and back on the road. I'm really having trouble putting these events in writing in this letter. Somehow when I see the words in black and white on paper they have a degree of finality and nothing last week or this week seems final or real , but I will keep trying. I have to make some decisions for Teddy and me. I will call you on Saturday and talk about my dilemma. Since that's two days away I hope you get this letter before I call, but nonetheless, I will call. I am thinking about coming to Knoxville and giving up this house at the Forks. We have nothing left at the Forks and the memory of Ellen is so full here I can't think of staying here without her.*

*I just can't imagine the changes that November has brought to our little family. At the beginning of the month I was worried about the world situation with Hitler storming around Europe and Japan around the Pacific. I was sure war was going to break out then I lost my job at the distillery and that was all I thought of and especially how I would care for Ellen and Teddy and the new baby. Then the bottom fell out of everything when she died and we lost the baby as well. It was a boy. We decided if the baby was a boy we would name him David, so David Everett Warring died a day before his mother. Looking back I guess we made a mistake by trying to have the baby at home like she did with Teddy. Now as I write these words it's like being trapped at the bottom of a well with no glimpse of daylight above, just being hopelessly lost.*

*Your Loving and Obedient Son,*
*Frank*

Frank tried to read the letter again, but couldn't. He sealed the envelope and he and Teddy walked the half mile to the post office along the road to Switzer. The snow, still deep, was melting fast in the 45 degree temperature and bright sunshine; father and son both wore rubber galoshes as they trudged through the melting slop. Supper that night would be from the food brought back from Carrolton at Thelma's insistence. There was ample food to get them through the approaching weekend; the weekend that would shake the foundation of the entire country and shatter world peace with a premeditated, manmade catastrophe in Hawaii.

# PART 1

## *Retreat, The Journey, December 8, 1941*

# PART 1

*December 8, 1941*

*Forks of Elkhorn to Knoxville*

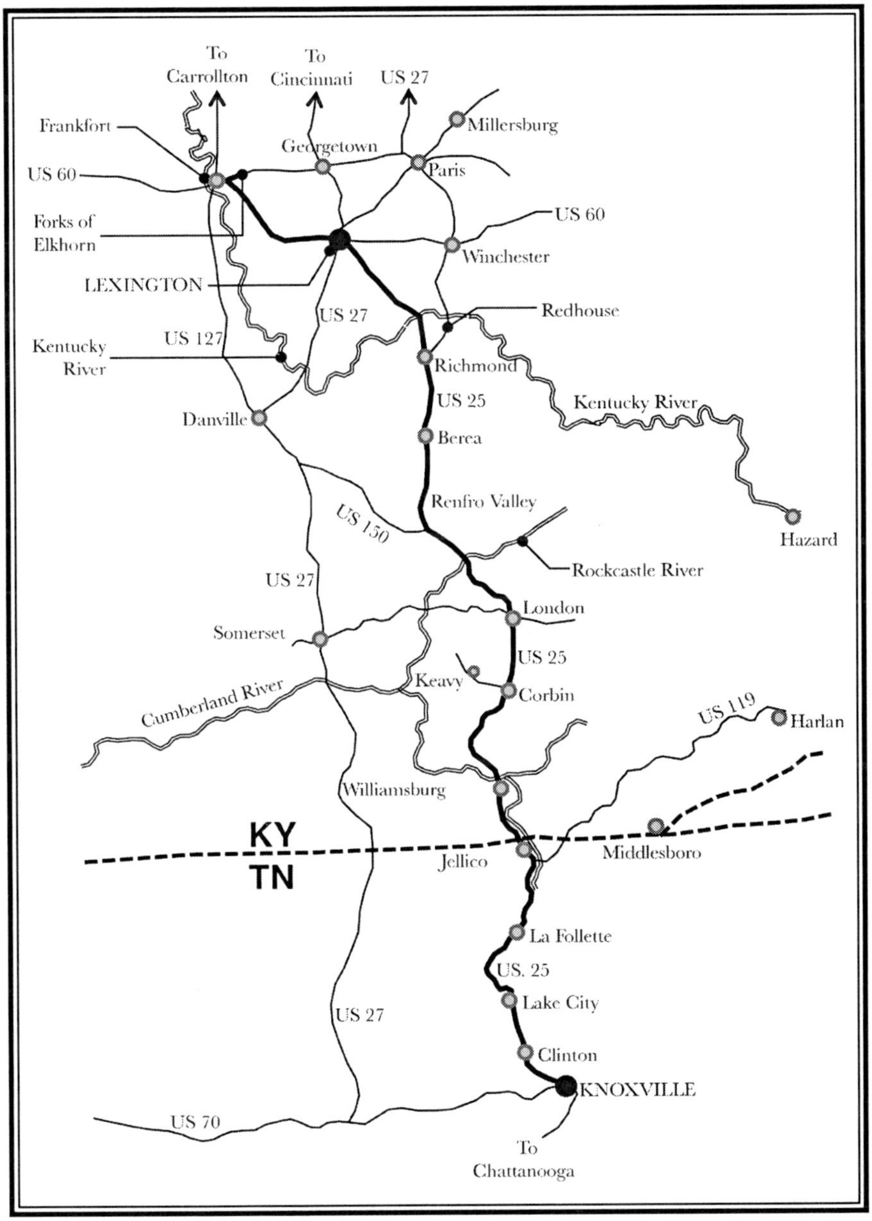

# CHAPTER 1

## *Forks of Elkhorn, Kentucky*

*The Forks of Elkhorn is a small community of homes and two businesses at the fork of the Elkhorn River a few miles east of Frankfort, Kentucky on US 460, the Georgetown Road.*

TEDDY SLEPT SOUNDLY on the cold winter morning. Little did he realize that by the end of the day he would say good-bye to the only world he had known and begin a new life in a strange place.

Warm comfort engulfed the boy as the illusion of being cuddled in his mother's soft, firm arms permeated his whole being. Teddy's slumber was interrupted by someone shaking his shoulder. He thought, *Mommy don't.* The shaking continued.

"Teddy, it's time to get up." Frank stood beside the bed with his hand gently rocking his son's shoulder. "Billy Ray will be here in a little bit. We don't want to be late; we have a long road to travel today."

Teddy rolled over rubbing his eyes as the room came into focus.

"You're a sleepyhead this morning. Were you dreaming?"

"Mommy was holding me." Teddy mumbled in the barely audible voice of an eight-year-old.

Frank involuntarily held his breath at these words. With a tightening voice he said, "Well . . . I'm sorry I had to wake you . . . We have to leave this morning."

The next sound from Teddy was something between a grunt and a grumble as he pulled back the bedcovers and his feet hit the cold linoleum floor. He hopped immediately to the rumpled rag rug by the door to his room.

Frank spoke over his shoulder as he left Teddy's small bedroom, "I've laid out your clothes at the foot of the bed, so go to the bathroom and get dressed . . . then you'll be warm again."

Frank stood at the counter pouring a cup of coffee as two eggs sizzled on the stove. "Would you like eggs this morning?"

"No."

"Cereal?"

"Yes . . . Corn Flakes." Teddy plopped onto his chair at the small breakfast table that also served as the lunch and dinner table at other times of the day.

"You're awfully quiet this morning."

"I'm still not warm," said Teddy as a visible shudder shook his small frame and he stuck his hands between his thighs to warm his fingers.

"How 'bout some hot Ovaltine?"

"OK." The thought of a warm drink sent a warming shudder across his narrow shoulders.

Frank turned on the large wooden cabinet radio in the living room, which shared the same room with the kitchen. The kitchen and living room didn't add up to a large room; in fact, it was rather small, but large enough for the small Warring family. After the radio warmed up Frank found WHAS on the lighted radio dial.

*". . . reports this morning are still coming in from the Hawaiian Islands about the extent of our losses, but Admiral Halsey said the losses of American lives and ships are extensive, and there will be more information later today. The White House has announced that the president will address a joint session of Congress today with—"* Frank snapped off the radio with an exaggerated twist of his wrist before the announcer could get the next word onto the airwaves. He found the radio's dial knob clutched in his fingers as he stared at the plastic circle.

"Daddy, the water's boiling."

Frank poured the hot liquid over the Ovaltine granules in

Teddy's favorite Lone Ranger cup and set it before him.

"Daddy?"

"Yes, son."

"What's a Jap?"

"Well, it's a person from Japan."

"The radio last night said the Japs hurt us."

"Teddy, I didn't know you were listening . . . But, yes, they hurt us."

"Daddy, what'd they do . . . I mean, are we hurt?"

"Well . . . uh, the 'us' the radioman was talking about is the whole country, not you and me, and I guess we all share some in the hurt . . . But, Teddy, it's very complicated and they won't hurt you."

"I know about the country, the United States of Ah . . . merica. We studied it with Miss Crenshaw. She taught us the Pledge of 'Legence. I pledge 'legence to the United State of Ah-merica and to the public for . . . for . . . I can't remember the next part."

"That's good, Teddy. Now, finish your cereal quickly; Billy Ray will be here soon." Frank, a medium-sized man with thick, dark hair, would find his cleanly shaven face showing traces of a five-o'clock shadow by midafternoon. He was dressed in heavy woolen pants, a dark plaid shirt, and sturdy winter oxfords. Teddy pulled the maroon sweater over his head, the one his grandmother Reed in Carrolton had knitted; it was a little big, but his mother had assured him he would soon grow into it.

As Frank finished washing and stacking the breakfast dishes on the drain board, the sound of the squeaky horn penetrated the thin walls of the house. It sounded a second time in a much louder blast of discordant noise.

"Teddy, put your pajamas in your suitcase and get your toy bag. I'll get your suitcase."

Teddy zipped up his jacket and stepped outside into the cold, dark morning air. He held his toy bag by both hands to prevent it from dragging on the ground through the patches of snow. He walked across the front yard to the waiting truck as his corduroy pants made the familiar swishing sound. His breath blew a thin cloud into the morning cold. Today he would not pretend to be smoking.

"Mornin', men, how you doin'? Mr. Frank, just throw them bags in the back and they'll ride fine," came the bright, enthusiastic voice of Billy Ray Vaughn sitting behind the truck's steering wheel.

After tossing the two suitcases in the truck bed among the tires, jacks, and odd pieces of machinery, Frank said, "Billy Ray, when are you going to get that horn fixed? It sounds like a sick sow; sometimes it bellows and sometimes it squeaks."

"Yeah, I know. I got a loose screw or somethin', I guess."

"You're right about that," murmured Frank. Father and son clambered into the old pickup with its missing front right fender. Frank and Teddy used special care not to step on the running board that dangled halfway to the ground by the passenger door. Teddy climbed onto his father's lap and pressed his nose to the side window as the truck drove onto the gravel road. The single outdoor light from Vaughn's Garage across the road cast a dim light on the small board-and-batten front of their house. Teddy saw the maple tree in the front yard with the tire swing Mr. Vaughn had fixed for him and remembered the time he swung too high and fell into the dust and knocked the breath from his chest. By the time he recovered his breath, he realized he had forgotten to cry, but there wasn't anyone in sight to hear him; Teddy didn't want to waste a good cry, although he had a good reason that time.

The truck rolled onto the blacktop of Highway 460 and headed west toward Frankfort. They passed the Kostigan's house and the Buck Run Baptist Church. Teddy saw for the last time the small cinder-block building of the state fish hatchery, and he could barely make out the dam on the South Fork of the Elkhorn River. Teddy couldn't see the swimming area behind the low dam, but he knew it was there and he remembered going there often with his mother on hot afternoons as he tried to learn to swim. Teddy knew he could learn to swim if he just didn't have to get his face wet.

"Did you hear what them Japs did to us, Mr. Frank? Just snuck in and blow'ed up the whole of the ships we had out in Hi'waya," Billy Ray blurted out.

The Gulf gas station, barely visible in the early, black morning was on the right, where Teddy spent an occasional nickel to buy a Moon Pie on Saturday afternoons and sometimes another nickel for a Hires.

"My Daddy says there's going to be trouble for them now and we goin' to have to go to war and kill them Japs."

"Yes, Billy Ray, I know."

"Did you ever hear of such a thing, just snuck in and BANG," barked Billy Ray. Teddy jerked around from the window and stared at Billy Ray. Teddy seldom heard a shout or a voice raised in anger, and he was uncertain what Billy Ray would do next.

"How old are you Billy?" asked Frank in a calm voice that reassured Teddy.

"I'm eighteen. I finished over at Franklin High last year and got me a diploma."

"Well, Billy, I think you're in for a little excitement in your life in the next few years."

"What'cha mean, Mr. Frank?"

"I bet you're going to be in the army or some other branch of the military very soon."

"Do you think so? That's what my Daddy says too. I guess I'll be a soldier or somethin'."

"Yes, I guess you will."

The cold air inside the truck was suddenly filled with a different but familiar aroma of the passing distillery. The sign for the Old Grand Dad Distillery lit by overhead lights flashed by as the truck moved up the hill out of the Elkhorn River valley. At six in the morning there was very little traffic on the road. The workers in the early shift at the distillery had already clocked in to begin their day's work. The truck rolled past the large McConnell farm with the white board fence. In the still, dark morning Teddy could barely make out the rhythmic passing of the vertical fence posts as the continuous ribbon of horizontal boards passed by. At the intersection with US 60, Billy Ray stopped for the red light by the Green Mill gas station and then steered right when it finally turned to green.

"Do you know anything about the army, Mr. Frank? I mean like, what do they do, or what'll I do?"

"Well, I was in military school, which was something like your high school. We learned to drill and march and we learned to say yes sir and no sir. I went to Millersburg Military Academy over near Paris."

"Well that ain't hard. I guess I can march all right."

"Billy there is a great deal of difference between my school experience and what you'll be faced with." Frank took care to speak very clearly to the teenager. "First of all, you'll have training in firing weapons, marching all day long, carrying a heavy backpack and digging fox holes and taking other defensive actions and, above all, in taking orders and carrying them out accurately. Your life and the lives of your buddies in your squad or platoon could depend on your doing what you're told."

"Well, shucks, I can shoot a gun—there ain't nothin' to that—and I bet I can dig a hole as good as the next guy. And anybody what has a mother like mine sure knows how to take orders. She don't cotton to no back talk or sassin', no sir; she 'spects you to do her tellin's just like she told you."

"You're probably right; your mother prepared you for war." Frank smiled. "But, Billy Ray, you have to realize, you may have to kill people. It's easy to justify killing someone who is trying to kill you, but you are still taking a human life. That someone you kill may have a wife and kids and a boy like Teddy."

"Well' I don't like the idea of killin' no person; rabbits and deer are alright, but on the other hand, if they're shooting at me, well, I guess I'll shoot 'em first."

"You'll get along fine, Billy Ray, but this war is going to change you forever. When you come back you will be a different person," said Frank. Frank thought to himself, *If he comes back.*

Billy Ray, with an unfamiliar serious look on his face, steered the truck past Kentucky State University, the university for Colored students, and finally down the hill past the armory into Frankfort. Teddy saw the new state capitol off to the left across the Kentucky River. In front of the truck, the Capitol Hotel building stood watch over Main Street as the truck swung into Ann Street toward the old capitol.

"Billy Ray, I want to thank you for giving us a lift into town; that's very kind of you. And also, thanks for the trip last week through the snow to the funeral home."

"Golly, Mr. Frank, that's alright, I had to come to town today to pick up a water pump for the Hudson. Daddy and me is working on and last week was fun driving through the snow. It weren't no problem."

The three travelers stepped down from the truck; Frank retrieved their baggage and faced Billy Ray.

"I left a note for your mother on the kitchen table and there are two boxes of books and pictures and things that she said she would ship to us in Knoxville. And, Mrs. Reed is coming down from Carrolton to pick up Ellen's clothes and things ..., and anything else we left in the house you can keep or throw away."

"I'll try and remember all that," the teenager chuckled.

Frank stared into Billy Ray's eyes and extended his hand, "And, also thanks for all of the kindness you and your family gave us while we rented from you. You're really good landlords."

"Shucks, we was real glad to have you folks stayin' there," Billy Ray's face flushed as he shrugged off the complement and took Frank's hand. "Daddy specially liked watchin' Mr. Teddy here do all his runnin' and chasin' around the yard." When Billy Ray said Mr. Teddy, he mussed his hand through Teddy's brown hair.

"We're really very appreciative." Frank and Billy Ray shook hands again. Frank surprised Billy Ray when he held onto his hand, "Billy, best of luck to you and be very careful in the army," offered Frank.

"You can count on me to be careful, 'cause my Momma would tan my hide if I didn't." Billy Ray Vaughn climbed into his truck, waved to the two travelers and smiled as he headed west on Broadway Street.

The steel gray sky of early morning light now illuminated the ring of hills surrounding Frankfort. Frank and Teddy crossed the street and entered the Capitol Café as a slow freight train began to rumble down the center of Broadway Street. Sprays of steam erupted from various parts of the lumbering engine; Teddy saw the engineer, sitting high above the street, lean out of the cab window to view the track ahead. Teddy stood inside the café door and waved at the engineer as the slow moving freight cars rumbled through downtown Frankfort in front of the Old Capitol. The engineer staring ahead and intent on a safe passage through the heart of the capitol did not see the small boy's greeting.

"What'll it be?" asked the plump waitress in the freshly starched apron.

"I believe a cup of hot chocolate for my boy and a cup of coffee for me."

"With cream?"

"Yes, please," Frank responded.

Teddy climbed onto the shiny stool with the bright red Naugahyde seat. His toy bag was at his feet beneath the brass rail that ran along the length of the counter. Teddy's feet dangled above the rail as he centered himself on the seat. The brightly lighted interior of the café had a number of regular customers who came every morning.

"Mable, can I have another donut?" asked a man three stools down from Teddy. The man's voice was gravelly and deep, a testament to the many cigarettes he had smoked each day over many years. Mable was not fast, but she was efficient. She laid paper napkins on the counter and placed the heavy mugs with their hot liquids before Teddy and Frank.

"Be careful, those mugs are hot. You're a good looking boy," Mable observed, looking at Teddy, "I gave you a marshmallow in your chocolate."

Teddy beamed as his father said, "What do you say, Teddy?"

"Thank you, M'am."

"You're welcome Sweetie," as she reached across the counter and tweaked Teddy's cheek.

Teddy scrunched his face and rubbed his cheek as Mable laughed and turned toward the plate of donuts under the glass dome cover.

"Have you boys heard any news this mornin' about the Pacific?" asked the man to Teddy's right.

Frank murmured, "I didn't listen very long to the radio this morning, the news is all bad, real bad." Frank stared absently at his cup of coffee as he continued to stir the bisque colored, steaming liquid.

"I know what you mean," said the stranger. "My son's in the Marines in San Diego and this is about as bad a set of news as we could possibly get. I guess we're going to war."

"Yes, I think so," offered Frank. "I did hear this morning that Roosevelt will address the Congress today, and I guess tell us all how bad it is. Whatever he says, it won't be good."

"Lord no ... those damn Japs ... those Sons-a-Bitches," murmured the stranger as a gray veil descended over his face and his shoulders visibly slumped. He idly stirred his coffee, cleared his throat and repeated, "Excuse my language, Lord no." After a short pause the stranger stuck his hand into his pocket and pulled out several coins and placed them on the counter. As he rose he said to Teddy with a brief flicker of a smile on his face, "Here young man, you look like you need a donut." He slid the plated donut in front of Teddy.

As the stranger headed for the door, Mable called, "Clyde, you didn't eat your donut."

"I know ... I guess I'm not very hungry this mornin'."

Teddy stared at his father, "Can I have the donut?"

"Yes Teddy. This is your lucky day, first a marshmallow and now a donut. You are going to gain weight before we reach your Granny and Granddad's house."

The clank of the café's ceramic dishes created a constant background noise as Teddy finished the donut and the last sip of chocolate. He turned to his father, "That was good. Yes sir, my lucky day."

Mable laughed as she approached the counter and reached toward Teddy with a damp cloth. Teddy started to pull back afraid of another assault on his cheek when Mable swiped his mouth clean, "The little fellow has a marshmallow mustache. You don't want to attract flies, do you?"

"No m'am." Teddy sat still as Mable scrubbed off the last vestiges of the sweet, sticky, chocolate and marshmallow.

The restaurant door behind Frank and Teddy opened and set the bell over the door to tinkling. "Frank, how you doin'?" As Frank turned he encountered the broad smile of Mal Sturdley who had just entered the cafe. The men shook hands as Frank turned to Teddy, "Time to go, son." Teddy slid off the stool, landed on his feet and hands as his knees bent easily with the jump to the floor. He grabbed his toy bag as Mal and Frank picked up the suitcases.

"The car's over here," said Mal gesturing to the left as the three left the café. Teddy climbed into the back of the car with his toy bag after his father pulled forward the back of the front passenger seat. Mal placed the suitcases in the trunk and slammed the trunk lid twice before its latch was secure. The 1938 Chevrolet pulled away from the curb and turned left.

"I need to make a quick stop over on Second Street before we hit the road." The car maneuvered through the rising light of the new day and headed across the river on the "singing bridge." Teddy stood on the floor of the back seat feeling the vibrations made as the tires crossed the open steel grate of the bridge's deck. The pitch of the singing, whining of the bridge dipped in tone as Mal slowed and then stopped at the end of the bridge before he turned left into Second Street.

"I love that ole bridge. It tickles my feet," announced Teddy.

"Yes, my kids love to cross it too. I'll be just a minute, I have to drop off an envelope," Mal said as he steered the car to the curb and turned off the motor.

# CHAPTER 2

## *Frankfort to Richmond*

SOON THE CAR was on the four-lane US 60 heading up the hill out of the Kentucky River valley retracing the route taken by Billy Ray into Frankfort an hour earlier. They drove past the armory and east toward the college. "Do you see that old armory?" asked Mal. "Do you reckon they keep gun powder and dynamite in there still?"

"I doubt it," answered Frank. "They probably store records and papers in there now."

Mal laughed in response. "Well, if it's state government paper, then this Keen Johnson administration is going to fill it up fast. Johnson, Roosevelt, and that Wilson Wyatt are thinking up so many programs that they'll soon start stacking paper in the yard outside the door." His laughing continued.

"Mal, you sound like a damn Republican with all that talk."

"Well, I talk like that because my daddy taught me correctly when I was a young 'un over in Floyd County."

"How'd you get along in Frankfort? I bet they don't know there's a Republican in their midst," commented Frank in mock seriousness.

"Well, sir, I keep my politics to myself and just try and get the best deal possible for tobacco in the legislature. Tobacco don't care what party you belong to as long as you are for tobacco."

"I didn't know there was anyone working against tobacco," said Frank.

"There's always that bunch of holier-than-thou people who lump together bourbon, tobacco, loose women, and gambling. Now you can legislate against loose women and gambling, but can you imagine people in Kentucky being against bourbon and tobacco? It doesn't make sense." Speaking loudly he blustered, "But hear this, Mr. Tobacco: I'm Malcolm at your service, ever vigilant and protecting your rights."

A slight smile flickered across Frank's face as he considered the power of a plant and what his friend must do, representing big and little farmers who depended on tobacco to make a living in farming. Frank had never started smoking like his father and his uncle Willard—and most every man he had ever known. He had grown up witnessing his own father's long-term, hacking cough and frequent spitting when outdoors, and he was not about to go down that same road with tobacco.

At the intersection with US 460, Mal steered the car to the right as they continued to follow US 60 toward Lexington and away from the sign that announced the road to the Forks of Elkhorn. A thin cloud cover hid the low-lying sun rising in the east.

"Frank, how you doin', I mean really doin'?" asked Malcolm.

The slight smile had faded from Frank's face. "Oh, I don't know. To be honest, everything in my life has gone crazy. I lose my job, then the baby dies before it ever had a chance to breathe, and then Ellen dies . . . ," Frank's voice faltered, "and now the war. My God, when will it stop getting worse?" Mal, stunned by the honest answer, stared ahead through widened eyes as he followed the four-lane road to the east.

"I don't know any more, I honestly don't," added Frank, speaking softly. He then glanced over his shoulder to see if Teddy might be listening, but Teddy seemed to be concentrating on directing the two toys cars retrieved from his bag along an imaginary highway on the cushion of the back seat. "Teddy is the only normal thing I have left in life," Frank added as his soft voice again broke slightly. "It's like I'm caught in a cocoon, like I'm being pressed from all sides." Frank blinked and turned to gaze with unseeing eyes out the passenger's side window.

"Yes, life has been mighty rough on you," lamented Malcolm, "mighty rough. What do you plan to do besides go to your folks?"

"I'm not sure. You know its damn funny, but last Thursday when I decided to go to Knoxville, I would have said I would try and get a job with the new Alcoa plant they're building down near Knoxville. It's going to be a big plant, don't you know. I talked to my parents on Saturday, and my dad just got a job offer from there as an electrician. He seemed confident that I could get on with them, particularly since I have a couple years of college. But now with the attack, I guess I'll wind up in the service. You know I went to military school for high school . . . that won't make it easy to stay out of the war."

"Do you really think there will be war?" asked Mal.

"Hell, yes," blurted Frank. "What other path can Roosevelt follow? Not only with the Japanese, but we're going to war in Europe as well, to fight the damn Germans. We're going to be fighting both to the east and west across two oceans at the same time. Before this is over, they're going to be drafting every man who can still put his pants and shoes on and walk a mile."

Mal swallowed and said, "Yeah, I guess you're right. I just don't want to think on it now, you know what I mean?"

"Yes, I know what you mean. But, Mal, you have a job and you're old, at least older than me," responded Frank as his sudden spark of anger subsided to be replaced by an ironic chuckle.

"Well, yes, I like to think of it as more mature, but forty isn't old. I can still walk and play a little basketball and run a little. Not like I used to, but I get around pretty good."

Frank looked at his friend and noted the growing double chin and rounded belly that pushed against his belt. "Mal, you're in the prime of life. I hope I look as well in eight years when I reach forty," chuckled Frank. Frank's smile faded and he added softly, "If I reach forty."

"Do you really think you'll have to go?"

"I don't think I'll have a choice. If I were single without

children, I wouldn't mind so much, but . . ." Frank paused as he felt a presence behind him. He turned and stared into Teddy's face barely two inches from his.

"You going away, Daddy?" Teddy blurted out. The words had hardly left his mouth when he burst into a deep, sobbing cry that shook his slim body.

"Teddy," Frank responded as he threw his arm over the boy's shoulder and pulled the child with a great deal of difficulty over the back of the seat onto his lap. On his way over the seat back, Teddy's right foot jabbed Mal's right shoulder and Mal raised his arm to prevent being kicked by the left foot. Teddy buried his face in his father's coat as the fear of losing his last parent took away his breath; the deep, erratic sobs continued.

Frank brushed away his son's thick brown hair and whispered, "Teddy, I love you very much." Before Ellen died, Frank could not remember telling his son that he loved him, but now the phrase had become a part of their life together. Teddy's sobs slowly subsided, but his face remained buried in his father's coat. The three travelers rode in silence as the car passed through Versailles.

In future years when looking back on that trip, Teddy would remember the incident in the car and the absolute and sudden feeling of dread that filled his whole being. Having lost one parent, he desperately wanted to hold on to the other. The fact that he was leaving the Forks, the only home his short memory could recall, and where he had lived surrounded by the loving care of his parents, was far less important than the fact he had to now clutch what remained of his once happy home: his father.

After a long period of silence, Frank spoke again, "Teddy, I may have to go and help our country fight the wars, not because I want to, but because I have to."

"I don't want you to go," Teddy's voice barked with unusual intensity. Teddy pulled his head back from his father and stared intently into his father's eyes. "Can I go with you? I won't be any trouble, I'll behave, I promise." The small boy's tear-streaked face earnestly sought reassurance of his future life with his father.

Mal spoke up, "Teddy, the army is no place for a boy. Now if you were an old boy, say seventeen or eighteen, they would be glad to have you, but a nine-year—"

"Eight," corrected Teddy.

". . . an eight-year-old boy would slow down the army." As Teddy lay his left ear against his father's chest, he faced Mal, "I can run fast, and I can keep up just fine."

"But can you carry a backpack and shoot a rifle at the same time?"

"I've had guns," Teddy protested. "Last winter I had two pistols and holsters and Billy Ray said they looked real and I got to shoot Jimmy's BB gun and—" Then Teddy realized he was talking about toy guns, not the real ones. "Real guns can hurt you; that's what Mommy said."

"Well, Teddy, that's the point of war: to hurt the people you are fighting, don't you see?" explained Mal.

Teddy's face fell as he began twisting the button on his father's coat, "I don't want him to go."

"Edward Franklin Warring, you are going to be all right, I promise. Don't worry, everything will be all right," whispered Frank. Teddy buried his face in his father's coat once again.

"Is that your full name, Edward Franklin? I thought it was Theodore," observed Mal.

"Yes," Frank answered for Teddy. "He's named after me, sort of. My name is Franklin Edward, but Ellen didn't want a junior since she lost her older brother, who was a junior, in infancy. Her family thought the junior name tag was a bad omen, so she reversed my names. Teddy is almost a junior but will be a far better and smarter person than his namesake."

"Aw, Frank, I don't know many people as smart as you," countered Mal.

"Well, if I am, a lot of good it has done me so far, working in the WPA and then in the office of a distillery and then losing that job."

"But that wasn't your fault. We all got hurt in the Depression;

then the Feds made the distillery reduce some jobs. And remember, you said 'so far.' Take it from me; the best years are ahead of you."

*God, I hope so, I truly do. It can't be any worse.*

The occupants rode on in silence as the sound of the car's tires traveling on the pavement provided the only noise. The sound soon changed to a rhythmic thumping noise made by the car travelling over expansion joints of the new concrete pavement. Horse farms with their clean grass pastures and grazing Thoroughbreds appeared. The board fences outlining the pastures were painted black and stood in contrast to the green-and-white horse barns with red roofs. Teddy, looking out the side window from his father's lap, saw two young colts racing about the pasture. A third larger horse stood passively as the youngsters kicked their heels and frolicked.

"Those are race horses," Frank explained to Teddy. "They will be getting them ready soon for the race track. When I was twelve years old, I used to exercise some horses. They were not as good as these ponies, but the owners were always hoping they would find a diamond in the rough, maybe a Seabiscuit, or the like."

"What's a Seabiscuit?" asked Teddy.

"He was a famous horse," Mal chimed into the conversation, "I guess he's still famous, but he's stopped racing now. I think he's a professional daddy now, raising a big family of young colts. When he was in his prime, he was the poor man's race horse: he ran funny, but he won. He beat War Admiral in a very famous race. Yes'sir, a poor man's horse." He chuckled.

"Did you ride him?" Teddy asked his father.

"Oh, no. I soon got too big to ride the better horses. To ride you need to be a small but strong boy or man. If you get too big or heavy, then you can't ride in a race because the horse would have to carry too much weight. Most jockeys, er . . . riders, weigh about a hundred or a hundred ten, something like that."

"Oh," Teddy said.

"Seabiscuit was born over near Paris, on Claiborne Farm, I think. We lived just up the road in Millersburg," added Frank, "but I don't ever remember seeing him on the farm. Seabiscuit was a late bloomer, but he really did shine for several years."

In downtown Lexington, Mal turned right onto US 25 and headed south toward Knoxville. Frank was gratified to pass the only Chinese restaurant in Lexington, the Hong Kong Chop Suey and Chinese Restaurant. He thought it may have gone out of business after all the years had passed since his college days. That's where Mr. and Mrs. Ito worked. He smiled as he recalled his college roommate George Ito, the math whiz. He and George had made numerous trips to Lexington from Richmond to get cheap and sometimes free, filling meals from the Ito's back in '29 and '30.

By ten o'clock in the morning, the car slowed as it entered Richmond. US 25 was now called Main Street. Off to the right of the street, several two- and three-story buildings came into view on University Drive.

"Teddy, do you see those buildings? That's where I went to college, Eastern Kentucky State Teachers College. I wasn't studying to be a teacher, but that is what most of the students studied. For two years I thought I was an English major, but then I met your mother. She was a freshman, and we fell in love and got married and dropped out of school. Our money had run out about the same time. That was in '30 just as the Depression was getting up a head of steam, and we decided we would rather be married and poor than be single and poor."

As they neared the courthouse, Frank said, "Mal, you can let us off anywhere around here."

"You sure, Frank?"

"Yes, this is still US 25 and everybody heading south has to drive through here."

Pulling the car to the curb, Mal turned to face Frank. "Can I loan you some money?" he inquired.

"No, no I have enough so we can take the Greyhound if we don't get a ride, but with you getting us this far and this being a road everybody uses to get to Knoxville, I think we'll take our chances and get a ride from someone. I want to save what money I can, and if I borrow from you then I'll only get further behind."

"Well, there's no hurry in paying it back; wait till you're on your feet again." Mal reached for his wallet in his back pocket.

Frank spoke firmly, "No, Mal, you're a good friend and I know I can count on you, but I don't need money."

"OK." Mal sighed and reached for the car door handle. Frank opened the passenger door, and he and Teddy stepped onto the sidewalk in front of Kresge's five-and-dime store.

Teddy stood still, transfixed by the large, bearded man dressed in the red suit trimmed in white who stood at the far end of the store beside the front door. His red hat had a white ball at the floppy end of its conical shape. His white beard and black boots completed the picture. "Who's that?" Teddy murmured in a soft voice.

Frank pulled the toy bag from the back seat and the suitcases from the trunk and lined them along the curb. "Mal, I can't thank you enough for the ride; this has been a big help."

"Frank, I hope you and Teddy reach Knoxville alright tonight. Sorry I can't go farther, but I need to call on some farmers around here and get back home by dark."

As the two men grasped hands and shook, Frank said, "You've got mouths to feed just like me. Work comes first, and I appreciate all you and Lois did two weeks ago and today as well."

"Say," said Mal, "are you going to get anything for your car that that damn drunk demolished?"

"I don't think so," Frank replied. "He is a day laborer who has only enough money to get drunk on, but no insurance."

"That's too bad . . . Bye, Teddy," Mal called out as he waved and climbed back behind the steering wheel and turned into the slow moving traffic.

# CHAPTER 3

## *Richmond*

"WHAT'S HIS NAME?" mumbled Teddy.

"Why that's, Mal, you know him."

"No, I mean the red man."

"That's Santa Claus. Your mother and I never did make much of him, but he's a Christmas make-believe man, or an overgrown elf or a fairy or something like that. He's supposed to live at the North Pole and come to homes at Christmas to bring presents. Some children believe he brings all of their Christmas presents, but we didn't live where there was a Santa in the stores, and we decided to give you the presents ourselves. Don't you remember Momma reading you stories about him?"

"Oh yeah, I kind of remember." Teddy stared at the stranger. "Is he real?" Teddy asked, still staring at the red image.

"Well, he's a real man alright, but he's a make-believe Santa. That beard is probably fake." Just then Santa turned in their direction and rang the large bell in his right hand. His left hand rested on top of a tripod supporting a bucket suspended above the sidewalk. A sign on the tripod announced Salvation Army. "Merry Christmas, ho, ho, ho," Santa bellowed at Teddy. Teddy, still transfixed by the image, walked slowly toward Santa.

"Merry Christmas, little fellow. How you doin' today?"

"Fine," said Teddy.

Frank, carrying the suitcases and the toy bag, caught up with Teddy a few feet from Santa.

"Looks like you fellas are a travelin'."

"Yes, we're going to see my parents in East Tennessee," said Frank.

"That's nice, always good to see family. You want to know where the bus station is?"

"No," said Frank, "we're going to try our luck at thumbing a ride, save a little money."

"Where did you say you were headed?"

"We're going down US 25 to Knoxville."

"Oh, yes, I know Knoxville. You know, son, Brother Culberson at the Army is headed that way today. He's driving a poor widow lady down to Corbin. I bet you fellas can get a ride with him. He's our colonel at the Army."

"You in the army?" asked Teddy.

"Yes'sir, the Salvation Army. We save souls for Christ."

"Daddy, you going to wear a red suit if you go in the army?"

"No, son, if I have to go I'll be in the US Army. That's a different kind of army; they don't save souls, sometime they have to take them," answered Frank with an ironic smile as he stared at Santa.

"You know, that's right," said Santa. "I was almost in the Great War; never did get to France and almost died from the flu, but our boys did do some killing over there in France. I was over to a camp on the south side of Louavul, Camp Taylor. I've never been that sick before and I hope not again until it's my time to go." Santa saw out of the corner of his eye two men approaching in long winter overcoats. "Merry Christmas," chimed Santa's sing-song voice. "Thank you, and God Bless you," as they dropped coins into the pot.

Teddy now stared at the two men as they walked away. He tugged at his father's sleeve. "Did they put money in there?"

"Yes, son, this Santa is collecting money for Christmas, for poor families," said Frank.

"And whoever else needs help in finding Christ," added Santa.

"Yes, that also," murmured Frank. "Getting back to your

colonel's trip to Corbin, how can we find out if he's got room in his car?"

"Oh, yes. Well if you fellas watch this pot of gold, I'll run into Kresge's and use their phone. He was supposed to leave about eleven; it's about ten fifteen now, according to the courthouse clock. That clock means its somewhere between ten and ten thirty now; it's just an estimate of time."

"We would be glad to watch over the pot," Frank assured Santa.

As Santa entered the store, a small withered lady stopped in front of Teddy, "Are you an elf?" she inquired.

"No, I'm a boy," Teddy said as he turned toward his father. "What's she mean, Daddy?"

"Santa's inside making a phone call," Frank told the woman.

Myrtle didn't bother to listen to the answer as she broke into a loud guffaw, laughing at her own humor. "He's a little elf," she repeated and laughed again with a gravelly smoker's voice.

"He'll be right back," Frank continued.

"Laws, the Salvation Army don't have any good Santas like they use ta," she said, looking at Frank. She opened her purse, pulled out a dollar bill, rolled it in a tight tube and pushed it through the slot.

"If the real Santa comes back, tell 'em Myrtle Kinner give him some money, will ya?"

"Yes, ma'am, I'll gladly tell him that," said Frank.

Myrtle shuffled off to the south as the Kresge's door opened and four young ladies walked out followed by Santa.

"Myrtle gave you some money," said Teddy.

"Myrtle, Myrtle . . . I don't think I know a Myrtle, little man," said Santa.

"Her last name was Kinner. I guess she wants to be included in your prayers," offered Frank.

"Oh, we pray for everyone who gives and those who don't. But this is your lucky day. Colonel Culberson will drive by here and give you fellas a lift all the way to Corbin. Just go across the street and stand in front of the courthouse, and he'll pick you up there."

"Thank you very much, Santa," Frank said as he extended a hand that Santa grasped with both of his red-mittened hands.

Teddy and Frank sat on the low limestone wall that separated the wide sidewalk from the sparse grass of the courthouse lawn. The occasional patch of sun that shone through the mostly cloudy sky offered a slight radiant warming of the temperature, but as soon as it was noticed, the sun would be blocked again by the low-lying clouds. Teddy watched the strangers walking briskly to and fro along the sidewalk. Frank, deep in thought, stared at an invisible spot on the sidewalk before him.

Teddy sat upright as he detected a faint rhythmic tapping sound coming from the direction they had followed on their drive into town. As he puzzled over the sound, it grew steadily louder and sharper in its clarity. "Daddy, what's that?"

"What's what?" asked Frank.

"That noise." Teddy stood on the sidewalk and then climbed onto the low wall. The sound continued to grow, and Teddy saw a car with a flashing light on its roof leading a large number of people as they turned from University Drive into Main Street. All of the marchers were wearing tall hats and marching in the middle of the street.

Frank, now standing, said, "Looks like a marching band."

The rhythmic throbbing of the snare drums and intermittent rim shots on the edge of the drums started to make normal conversation difficult as the band drew within a block. The man leading the band suddenly blew his whistle and the band erupted into "Stars and Stripes Forever." Teddy stood with his mouth open as the sharp brass sounds dominated his being. The band, now only half a block away, slowed their pace but not the throbbing of the music. As they completed the song, the band standing in front of the courthouse responded to signals from the strutting drum major, turned in unison to face Teddy and the seat of government.

A John Philip Sousa march erupted from the band as the trombones followed by the flutes and piccolos contributed to the loud music, and the drums—always the drums—beat out their enthusiastic rhythm. Teddy tugged on his father's arm as other pedestrians stopped on the sidewalk blocking his view. Frank picked up Teddy and held him so his head matched his own eye level. Teddy's right arm started to involuntarily keep time with the music, almost as if he were directing the band. Other observers standing nearby were amused by the vigorous young conductor's efforts. With the completion of the song, the drum major snapped to attention, blew his whistle, and the band turned smartly to its street-marching formation and stepped as one as it marched to the south to play yet another Sousa tune. The bass drums continued to throb in the chests of the admiring onlookers on the sidewalk. Scattered applause broke out, including Teddy's enthusiastic clapping, as a second police car crawled by behind the band.

Teddy suddenly struggled from his father's arms and ran to the curb to watch the band march on down the street. As they passed from view, he raced back to his father, "What was that?"

"That was the Eastern band, Teddy. They march at football games."

A smiling stranger standing beside Frank volunteered, "They've been invited to play in the Rose Bowl and are trying to collect donations to pay for the trip. All the stores downtown have contribution jars. They've started to play downtown most every day now to get people excited."

Frank smiled, "Well, it worked to get my son excited."

"Yeah, they're the best band in the state this year, better than UK even."

"They've come a long way since I was here in school," Frank said.

"When did you go here?" the young man asked.

"I started in '28 and stopped after '30; the times got too hard," replied Frank.

"I remember some of that. I was a little boy then. I remember my folks worryin' a lot then; they still do, but it's not so bad now with 'em." The young man pulled his jacket tight and fastened the front zipper as he talked. "I go to school here so far, but I called my cousin last night, and we decided with what the Japs did an' all, we would sign up for the army. I'm going down to Jellico, and then tomorrow me and him are going, I guess, into Knoxville and see if we can join up."

"Oh," said Frank, "we're headed south as well. Going down to Knoxville to visit my parents."

"That's great. I'm gettin' a ride with my buddy Bobby. He drives for the Splinkler Brothers and has to take a load of gravel down to London this afternoon, and Billy Jack, my cousin, is goin' to meet me there and we'll go on to Jellico. I'm all fired up about them Japs. I can't wait to get into the army and kill some of 'em for what they did to us."

The two men talked on about their college experiences as Teddy listened briefly before his mind began to wander. The sound of the band still filled the three dimensions of his body as he felt all over again the sound, the feeling, and the throbbing that resonated in his chest and head. He loved that music; it was the first time he had ever heard such a thing as a live band.

He then remembered the sound of the organ in church, but it paled in generating that feeling inside his body. He liked the church songs, but the organ in church wasn't the same as the band standing right in front of him. Then he recalled his mother singing in church every Sunday and his father's deep reverberating voice on the occasional times he accompanied them. Teddy could place his ear against his father's chest and hear and feel the deep sound of his father's voice vibrating in his chest. Usually his father would stay home and read the paper on Sunday mornings. That was his quiet time, according to Teddy's mother, and that was after he had made everybody pancakes. They had pancakes for breakfast every Sunday, as far back as Teddy could remember.

Thoughts of his mother filtered back into Teddy's memory. He was suddenly seized with a tightening of his breath, and he thought he might start crying even though he didn't want to. He remembered being sent over to Mrs. Kostigan's house to stay when his mother started feeling sharp pains. That was just before Thanksgiving. Teddy knew she was going to have a baby, and he thought he knew what that meant since her stomach had gotten very large. She would let him feel her stomach and he actually felt a little jerking movement beneath her dress. His mother assured him it was his baby brother or sister beginning to kick up a storm. He also got to place his ear against her stomach, and he thought he heard a heart beating when she asked, but he wasn't actually sure if he had heard it.

At supper on one of those early fall nights, the three talked about names for the baby, for either a boy or girl. His mother finally got her way, and they decided they would name the boy, if it was one, David Everett, for her father. Then they had an easier time picking Mary Elizabeth. That was for Frank's mother Mary and Ellen's mother Elizabeth, if it was a girl. Actually Ellen's mother's name was Thelma Elizabeth, but Ellen preferred the name Elizabeth more than Thelma. Teddy often thought about having a baby brother or sister; he preferred a brother since he could teach Baby David to play baseball and basketball. That would be fun to do. But he now knew Baby David wasn't coming and he wasn't going to see his mother again. In fact, when he went over to Mrs. Kostigan's, that was the last time he had seen her. She gave him a kiss on the top of his head as he was led out of her bedroom. He noticed how warm she felt, it was as if there was a warm halo surrounding her.

Teddy had to spend the night before Thanksgiving in the Kostigan's home. That was very strange since the only places he had ever slept when he was not at home was with his mother and father at his grandparents' homes in Carrolton or Millersburg. Mrs. Kostigan's daughter, Betty Jane, had slept in the twin bed next to his, and he heard her crying during the night. He couldn't figure out what made her so sad. It may have been because she was a girl. The next morning Teddy had bacon and eggs for breakfast, and that was another thing he noticed: none of the Kostigan's ate any breakfast on that Thanksgiving morning. They were strange people. He finished eating just before his father came to the house and said that Teddy's mother was still very sick and that Baby David had not made it. When Teddy looked puzzled by the comment, Frank told him plainly that David had died. Teddy was upset but cried only a little; after all he had never met David, and he guessed he could get another brother.

All of the Kostigan family members were at the house, including an aunt from Lawrenceburg and a grandmother from Wilmore. Teddy had not met either woman before, but they seemed to go out of their way to pat and hug him whenever they had a chance. He saw the women speaking in hushed tones with Mrs. Kostigan as they set the table and worked in the kitchen. Betty Jane also helped, but Teddy could see that she was still very sad and regularly wiped her eyes on her apron. In the early afternoon, the family had a quiet dinner with turkey and the traditional trimmings, but again a hushed tone softened the conversation among the diners. Frank came over to the house for a few minutes and had a small sample of the meal before he excused himself and returned home to Ellen.

Teddy continued to stay at the Kostigan's despite his suggestion that it was time for him to go home, but his father said it was better that he stay until his mother felt better. Thanksgiving night an ambulance arrived with flashing lights as the older members of the Kostigan family stood watching on the front porch. The ambulance left the Forks community heading west for the hospital in Frankfort with Ellen in the back on a stretcher and Frank, crouched on a side seat, holding her hand. Teddy slept through the near silent leaving of his mother. In the midafternoon on Friday, Frank returned from the hospital to the Kostigan's house. He sat with Teddy in the living room and told him that God had taken away his mother. Mrs. Kostigan said it was to a better place, but Teddy didn't think so if he couldn't go with her. When his father made the meaning of his statement clear, Teddy, stunned into silence, sat staring with unseeing eyes at the wall, unable to see anyone who stood in his line of vision.

Then after a few minutes, he started to cry and so did everyone else, including Mrs. Kostigan, Betty Jane, and Betty Jane's younger brother. Everyone except Frank who held his son on his lap for a long, long time. Teddy wondered if he had had a part in his mother's death. Did he do something or fail to do something? Was God punishing him for a sin he had committed? He should have prayed harder for his mother. Had he let her down by not praying when she got sick? Now Teddy sat on the low courthouse wall in Richmond, head bowed, and started to cry softly as he felt his mother's last dry kiss on his head.

The hissing sound of air brakes grabbed the attention of the chatting men as the large dump truck rolled to a stop at the curb. The red sign on the door proclaimed Splinkler Brothers, Contractors and Hauling. The young man talking to Frank stopped, grabbed his canvas duffel bag, and walked to the truck. He waved good-bye to Frank as he climbed up into the seat high above the traffic.

As the truck pulled away from the curb a yellow Studebaker sedan followed the truck into the same stopping place, and a large man emerged from the car. He ambled toward the courthouse, tossed away his burning cigarette, and saw Frank standing by the low wall. "Are you the fellas that need a ride south?"

"We certainly are," said Frank as he extended his hand.

"Brother Culbertson, sir. Glad to make your acquaintance. This your boy?" asked the newcomer as he bent down toward Teddy.

"Certainly is," said Frank, smiling, looking down, and then seeing for the first time Teddy's wet cheeks. Frank hugged the boy against his leg and said quietly, "We've had a couple of rough weeks, and Teddy and I are still very sad."

"I'm so sorry to hear about that," Brother Culbertson extended his hand and patted Teddy's head.

Frank bent and picked up their luggage as the three walked to the car. With the bags in the trunk, Frank opened the passenger door and pulled back the rear of the seat as Teddy climbed in. Teddy was surprised to see a woman sitting in the back seat behind the driver; she was sitting as far away from Teddy as the small backseat would permit. Teddy stared at her; she turned briefly toward him and with a fleeting smile nodded her head in recognition of his presence. Brother Culbertson climbed into the front seat and turned on the motor. "So you fellas goin' to Knoxville?" he asked.

"Yes," replied Frank, "and we appreciate a ride to Corbin."

"Glad to have you along. Let me introduce you to Mrs. Ida Mae Combs. I'm giving her a lift down to her sister's in Keavy, that's just outside Corbin."

"My pleasure," said Frank, turning to face the woman in the back seat. He saw a thin-faced woman probably in her late fifties with her thin body wrapped tightly in a dark-brown coat made of a very heavy, rough wool. Mrs. Combs nodded and said in a barely audible voice, "Nice to meet you."

Brother Culbertson drove around the courthouse block before the car was headed south on US 25 toward Berea.

# CHAPTER 4

## *Richmond to Corbin*

FRANK SAW THE last familiar sights of Richmond slip behind the car as they traveled south. He had taken this road south of town only one time before, as far as he could remember. When he was here in college, Frank always travelled north to Paris and then Millersburg. His parents had moved to Knoxville from Millersburg in February 1939, and so far he, Ellen, and Teddy had not had money enough to visit them. They were going now because Frank felt he had nowhere else to go.

He so wanted to be with his parents and feel again the comfort of their hospitality. He wondered if he would feel safe. He doubted it. He couldn't recapture the feelings of security he had had as a boy. He was just too old to go home and start over, yet that was what he was doing. He no longer had reason to pay rent on the house at the Forks of Elkhorn, now that Ellen was gone. He was sure Mr. Vaughn would let him stay for a while without paying, but what was the use? He no longer had a job at the distillery, such as it was, and no car to get to a job if he found one. Life had played a dirty trick on him, taken away his ability to earn a living then taken away his wife. Now those damn Japs and Germans. *Damn them. Damn the too few jobs. Damn God for taking his wife, damn everything . . .* Without saying the words to himself, he knew his all-consuming thought was, *What am I going to do?*

Frank looked at his hands, unclenched his fists, and found that his fingernails had dug four small cuts in the base of his palms. He pulled his almost-clean handkerchief from his back pocket and dabbed at the wounds.

As they slowed to pass through Ferristown, he thought of Richmond and his sophomore year and how he had spotted Ellen during the third week of classes in September '29. Wow, she was something. It was odd the effect she immediately had on him. She was good looking; not the prettiest girl in school, but it was her dark-brown curls, the laugh he heard her exchange with other girls, her smile intended for others, and just a certain indescribable "thing" about her.

Yes, it was her "thing" that attracted him to her. He couldn't define what made up the "thing," but he recognized it none the less. It was something he felt inside. He finally managed to meet her in the library where he was working when she came to the reference desk and the librarian asked Frank to explain the card catalog files to Ellen, as well as the Dewey Decimal System, while he was at it. Frank certainly did his best during the shoulder-to-shoulder explanation leaning over the card catalog index files. In fact he took so long that Ellen had to leave for her next class before she had a chance to use the shelves of the history section.

Frank made sure he was at the desk the next time she came into the library; he had to work extra hours so that he would not miss her. When she arrived, Ellen was in the company of two other girls, but soon she and Frank were huddled together looking at the cards under American History, The Revolution. Again, Ellen didn't get into the stacks before she had to leave. The next afternoon when Frank arrived at the Library to do some of his own research, he found Ellen already at work at a reading table. She laughed when she saw him and made a joke of needing to be there when he was not present so she could get some work done. Frank had turned a bright crimson as they both laughed and received a reproving "shush" from the librarian. Ellen, of course, had noticed the attention he was paying her. She was flattered and in Frank shared a mutual interest. That Saturday night Frank didn't need the cover of the library to see Ellen; she readily accepted the opportunity to see the latest movie at the Crown with him. Frank paused from his reverie; he had no recollection of the film . . . What was it? He couldn't remember. He only remembered feeling her warmth sitting next to him, that he put his arm around her and she didn't shrug him off—in fact, she snuggled closer.

The following two days Frank walked around campus in a daze. His roommate, George Ito, wondered if he was sick. "Frank you feeling OK? You look like you're sicker than a dog or have seen something no other human being has ever observed." At supper Frank admitted that a girl was at the heart of his problem and that it was not a problem, actually, but a sort of a reverie, a feeling from which poems were born. George groaned. George could accept the girl part, but he had a problem with the reverie part of the explanation and especially the poem part. He worked out on paper a complicated equation with many factors that he assured Frank would determine if the match with Ellen was a good one. The wrangling over the value of the factors continued for an hour until Frank finally got the picture that George was stringing him along with math double-talk. The discussion ended with a rolling, tumbling, laughing rough house between the two friends. George was a math major who wanted to transfer to UK in Lexington as soon as he completed his sophomore year. He maintained that Asians made better mathematicians than Westerners. George's father and mother had been born in Japan and came to California before George was born. They settled in Sacramento in a small Japanese enclave. However, they made no noticeable economic advance, and his father thought there would be better jobs in the East.

George's dad, Maturi, made what his brother thought was a miscalculation since many Americans were continuing to come West. It was 1921. But Maturi was the head of his small family, and he decided to buck the population trend and they settled in Lexington. A stroke of good luck shone on his father, as Maturi described it, when he landed a job in the only Chinese restaurant in Lexington. The Chinese owner wasn't particular about the

Japanese heritage and hired both parents to wait on tables because the locals would assume any Asian was a Chinese. George's mom eventually went to work in the kitchen and learned to cook Chinese-American food as well as the Chincsc cooks.

Their jobs had lasted at least up to the end of George's sophomore year, 1930, despite the looming hard times of the emerging Depression. Frank had kept in touch with George when he transferred to UK and graduated in '32. George then went to graduate school at UCLA, and the contact between the two friends grew weaker over the course of the Depression. The last Frank had heard, George was married and teaching at Fresno State, but that was *let's see, three years ago*. Frank hoped George would be all right as a result of this big problem with Pearl Harbor.

The relationship between Ellen and Frank continued to blossom through the fall, winter, and spring of 1930. As the winter semester wore on, they had growing difficulty keeping their hands off each other. There was first the constant holding of hands, then finding every opportunity for light touches and caresses, then they progressed to petting and more touching; neither had the least hesitancy about the touch of the other, they forbade nothing. They began to regularly give in to their natural urges or, as Ellen said, their biological instincts, as the weeks slipped by. As their love grew, Frank's parents' financial problems increased in the depressed economy as farm prices stayed low and his dad's opportunities to work outside the farm as an electrician all but dried up.

The farm was owned outright without a mortgage by his father and uncle, so they were assured of having food on the table but they had difficulty earning enough hard currency to buy those things not produced on the farm, let alone pay Frank's tuition. By Easter, Ellen and Frank knew that Frank could not return to school in the fall, and faced with life alone on campus, Ellen suggested a way out of their emotional dilemma. At the end of April they drove to a justice of the peace in Covington and spent a one-night honeymoon in Newport before returning to Richmond to complete the semester. When school ended, they announced their marriage to their parents and close friends and moved in with Frank's parents on the farm. There, Frank worked the farm with his father until the WPA was organized, then traveled to Louisville and then Covington helping run public works construction projects.

In early 1932 Ellen had a miscarriage before delivering Teddy in 1933 in the farmhouse of the Warring's Millersburg farm. Frank moved his three-member family to the Forks of Elkhorn in 1936 when he landed a job—low paying, but still a job—with Old Grand Dad distillery. Things were looking up, finally; that is, until now when nothing was going up and all of the pieces of Frank's life were plummeting into a bottomless void.

The passengers in the car were very quiet as they completed the twelve-mile trip to Berea. They passed Berea College's small campus, Boone Tavern, and on through the small downtown. The town's nice homes were now behind them as they traveled south; small scattered homes, many with old cars and trucks parked in the front yards, slipped past. Brother Culbertson had fallen in behind a slow-moving Model A Ford with dull black paint that absorbed the brief flashes of sunlight breaking through occasional openings in the clouds. When the road finally leveled out and provided clear visibility ahead, he accelerated and drove past the ambling car with two elderly people in the front seat. The tinny, rumbling, thudding sound of the Ford diminished as they pulled away from it.

"I think we should go faster than thirty miles an hour." Brother Culbertson chuckled and glanced over at Frank. "You seem to have a lot on your mind, young man."

"Yes," Frank said in a weary voice, "I guess I do."

"Well, I hope it's not all bad, but after yesterday and what happened out west in the Pacific, everybody is feeling down today."

"I certainly agree with that," Frank said in a soft voice.

"Yes sir, those Japanese killed a lot of our sailors, and now we have no choice but to go to war."

"That's the way I see it," Frank confirmed.

"Those Oriental types, those Japanese, have been growing stronger over the years, and now they seem intent on driving us and the British out of Asia." He paused and then added, "I guess they want to have Asia for the Asians . . . but," now spoken seriously as his voice dropped in tone, "they did a terrible disservice to everybody by starting a war. To them and us."

Frank studied Brother Culbertson for the first time since they had briefly shaken hands in Richmond. "That's a little different way of describing our problem. Other people I have talked to this morning were calling them names, Japs this and Japs that, and now we are going to go kill them."

"I know, that's the kind of reaction I expect, but you see we at the Salvation Army believe in the essential goodness of all mankind, even Orientals, not that we have many in Kentucky, but still they are human beings. And our job is to help all people turn to a Christian life and find peace and eternal life in heaven."

"What if they aren't Christians, like the Buddhists or Shinto folks in Japan?"

"They're still human beings," said Brother Culbertson, "and they deserve our respect, at least until they attack us and stab us in the back. We have to defend ourselves."

"That's interesting," said Frank. "I had a friend in college, my roommate, his parents were born in Japan, so I guess he's by definition a Jap. But he was born and raised here in America and I know he's an American, as much of an American as you or me. No matter what the Japanese government does, I will not think unkindly of him. He was, or still is, a good friend; he just lives so far away that I haven't seen him for years. And I'm sure he'll want to go to war against Japan as much as the rest of us."

"Young man, you and I are probably two of only a handful of people in the state this morning that feel that way. Almost everyone will want to lynch any Jap they can find. The prospect of war has upset you a great deal, hasn't it?"

Frank replied, "Well, for me it's not just the war, although that's part of it. Teddy, my son," said Frank, flicking his hand toward the backseat, "lost his mother two weeks ago, and we are going to my parents' home to try and start life over."

"You say he lost a mother, did you lose a wife?"

"Oh yes . . . Oh, God, yes! . . . I lost my whole focus . . . I can't figure out what to do now except go home to my parents. Imagine that, me going home at thirty-two with my tail between my legs." Frank's last words trailed off as he lost his breath and could not have uttered another word.

"You have my deepest sympathy, and I'll include you in my prayers tonight when I get back to the mission."

"Thanks," mumbled Frank. After a moment of thought he continued, "Should I call you Colonel or Brother?"

"Well, Bob is a little more fitting to our present situation, don't you think?"

"Yes, Bob . . . Bob, I'm very upset. I guess I'm upset with God. I've found myself damning him. I know it's not right, but I do and I can't help it. My wife died in child birth and so did the baby, and there wasn't anything I could do. There wasn't anything the doctor could do either; it was as if God had made a decision and be damned with who it hurt." Frank paused, "I've lost my job and all I have left is Teddy," he said softly.

"I can't start to understand what God does or why he does it, son, but I have faith that there is a reason for things that happen," Bob said.

"I just don't know . . . but . . ." Frank's anger suddenly flared and he stared at Bob. "Is it God's reason, is he acting on us, or is he just sitting around and watching the people of the world screw up things? I can't understand that. I read that they have invented a new shot for infections, penicil . . . something like that to replace sulfa, but the doctor tending Ellen couldn't get it in time to fight her infection. He said the medicine was still new and hard to get, and the sulfa didn't work. Now Bob was that God acting or the odd occurrence of the calendar. What if Ellen had conceived a month later or two months later? Would that have made a difference, would the new shot have been available?" Frank paused, his anger still dominating his reasoning. "Is God playing with us? Who's really in charge of life, Bob? Not the doctor, not Ellen, and certainly not me, and I bet you aren't either. Is anybody in charge that cares?" Frank continued to stare intently at the driver.

"Well son, I believe that God cares; that's my faith speaking. You're right about your other questions, nobody on earth being in charge . . . What can I call you, since we are certainly on a first-name basis?"

"Oh, I'm Frank . . . and . . . I'm sorry for saying those things . . . It's just that I can't begin to accept her passing . . . her . . . death. I can't accept that; it's not fair."

"Frank, I guess my reading of the Holy Scriptures tells me that God didn't promise us an easy life and, as you say, necessarily a fair life, but if we believe in him and his Son, Jesus, at the end we will gain salvation. It's easy to see that not everyone has an easy time of it, and by looking in history we see the same wars and hardship constantly visited on us, over and over again, kind of like the plagues in old Egyptian times. And a lot of us are constantly committing sins, doing what we know we shouldn't. We do that in light of the consequences that will come. And those sins cause serious grief for our fellow humans. In that regard we're all still like children, doing what we know we shouldn't."

The rare stretch of straight road that lay before the car gave two cars following the Studebaker the opportunity to jam their accelerator pedals to the floor and pass Bob on the two-lane road. Bob, undisturbed by the noise of the passing cars, continued, "It seems most of our problems are brought on by ourselves without God's help or interference. I guess he's not a dictator like that Hitler fellow, but I guess he's put us in motion with birth and he sort of wants to see how we do, how we get along, how we treat each other. Now I've heard some of my brethren say that God is in full control and has a plan and even decides when a bird's feather falls to the ground, but I guess I don't see that—at least if he knows, he doesn't stop it and doesn't necessarily care. I just don't think that every tragedy we face is brought on by God and fits his big, big plan. No, I guess I believe that we are responsible for our own lives, our own decisions. We all face different obstacles. Some people have easy times and some are faced with a lot of hard times, so I guess we're not all equal. But we're all responsible for our choices.

"Now you take the Old Testament. It strikes me that the Book of Job may have some answers for you, Frank. Job had a great life with plenty of wealth, but God took it away from him. Now Job and his friends were at first trying to figure out what Job had done wrong to bring down the wrath of God. But Job eventually realized that his faith in God was still what he believed, even though he had nothing left. He was like a beggar. But, he kept his faith and God restored his wealth and increased it. Now that story tells us not to expect rewards here on earth just because we say we believe. No, it tells us to keep our faith no matter what we face, no matter what obstacle blocks our way."

Bob glanced at Frank who stared straight ahead at the ribbon of asphalt that preceded the car, "Now you've been facing a lot of hard times; they just seem to keep piling on, don't they? I know how that is, and when it happens we just can't see why God lets it happen. But, son, I tell you that someday the sting of your loss will not be as sharp as it is now, and between now and then you have a lot of life to live and a lot of decisions to make. You have been given a large obstacle to overcome and to lead your boy and yourself through it. God seems to have a way of opening up a path for us to follow when we least expect it. Sometimes he opens more than one path and we must choose which way to go, but those are some of the challenges we all face. I'm sure you'll find your way, especially if you pray for God's guidance and listen to his voice that you hear sometimes deep inside you." Frank's gaze remained fixed on the road as Bob's words began to sink in.

Having heard God's name mentioned several times, Ida Mae unconsciously turned her head to the left to place her right ear, her "good ear," in a position to pick up more of the front-seat conversation. In doing so she eased away from the side window and leaned into the center of the narrow back seat. Teddy looked up from the sheet of paper in his lap and noticed her movement; he pressed his legs against the right side of the car to keep a space between himself and the strange woman. He didn't want to touch her or have her touch him. He had tried to draw a picture on a sheet of paper Mrs. Kostigan had given him before he left the Forks. She had also given him a six-color set of Crayola crayons to draw with. But the bouncing and swaying of the car made it very hard to draw the way he wanted to. Their house at the Forks just didn't look right. He put the paper and crayons back in the bag and opened the book he had been using as a drawing surface. He started to turn the pages of the familiar story about the Hardy Boys.

Bob's oration in the front seat continued, "Frank I've had two parts of my adult life, before and after I joined the Salvation Army. I did my share of sins in life, when I was a young man, younger than you. I got a job on a river barge, and at first we went back and forth between Cincinnati and St. Louis, occasionally St. Paul. Then I got transferred to one of the company's other boats, and we went to New Orleans. Lord have mercy on my soul. On that first trip I got into every sin and vice known to man down there—there were women, gambling, drinking, and the like. I was a sorry sot by the time we left, and the captain warned me that if my drinking and carousing continued, he would fire me. He said it was a week before I could carry my work load on the boat, and he wouldn't stand for it.

"Well, sir, I was a slow learner," Bob frowned at the memory, "cause on the next trip to New Orleans, I did the same thing and got held by the police for about six hours and I almost missed the boat. I got on board and thought I had avoided the captain's attention, then I started to get all of the really dirty jobs, and I suspected something. Then bang, we reached Paducah and he hired another boy and put me ashore with only half pay. He said I could always sue him for the rest of the pay if I wanted to, but I didn't know anything about courts and lawyers, and I think he knew it. That captain did me a great favor, because as I bummed around Paducah picking up odd jobs, I sensed what my life was and decided to ask God for forgiveness and to help me find my way.

"Now I don't know what part he played in my life—that's my life so far, of course—but I give him credit for turning me around, 'cause I did straighten up and I got to Louisville and tried to join the Salvation Army. At first they thought I was just another sinner who would fall off the wagon, but I wasn't and I kept coming back until the colonel asked me if I really wanted to join the Army. I said yes, and I cried and kissed his hand. I swear to Go—" Bob glanced over his shoulder to reassure himself Teddy was not listening before continuing, "I swear I kissed his hand just like in the Bible. I felt a great burden lift from my shoulders, and ever since, no matter what happens, I am as happy as can be for I have found the salvation that suits me, helping my fellow man. And, Frank, I had to make that decision to change for myself; no one could make it for me. I had to do it. Joining the Salvation Army was the path he opened for me. But God had put out a lot of sign posts to lead me to him through Jesus, and I just started to follow the signs that were always there marking the path."

"Gosh, I'm sorry I've been preaching at you, sometimes I get carried away."

"No, that's alright Bob," mumbled Frank, "I think I'm in a kind of state of shock, or something. I'm just sort of numb . . . But thanks for your words."

Frank stared out the window as they traveled down the hill toward Conway. He had a great deal of difficulty focusing on his problems. Indeed, *where do I start?* All of the passengers once again fell silent.

With the silence, Mrs. Combs, who had overheard all of the last part of the conversation, leaned back in her seat; a handkerchief that she once held loosely in her hands now was knotted in a tight wad. At eight Teddy failed to connect the knotted handkerchief with the inner turmoil in Ida Mae.

She thought, *I could tell them men in front a thing about hard times and Almighty God, praise the Lord.* She knew he was a mighty God capable of casting lost souls into everlasting hell, but she wasn't afraid of him; he was her friend and she was glad. She had heard every Sunday and Wednesday since she was a little girl about the might of God, and she knew it was true. And she knew God was going to smite down the evildoers either on earth or in hell, or maybe in both places. She couldn't remember how someone in hell would be smited down again; she had forgotten what preacher Gingham said. She couldn't stand to listen to those who doubted the word that Jesus Christ was the Living God and he was coming back on judgment day and making judgments, picking the deserving and casting the rest into everlasting hell. And judgment day was coming soon, she knew that. *"And he will be dressed in a suit of armor made of, made of . . ."* She couldn't remember what Preacher Gingham said the armor was made of, *the steel of the righteous, maybe, but he will raise the faithful dead from their graves and those that have been saved and take their hand, and I'm goin' to be among them that gets raised up because I am saved and it's goin' to happen as soon as I die.*

She was ready to die now that Lester was dead following a heart attack at their home up at Redhouse. And she knew that the Redhouse Free Will Baptist Church was better than all the other Baptist churches in Richmond and all of the other Baptist churches all over the world, and you could throw in the Catholics, Presbyterians, and Methodists, and . . . and all of the other make-believe churches as well. *Lester and me and Preacher Gingham and, of course, Momma and Bonnie Mae and her Harold will all have the last word, you wait and see. And we will all go to heaven, and if we find Poppa up there we will send him straight down to hell where he deserves to be, what with all his drinkin', smokin', singin', and stayin' out all night, and probably whorin' as well.* She shuddered at the thought of her father.

Out of the corner of his eye, Teddy noticed the rapid jerking motion of the woman next to him and he laid aside the book. "Are you all right?" he asked.

"What?" she asked.

"You all right, or are you cold or something?"

"No, I'm quite all right, thank you."

"I saw you shake and I thought—"

"I'm perfectly all right," she barked. She added to herself, *Now be quiet, little boy.*

Teddy continued to look at her until she turned to face the window, and then he stood, leaned over his father's shoulder. "Daddy, I'm getting hungry."

"I know, son, we should be in Corbin soon and we can eat there. We want to ride with Bob, er . . . Brother Culbertson as long as we can."

"OK," said Teddy rather dejectedly as he resumed his seat and picked up his book.

"Teddy, do you remember, Mrs. Kostigan gave you some peanuts? They're in your toy bag."

"Oh, yeah, I forgot." Teddy immediately pulled out the small paper bag of peanuts and proceeded to crack the first shell and deposit the crunchy morsels in his mouth. After the fourth peanut shell had been opened, Mrs. Combs said, "For goodness sakes, boy, put your empty shells in the bag . . . stop making such a mess on the seat."

Teddy quickly scooped up the shells but was oblivious of the shredded nut wrappers and small pieces of shell that still littered the seat. A clean world looked far different to a boy of eight than to eyes as perceptive as those of Mrs. Combs.

"And those little crumb things too," Mrs. Combs said as she pointed to the paper-thin nut wrappers. Teddy picked up at least half of them, but in so doing, created twice as many smaller pieces when he lifted them up from the upholstery. . Exasperated, Mrs. Combs thought, *Why am I in a car full of men and that boy. They're so messy; they're always clutterin', causing problems.*

"Teddy," said Frank, "we're coming into Renfro Valley. I used to listen to the Saturday Night Barn Dance show with your Moth

. . . your grandparents. They had Pee Wee King and his band on the show and they were great, good old honest-to-goodness Bluegrass music."

"Yes, sir," chimed in Bob, "ole Pee Wee and the boys can cut a mean tune, almost wear out the radio." Bob chuckled at his humor. "Wear out the radio," he repeated and he laughed out loud. "He plays mostly up in Louisville now, I hear."

Suddenly from the back seat, "And that's another thing my daddy did was sing those high lonesome songs and attract the devil. That's what my momma said." Mrs. Combs abruptly broke into the conversation; her shrill pronouncement startled the males in the car. Teddy noticed that as she said the word "Daddy," a spray of spittle shot from her mouth and arced toward her lap and onto the floor of the car.

"Yes, yes now, Mrs. Combs," glancing over his shoulder again, "I've heard about your daddy, and I'm sorry for the hurt he inflicted on you," Bob said in his most consoling voice.

"Hurt wasn't half of it," she said with a great deal of force. "He took my brother and my brother's son to hell with all that carryin' on of his. He infected both 'em. He fouled all the children in the nest but me and Bonnie Mae, and I was saved by my precious Lester and Bonnie Mae had her Harold."

Teddy again saw the oral spray arc into the air. He stared at the woman open mouthed as the book slipped from his lap to the floor. He scurried to retrieve it before she noticed or said something else he didn't understand. *Why was she so mad*? She was very hard to figure out. She had sat quietly in her seat while he read a chapter of *Hardy Boys and the Mysterious Cave*, but now she was almost screaming when she spoke of her father. He picked up his book and held it close to his nose, not to read, but to shield his face from the strange woman.

She was quiet for several minutes and Teddy thought, *Now that she's calm, maybe she would like a peanut.* "Would you like a peanut?"

"No, I don't want that nut, and you haven't cleaned up your seat yet. You made a mess," she said with vehemence as she swept the peanut detritus into her other hand and deposited it into his toy bag.

"Now, Mrs. Combs, please be kind to the little boy; he's hungry and a long way from home," urged Bob.

"I don't care where he's from or if he's hungry. He's still made a mess with them peanuts," she growled. Teddy wondered if her coat or the floor were getting damp now that she was talking and spraying. He liked her better when she was quiet.

"Ida Mae, you know your mother was a person full of love and kindness first, and then second she believed in judgment and punishment. She and I talked many times about the love of God and his son and how it should always be the first thing we should remember when we get angry. By spreading love we can promote peace on earth, that's what she believed. Remember that?"

Ida Mae sat very still and looked out the side window of the car. *Momma was never in a car with such men and a boy as this. They make me so mad. If my Lester were alive, I wouldn't have to be here, but he ain't. He's dead.* Ida Mae abruptly yanked her coat tightly around her waist and continued to hold it cinched snuggly to her body. *Lord why did you have to take him so soon, answer me that? It weren't his time to go; it should have been me. Now I'm left to contend with life without him . . . I'm on my own. Give me strength to get to the judgment day, that's all I ask. Now today I just want to get to Bonnie Mae's so I can talk. I can't talk to these men; they just don't believe right. Once I get to Bonnie Mae's, I'll be free. I'll love it there in Keavy, no men, thank you Lord Jesus.* She paused. Thinking was often difficult now, and she was getting mixed up in her head, and she knew it. *Momma was in favor of love, that's a fact for sure, and I used to follow that road, but lately things have been so hard with Lester gone, I'm at a loss.* After a long pause, *Oh all right . . .*

"Little boy, I'm sorry I snapped at you," she said in a sudden sharp voice as she released her coat, and then in a somewhat softened tone, "I'll have one of your peanuts, and thank you."

Teddy, surprised at her latest abrupt pronouncement, at first didn't hear all the words. Or maybe he heard them, but they were slow to register since he was watching her body to see if she was going to do something physical, like grab his hair or hit Bob. After a short pause though, he extended one peanut to Mrs. Combs. "You can have another if you want."

"One is all I need, thank you." She cracked the shell and deposited the nuts in her mouth, began to chew, and dropped the shells in Teddy's toy bag.

Disturbed by Mrs. Comb's tirade in the back seat, Frank was ready to do whatever was necessary to protect Teddy, but Teddy was doing all right. This had turned into a strange ride to Corbin. He hoped saving the money was worth the strain on Teddy. As he turned to gaze out the side window, the car topped a rise and headed down into the Rockcastle River valley. "Uh, oh," said Bob. Frank looked ahead and saw they were confronted by a solid line of cars all with their brake lights blinking on and off as the cars coasted slowly down the hill, single file.

"Must be an accident or the state highway boys are fixing the road," Bob intoned.

During one of their frequent complete stops, Frank stepped out of the car and then up onto the running board as he tried to look over the line of traffic. He reentered the car. "I see a police car up ahead with its light blinking; something must be wrong."

"Sometimes they have a police car on this road for repair work, not always though," Bob added. They continued the slow crawl; five minutes turned into seven and then ten as they got within five cars of a state trooper standing in the center of the road waving a flare. Frank noticed a Desoto on the left shoulder with a badly damaged front fender, smashed windshield, and gouges down its side past the rear door. Teddy was standing on the floor behind his father peering over Bob's shoulder. As they pulled even with the policeman Bob asked if anyone was hurt.

"One on the way to the hospital, the driver of the Desoto, and the other two didn't make it. The other driver was crushed by the steering wheel, and the passenger went through the window and was dead when he stopped rolling. Their brakes must'a failed coming down the hill. Move on, please."

Both Frank and Bob were struck by the gruesome detail of the accident. Where was the other car? They couldn't see it. As the traffic crawled past the officer, they noticed off to the right side of the road a track of disturbed ground, and it was obvious that a large, heavy vehicle had rolled off the road and plowed a path through the twenty-foot-high scrub growth into the edge of the forest that lined the highway. As they crept farther along, the back end of a large dump truck was visible sitting among a cluster of trees and shattered tree limbs. The body of the truck was tipped to the side and a large pile of gravel had been spilled on the ground along the path the truck had followed. The side of the truck came into view, and Frank saw with dread the red sign on the door, Splinkler Brothers, Contractors and Hauling. The truck cab had rammed into a three-foot oak without inflicting any noticeable injury to the tree. The hood of the truck was jammed between what was left of the cab and the tree. Part of the engine now rested inside the cab; the truck had experienced a catastrophic and complete stop on a dime. Gravel was scattered on the ground in front of the truck; it had catapulted from the truck bed over the cab upon impact with the tree. Frank looked on in shock as they eased along the road.

"Mercy, what a tragedy. Two lives taken, God help them," muttered Bob.

"I met the truck passenger in Richmond," came a soft voice from Frank as he stared at the dashboard.

"Did you say you know him?" the stunned Bob asked.

"I just met him today before you came . . . That truck pulled away from the curb to make a place when you picked us up at the courthouse. The young man was a student at Eastern, and he was hitching a ride to Jellico to meet his cousin. They were going to join the army to fight the Japs . . . or Germans." Frank's voice trailed off as he continued to stare ahead. *What else can go wrong? Am I cursed, do I curse people around me?*

"Lord, watch over those servants and bring them peace," prayed Bob for the dead as he continued to steer the car south on US 25.

In a velvety blunt voice, Frank asked, "Why did that young man have to die, Bob? Did God have a better plan or place for them to go?"

Also speaking softly, "Frank, I can't read God's mind, can't understand why things happen, I only know that for those of us who survive from day to day, love and forgiveness are the paths to follow. That's what Jesus taught us."

Bob had approached the day's trip with the expectation of a pleasant drive to Keavy to drop off a poor unfortunate woman who had recently lost her husband. The drive south had turned into a confrontation with life and his beliefs. He supposed when he talked he sounded more convinced of his beliefs than he was certain of in his own mind. He knew on the return trip to Richmond in the afternoon he would remember and relive all that had happened, his conversation with Frank, the Book of Job, and would again think about his outlook on life. The return trip would result in many rethinkings.

# CHAPTER 5

## *Corbin to Knoxville*

THE CAR PASSED through London and Lily and down the hill into Corbin about twelve-thirty. Teddy and Frank got out of the car with their luggage in downtown Corbin, determined to find someplace to eat. Frank was surprised when Brother Culbertson gave him a bear hug and wished him happiness and peace in his life. Frank thought, *That would be a big improvement over the present.*

"There's a restaurant down the street a couple of blocks, I think, that might be a good place to get a bite to eat." Bob smiled.

"Thanks for everything," said Frank.

Teddy and Frank walked three blocks before finding Sanders Diner, a typical small-town eatery. After using the restroom, they sat by the front window at one of the last empty tables. Frank looked over the one-sheet menu and waited for the waitress. She finally came bustling around the counter and dropped her order pad on their table, prepared to write.

"What'll it be, gents? Most folks get the fried chicken, but we have good burgers and dogs and chicken salad and other sandwiches." Quietly she added, "I wouldn't get the meatloaf special; it's not very special today, know what I mean, huh?" Teddy noticed she had a name stitched into the shoulder fabric of her dress: Doris.

"Got it," said Frank. "Teddy, would you like a hot dog or chicken?"

That was a hard choice since both were his favorites. "I guess

. . . ah . . . chicken," ventured Teddy tentatively.

"How about a couple of legs for him and I'll have a chicken salad sandwich on toast. And to drink, a glass of milk and a cup of coffee with cream."

"OK," said Doris. She picked up her pad, turned, and walked to the kitchen. Teddy noticed that when she walked away, her tight skirt kept rising and falling with her striding legs.

Teddy turned and looked at his father, "Daddy, why was that lady in the car so mad?"

After a pause, Frank said, "Some people get a hard shell around them that gets thicker as they grow older. They don't always see and hear things the way you and I do. She has had an unhappy life, and she wanted someone to blame, I think. She's unhappy with her life right now. I hope she's happier with her sister."

"Me too . . . ," said Teddy. "Are we having a hard life, Daddy?"

The question caused Frank to pause and quickly think about his response. "Well . . . we definitely have had our problems too, but we shouldn't let them get us down; we still have each other and Granny and Granddad and your grandparents in Carrolton." Frank was grateful that he was talking to a child and hoped his true feelings were not obvious to Teddy. His false attempt at being positive was disingenuous, he knew that, but it was for Teddy's sake that he acted as he did.

"I don't want to grow a shell like that old woman. I don't want you to grow one either."

Frank smiled. "Teddy, I'm certain you won't ever grow a shell, and if you notice I am, then you have my permission to hit me alongside the head and tell me to straighten up."

Teddy laughed. "I can hit you in the head?"

"You can hit me, but first make sure I really have a hard shell," smiled Frank.

"Ker pow," said Teddy. "Can I use a baseball bat?"

"No, I prefer your hand; it will do less permanent damage. Remember, you want to change me not ki . . . hurt me so I can't change."

"OK, can I have a boxing glove on my hand and hit you like Joe Louis?" Teddy giggled.

"Well, that might be all right." Frank laughed aloud, and as he continued to smile, he realized that this was the first time Teddy had laughed since his mother's death.

The noise in the restaurant stayed at a steady drone occasionally broken by a peal of laughter or an occasional loud word and at times a sudden reduction in volume before the clanking of dishes and the clicking of cutlery resumed.

Frank noticed that a man behind the counter was stretching to a radio on the upper shelf over the pass-through window between the counter and kitchen. After several attempts to find a station, he said in a partially audible voice above the din, ". . . resident's goin' to speak." A man at the counter spoke up much louder, "Quiet."

A hush descended over the stools and tables as the radio voice broke through the din. "Louder," came a voice from the table in the corner. The counter man stretched again, and the radio blared before he found a suitable volume for the patrons.

The first recognizable sound that came from the radio was the sound of clapping and then very loud applause that was soon joined by shouting voices. A voice now came through the speaker:

> *"The president is being escorted to the microphone by two aides, one on each side. He will speak momentarily to the joint session of Congr— here's the president."*
>
> *"Mr. Vice President, Mr. Speaker, members of the Senate and House of Representatives. Yesterday, December 7, 1941—a date that will live in infamy—the United States of America was suddenly and deliberately attacked by naval and air forces of the Empire of Japan.*
>
> *"The United States was at peace with that nation and, at the solicitation of Japan, was still in conversation with its government and its emperor looking toward the maintenance of peace in the Pacific."*

"What's he saying?" whispered Teddy?

"Shush," was Frank's sharp reply.

*"Indeed, one hour after Japanese air squadrons had commenced bombing in the American island of Oahu, the Japanese ambassador to the United States and his colleague delivered to our secretary of state a formal reply to a recent American message. And while this reply stated that it seemed useless to continue the existing diplomatic negotiations, it contained no threat or hint of war or of armed attack.*

*"It will be recorded that the distance . . ."*

Teddy's eyes wandered around the restaurant. Everyone was listening. What was going on? Most people stared at the radio as the voice spoke. One lady at the counter had her head bowed with her forehead resting on her folded arms that lay on the counter. One fat old man dressed in brown work pants and a matching brown shirt spilled over the edge of his stool obscuring the stool's cushion. Another old man sitting at a table had turned sideways in his chair to face the radio. One hand was on the chair back and the other on top of the cane he held to the front of his body.

*". . . has caused severe damage to American naval and military forces . . ."*

Teddy recognized that the president was talking about our country and Japan, and he guessed it was because of what happened last night. *The President had an odd way of saying words*, he thought.

*"Yesterday the Japanese government also launched an attack against Malaysia. Last night Japanese forces attacked Hong Kong. Last night Japanese forces attacked Guam. Last night Japanese forces attacked the Philippine Islands. Last night Japanese forces attacked Midway Island.*

*"Japan has therefore undertaken a surprise offensive extending throughout the Pacific area. The facts of yesterday and today speak for themselves. The people of the United States have already formed their opinions and well understand the implications to the very life of and safety of our nation."*

With this statement the radio erupted with applause and shouting soon matched by a sudden outburst from the restaurant's patrons.

Teddy was stunned by the outburst. He sat up straight and noticed his father was not making a sound but staring quietly at the floor of the restaurant with elbows resting on his knees. The people in the restaurant were like the old lady in the car. They were angry.

As quiet descended on the restaurant the president continued.

*"As commander-in-chief of the army and navy, I have directed that all measures be taken for our defense, that always will our whole nation remember the character of the onslaught against us.*

*"No matter how long it may take us to overcome this premeditated invasion, the American people, in their righteous might, will win through to absolute victory."*

Again the restaurant and radio erupted with shouting and clapping.

*"I believe that I interpret the will of the Congress and of the people when I assert that we will not only defend ourselves to the uttermost but will make very certain that this form of treachery shall never again endanger us.*

*"Hostilities exist. There is no blinking at the fact that our people, our territory, and our interests are in grave danger. With confidence in our armed forces, with the unbounding determination of our people, we will gain the inevitable triumph. So help us God."*

Again the eruption of the noise. The old man jabbed his cane into the air and the fat man almost lost his balance on the stool as he shook his arms. He finally grabbed the counter and hooked his toes around the stool's pedestal base. After a brief interval the counter man frantically waved his arms to hush the patrons.

*". . . 1941, a state of war has existed between the United States and the Japanese Empire."*

The noise this time continued as the radio was switched off. Teddy noticed one other patron who did not share in the shouting and swearing. He sat by the door with a plate of partially eaten chicken and mashed potatoes. He was also different from others in the restaurant because he wore a brown suit, the only suit Teddy could see, and had a thin mustache, again the only one in the restaurant with facial hair. It took several minutes for the noise level to subside to a medium roar.

"Daddy, are we going to war? Do we have to fight the Japs?"

"Yes, son, we have to fight the Japanese because of what they did to us."

"Do you have to go?" came Teddy's quiet question.

"I don't know, son," said Frank as he reached across the table and patted his son's hand. "I don't know."

A cloud of doubt crossed Teddy's face as Doris delivered the food. "Here it is, boys, be careful. The chicken, it's hot, just come from the fryer. There are napkins in the holder. Weren't that a great speech? That Roosevelt is a great leader. Got us out of the hard times, and now he's going to lead us to victory. I didn't vote for him, but I'm sure glad he's in charge now." Doris chuckled as she turned to the counter and Teddy saw her rear end bounce toward the kitchen.

Teddy stared at the chicken. He didn't feel particularly hungry, but then the aroma of warm legs changed his mind as his hunger returned. After a bite, he thought *This chicken is as good as Mommy's.*

Doris had left the check, and when they finished, Frank pulled forty cents from his pocket and laid it on the table. They rose and Frank gathered the luggage as they walked to the door. Doris was standing at the table of the man who had been silent like Frank during the loud noise making. "You boys traveling?" she asked. Frank told her of their trip and said they needed to look for a southbound ride on the highway. "Hope you get one soon," she called after them as the glass door closed.

Frank and Teddy stood by the edge of the pavement on US 25, Frank with his fingers curled and thumb extended, Teddy by the suitcases and his toy bag a few feet away on the gravel shoulder. Several cars passed, then one stopped. The driver said he was going to Williamsburg and then Somerset. Frank declined the ride offer as far as Williamsburg, confident one going all the way into

Knoxville would come along. Four more cars passed before a Ford rolled to a stop. The driver reached across the empty passenger seat and rolled down the side window. "I believe you're headed to Knoxville. Hop in."

Frank was puzzled. *How did the stranger know of their plans?* Teddy recognized the man in the brown suit and thin mustache.

"I overheard you in the restaurant talking to the waitress. I'm going down there with a stop first in Williamsburg," the stranger said. "You'll have to put your suitcases on the back seat because the trunk is full of samples." Frank and Teddy climbed in with the suitcases stacked on the back seat behind the driver.

"Thank you very much," Frank said as he shook the outstretched hand.

"Glad to have the company. My name is Mark Carroll. I sell jewelry to drug stores, dress stores, and small-town shops. It's not too expensive, most ladies like the selection we have, and business is getting better these days. We have bracelets, earrings, little necklaces, and pins—costume jewelry. It's a great selection."

"I'm sure it is," responded Frank as the car pulled into the street and sped up as it climbed the hill.

Teddy settled back into the rear seat and pulled out his book. He was a good reader for an eight-year-old. His teacher in Frankfort said he could handle sixth grade reading although he wouldn't understand all that he read. Ellen had started reading to him at bedtime as a baby of three months and then continued the practice until a week before the birth of her second child.

"If you're interested in buying something, I can give it to you wholesale."

"No, thanks," replied Frank.

"What do you do for a living, if I might ask?"

"Well, as of a few weeks ago I was with Old Grand Dad distillery in Frankfort, but now we're headed to Knoxville to my parents. I don't know about work now that the war is on."

"Yeah, ain't that something what the Japs did to us? I noticed in the restaurant you weren't clapping for the president."

"I have a lot on my mind."

"I see," said Mark. "I thought you didn't necessarily agree with what you heard."

"Are you kidding? 'Course I agreed. I'm just worried about how it will affect me and Teddy."

"Well, sure, none of us are for Japan, but I didn't get too excited either. Up till yesterday I thought Japan was doing a pretty good job of cleaning up the Pacific, you know taking care of those gooks in China. The Japs really are giving them the business. Don't get me wrong, I'm no fan of the Japs, but they should be in control in Asia. But now they made a big mistake by attacking us, I guess we'll have to teach 'em a lesson.

"Now you take Germany. I think that Adolph Hitler fellow has some pretty good ideas. At least as far as the communists and Jews are concerned. He's doing well in Russia, and I don't think those Commies can stand much longer. I expect Hitler will march into Moscow very soon."

Frank looked at the driver to make certain his leg was not being pulled.

Mark lit a cigarette and opened the driver's side window a crack, the smoke drifting outside. "It won't bother me if the Germans go ahead and take England. Those people are very uppity, and they have a lot of Jews in their government. Would you like a cigarette?"

"No thanks," replied Frank.

Frank was at a loss for words as he stared straight ahead and listened to the "world according to Mark" unfold. He did recall the childhood rhyme "Liar, liar pants on fire" and smiled. The problem with Mark, Frank realized, was that he accepted propaganda as fact and incorporated it in his understanding of life. What a sap.

Mark glancing at Frank mistook the smile for one of agreement rather than derision. "I don't know why Hitler joined with those wops in Italy; they can't fight their way out of a paper bag. They haven't fought a decent war since the Roman days. Now, you take the Austrians. It was a good thing that Germany invaded them, since Austrians are really Germans under a different name and now Germany has more people and soldiers. I expect Germany will also take the Middle East and get their oil by next spring. They have this Rommel fellow who is a good general. I read about him in a newspaper I get that tells what is really going on over there. The papers in this country are controlled by the Jews, and they don't tell us the truth about Europe. You know we have Commies in this country just like in Russia, yes'sir, and I think Roosevelt is a sympathizer. And he has a lot of Commie friends in Washington with him plotting on how they can take over the country and unite with Russia. It will be a cold day in hell before us loyal Americans stand still for that. We know what he's up to, yes'sir we do."

Mark began to cough and finally rolled down the window and spat into the air whistling past the car. After a few quiet minutes he cleared his throat and continued, "Now you take that Catholic priest fella, Father Coughlin, he opened my eyes to a lot of things. He used to support Roosevelt, but he saw the light and started a radio show and newspaper and told us what was happening. The Jews were behind the communists takeover in Russia, yes'sir, they were. Now, I don't buy everything Coughlin says about capitalism, but he was sure right when it came to Jews and the problems we are facing today. But that damn Roosevelt and his FBI and his other government agencies that he controls, they drove Coughlin off the air, cancelled his radio show, yes'sir they did. I could go on and on about the injustices brought down on Coughlin, I could."

*No doubt*, thought Frank, *but please spare me the pain of listening, you son of a bitch.*

Getting no response from Frank, Mark finally lapsed into silence as the miles sped by. He was driving sixty miles an hour uphill and faster downhill. The highway was winding through the hills on the edge of the Cumberland River watershed. They sped through the small community of Gold Bug as they approached Williamsburg. The road finally leveled out as they entered the town on the banks of the Cumberland River.

"I've got two stops to make," said Mark. "Won't take more

than thirty or forty-five minutes and then we'll be on our way. I'll park here and walk around the corner to Bailey's Drug and Pretty Miss clothes store. I'll be back in a bit. There's a coffee shop there on the corner," gesturing to the west, "in case you need a little lift before I get back."

"Fine," said Frank.

Mark hoisted three large, black boxes form the trunk and stacked two on a heavy wire rack with two wheels and a handle. The third box he carried by its handle. As he walked down the street and around the corner, Teddy noticed the wheels on the wire rack wobbled, causing Mark to stop and adjust his load.

When Mark neared the corner, Frank turned and said, "Teddy get your toy bag and get out of the car."

"I thought we were riding to Knoxville with that man."

"No," said Frank, "I've changed my mind. I think we can get there quicker if we get another ride." To himself Frank thought of the real reason he wanted to leave now, *I don't think I can take much more of his shit before I say something, and then he would probably put us out on the side of the road in the middle of nowhere. I can't let that happen.*

Teddy didn't suspect his father's real reason for switching rides; he had been reading and hadn't heard Mark's soliloquy, not that he would have understood if he had.

They walked two blocks farther along Main Street, and Frank once again extended his thumb. After fifteen minutes, which seemed like thirty, a lady in a Cadillac stopped. She rolled down her window and inquired as to their destination, and the travelers were soon seated in the comfortable car as it moved south toward Knoxville.

"How old is your little boy and what's his name?" she inquired.

"That's Teddy and he's eight, ma'am. And I'm Frank."

"Well, I'm Belle. Your boy is so cute. He's the reason I picked you up. I believe that a man with a child is safe for a woman to pick up. Now, if you had been alone, you would still be in Williamsburg."

"I understand . . . we appreciate the ride very much. We've been traveling all day, headed to my folks in Knoxville." In response to the driver's probing questions, Frank repeated their story, including the loss of Ellen, his job, car, and the uncertainty of his future caused by the war.

"There's not much I can say about your personal losses except that I am deeply sorry. As far as the war is concerned, we're going into hard times, and we're all going to be making sacrifices," she said. "My husband is the sheriff here in Whitley County, and he expects to lose some if not all three of his deputies to the army. We listened to the president's speech today, and we're definitely in a war, no ifs, ands, or buts."

"Yes, ma'am, we heard his speech while we were eating lunch in Corbin."

The driver liked to talk, and Frank tried to carry on a conversation with her. Talking was not at the top of his favorite things to do, especially today. "Does your husband enjoy law enforcement?" he asked as a leading question.

"Yes, he does, but at fifty-seven he says the strain is getting to him. The hours are so unpredictable. He is toying with the idea of running for Congress in the fifth district."

"Oh," said Frank, "the US Congress?"

"Yes, you know you have to have political friends to be a sheriff, and he believes he can win down here in southeast Kentucky."

"He must be a Republican," Frank guessed.

"Yes, yes indeed, in central and west Kentucky we are known as the Damn Republican Party but around here we just call ourselves Republicans."

Frank smiled, "That's the name they use in Frankfort, the damn part, I mean. I was surprised to learn that one of my best friends is a Republican; he's the fellow that gave us a ride to Richmond. We met him and his wife in church and I've known him now three or four years, and I never knew about his politics."

"Yes, there are a few of us hiding under logs and behind trees in Kentucky," she laughed with a deep hearty rumble that belied her decades of smoking. "You seem to keep up with things. How much schooling have you had?"

Frank told her of his Eastern Kentucky experience and meeting Ellen. "I'm not surprised that you went to college," she said. "You speak well. I started college up at Wellesley near Boston, went a year and a half, but the Great War was getting hot and my daddy thought I should come home, so I finished at UK in '20. Then I came home and asked Daddy, 'What do I do now?' and he said get married, of course." She broke into more laughter. "So I found Roger, or he found me. I don't know who saw who first, but like you experienced, we just knew we wanted more than holding hands in the parlor, and marriage was the next step. I was Roger's second wife, so I got two children in the deal, along with a partially used husband." She chuckled again.

"His first wife got a big taste of religion from a Pentecostal preacher, and they must have enjoyed the taste—the wife and preacher that is—'cause before Roger knew it they ran off together. Last he heard they were in Kansas preaching love and redemption, and that's when he gave up on her ever coming back or him wanting her to come back. That was when I found him. Then we had three children of our own. Now, Roger isn't perfect, or as they say in Whitley, *He ain't too good,* but he was good enough for me. We have five children altogether and three grandchildren so far."

"That's a good size family in these hard times," said Frank. "My parents were married in '07 and had six children. My brothers, sisters, and I teased my father about keeping our mother pregnant all the time in the early years except when she was caring for a little baby."

*Actually, your mother had something so say about having those babies*, she mused. "She must be a good mother."

"She's the best, but she's the only one I've had. But looking around I'm very satisfied when I compare her to other women I've known"—Frank chuckled—"as if I had a say in the matter. My dad was a farmer. He and his brother have a farm my granddad had lived on all his life. It's on the Licking River in Nicholas County just east of Millersburg. Back when the rural electric people came through the area in the teens, Dad watched them string up the electric service and said, 'I think I can do that,' and he did: he started fooling around with electricity. It turns out he had a knack for understanding electricity. He was not afraid of it, and he soon had the farm wired and started helping others in the area. Then he took some classes from the county extension agent and got a few jobs in town doing electrical work. He met a man who was an electrical contractor, and Dad started working for him from time to time. Then when the Depression hit, he farmed some and did electrical work some to earn a little money, not much, but a little. I guess it was in '37 when he went to Knoxville to work for the contractor, and then he went back in '38 and was working on a store on Cumberland Avenue in Knoxville when this guy came over to look at what they were doing. He said he was an engineer with a plant located across the street, and soon after he offered Dad a job as assistant plant electrician. Now, that posed a dilemma, and after talking about it for a while, Mom agreed reluctantly to move to Knoxville as long as they set their sights to come back to the farm someday. Dad agreed and they moved, and he no sooner got there than the head electrician was electrocuted on the job and Dad moved up to fill his shoes."

"My, that job sounds dangerous," said Belle.

"Well, it is unless you know what you're doing. Dad said the fellow he replaced would take short cuts and one of his short cuts killed him. Dad knows better than to do something that he's not totally familiar with. He had the TVA people come out several times to go over procedures on how to avoid problems." Frank chuckled. "Problems like death."

They rode in silence for several miles and without realizing it, the more Frank talked, the more comfortable he felt with the driver. If only temporarily, the heavy burdens resting on his shoulders were less apparent.

The landscape along the road had changed, the hills were

taller, the sheer rock outcroppings more plentiful, and the valleys deeper. The road was also curvier going from the right to left to right to left and repeated over and over again. Frank broke the silence, "If your husband runs, does he think he'll win?"

"The first step, and the hardest, is winning the primary; we don't think the man in the job now will run again. He's from Middlesboro and has been pretty sick. If Roger can win the primary, then he will be hard to beat in the general. The fifth is pretty safe for Republicans. He's been out calling on the judges in the other counties in the fifth to check out his chances. So far it looks like he would have one opponent, a young lawyer from Harlan. He will be a tough campaigner; they don't call that town Bloody Harlan for nothing." This time she smiled, but did not laugh. "You see, my husband got some of the idea about running for office from my family. They are politicians going back to my grandfather, who was a Congressman from Pikeville. He made money in coal and could afford to run. Then my daddy was the county judge in Pike County, and I wind up in Whitley County married to a would-be politician. I was Belle Cooper back in the early days. Last year Roger put two and two together and came up with Congress as a way to change our life. I'll be happy either way, in Williamsburg or Washington. I was a little surprised when he told me of his dream about Congress, but I said let's go."

"I think you could get along just fine in Washington," said Frank.

"Laws, yes, I'm no shrinking violet. Now if you want to meet a promising politician, go see my cousin John Sherman Cooper. He is a real comer in the Republican Party from over in Somerset. He's talked about making the governor's race again, but he hasn't decided yet. I guess you remember he lost to Johnson in '39. Daddy said he should run for Senate. We have those two Democrats up in Washington now, Happy and Alben. Alben has been there so long there're likely to find moss growing on him. I think Happy can be beat; that race is two years away."

"I bet you are the real politician in your family."

"Well, I've been known to give Roger advice from time to time, and if he's elected I won't stop." They both broke into laughter. Belle continued, "You know politics is a blood sport in Kentucky; people are always jockeying for position for the next election. The best thing that's happened was when they limited the governor's term to four years—that way no one gets stuck in the office." The laughter resumed.

"Daddy, I feel sick," said a voice from the back seat.

"Oh, Lordy, hold on child," said Belle as she started looking for a place to stop the car. A wide shoulder on the right-hand side of the road appeared, and she skidded to a stop on the gravel shoulder. "Open the door for him, I don't want to have to hose out the car."

Frank was already out of the car before Belle finished speaking and pulled open the back door and lifted Teddy from the car. He led Teddy in a halting trot toward the rocks along the bottom of the hillside as Teddy's stomach launched its first heave. Teddy's attempts at holding down his lunch failed. The first eruption was rather small but his stomach gained strength and hurled out a surprisingly large volume for the boy on the second and third try. The vomit spewed on the rocks and spattered his shoes.

"Here, let me have him." Belle came running from the car with a fist full of Kleenex and held Teddy's forehead as he bent over and continued to launch smaller and smaller quantities of lunch and bile. Frank stood helplessly by but was grateful that Belle had stepped in to help.

"There you are, little man," she said as she wiped his forehead, mouth, and then his shoes. "Do you think you're finished?"

Teddy had no idea how to answer the strange woman's question. His stomach felt calmer, but was he finished? "I'm not sure," came his reply.

"Walk around a little and see if you feel better, honey."

"Howdy, folks," came a voice from the road. Frank and Belle turned to see Mark Cooper striding from the highway. "I wondered what became of you," he said looking at Frank with a slight grin.

"I decided to try and get another ride since you had business to attend to. This nice lady offered us a hitch, then Teddy got carsick"

"Hello, Mrs. Carroll, I thought that might be your big caddy."

"Mr. Cooper," an icy frost cooled her reply.

"I see the boy is sick. Glad he wasn't in my car." Mark laughed and returned to his car, started it, and shot off the shoulder of the road kicking gravel in their direction. His thin laugh reminded Frank of the movie serials that he had seen as a boy: the villain had that sinister "hee hee" laugh with a hint of a sneer, so like Mark's.

"That detestable man."

"So you know him. Are you related?" asked Frank.

"I wouldn't say know him as much as I know of him. And we are not related even though we shared the last birth name. These hills are full of Coopers, . . . Carrolls, Combs, Caudills, and the like, and thank God those of us with the same last names don't have to claim a blood tie to all of 'em. His side of the Cooper family must have lived in a rat hole somewhere, but not in Pike County. He is a hate monger that tried to poison our county party with his filth, about four years ago, maybe five. We have some pretty conservative people who don't like government, but they're not the likes of him. You should have seen the pamphlets he was trying to hand out, filthy Nazi literature. We had to drive him out of the county, or rather Roger did. It's for people like that Mark that we enjoy having a strong-willed sheriff in Whitley. Roger grabbed him by the back of the collar and escorted him out of the meeting. Gave him the old fashioned bum's rush. That vermin told Roger 'you can't do this; we have freedom of speech, it's America.' And Roger said 'yes I can, this is Whitley County, and I don't want to find you in town again.' I do see him in town every once in a while when he's selling those cheap trinkets of his, but he knows better than to stay overnight or to try and butter-up people about his beliefs. You know, he was calling everyone in Washington a communist or a dupe who could be fooled by the reds. Now, I admit Roosevelt did some awfully questionable things from '32 up to '40, but he managed to get them through Congress and didn't get slapped too often by the courts. He is not a communist, just a damn good, damn Democrat, and he's awfully lucky."

Surprised, Frank looked at her. She stood on the gravel shoulder with her fists on her hips and glared at the road to the south as if she hoped Mark would return so she could pop him one. She was rather heavy in the hips. The weight had probably accumulated gradually over the years. She, in fact, reminded Frank of his mother. Belle was much more worldly and better educated, but the women underneath were very similar. Belle knew about politics and his mother knew about farming, and they both understood a lot about life. He remembered his mother facing down a deputy sheriff once when she knew he was throwing around his weight. The farm hands were hesitant to confront him, but she marched right up to that jack-leg and ordered him off her property before she got mean. He claimed he left because he didn't want to hurt a woman, but everyone knew he had met his match. He knew Belle would have done the same thing given the circumstances.

"I guess no one wants to mess with you, at least not more often than the first time," said Frank.

"I have a reputation to protect," she said and turned with a smile on her face. She had conquered Mark. "Did you know him?"

"We ate in the same restaurant in Corbin, and he gave us a ride to Williamsburg. He had business there, and I decided to leave and find another ride rather than to wait and have to listen to his diatribe all the way to Knoxville."

"You used good judgment not to be around him any more than you have to."

They returned to the car, and placing her arm around Teddy's shoulder, Belle said, "Why don't you ride up front with me? I'm sure your father won't mind. There's less swaying in the front seat than in the back; it's these mountain curves that make little people sick." Once inside the car she reached inside her purse and pulled out a roll of Tums and said to Teddy, "Here, eat two of these. They may not cure the sick, but they will make your mouth taste better." Teddy did as he was told.

Belle pulled the car back onto the roadway and continued south. The road followed the west bank of a small rapidly flowing branch of the Cumberland River, curve after curve after curve. The L&N Railroad ran on the narrow east bank. Teddy saw the railroad tracks disappear into a tunnel as the steep hillside dropped vertically into the stream's edge. A little farther to the south the tracks emerged from the hill and followed the stream's constantly curving path. The car had passed through Jellico and Chaska; the road sign said the next towns would be La Follette and then Lake City. The road left the stream valley but was still curvy with one hill after the other.

As Frank relaxed in the comfort of the back seat, he tried to review his problems and what he faced in the month ahead. He realized that he had an aching feeling, a need to respond to the nation's catastrophe that had occurred at Pearl Harbor. He knew he was qualified for that. Was that response just a way of taking him away from his responsibilities with Teddy and his other problems? Would he be running away? He had left The Forks, but there was nothing left for him there, nothing. That wasn't running, but yes it was in a way . . . , *I don't know. Uncle Willard would call me a Pitiful Puss if he saw me now. I guess anybody looking at me would feel sorry for me. Is that the problem, I feel sorry for myself?* If he did go into the military he could think of no solution to the dilemma of Teddy. He knew his parents would care for Teddy, but Teddy needed more than a grandparents' care; he needed a parent. Frank could think of only a few choice swear words to say, but that was of no help.

"Teddy, is your name Theodore, like my son Ted?" asked Belle.

"No, ma'am, it's Edward Franklin Warring, not Theodore. How old is your son?"

"He's twenty-seven, or is it twenty-eight? Well, older than you. He works in Cleveland, Ohio. He sells insurance."

"Oh," said Teddy. "Was he called Teddy when he was little?"

"No, he was called Button. When he was born, everyone said he was as cute as a button, but when he went to school we knew he needed a better name for a boy." Teddy broke into a giggle when he heard the name Button. Belle continued, "And so we switched to Ted and he's been Ted ever since"

"Button," Teddy repeated and continued to laugh. "Button."

Frank realized he had enjoyed the brief respite from his misery offered by Belle. He thought, *She must have been some girl as a young bride and mother*. He wondered how much spunk she exhibited then . . . probably a lot for a young person. Then his thoughts returned to his dilemma, rather, Teddy's and his dilemma. He gazed out the window at the passing hillside, *Lord, I'm lost . . . I don't know where to go, or what to do.* He paused, *I remember as a boy with the fishing canoe, Daddy always stressed that when I got in shallow water and the rocks started rubbing the bottom of the boat to get out of the boat and pull it to shore or push it back into deeper water, don't hurt the bottom of the boat, don't make it leak. Well, Lord, I'm rubbing on rocks now; I'm on the bottom and I don't know where the shore is or which way is the deep water, I just don't know. Tell me, Lord, . . . which way to go. Help me find that path.*

Frank laid his head back on the plush upholstery and heard the light laughter coming from the front seat as the repartee between the eight- and forty-eight-year-old continued. His mind went blank as he concentrated on not concentrating. He closed his eyes and did not sleep.

# CHAPTER 6

## *Knoxville*

As THE CAR traveled down the Clinton Highway and entered downtown Knoxville, Belle asked Frank where she could drop them. "My dad said we should go to the Farragut Hotel and call him and they would come right in to get us." As the hotel doorman opened the front car door, Teddy stepped onto the curb and gazed at the number of large buildings on Gay Street. This place was larger than either Frankfort or Lexington. Frank had the luggage on the sidewalk after telling the doorman they did not need a bell hop. Belle approached Frank and gave him a hug, which surprised both Frank and Teddy, then she hugged Teddy, who grunted a little at the attention. He wondered why women were always grabbing, pinching, or hugging him. They waved good-bye to Belle as she drove toward the Tennessee River, then father and son entered the hotel lobby.

"Sit here with the luggage while I go to the pay phone in the shoeshine shop and call home." Teddy did as told and sank into the deep leather cushions of the chair in the center of the lobby. His feet were about a foot from the floor when he sat with his back against the back of the chair. Frank returned and said, "Granny and Granddad will be here as soon as he gets home from work. It'll be about an hour, I think."

Frank sat in the chair opposite Teddy and stared at his hands. Teddy pulled his two toy cars from the toy bag and began running them along the arm of the chair. Soon he was driving them down the front of the chair to the floor. The cars drove in front of a side table and then started up the arm of the chair on the other side of the table. It was then he looked up into the eyes of a girl staring at him over the back of the chair. He stood up holding his cars and stared back.

"What's your name?" came her query.

"Teddy . . . What's yours?"

"Mary Ann."

Teddy felt a presence now at his side, and when he turned, there was another girl. He looked back at the first and then the second girl and saw the same person.

"I'm Barbara Ann," said the second girl.

"Are you sisters?" asked Teddy.

"Of course we are," came Mary Ann's response. "Who do you think we are?"

"I don't know," said Teddy, "maybe cousins."

"No silly, we're twins."

"Do you want to play cars? I have two."

"I don't like cars," said Barbara Ann. "There're boring."

Teddy stared at the cars in his hand, "One is a Fiat and one a Ford."

"What's a Fi-at or whatever you said?"

"Daddy say's it's an Italian car."

"That's stupid," said Barbara. "Let's sing songs."

She proceeded to launch into a verse of "Mary Had a Little Lamb." Mary Ann joined her partway through the song, and they ended in more of a yell than a harmony.

"Shush girls," came the voice of a thin woman in a nearby chair who was reading this month's edition of *Collier's* magazine. "You're making too much noise."

Then the girls started to whisper the words to *Mary Had a Little Lamb* and broke into giggles as they hissed through the ending. "Do you know any songs?" Barbara asked Teddy.

He thought and then started the song he knew best. He waved his hands in a series of patterns as he sang, "Oh I had a little chicken and it wouldn't lay an egg; I poured hot water up and down its leg; and the little chicken squawked and the little chicken laid; the little chicken laid me a hardboiled egg, hump diddy eye eye, some chick."

The girls squealed and clapped their hands. "Sing that again," demanded Mary. He did and then the girls tried to learn the song and hand movements. All three children at one point during the song lesson giggled uncontrollably. Barbara, afraid of her mother's scolding, said "Shush," and they sang in whispers, which increased the giggling.

"Let's play musical chairs," said Barbara.

"There's not enough of us," complained Mary.

"There are too." And she proceeded to align two straight-back chairs she retrieved from a writing desk. Then she started to parade around the chairs singing and humming a series of notes. The other two children joined in, and Barbara stopped singing when she was in front of a chair. Mary was eliminated, and Teddy was eliminated when she stopped singing the next time. "I win," exalted Barbara. They played two more times with the same result, and Teddy and Mary revolted against Barbara's rigged game.

"Where do you live?" Mary asked Teddy.

"At the Forks of Elkhorn," he replied.

"Where's that?" the girls said in chorus.

"Near Frankfort. That's the capitol of Kentucky."

"We're from Birmingham. That's the biggest city in Alabama. We're here for a job interview at the university."

"Oh," said Teddy, "what's that?"

"The University of Tennessee, silly. That's a college," chimed in Mary. "Our Daddy teaches math, and we may move here."

"What's math?" said Teddy.

"It's, ah . . . like arithmetic only harder," said Barbara

"Mommy, he doesn't know what math is," Barbara called to her mother.

"Shush, Barbara, some country people don't know such

things," she replied without looking up from her magazine.

"He's not from the country, he's from Fort Elkton or someplace like that."

"Shush, girls, don't make fun of people."

Teddy was embarrassed by her reference to him, and he turned slightly pink.

The children chattered on, or rather the girls did, and Teddy added a few words from time to time. Frank had begun to notice the interaction of the three children and was pleased to see Teddy laugh and giggle. He was being a child again. Frank hadn't seen such reaction in the last few weeks, and he was glad. Frank noticed the girl's mother had not looked up from her magazine when she spoke and had a stern look on her face and at times a visible frown. She did not seem to be a happy person, maybe like he had been over the past month. Two businessmen stood by the shoeshine shop and chatted with gestures emphasizing their conversation. An elderly couple walked through the lobby toward the elevators, and the clerk behind the desk was checking a young couple into the hotel. Frank realized that this was the first time he had looked upon his surroundings since he sat down. He felt relaxed and relieved to be in Knoxville.

The girls suddenly ran from Teddy toward a man who had just entered the lobby. They tugged at his coat as he carried a briefcase over to the mother of the girls. *He must be the father*, thought Frank. The couple started to have an animated conversation, and the mother rose. The family walked to the elevators with the girls hanging on their father's coat. Neither parent looked as if they were enjoying the afternoon.

Teddy waved and called, "Bye." The girls ignored him. Teddy then turned and walked over to the chair opposite Frank and plopped down.

"It's been a long day, hasn't it, kiddo?"

Teddy understood the term "kiddo" was a signal his father gave him when he was feeling good. "I'm fine. Daddy, can I change my name?"

"Sure, son, what name do you want? Ralph, Waldo, Cedric, anything you want is OK with me."

"No, Daddy, none of those made-up, funny names. I want my own name."

"Well, how about Eddie or Ed for Edward or for Franklin there's Little Frank, or—"

"I want to be Ted now," said Teddy. "That sounds better."

"Oh, you're growing up, are you?"

"I don't know. I just don't want to be Teddy anymore. That's a baby's name."

*I guess you're right*, thought Frank.

"Granny!" shouted Teddy as he sprang from his chair, raced to the door, and launched himself onto a stocky lady by wrapping his arms around her neck and his legs around her waist. Frank's mother momentarily lost her balance and stepped back to absorb the blow. "I'm so glad to see you," Teddy said in her ear.

Frank's father, Will, walked past the embracing couple and took Frank in a bear hug. The two men remained in their embrace a longer time than most greeting hugs. "How're you doin', kiddo?" He gazed in his son's face and held him at arms' length.

"It's been rough, Dad, very rough," was all Frank could manage to say as his throat closed to further conversation. His father pulled his son into another embrace and this time Frank returned it with equal fervor. After a moment they parted and Frank observed, "I've forgotten what a strong old farmer you are."

His father smiled and replied, "Same to you, boy."

The men laughed as they walked to Teddy and his grandmother; she lowered Ted to the floor. Mary wrapped her son in a warm embrace, than released him saying, "This young man says he wants to be called Ted from now on. Lands sakes, I can't keep the names of my grandchildren straight. You'll have to help me remember your new name. I may forget," she said smiling at Teddy.

"Let's go home," said Will, as the family exited to Gay Street.

# PART 2

## *Refitting*

# PART 2

*Knoxville, Tennessee, 1940s*
*(Partial Map of City)*

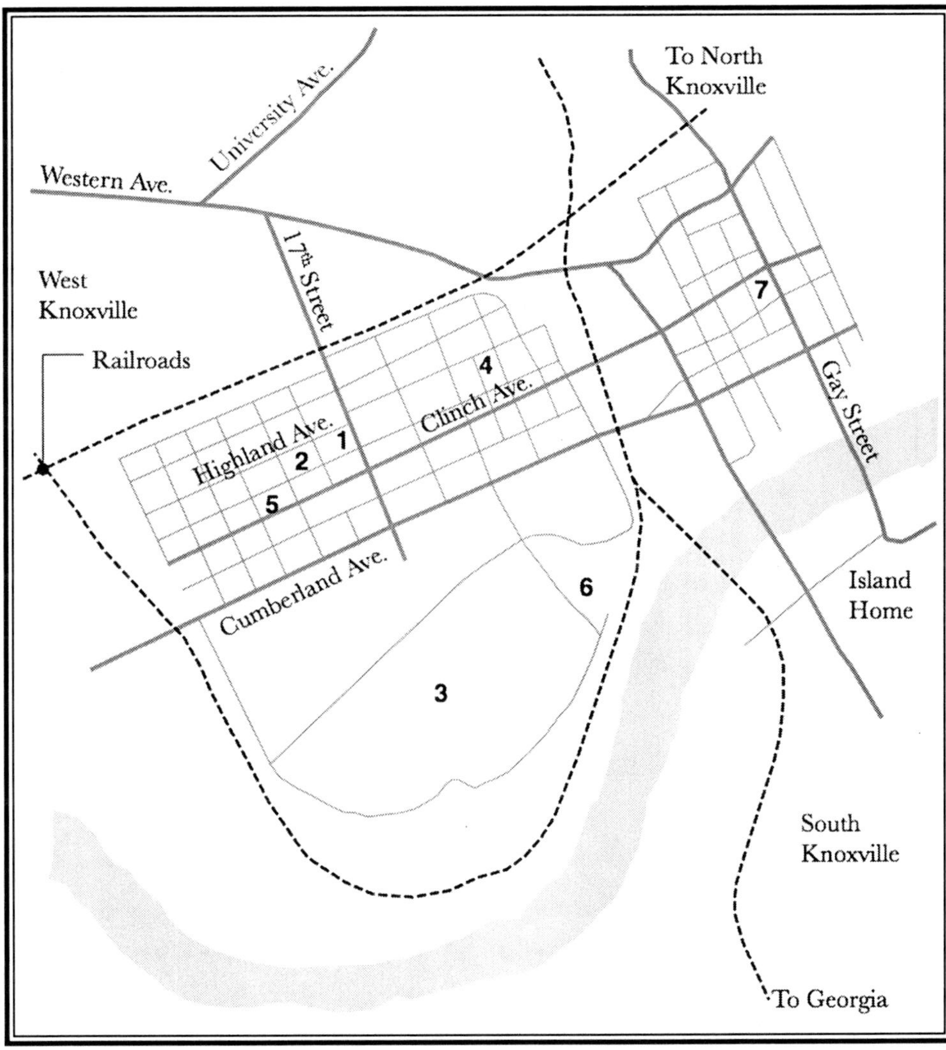


LEGEND:

1. *1702 Highland Ave.*
2. *Roberts Grocery*
3. *Univ. of Tennessee*
4. *Van Gilder Elem.*
5. *Civil War Trenches*
6. *Shields Watkins Stadium*
7. *Downtown Knoxville*

# CHAPTER 7

## *Morning in Knoxville*

## *January 20, 1942*

AT SIX THIRTY in the morning, Frank climbed the front porch steps of the house at 1702 Highland Avenue and entered the front door leaving behind the cold winter air. His mother was in the kitchen fixing breakfast for Will and Ted, who were still upstairs. "Morning, Mom. Everybody have a good night?"

"Oh, yes, everything calm." Mary stood at the electric stove frying bacon while the smell of baking biscuits filled the air. "How was your night? Any problems?"

"No, like here, calm." Frank poured a cup of coffee and sat at the small kitchen table. Fast-moving feet were heard on the stairs that descended from the second floor and ended by the kitchen door into the dining room. Ted jumped the last three steps and landed on his hands and feet in a squatting position.

"Hi, Daddy," he said as he jumped into the kitchen and landed on his father's lap. This was Ted's custom now to greet his father in the morning with a brief visit in his lap, being close to him.

"Did you finish your homework from school?" asked Frank looking over Ted's shoulder at the side of his face?

"You bet. It was easy. Granny helped a little. I had to learn five words to spell and do a counting problem. They were easy."

"All I did was listen to his words that he spelled right the first time, except for ocean—that was a little harder, Mary added."

"O-c-a-n, ocean," said Ted.

"Not quite," said his father.

"Oh yeah . . . o-c-*e*-a-n, ocean," Ted said with emphasis on the *e* and delivered with a smile. Frank was struck by the personality that was emerging in Ted: happy, so much like his mother.

"Well, if you can't spell the word correctly, you can always smile at the teacher and still get a good grade." Frank chuckled.

"Ah, Daddy, anyway ocean should be spelled o-s-h-u-n, just like it sounds," Ted said as he hopped off Frank's lap and pulled a cereal bowl from the cabinet shelf, the box of Corn Flakes from the lower cabinet, and the milk bottle from the Crosley refrigerator that sat by the back door.

"Want some bacon, Teddy?" asked Mary.

"Yes, please," Ted responded as he poured milk on the flakes, sprinkled sugar, and began spooning cereal into his mouth.

"Frank, here's your plate," said Mary as she placed a plate of warmed-over beef stew and a freshly baked, hot biscuit before him and gave her son a squeeze on the shoulder.

"Thanks, Mom."

"The stew's from last, night and it may be better today. Stew usually gets better the second time around . . . I hope it's hot enough."

"It's really good," said Frank with a full mouth of food.

Mary smiled. She no longer reminded her son not to talk with food in his mouth. After all, she had not broken him of the habit after raising him, nor had Ellen after almost twelve years of marriage. Mary paused, *Imagine, they were married twelve years; then she's gone in a snap of the fingers.* Mary's sad reverie was broken by Will entering the kitchen.

"Morning, Dad."

"Morning, Granddad," Ted mimicked his father.

"Good mornin' to one and all," said Will as he kissed the back of Mary's neck, picked up his plate of breakfast from the top of the stove, and sat at the table. "Ouch, these biscuits are as hot as blue bejeabbers."

"Watch out for the hot biscuits," came Mary's belated warning, delivered with a sly smile.

"Now she tells me," Will said with mock gruffness as he spread butter on the steaming bread. Ted laughed at both grandparents.

"Ted, if you're finished, go up and brush your teeth," said Frank. "Get your school papers and jacket. I'll walk you to school this morning."

Ted raced up the stairs as Frank leaned toward his father. "Dad, I need to talk to you, maybe tonight after supper and before I go to work. I have been thinking . . . well, maybe worrying. I'm all mixed up. Can we talk?"

"Of course, son, either before or after supper would be fine. I'll be here."

"Thanks," said Frank as he rose from the table with downcast eyes and headed toward the front of the house.

Ted raced down the stairs, grabbed his lunch sack with the peanut butter and jelly sandwich Mary had made, and raced after his father. Mary called out, "Have a good day, Teddy." After a pause, "Laws, he's so sad, he just don't know what to do next or where to turn."

"You mean Frank?" murmured Will.

Mary nodded.

"I know. I wish I could help, but I can't."

Mary mumbled as she carried dishes to the sink, "Only time will mend a broken heart."

Ted and Frank sat on the front porch steps as Jerry and Floyd walked up the slight hill on Highland Avenue toward Seventeenth. "Morning, boys," said Frank, "mind if I get a little exercise and walk to school with you?"

"No, sir," came the two responses as the four crossed Seventeenth, turned left, and then to the right onto the offset extension of Highland and started their downhill walk to Van Gilder Elementary School at Fourteenth Street.

Ted asked Jerry and Floyd, "Did you get your homework done?"

"Oh, sure," came Jerry's response, "ole Miss Wolf gave us easy words this time. My father grilled me on' 'em." Floyd didn't respond but looked a little worried as they crossed Sixteenth Street.

Frank left the boys on the steps of the school and then reversed his path and started walking back up Highland toward Seventeenth Street. As he walked, hands in his jacket pockets, he rewound the story of his life during the past three months. Ted had started to adjust to Knoxville after Christmas when he began to make friends in school and in the neighboring homes on Highland Avenue. Before Christmas there were heartbreaking exchanges with Ted that echoed the depth of loss he felt with his mother's passing. Frank absorbed the depth of Ted's anguish and understood that the loss of a parent at eight and a wife at thirty-two were equally devastating. Why had Mommy died? Why had the love of his life died? Frank had no answer for Ted or himself with any deeper reason than the cold medical facts, which he did not clarify for Ted. Neither of them was satisfied or comforted by the cruel turn of events during the Thanksgiving holiday.

In an effort to have Ted take some kind of action about his grief instead of only the push and pull of the conflict, Frank suggested he write Mrs. Kostigan a letter to see how she was doing now that he had moved to Knoxville. Ted agreed. Frank's only contribution to the letter was the spelling of Mrs. Kostigan's name. During the letter writing, he also provided Ted with the spelling of the name of his new school.

*dear Mrs. Kostigan how are you I am fine but pretty sad most of the time. my granny said you were a kind lady to keep me and you have good brekfists to my school is Van Gilder Elementary School and is near my house Granny hears my less-ons sometimes. Gerry goes to school there You must come see us and stay a while how is Betty jane I hope she has stopped crying. Ted Warring your firend*

The letter seemed to have a positive effect on Ted as Mrs. Kostigan answered promptly with news of Betty Jane's recovery from crying, Billy Ray's induction into the navy, and the small fire in the kitchen of the Buck Run Baptist Church that scared everyone because of the time it took the volunteer fire department to reach the Forks. In reply, Ted sent her one of his art papers from the third grade that she could keep "for herself." It showed a "Jap plain" going down in flames with a long trail of black smoke.

With the beginning of the new year, 1942, Frank noticed a slow turn in Ted's attitude as life at school and home became his new normal. His new friends helped in a way that they could not understand, and Ted's raw wounds began to slowly heal. Laughter with his friends turned out to be a healing balm for Ted.

Frank recalled Ted's first day of school in mid-December. Father and son walked along Highland Avenue toward Van Gilder Elementary School. Ted walked slowly at times and then had to run several steps to catch up to his father. Frank set a consistent pace, not wanting to give in to Ted's efforts to slow their progress. They crossed Fourteenth Street and turned onto the school property, a two-story, brick school building facing Highland Avenue with a playground along Fourteenth and Laurel Avenue at the back of the building. Frank paused. "Teddy do you see the street signs? Notice we have walked along Highland Avenue to Fourteenth, and there is the school."

Ted glanced at the street sign and nodded to his father.

"Are you sure you know how to get back home," asked Frank?

"Yes," Ted said, slowly pointing back up the hill toward Seventeenth. His eyes then stared at the sidewalk.

"Be careful crossing the streets and remember to look both ways for cars. Teddy, I know you don't want to go to a new school, but we need to get you started so you can finish third grade. You'll make some new friends just like Buddy Ellis and Tommie Bauman at the Forks."

"I didn't really like Tommie. He hit me in the stomach."

"Well, I'm sure you'll find better friends here than at the Forks. Let's go in and see who we meet."

Ted trudged slowly up the front stairs and through the door held open by Frank. The school office was to the left of the entrance. On the wall bulletin board by the entrance were letters proclaiming Art Work, Mrs. Wolf, 3A. Under the letters were sheets of manila art paper with pieces of construction paper glued in patterns to depict the pilgrims' arrival in Massachusetts in 1620. Each student had developed a different theme: one showed Indians, another a turkey and a feast table, and others chose different ideas of how the first Thanksgiving feast might have been. Ted stood and looked at the sheets of paper and did not accompany his father into the office. After the door had closed, Frank opened it again. "Come on, Teddy."

The school secretary sitting behind the counter rose. "Yes, can I help you?"

"I have a new student for you, Teddy Warring."

"Daddy . . . , Ted," came the soft voice at Frank's side as Ted tugged at his father's sleeve.

"He prefers Ted rather than Teddy. Sometimes I forget."

"Oh, yes, we've been expecting you. I'll get Miss Pritchett, the principal. She'll want to meet both of you. In the meantime have a seat there." She motioned to a row of hard wooden chairs lining the office wall facing the counter. And so a new chapter opened in Ted's life.

# CHAPTER 8

## *Evening in Knoxville*

## *January 20, 1942*

FRANK HAD JUST awakened from his daytime "night's sleep." After shaving, washing, and dressing, he went into the room he shared with Ted. The room sharing was not a problem since Ted slept at night while Frank worked and Frank slept in the day when Ted was in school. Frank turned on the late afternoon news at station WNOX, the CBS affiliate in Knoxville.

*"This is The World Today with Douglas Edwards . . . At least three men have been detained by the FBI for questioning about possible seditious activities, according to reports out of Washington. One of the three was Mark Cooper from Lexington, Kentucky, a salesman for the Rumbold Jewelry Company in Cincinnati. Cooper is reported . . ."*

An ugly chuckle came from deep inside Frank as he recalled Mark's view of the world and Belle's warning about the literature he had tried to distribute in Williamsburg. He wondered if Belle had a role in his arrest. His attention was suddenly disrupted. "Do you have any clothes to wash? I've got Teddy's," asked Mary from the open door to the hall.

"Oh, no thanks, Mom," came his reply as reality of the afternoon seeped back into his consciousness.

Mary saw Frank's ashen complexion and the rings under his eyes. *He's so troubled. There's no place to turn, and I don't know how to help him. I used to be able to help when he was a boy, but not now, not this time with Ellen gone.* Mary caught her breath as she started for the stairs with a bundle of dirty clothes.

Frank tied his shoes. *"On the war front, yesterday's attack on the oil refinery in Ellwood, California, was carried out by a Japanese submarine, according to naval officials in San Diego. The fires started as a result of the attack have been contained and are expected to be doused completely by this evening. The search for the attacking submarine continues as naval aircraft patrol the Southern California coast. In an effort to reassure the American public, the same office of public affairs in San Diego said that additional aircraft surveillance will be extended north along the coast to the Canadian border by the end of the year.*

*"We have reports today from Washington that in a meeting of the country's new war council, President Roosevelt ordered Pacific commander Douglas MacArthur out of the Philippine islands to a base in Australia. MacArthur, whose headquarters were moved to the Bataan Peninsula from Manila in December, is reportedly resisting the move and is in further consultation with the War Department. The American defense forces on Luzon are continuing to retreat to the Bataan Peninsula under heavy pressure from the invading Japanese force and face a possible complete collapse. Because adequate US naval forces are not available to counter the Japanese navy, the rescue of American soldiers seems doubtful at this time and the nation braces itself for the worst.*

*"Meanwhile as the nation continues to establish its foundation for waging war on two fronts and to forestall cooperation with the enemy if the Japanese army invades the West Coast, President Roosevelt today ordered the internment of Japanese-American citizens in the western United States."*

Frank's attention was riveted on the radio dial. *"The action is viewed as the next step following his signing of Executive Order 9066 on January 19th that allowed the US military to define areas as exclusionary zones in the western states. The War Department, in conjunction with the Department of the Interior, has begun making plans for the location of internment camps removed from the coastal regions of California, Oregon, and Washington. The number of Japanese confined to the camps may exceed one hundred thousand. The order is also expected to affect people of German and Italian extraction on the East Coast.*

*"In Europe today Princess Elizabeth registered for war service with the . . ."*

Frank snapped off the disturbing news and sat motionless, staring at the radio. With his recent schedule of work during the nighttime hours, he had missed news of the president issuing the Executive Order allowing for the internment of the Japanese out west. Frank immediately thought of George Ito, his college roommate and about the only person of Asian descent he had ever met. *What about George and his family? Surely they won't put him in a camp. He's an American . . . He's always been an American . . . he has a wife and two children . . . His wife has Korean parents. What about her? Will half-Japanese, half-Korean children have to go to jail too? Damn, what's happening to us?*

The questions swirling in Frank's head were suddenly disturbed again. Ted, Jerry, and Floyd entered the room discussing the differences between Tonto and the Green Hornet's man servant. "Tonto's a better fighter and he can ride and shoot better," Jerry observed.

"Oh, hi, Daddy, I didn't know you were here," said Ted.

"Just listening to the news . . . What're you doing?" Frank asked with an expressionless face hardly able to focus on the conversation.

"We wanted to listen to the *Lone Ranger* and then *Captain Midnight*," Ted said.

"Oh, sure . . . go right ahead. After all, it's your new radio. I'm through with the news." Frank rose, picked up his wallet and keys from the dresser, and walked from the room and down the stairs. As he reached the bottom, he could hear the opening music of the "William Tell Overture" as the episode of the *Lone Ranger* began.

Will parked his truck in the back yard under the maple tree and ducked under the clothes line with the drying clothes, the result of Mary's afternoon labors. He entered the back door of the house; it was about five thirty. Mary greeted him, "Frank's in the living room waitin' for you."

Will looked puzzled and then recalled the morning's conversation and walked down the hall to Frank. Will settled in his favorite chair with the smoking stand on the chair's right-hand side. Frank was standing at the front window that provided a view of Highland Avenue, but Frank's eyes were not registering on the quiet residential street. He turned and walked over to his father and sat on the footstool in front of Will. Staring at his hands Frank said, "Have you ever been totally lost, not knowing what to do . . . and what not to do? That's where I am . . . I just can't find my way . . . I see no future for me." The gray shadows on his face spoke of the sleepless days and unfocused waking hours.

"She was the dearest person I've ever known, son. Your mother and I regarded her as our daughter. We're not surprised at your grief, at your loss. I hate to think of what I would'a done had Mary died." A visible shudder shook the older man.

Frank continued to stare at his hands as tears began to form in his eyes. Frank blinked, but the tears continued flowing despite his effort to hold them back, his body shaking with a spasm of grief. Will eased himself out of the chair and onto his knees in front of his son and held him tightly as the shaking continued.

After a few minutes Frank mumbled, "I'm sorry, Dad . . . I guess I haven't cried yet, and now I have to do it in front of you."

"There's no better place than here and now," whispered Will as tears rimmed his eyes as well. Mary came down the hall and entered the living room to behold the two weeping men and she joined the crying huddle, kneeling beside her son and husband.

"Frank I know you are deeply troubled. You've had a lot thrown at you all at once; it's like you're in the middle of a terrible storm," Mary whispered amid her tears.

After several minutes Mary, in an attempt to change the mood, said in a halfhearted manner and with a hint of mirth amid her tears, "You men sure know how to get to the bottom of a situation." Then she gave a short laugh.

Frank and Will both began to chuckle with their wet faces and tear-streaked cheeks. They heard a commotion on the stairs caused by the noisy descent of Ted, Floyd, and Jerry. Mary pulled Kleenex from her apron pocket, and the three began dabbing eyes, wiping noses. Floyd was the first to walk past the living-room door and observe the three adults on their knees and said to Ted and Jerry, "They must'a dropped something on the floor. They're looking for it."

"Wha'dja lose?" asked Ted.

"Granddad dropped his pen," replied Mary as she collected her thoughts. "We'll find it; you all go on outside." None of the three adults faced the door to the hall, knowing their tear-stained appearance would relate to the boys a different reason for their posture on the floor.

A race broke out between the boys to see who could reach the front porch first and then continued on toward Eighteenth Avenue and Jerry's house to shoot his basketball at the hoop nailed to the garage.

After a prolonged shuffling, the three adults made it to their feet and Will sat once again in his chair, and Mary with her left arm circling Frank's waist stood beside her son in front of the burning gas grate in the fireplace. Frank cleared his throat, looked at his feet, and began again to describe his dilemma, "I feel lost, as I know you both already know. With this job as a night watchman, I feel like I'm treading water. I've no reason to go back to the Forks with Ellen gone, and of course, I don't have a job there either. With the war starting, I feel like I should help, but there's Ted. He's all I have left of my family, and I don't see how I can leave him."

"Frank," said Mary reaching up to touch his cheek, "I don't want you to go, but you know we will take care of Teddy no matter what until you return, even if we go back to farmin', which I hope will happen someday."

Will nodded, "He's fit in real well here in Knoxville, especially now that he has friends, and he seems to be gettin' on in school pretty good."

"Yes, he's adjusted better than I ever will." Frank looked at his parents. "But still, can I sacrifice his happiness by not being here just so I can feel like I'm doing something useful in the military?"

"Frank, there's not a one of us in America who won't be sacrificing till this war is over. Some will sacrifice more than others. Just think of the parents of those poor sailors in Pearl Harbor—they sacrificed their children." Realizing the implications for his family of what he just said, Will felt a shiver go down his back.

"I went down to the army recruiting office two days ago just to talk," said Frank holding his mother's right hand and looking at his father. "A sergeant there said the draft was going to start pulling in more men, and he didn't think my watchman job would exempt me, but being a father might. He said with my military school and two years of college, I should volunteer and apply for Officer Candidate School. That's a new training program the army has set up for training second lieutenants. You used to have to go to West Point to be an officer, but there's not enough young officers coming out now and they have this additional school. He said I was a shoo-in unless I was a real f— excuse me, unless I really messed up. If I was an officer, my pay would be higher and I could send it home for you to use for Ted. And if the worst happened, there would be some life insurance to help with his future."

"Lands sake, don't talk that-a-way, don't even think about dying," blurted Mary. "Don't consider it."

"Now, Mary," said Will, "life is life and it's gotten real hard all of a sudden. We thought the Depression was bad, but I don't think we've seen anything yet till this war. We have the draft startin', rationing startin', and they say they're goin' to set prices and stuff so who knows what all is goin' to happen—and that's on top of people gettin' killed. You know about Mrs. Reese's boy missin' after the attack on Pearl Harbor. He was on the Arizona, and all missin' means is that they haven't found his body yet."

"I don't want to hear about it," said Mary as she broke off from Frank and walked resolutely back to the kitchen. Frank and Will heard very loud banging of pans coming from the kitchen as she set about assaulting the evening meal. Frank and Will followed her to the kitchen.

"All right, Mom," Frank said with a sigh. "I still have to decide what to do."

"Now, Frank," lectured Mary as she gestured while holding a frying pan, "I have always believed in prayer, and I think you should empty your heart to the Lord and ask him what to do."

"Mom, I've tried that and I got no answer," replied Frank.

In a softer tone she said, "Well, give him time for heaven's sake, give him time. He may have a few other things to do, you know. Besides, sometimes he doesn't seem to work on our schedule. He'll tell you sooner or later. Promise me that you'll pray on it one more time tomorrow morning when you go to sleep and then sleep on it and see what you think then."

"OK, Mom."

"Son, you're a good man," Will said softly and halted, then staring directly into Frank's eyes, "and we're very proud of you. You're a good father . . . we will stand with you no matter what you decide. Whether you go or stay will make no difference in our feelings for you and Teddy."

"Thanks, Dad, I love you both so muc . . ." Frank uttered the barely audible response, and the three had a second brief scrum in the center of the kitchen. This time they were on their feet and with tears held at the back of their eyes.

The next day, Saturday afternoon February 28, Frank got up from his night's sleep and prepared for the day. He did not have to work that evening, but he knew he needed to keep his schedule intact, sleeping in the day and being awake at night, so he could go to work Monday evening. After eating a quick breakfast he walked outside to find Ted. The Gooch's house across the street had large bushes in the side yard, and as Florabelle and Marie McGruder walked around the corner of Seventeenth, loud screams erupted as Ted, Jerry, and Floyd sprang from the bushes wielding long, willowy sticks that sliced overhead arcs through the crisp winter air. The girls screamed and led the race toward their house two doors down the block from where Frank stood. Frank walked down the sidewalk and found the boys securing new hiding places beside the front porch of the McGruder's in hope that the girls would reappear.

"Ted," called Frank, "come on home. We have to go downtown."

Ted dropped his willowy-stick sword and immediately ran to his father. He liked the idea of going downtown, that was a rare treat on Saturday. "Where're we going?" asked Ted.

"We have to buy a few things."

At seven o'clock that evening, Ted and Frank climbed the steps and entered the house on Highland Avenue. Will and Mary were sitting in the living room listening to the radio; Mary knitted as she listened, "*. . . the Tennessee Barn Dance brought to you by Cass Walker . . .*" Mary turned off the radio. Ted carried a large wrapped package that was about an inch thick. "Look what Daddy bought me," said Ted as he fell to his knees in the center of the room and tore the paper from a world atlas and handed it to his grandmother. Then he relieved Frank of a second package, a large cubical box. Ted strained to open the box and then pulled out a world globe on a short revolving stand and placed it on top of the box in front of his grandfather. "This is the world, and see it turns just like the earth turns and you can find every place in the world on it."

"My, my," said Mary, "what're you goin' to do with all of this?"

"I get to help Daddy follow the war all over the world," said Ted. "I've got my radio, and we can listen to the news and tell what's happening."

"I see," said Will, as he glanced at his son.

"I thought it would be a good way to study geography if we got these things," Frank said without looking at his father.

"Yes, I guess it will be," offered Will.

During the next two weeks, the family resumed their routines with work, school, and home life. Frank's attitude had improved, and he spent more time with Ted as they listened to the news, read the newspapers, and plotted the dismal progress of the war on the maps and globe. During early March the news continued to be bad from around the world. General MacArthur had left Bataan by PT boat and reached safety in Australia, the RAF launched air bombing raids against the center of German industry in Essen, and the Japanese continued their march to dominate Asia. President Roosevelt ordered the relocation of all Japanese-Americans on the West Coast, and Frank knew what that meant for George Ito.

On one Saturday afternoon in the middle of March, Frank and Ted plus Jerry and Floyd rode the streetcar downtown and attended a double-feature movie at the Tennessee Theater—*Along the Sundown Trail* and *Billy the Kid's Smoking Guns*. Between the features, a cartoon, *Daffy the Commando*, was run. Frank recognized the film as Walt Disney's efforts at propaganda to boost the will of the viewing public. By the time they reached Highland Avenue at the end of the day, Frank's head was reeling from an extended dose of young boys having a very good time with ample horseplay and giggling. The ride home on the nearly empty streetcar was particularly boisterous.

The next afternoon after Ted and his grandmother attended church services and Sunday school at the Fifth Avenue Presbyterian Church, Frank and Ted walked over to the open ground near Fort Sanders Hospital. Ted wanted to show his father something "really special" about the Civil War. As Frank looked at the rolling ground, the remains of Civil War trenches were clearly evident. They sat on a mound that had been the top of a trench. Ted and his friends regularly played cowboys and Indians among the trenches. The soft earth easily absorbed their agonizing death falls when they were gunned down by the enemy. The mounds also allowed the victim to roll down to the bottom of the trench in the soft grass, thus adding a dramatic emphasis to their repeated deaths. Ted told his father all of this.

"Do you know what happened here about seventy-five years ago?" asked Frank.

"Yes they were fighting the Civil War. Jerry says it was really the War between the States."

"I guess both names are correct. The folks in the South don't want to admit now that they were rebels so much as they were fighting for their rights. The folks in the North said they were rebels and called it a civil war. They both are right. I don't know if there was actual fighting here, but there was fighting all over the South and around Washington DC. There were a lot of people fighting hard for what they thought was right."

"Yeah," said Ted, "it must'a been pretty bad. Jerry said there was fighting here when the South attacked the Yankee's fort here at Fort Sanders. That was before it was a hospital."

"It must have been pretty bad," said Frank. "But look at this place now. We are at peace with each other, and the grass has grown to help cover our wounds from that war. Someday these mounds will be worn down and gone altogether."

"Yeah," said Ted watching ants carry tiny bits of food in a long line that wound between the stems of grass, up the side of an anthill and disappeared into a center hole.

"You know that's what's happening now all over the world. People are fighting for what they believe in. Unfortunately the Germans and Japanese are fighting for the right to dominate other countries, and those countries are resisting as well as they can."

"Yeah," said Ted. Ted began to sense that his father had something to say to him.

"We're helping those other countries, as well as protecting our country. Do you remember on the drive down here we talked a little about the war and what might happen to me?"

"Yeah . . . ," said Ted slowly as the memory now brought a feeling of dread.

"Well . . . , Teddy I have to make a decision about our future, and I wanted to talk to you about it." Ted remained silent, not wanting to hear the next words from his father. "I'm going to have to go in the service and be away from you, Granny, and Granddad for a while. Then when I come back, we will get our own house near here and you can finish elementary school at Van Gilder."

Ted's eyes betrayed his attempt to be brave as tears began to roll down his cheek. Frank encircled him with his arm and held him tightly against his side. "Ted, I have to go fight for our country because it's the right thing to do. I just can't stay home; I have to help. You can help me by writing letters to me while I'm away, which I will need very much so I can tell how you are doing. And you can tell me how Granny and Granddad are doing as well. Do you think you can do that?"

Ted, with his head bowed, nodded.

"This war will be over someday, and everything will be all right again, I promise," said Frank, not letting the specter of his not returning enter his mind. *God, grant me courage to do what's right and to live, to be with my son, to see him reach my age. Wouldn't that be wonderful?* thought Frank. *Ted as a man. Yes, I want to survive and live.* Frank was uncertain where his prayer stopped and his thinking of Ted as an adult began and whether they were all part of the prayer. Maybe God would sort out his thoughts. After all, Frank knew he wasn't very good at talking to God, and he knew God knew it as well.

# CHAPTER 9

## *Knoxville*

## *Spring 1942*

"MARY, THIS IS Leroy Ames. He's started working with me at the plant as assistant electrician."

"Evenin', Leroy. Will told me he was goin' to invite you to supper. We're mighty glad to have you."

"Evenin', Mrs. Warring, I certainly appreciate a good, home-cooked meal; it's been two weeks since I left home to come to Knoxville, and I miss whatever you've fixed us tonight."

Mary laughed. "Don't be too sure you missed it until you've tried some of my cookin'. You can wash up here in the sink or in the bathroom at the top of the stairs."

"Thank you, ma'am. I'll just knock off the top layer here in the sink."

"Will, would you stick your head out the front door and call Frank and Ted? I think Frank's on the porch."

"Will tells me you have a wife and some children up in Cadiz, Kentucky,'" said Mary.

"Yes'sum," said Leroy as he dried his hands on a dish towel. "My wife is tending her daddy. He's in a bad way and needs help to feed himself. They think he may pull through and get back on his feet again, but the docs ain't sure. He's seventy now and has been slowing down for some time. He was a miner and that was hard on him, and his lungs are all full up and don't work so well."

"I'm sorry to hear that," said Mary. "I hope it works out for him. But you're down here by yourself?"

"Yes'sum, we just needed the money, especially with the war starting, and this will be a good job for allowing me to do electrical work, which I love. If her father don't make it, she and the two girls may move down, but that's not decided yet. She don't want to consider the possibility he might die, the possibility of her daddy not bein' around, don't you know."

"Yes, this is a hard time for your wife. I hope everything works out for her too."

Soon the family of four and their guest were gathered at the dining-room table for a brief and almost unintelligible blessing offered by Will in a rapid staccato voice. The meal of white navy beans seasoned with ham plus sliced onions and cornbread sticks were enjoyed by all, especially Leroy and Ted. After clearing the table of dirty dishes, Mary brought in bowls of freshly baked short cake topped with peaches she canned the previous summer and cream whipped to a mound of white perfection.

"I can't wait for the fresh strawberries to come in and then the peaches," Mary said, smacking her lips. "They are the best part of summer of course, along with corn on the cob and green beans we buy down at Market Square now that we don't have the farm. We've got a little garden, but it's not big enough to get us through the summer. Besides it's still too early for those goodies." Mary chuckled.

After cleaning his dessert bowl, Leroy said, "I am fuller then a tick. That was mighty good."

"Leroy is living in temporary housing arranged by the company, and he needs to find something more permanent," said Will. "Since he's an electrician helping me at the plant and bein' married, he probably won't be drafted, which is good. The thermostats we make now at the plant help us to be essential for the war. And"—he pronounced with a long emphasis on the word—"before long we may begin casting cannon shells, big brass ones, made just for the Germans and Japs." Looking at his wife, he continued, "Now, Mary, we have that shed at the back of the lot that a hired man used to live in, according to Mr. Gooch from across the street, and I was thinkin' I want to fix it up nice so it will be a little more comfortable, and then Leroy can stay there. That way we can ride to work together and save gas. So what do y'all think?"

"Holy cow, Mr. Warring, that's mighty nice of you," said Leroy. "I don't know what the shed needs, but I would sure like to help fix it up. You may not know it but I am quite handy with a hammer and saw, been building things all my life it seems. I'm not so good at plumbing, but I can help with most of the rest, electricity and plastering and painting and things like that, don't you know."

"Well there's already some plumbing in the shed. You can see where they pulled out a toilet that used to be there, and there's an electric light. Oh, and there's a coal heating stove and a chimney pipe. Mary, what do you think?" asked Will.

Sitting back in her chair with her arms folded across her chest, "I know by now after forty years of bein' married to you that when you have thought about something and made up your mind, then you are goin' to do it."

"No, now, Mary, I want your honest opinion."

"I think it's a good idea. That way I'll have another man around the house for me to boss," she said with a sly grin. "Besides, Leroy likes my cookin', so he's a right smart fellow with good taste." Mary's smile grew larger as she talked.

"We may need to hurry and start before they start rationing building materials," said Will. "Leroy, do you think we can start this weekend?"

The die was cast and in the last week of March on a clear Saturday afternoon after lunch, the construction crew gathered—Will, Leroy, and Ted. Frank would join them after he woke from his night's sleep. Will and Ted had piled the junk that had been stored in the shed in the backyard. "Now I've got a problem," said Will scratching his head. "Some of this machinery I brought from the farm and want to keep, and I need a place to put it."

"Can we put it back in the shed?" asked Ted.

"If we do that, we don't have room for Leroy."

"Oh, yeah," mumbled Ted.

Leroy wandered into the shed and after a few minutes emerged. "Let me run a few ideas by you, Mr. Warring."

"Now, just a minute, Leroy, if we are going to build this thing, you're goin' to call me Will. None of this "mister" business."

"Yes, sir," said Leroy. He walked to the shed door, and all three entered the twelve- by twenty-foot cinder block building. "You see we got one window near the door. Now, if we built a wall to separate this main room from the back of the shed and then knock a new door into the back part from the outside, you could store the machinery there and this part would be the living space," Leroy said as he swept his arm around the nearby floor space.

"I don't know," said Will, scratching his jaw. "I don't think you would have enough room here with the back part walled off."

Leroy looked up into the space above the rafters, "Well, we could put in a little stair and a floor up on the rafters and make a sleeping room up there so a fella would have a little two-story apartment, like."

"Is there enough headroom up there?" asked Will.

Leroy pulled a ladder into the shed from outside. "Ted, climb up there and hold the end of this tape measure against the rafters. Now, you have to be careful up there. Be sure to stand on one of those boards that runs across the rafters."

Ted liked being included in the important work and scrambled up the ladder.

"Stop there," said Leroy, "and put the end of the tape at the bottom of the rafter so we know how much room we have down here." After doing as told, Ted climbed the rest of the way into the open attic space and Leroy directed the placement of the tape end in several locations. Leroy had a board where he wrote numbers and said to Will, "We can do it OK. We'll have headroom down the center of the attic gable, 'bout six feet wide. It's a good thing that roof is high and steep, 'cause that way we get more headroom. You know, we can also have the room extend over the back part of the shed so the upstairs room'll be very roomy. We just need to put a floor over the entire attic space and maybe cut a window in the end of the gable for a little natural light and air. What'cha think, Mr. War . . . Will?"

"I guess that's a plan, but I'm goin' to have to get some more building supplies: a window and door and some floorin'."

"Will, if we can take your truck and go over to a place on Western Avenue, that's near where I'm rooming now, there's this salvage materials place and we might be able to pick up some things over there."

"Might be," said Will hopefully.

Three hours later the three clambered out of Will's truck and began to unload several items from the truck bed and add them to the pile already in the backyard. They had a small Palladio-style arched window that would open with two hinges across its flat bottom, just right for the second-floor sleeping area, and a two-part Dutch door and frame just right for the outside entrance into the new storage room. There was also a commode with an overhead flush tank, coils of electrical wire of various sizes, and a slop sink with a drain board that could be rigged up for a small kitchenette area.. "These were real bargains," said Leroy.

"You're a born scrounger, Leroy, you know that?" said Will.

"I prefer frugal, if you don't mind," said Leroy with a big grin on his face.

"I sure hope we can fit these into the shed and make it a decent place to live."

"We'll do 'er, all right," reassured Leroy.

After two weeks, Will walked into the shed to inspect their work so far. Leroy was correct, *he was "handy with a hammer and saw*," he thought. So far, they had built the interior wall separating the new storage room from the living area, cut an opening and hung the outside door, only they placed the Dutch door on the apartment and moved the original shed door to the new storage room. Will soon learned to let Leroy do all the sawing, while he, Frank, and Ted did most of the nailing. Will also learned the value of concrete nails used by Leroy to anchor the new interior wall's plates to the concrete floor and lag bolts to anchor the last double stud to the cinder-block walls.

Leroy and Frank had applied the rough sheathing to the inside wall of the storage area and then nailed the plaster lath strips to the living-area side of the inside wall. Leroy did the plastering; no one else tried to help. The toilet was to be placed in the corner of the "living" room next to the new wall, and they planned to build a short wall to help provide privacy for its use. Will hoped they could hang a curtain over the toilet area entrance so he could avoid having to buy another door.

As Leroy and Ted entered the room, Will said, "I guess we'll build the stair here," standing in the center of the room. "That way, you won't hit your head on the roof joists when you go up 'em."

"Yes, sir, I guess we could, but then again we could turn the stairs ninety degrees and start them here by the front door and climb up part way then have a little landing and double back and finish the stairs going toward the high part of the room up there. That way the stairs won't be in the middle of the room where they would sorta be in the way, don't you know."

After considering the logic of the proposed arrangement, Will said, "Damn, you're right again, Leroy. All right, are we ready to start cutting the stairs in?" inquired Will.

"Yes'sir," said Leroy. "Let's measure first and then frame around the rafters we're gonna cut, then cut out the rafters to make a place for the stairs to go through the opening."

"Huh?" said Will.

"I'll show you," said Leroy as he unfolded the ladder and climbed to the rafters.

April 14, 1942, was a day each member of the Warring family would remember until their final breath. They rose early and had a hardy breakfast of ham, eggs, biscuits, and grits. Frank did not eat any grits; he quipped that he preferred wallpaper paste to the corn specialty. Mary did not chastise him. Since Ted and Granny had bathed the night before, their preparation time for leaving the house was reduced to a minimum. They boarded the street car on Seventeenth Street and were soon downtown at the post office federal building. Ted held on to his father's hand as they entered a large room of families and individual young men. Most everyone looked apprehensive, considering the seriousness of the unfolding sequence of events that had brought them together. The assembled crowd grew and waited. At eleven o'clock a military officer stood at a microphone at the far end of the room and directed all the young men to come forward and stand in rows of fifteen facing the low dais. To do so, they had to duck under a rope stretched across the middle of the room. The families and friends crowded behind the rope.

Straining to see, Ted forged a path around legs to the front right side of the gathering so he could see his father in the third row of men and glimpse the people gathered on the dais. An officer began speaking and the meaning of his words eluded Ted. Then the officer introduced a man called a "federal judge." The judge raised his right hand and administered the oath that inducted all the young men, including Ted's father, into the United States Army.

Ted did recognize several words that were said about the constitution and knew that when all the men said, "I will," in a resounding voice, something very important had occurred. The men were instructed to be at the L&N railroad station at "Oh eight hundred hours on Twenty One April, that's eight o'clock next Wednesday morning if any of you need a translation," came the officers parting words.

At the conclusion of the ceremony, there was scattered clapping from the families and also a sigh in recognition of what had happened. The conversation level then increased as the new soldiers, their loved ones, and friends reunited at the rear of the room. Frank, Ted, Mary, and Will made their way to Gay Street and walked several blocks to the S&W Cafeteria. Ted had never before been in a cafeteria and received instructions on sliding the tray along the stainless steel bars and selecting individual dishes to eat.

"You can have whatever you want today," said Frank, "just make sure you can eat all of whatever you get." Ted passed by the salads and most of the vegetables but did ask for the fried okra to go with his fried chicken, mashed potatoes with gravy, and a dinner roll. At the dessert section he selected a piece of chocolate cake and a piece of pecan pie to go with his carton of milk.

During lunch, Will told stories of adventures that Ted's great uncle Willard had experienced in the Great War. As everyone finally stopped eating, Ted laid down his fork without a single bite taken from the piece of cake. "I'm fuller than a tick," he said. Mary had a small paper sack in her purse in which she deposited the cake, as well as the extra roll left from her lunch and crackers wrapped in cellophane from Will's plate.

"That's mighty good food," said Will. Then with a smile, "My compliments to Mr. S and Mr. W."

"I think they're women," said Mary. "Men can't cook like that."

"Maybe so, old girl." Will laughed. Mary swatted his backside as they walked to the door while Ted laughed.

The following Wednesday the family again rose early, but this time the breakfast was quick. They boarded the streetcar shortly after seven o'clock and reached the train station in a half hour. Ted carried his father's small duffel bag, which contained only what he was to bring: a change of underwear, toothbrush, and razor. He would soon have a standard set of government issued clothing and could send home the clothes he wore. The good-byes were long anticipated, but nonetheless painful. Ted and his grandmother cried, and Frank held Ted as long as he could before he had to board the train.

At 8:05 the steam engine positioned well beyond the roof of the covered boarding area started to turn its drive wheels, and the conductor's shout of "all aboard" signaled their departure. Ted watched the train until it disappeared around a distant curve heading for the Tennessee River bridge and Fort Benning, Georgia.

On the ride back to Highland Avenue, Mary asked Ted if he would like to stay home or go to school a little late that day. "I want to stay home," was the reply. Ted spent the afternoon sitting on the porch watching the few cars go by on Highland and the greater amount of traffic on Seventeenth. Ted said little at supper, picking at his food, and then went to bed early. Mary went up to his room after she was certain he was in bed. "Would you like to say a prayer for your father?" she asked sitting on the bed and stroking Ted's hair.

"Yes," was the reply, and the two knelt beside the bed, their heads bowed and hands held together as Ted recited the prayer taught him by his mother, but one he had not said since her death. "Now I lay me down to sleep and pray the Lord my soul to keep. If I should die before I wake, I pray the Lord my soul to take. Bless Mommy and Daddy and Granny and Granddad and Mamaw and Papaw and Mrs. Kostigan and Betty Jane."

Ted kissed his grandmother's cheek and climbed in bed. Mary kissed his forehead, said, "Good night Teddy," pulled the covers up to his chin, and then walked quickly from the room before he saw her tears. The two would repeat the ritual of the evening prayer every night for the next three-and-a-half years.

The following Friday, Will announced that a fellow named Isaac was coming over to take care of the plumbing hook-ups at the apartment. Early Saturday morning while Ted walked around the shed with a small hammer looking for a loose nail he could bang on, a rickety truck rolled into the backyard and stopped beside his grandfather's slightly newer and slightly less-rickety truck. A medium-sized black man wearing denim overalls eased out of the driver's seat and walked toward the shed. He spotted Ted and asked, "Is Mister Will 'round?"

Ted paused then replied, "Yes, sir, just a minute," and raced into the house to fetch his granddad. When he returned, he confided to the stranger, "Granny said he's on the pot and will be out soon."

"Umhum, my name is Isaac," said the stranger, not betraying the smile he enjoyed at the youngster's straightforward information about his grandfather. "I do the plumbin' work," said Isaac, "and I believe Mister Will need's some work done."

"Yes'sir, Mr. Isaac, it's right in here," said Ted as he proceeded to show Isaac the proposed toilet and sink location and the fixtures lying on the floor.

After studying the location of the former toilet that had long ago been removed, Isaac pulled from the floor drain wadded up newspapers that formed a sufficient but not complete drain plug. Ted started to notice the odor emanating from the opened hole in the floor. "Phew," he exclaimed.

"That's sewer gas," said Isaac. "That's a good sign 'cause its means the drain is still open to the sewer. Now, if we didn't smell nothin', that would mean the pipe was probably stopped up or busted and we would have to dig up the yard. That smell is good. Umhum."

Just then Will entered. "Hi, Isaac, how y'all this mornin'."

"Jus' fine, Mister Will. This young man showed me where the toilet and sink go. Is there anything else?"

"No, that's about it, and of course we need the water line extended to the sink from where it's stubbed off."

"'Course, neither one works without water. I guess there's no hot water at the sink?"

"Yeah, we don't need hot water for the old boy who's going to stay here. He can use our house when he needs his Saturday bath," said Will.

Will returned to the house, and Isaac went to the truck and returned with a substantial wooden tool box with many pipe wrenches and other plumbing items piled six inches above the top of the open tray. After Isaac set it on the floor, Ted tried to lift the box but could only manage to budge its weight slightly. "That's pretty heavy," said Isaac. Ted grunted in agreement.

Isaac next brought in pieces of pipe and a steel tripod, which he erected on the floor. "That's for cuttin' and threadin' the pipes," said Isaac. "See, this vise holds the pipes, and I saw or thread the end while it's held tight."

"Uhhuh," said Ted, not understanding for certain what Isaac meant by "threading" the pipe.

"Young man, do you have a place to hook up a garden hose at the back of the house?"

"Yes, sir."

"Can you hook up the end of my hose so's we can test how good this drain really works? We wants to make sure it will let out water as good as it lets in the stink." Isaac had pulled a coil of hose from his truck and handed its end to Teddy.

"Yes, sir." Ted grabbed the end of Isaac's hose and started racing toward the house. About halfway across the backyard he slowed down as the drag of the unrolling hose was increasing. By the time he reached the outside water tap, he was pulling with all his might as he finally got enough slack to successfully screw the hose end to the tap.

Isaac stuck his head out of the apartment door and said, "You can turn it on whenever you're ready."

Ted did so and immediately turned it off as the hose squirted his shoes and socks with the first blast of water. After two more attempts by Ted, Isaac saw the trouble he was having and walked to the house and gave the hose a turn to seal the connection. Ted noticed the hard muscles in Isaac's forearms that turned the hose well past the point he had reached.

"That'll do 'er," said Isaac, and the pair walked back to the apartment. Isaac had the other end of the hose stuck down into the floor drain. "We'll let 'er run for a minute or two." When satisfied with the drain's performance, he pulled out the hose and turned off the nozzle. "I better go turn off the house faucet so's it don't bust my old hose."

Isaac had soon pulled from his truck additional large and small pieces of pipe. "Now, first I'm goin' to weld a piece of pipe as a extension on the drain so's I can attach the toilet."

"OK." Ted followed Isaac's every move.

After cutting and threading one end of the large drain pipe, he said, "Now, I got to weld the other end of this piece on the floor drain. You musn't look at the fire when I turns on the welder 'cause it'll hurt your eyes. Promise you won't look?"

"Yes, sir. Won't it hurt your eyes?"

"I got this mask with special glass to protect my eyes."

After bringing a tank of gas on a rolling frame into the apartment, Isaac started the welding step. As Ted stared at the wall with his back to the welding operation, he heard the pop and crack of the torch's ignition and heard the crackling, sputtering of the torch uniting the pieces of pipe.

The sputtering, flashing light cast Ted's shadow on the cinder-block wall, and Ted jumped and waved to see his shadow mimic his every movement. "That'll do it," said Isaac as the welding flame was turned off with a sharp crack. Soon he was fitting the toilet onto the drain and bolting it in place.

"I ain't installed one of these old overhead tanks in several years." He began fastening the drain tank to the wall and attached the connecting water line. An hour after arriving, Isaac was ready to test the operation of the toilet. "Les see if it works, young man. Pull that cord." Ted did as requested, and the toilet functioned as well as an old used toilet could, and with plenty of noise.

"Now for the sink," said Isaac. During this operation Ted got to try his hand at turning the die on the end of the pipes to cut the threads; he now understood the purpose of the threads. He made two complete rotations of the device before he guessed Isaac had better finish the job. Isaac showed Ted how to apply the pipe dope to the threads to help ensure a watertight connection. Ted also started turning the nuts on the connections, with Isaac completing each one. Isaac showed Ted how to sweat the pipes so that the solder would run into the seam of the water-line connections.

As Isaac and Ted started to carry supplies and equipment to the truck, Ted confided, "We have leaky sinks at my school."

"What school's that?"

"Van Gilder."

"I knows where that's at."

"Did you go there," inquired Ted?

"Lordy no, I went for three years to a colored school in Dibrell, that's a little town down near McMinnville."

"Oh," said Ted. "Didn't you like school?"

"Oh, I liked school jus' fine, but I had to help my daddy on the farm. I must'a been 'bout your age. We was mighty poor."

"I think we're poor too," said Ted.

"Well, most everybody I know in the depression was poor. We was poor before it started and poor during it; depression made no difference. We doin' a little better now that I'm doin' plumbin' work. Now my son, Isaac Two, he graduated from high school, and his son, Isaac Three, he's in first grade now. He's learnin' to read. We just call him Three and his daddy we call Two, saves time you know."

When packing the truck was completed, Will came into the backyard and Ted ran to the house. "Did the boy get in the way?"

"No, sir, he was a big help. He sticked right with me, a big help. He was interested in everything I did."

"Well I hope he didn't slow you down too much. His daddy left for the army about a week ago, and he's been very quiet ever since. I was glad to see him get interested in what you did."

"Oh, that Mister Ted, he's a fine young man. My youngest son, Aaron, he's eighteen and has gone in the navy, he's been up in Illinois now a month. I know he's gonna be a cook on a ship, but that's alright; a ship needs a cook as well as it needs a captain to fight a war. His momma says if the navy can teach Aaron to cook, they would have performed a miracle." Both men laughed. "She say he can't even peel taters or slice onions or boil water." The laughter continued.

They walked into the apartment, and Will checked out the results of Isaac's labors. "Looks fine," said Will. "What do I owe you?"

"Well, 'cause you're Mister Kaderly's friend, that would be

ten dollars."

"We're not exactly friends, although he's a friendly enough fella. I work for him, and he said you was a good plumber and had pretty good costs. I think he's right on both scores."

"Thank you, sir. Let me know if I can do anything else for you."

"I sure will. Can I help you with gettin' your things on the truck?"

"No, thanks, I think we got her done."

The kitchen door slammed, and Ted came running out of the house, clutching several books. "Mr. Isaac, here's some books for Three that I'm done with," said Ted as he handed Isaac several colorful young children's books. "Mrs. Kostigan and my mamaw in Carrolton gave them to me when I was a little boy, and now I'm bigger and in harder books. These have easy words like Dick and Jane and run and jump and things like that."

Ted had noticed the light skin on the palms of Isaac's hands and the deep mahogany color on the backs; he looked at the colorful hands. "Have you always had light palms?"

"Oh, yes, God made me black on the outside and pink on the inside, pink on the inside." He chuckled as he turned his palms up for Ted to see. "All God's chil'ren are pink on the inside, yes sir."

Ted laughed. "Pink on the inside," he repeated.

"Well, thank you very much, Mister Ted. I know Three appreciate them books. It was a pleasure workin' with you today." Isaac extended his hand enclosing Ted's in a one-sided handshake. With that, Isaac backed the truck into Seventeenth Street and drove toward Forrest Avenue. Ted waved.

Now that the plumbing was completed, the floor laid on the rafters making a solid second floor, insulation placed between the roof joists, sheathing nailed in place to cover the insulation, and the stairs completed, the living area was beginning to look like a "real" small apartment. Leroy moved in before the kitchenette was completed, but that caused little concern since he ate evening meals in the house with the Warrings after they agreed on a nominal boarding fee that Leroy insisted on paying. Mary devoted all of the five dollars he paid every week to their food purchases, and they ate as well as the ration stamps allowed. On rare occasions, Leroy did not have evening meals with them but said he was going out on the town; this occurred about once a month.

# CHAPTER 10

## *Knoxville*

## *May 1942*

*Dear Daddy,* *may 3, 1942*

*school is almost over this year. I will go to the forth grade next year I shall be in Miss Simpson class. No body likes her I will try and be her friend. How is the army are you doing all right. Granddad said to tell you that shutout won the KY derby and his horse came in second alsab or absal or some thing like that. I and gerry and Floyd and ~~florab~~ the girls down the street are going on a picnic because school is almost over georgie and david may come also they do not live on highland. Miss wolf had us rite letters to pen pals so I know now how to rite a letter better now.*

*Sincerely, your son and friend Ted*

FRANK REREAD THE letter several times and enjoyed each time anew. His boy was not yet a budding literary genius, but there was still time for the fruit to blossom. As Frank lay on his cot, he ached. "Dog tired" as they say in the army. His unit had marched ten miles today with a full backpack, a full complement of winter clothing, rations for three days, and trenching tools. Some soldiers also had to carry a field radio, another ten pounds. Frank was in the midst of basic training. He felt like he was by far the old man among boys of eighteen, nineteen, and very young men in their early twenties. At thirty-two he was older than the corporal who put them through their rigorous exercises. Four draftees had already been dropped from their numbers; they could not keep up the rigorous physical training. Each day Frank told himself that the day ahead was a challenge to be overcome, and so far he had succeeded, but each day he had a little doubt in the back of his mind that he could keep up with the rank.

Fort Benning was south and west of Atlanta on the Alabama state line. The little town of Columbus, Georgia, was now bustling to support all of the new activity on the army post. From his limited trips to Columbus, he was impressed with how much the town depended on the army to thrive. There were trailer parks, pawn shops, and used-car dealers aplenty. He wasn't sure of the more personal services that a young soldier could find in the town, but he was certain those were available as well; he wasn't in need of those services.

In Frank's two brief leaves spent in Columbus, he wound up at the USO club where he could talk to local townspeople who were not out to make a buck off the soldiers but seemed to care about the sacrifice they were making and would probably make at greater cost in the near future. He did dance with two town girls. They were attractive, but oh so young, probably eighteen or nineteen. They had little in common to talk about once he answered the questions "what's your name" and "where're you from."

Life on the post was not strenuous work all day every day, although at times it seemed that way. There were training films and lectures and demonstrations of the equipment they were going to have to know how to operate as infantrymen. Aside from the M1 rifle, the chief weapon of the infantry, they were introduced to other weapons: Browning automatic rifle, mortars, and air- and water-cooled machine guns. They were truly awful weapons. The post also had a PX for the purchase of personal items, as well as low alcohol beer, a reluctant favorite of many of the men. Frank even developed a taste for the brew since he could not secure his favorite drink, bourbon. The service club was another more frequently used facility that found many men there in the evenings if they had the stamina for prolonged hours of being awake. Frank used the club on occasion but preferred the comfort of his cot and the almost quiet of the barracks for reading or writing letters. At the club there were card and pool tables, a small library, and a place just to relax and talk.

Once in a while, the USO sponsored dances with the town girls brought in, and on even rarer occasions they brought in entertainers from New York or Hollywood for shows given on the open-air parade grounds. Frank had been up close to June Allison, a sweet-looking young girl and one he might have admired more had the situation been right.

During their training, his platoon of fifty men occupied two floors of the same barracks. Each day was filled with meaningful and meaningless tasks, all in an effort to keep the troops busy at all times: there were no idle hands during the full day's activities; the only downtime occurred during the evening hours after supper. According to the sergeants, training was conducted in all the basic skills needed by the soldiers, including military protocol, weapons, bayonet use, hygiene, food service, water purification, forced marches, map reading (at which Frank excelled), camouflage, and other field survival activities such as erection of tents and digging foxholes. Frank was typically exhausted at the end of the day.

Mary worked in the kitchen on Saturday morning with Ted fixing his picnic lunch. "Now, we have a fried chicken leg, some peanuts, and two Oreo cookies, do you think that's enough? Do you want the last leg as well?"

"I think one leg is OK, but can I have maybe four cookies? Then I can trade two if anybody has something better for dessert"

Mary smiled. "I guess we can spare them. Here's two more. Oh, and here's an apple; there're good for you. And you like radishes, so I'll put two in—one for you to trade in case someone has a vegetable you want to eat."

Ted wrinkled his nose but didn't say anything. Maybe he could trade the apple, but he sure wasn't going to trade for vegetables. He strapped on his Red Rider holster with a cap pistol, but no caps, picked up the larger than normal bag of food, and went to the front porch to wait for Jerry, Floyd, Florabelle, and Marie. The girls were already on the sidewalk approaching his house. They joined him on the porch. "Whatcha got in your bag?" asked Marie. "We got baloney sandwiches and peanut butter an' crackers an' a box of Cracker Jacks that we haveta share."

"Good," said Ted, "I like Cracker Jacks."

"I mean me and Florabelle have to share' 'em, not everyone else. There wouldn't be enough then."

"Oh," said Ted, "well maybe I could get some Cracker Jacks for an Oreo?"

"Maybe you could," said Florabelle, already positioning herself for a round of bargaining. Florabelle was a year older then Ted, Jerry, and Floyd, and Marie, a year younger. The girls went to the only Catholic grade school in Knoxville and would be in the fifth and third grades in the fall.

"Hi-ho, Silver," said a boy's voice shouted from in front of the McGruder's house. Floyd came galloping up the street on his make-believe steed carrying his picnic bag in his left hand and the fictional horse's reigns in his right. "Howdy, podna," he said as he came to a stop at the foot of the Warring's porch steps. Ted pulled his cap gun from its holster and tried to twirl it on his curled index finger, but the gun clattered to the step below where he sat.

"You need more practice," lectured Florabelle. She picked up the gun and proceeded to twirl it three times before handing it to Ted, who returned it to the holster without comment. When Ted looked toward Eighteenth Street, he saw Jerry coming out of his house running toward Seventeenth.

The five children walked south two blocks then west three blocks to the open Civil War site. "My Dad said the hospital is gonna grow bigger and this block will be covered by a building," said Jerry.

"Where're we gonna go then?" asked Floyd.

"We could cross Clinch and Cumberland and play on the University's grass," said Florabelle.

"My Mom won't let me cross Cumberland," said Jerry.

As they walked across Eighteenth Street, Ted spotted Georgie and David. He waved and called their names.

"Who invited them?" said Florabelle. "I hope they brought their own food; they're poor."

"I did, and I bet they did," said Ted, defensively.

"Hi, Georgie, whatcha got to eat," Florabelle said in a slightly mocking voice. Ted suddenly wished he had brought the extra chicken leg that Granny had offered.

"I got fried baloney and sliced tomato sandwich and cookies and celery," Georgie responded, having not heard Florabelle's comments about his economic status.

"Ucky celery," she said. She did not let on that fried baloney was her favorite sandwich, and she wished she had insisted her mother fry her sandwich meat.

"Florabelle likes fried baloney," said Marie.

"I do not," said Florabelle.

When Marie insisted, Florabelle chased her and gave her a nuggie on the left upper arm and told her little sister to shut up in a harsh whisper at which Marie started to whimper from the blow more so than the reprimand. The five boys sat on top of a trench and started pulling food from their bags. The girls joined them, and the trading started in earnest. Ted secured two peanut butter crackers, which he promptly traded to David for gumdrops. He was unable to get more than five kernels of Cracker Jacks for an Oreo, so he held on to the remaining three cookies. He did get a quarter of a fried baloney sandwich from Georgie for a radish, which Georgie tasted then promptly hurled into the street. "My mother eats radishes, and I thought they would be good but they're too hot, dadburnit," said Georgie.

"Don't swear, Georgie," Florabelle said reprovingly.

"Those ain't swear words. Now, if you want to hear swear words, just ask," said Jerry. "My brother's in high school, and he knows a lot of stuff. Anybody want to hear?"

"You say those kind of words, and I will personally kill you,

Jerry," warned Florabelle.

"You can tell us later," laughed Georgie, "after Florabelle leaves."

After the children had finished their lunch, Jerry produced with a flourish a sheet of paper from his back pocket. "I have a joke that my uncle brought over to our house. He told Daddy, and Daddy about split his pants laughing so hard. Uncle Cletus left the paper, and I borrowed it."

"Tell it," the boys said in almost perfect unison.

"Well you are s'posed to talk in a accent," started Jerry.

"What's that?" said Floyd.

"It's when you don't talk like everybody else, like somebody from Ohio talks funny when they're here, like my cousins."

"You all know nobody in Knoxville has an accent," said Florabelle. "We all talk normal."

"Well let's pretend I'm talking in an accent." Jerry continued, "A army pilot is talking to a class of school children and said he was in a dogfight with Germen airplanes."

"What's a dogfight have to do with Germans?" interrupted Florabelle. "Were they German shepherds?"

"No, no," said Floyd, becoming frustrated. "Dogfight's what they call an airplane fight."

"That's stupid."

Jerry ignored Florabelle's last contribution and continued with the joke. "And the pilot said there were a lot of fokkers attacking him. And he shot one down and then another fokker got on his tail, and—"

"What's a fokker?" said Floyd.

"That's right," said Jerry excitedly, "in the joke someone hearing the joke asks the same question, and the teacher said fokker was a German airplane. And then the pilot said, 'But these fokkers were flying Messerschmitts.'"

"Then what?" said Florabelle

"That's it," said Jerry.

The children looked at each other and none laughed. "That's

not funny," said Ted.

"I got one," said Floyd. "There was this lady who lived in a big house with a banister on the stairs and she slid down the banister every morning, and at the end of the week she was de-furred." Floyd chuckled.

Again the children stared at Floyd, and he gestured with a shoulder shrug that the joke was over.

"Only men get deferred, not women," Florabelle said indignantly. "That's not funny either."

"Now this is funny," said Georgie as he grabbed the sides of his mouth with the index fingers and stuck out his tongue trying to lick his nose. The children giggled and each in turn produced their own version of a distorted funny face and nonsensical sounds. They all laughed very hard and were soon rolling down the grassy sides of the trench doing somersaults and other rolling acrobatics.

# CHAPTER 11

## *Knoxville*

## *June 1942*

*2 June, 1942*

*Dear Son,*

*I was glad to receive your letter. I read it over and over, and it placed me back home with you, Granny, and Granddad. You asked how the basic training was going. Well, it is going fine. It is hard, but I am keeping up with the young soldiers just fine. The corporal who runs our exercises is younger than me; in fact I am the "old man" of the training class. The corporal used to pick on me and everyone else who had been to college, but he has left me alone after he recently found out that I have applied for Officers Candidate School. That training will also be here at Fort Benning. So I will spend the hot summer and fall in Georgia.*

*I have discovered that I am a pretty good shot with the M1 rifle; I hit fifteen of sixteen bull's eyes on our last trip to the firing range. That makes me a marksman. We had a USO show last week. There were singers and dancers and Stan Hack, Johnny Mize, Joe Medwick, and Grover Cleveland Alexander (they are famous baseball players), and the actress June Allyson. I don't believe you have seen her movies, but she seemed very nice.*

*In your next letter you may want to remember to start each sentence with a capital letter and end it with a period (.). Also, a person's name starts with a capital letter.*

*I know you will enjoy your summer vacation. Maybe Granddad can take you fishing. Give my love to Granny and Granddad and keep plenty for yourself.*

*Love, Daddy*

TED ADDED HIS father's letter to his new scrapbook that contained the three previous letters he had received. Father and son averaged writing each other on a staggered two-week schedule with a letter arriving at one end of the communication link almost every week. Ted also pasted in the scrapbook stories from the *Knoxville Journal* that he thought important. There was the story of Colonel Doolittle's raid on Japanese cities that President Roosevelt said was launched from "Shangri-La." Ted asked his grandparents the location of Shangri-La since he could not find it on his maps or the globe. They were mystified as well, but his third grade teacher cleared up the non-location of the mythical kingdom.

He next had an article telling of the epic battle of the Coral Sea, where after a four-day battle the Americans claimed victory over the feared Japanese Navy. That victory was a real accomplishment. The Japanese then invaded the Aleutian Islands, which Ted found as an extension of Alaska that pointed toward the islands of Japan. Ted wondered if there had been Japanese people already on the Aleutians like there had been in Hawaii when Pearl Harbor was attacked.

At the end of May he pasted in the story of the British bombing of Cologne that demonstrated the new technique of "carpet bombing." Ted talked to his grandfather about the meaning of carpet bombing. Between the two of them they developed a good understanding of the tactic, although the devastating effects of such a raid were not mentioned.

Will, having read his son's letter to Ted, decided that it was a good idea to go fishing. He bought two bamboo poles at Woodruff's Hardware on Gay Street along with lines, floats, and hooks. Will didn't bother with buying a reel since he wanted to test how well the outing went before investing more money in the pastime activity. As instructed, Ted dug around the edge of Mary's vegetable garden until he had found a nice selection of worms; some were quite large and wiggly. He placed all of them in an empty Campbell's soup can along with a little dirt. Granny told the fishermen to be sure and return the can so they could save it for the scrap-metal drive for the war effort.

The two piled into Will's truck and drove to the edge of the University's Shields Watkins football field. They made their way across the railroad track and down to the river bank and secured a comfortable place on the edge of the water. The day promised to be hot, and Will brought his straw hat, a milking stool left over from his farming days, and a wicker creel to store the fish in the event they actually caught some. There were others fishing along the shore: two colored men and a boy to the right and an elderly man and woman to the left. Neither the fishermen to the right or left were close enough to interfere with Ted's nor Will's fishing efforts.

Will reminded Ted how to fasten a cork float about two feet above the end of the line and then the hook at the end. The line was fastened to the pole, and then came the baiting step. This was an unusual experience for Ted, one that he did not particularly enjoy, but he would not admit that fact to his grandfather. Ted had been fishing with his father on the South Fork of the Elkhorn, but his father had performed most of the preparatory activities; Teddy had been too small to learn the intricacies of the operation.

The two were soon swinging their lines into the slow moving river with little results. After throwing his line in the water Ted watched it drift lazily downstream. He would then swing it ashore, check to see if the worm was still intact, swing it back into the water again, and the river would repeat its lazy action. After half an hour Ted's attention began to drift, and he watched two row boats in the river some distance from the shore. The fishermen occasionally created a clamor as they landed a wriggling fish. Their success was somewhat reassuring, but things were still very quiet along the bank.

Ted next looked to his right and studied the two men and the boy. Something looked familiar about one of the men. As Ted mused, Will's voice penetrated his thoughts, "Look at your float." Ted did look but didn't see the float. Then it popped to the surface, and the fishing line went taut as something under water had seized the hook. "It's a live one all right," Will said. "Now walk toward the bank when it pulls on the line and walk back up here when it stops. That way you can tire it out." Ted did as his grandfather said as well as he could, but the fish was persistent, and before he knew it he was ankle deep in the river.

"That's it, play it easy," encouraged Will. The fish became visible for the first time as Ted walked back up the bank. "Let me have your pole for a minute," said Will as he lifted the pole high and swung the fish, flipping from side to side, onto the bank. The vigorous on-shore flopping of the creature soon attracted the attention of the other fishermen along the bank. Will held on to the line and walked his hand down to a point close to the fish and then held it triumphantly over his head. He then handed the line to Ted. "Now, this is a hard part but an important step," said Will. "You need to take out the hook. You have to grab the fish behind the head like this and keep its mouth open while you pull out the hook. See, I'm pushing the hook away from the barb so it will release from the fish's mouth—and out flips the hook. Here, you put the fish in the creel."

Ted took hold of the wiggling creature with hesitant hands, and the fish was soon thrashing on the ground near the water's edge. "Don't let it get back in the river," said Will as they both scrambled for the flailing fish. Ted was the first to secure it, and this time held it with determined hands. He dropped it in the creel, closed the basket's lid, and raised his arms in joy. He became aware of others now standing around him. The elderly woman from the left had walked over to watch as had the young colored boy from the right.

"That'll be good eating, son," said the woman. "Congratulations."

"That was my first fish that I ever caught by myself," said Ted. The small boy grinned and walked back to his companions.

Ted baited his hook again, this time not worrying as much about the worm, and eagerly cast his line back into the river. Will had to replace his worm as parts of his bait kept disappearing. "I think something is nibbling at my worms, but it won't take the hook."

Ted was the next one to feel a strike on his line, and this time Will watched his grandson complete the entire operation of landing the fish, recovering the hook, and putting the fish safely in the creel. Ted was feeling very special now even though he had waded into the river up to his knees in landing his second fish. "The fish gods are smiling on you today, boy." Will laughed.

Time slipped by with Will catching a very small fish that he threw back into the river and a second larger fish that was still smaller than Ted's but yet big enough to keep. As the heat of the day grew, the older colored man to the right walked over and said, "I thought somethin' looked familiar 'bout you two fishermun, yas'suh."

Ted exclaimed, "Mr. Isaac, it's you!"

"Yas'suh, it's me alright."

"Howdy, Isaac," said Will, and the men shook hands and complained about the heat. The small boy who had been with Isaac ventured to follow his grandfather and approached the group slowly.

"This here's my grandson, Isaac Three," Isaac said proudly.

"Hi, Three," said Ted, "how's your reading coming along?"

"OK," came the shy and almost inaudible voice as Three stared at the ground.

Ted raised Three's hand toward Isaac and said, "Pink on the inside."

Isaac puzzled at first, then recalled the incident with Ted during his plumbing work at the Warrings and laughed. "Yas'suh, pink on the inside." Will recalled the "pink" experience with Isaac as well and laughed.

"And that's my son Isaac Two, and Three's daddy, over there landin' all the fish today. I ain't had nary a nibble, no'suh, not a one."

Ted showed Three the three fish in their creel, and then the boys walked over to inspect and admire Isaac Two's catch for the day. The two boys were soon gesticulating about the fish that had been caught and just as soon running along the bank and then rolling down its slope almost to the water's edge. Will and Isaac exchanged stories of past fishing experiences and agreed that this was not their day to match past glories in catching the large fish they both recalled from their expanded memories.

"Doggies, I think I've had as much fun as an old man needs in one day," Will said to Isaac. "Think I'll go home and try to cool off."

"Sounds like a good idea," agreed Isaac as he wiped his forehead with the red bandana that lay limply around his neck. "Good idea."

After telling Ted that it was time to go home, the two tired fishermen trudged to the truck with their fishing paraphernalia. Ted carried the creel. On entering the kitchen door, Will said to Mary, "Not as young as I used to be."

"Gracious, Will, look at you. You are red as a beet. You're not used to the outdoors like you were on the farm. You've been inside for the last four years and you lost your color. Go up and take a cold bath and leave off your shirt and sit in front of the 'lecteric fan, maybe you can get cool."

"I will, soon as I show Ted how to clean the fish."

"I'll show him, you get on upstairs," demanded Mary. Will did as he was told, and Ted and Mary cleaned the fish for supper.

After the cooling bath, Will sat in the living room in front of the GE oscillating fan, the first one he and Mary had owned. Relaxed, sitting in his comfortable chair with a smoldering cigarette and his eyes closed, he reflected on how tired he had been and how much better he felt now. Being cool was a distinctly comfortable feeling on these terribly hot, sticky summer days. He chuckled at Ted's comment on *being pink on the inside.* Teddy had quite a memory recalling things that Will often ignored. He remembered Isaac's comment about being pink when he installed the plumbing in the apartment, now that Teddy had reminded him, but it took Teddy's prodding to bring it to the surface.

*That Isaac is a nice fella, all right. He was like ole Pres.* Will had known ole Pres in Millersburg. Alphonso Thomas Jefferson was known by the colored folks as Pres, a name that Will had overheard and adopted for Alphonso. Pres worked on Will's farm from time to time along with Will and his brother Willard in planting and harvesting tobacco. Pres was the best at stripping the leaves and hanging the racks in the barn for curing. *Yes'sir, the Pres was a friend and a good worker.* Pres would call Will "Mista Will" and Willard "Mista Other Will," and then he just shortened Willard's name to Mista Other. Pres and Will would tell each other jokes on the people of their own kind: Pres would tell stories of colored people and Will, stories of the whites. That had been a lot of fun. *Yes'sir, Pres was quite a fella.* Will decided during the time he knew Pres to stop using the name "nigger," one he had heard and used all his life. He knew it was meant to keep the colored in their place, but he just didn't think it applied to Pres, and if it didn't apply to Pres, then maybe he shouldn't use it at all. So he stopped.

Will had gone to Pres's funeral after he took ill and died of a fever in the winter of '36 (or was it '37?) he wasn't certain, but he remembered Pres's church jammed with his family, of course, and colored folks and about a dozen white people. That was Will's first venture inside a colored church after living within four hundred feet of one most of his life. He couldn't help but hear the vigorous singing and, at times, rhythmic clapping as he passed the church during a service, but he had not ventured inside. After all, that was their church not his. During Pres's funeral he was struck by the deep devotion of the members of the church to their faith and their belief in God and Christ. At the time, Will recalled he wasn't as certain in his faith as they were in theirs, and he remembered wondering if that made a difference to God. Maybe on the day of his death he would find out. Yes, he mused, on the day of his death *all of the mysteries about life would be answered for better or worse.*

Will opened his eyes and was aware that his cigarette had burned down to a very short butt with a long ash curving toward the floor. He jerked his hand up to the ashtray and in so doing knocked the fragile ash onto the carpet beside the chair. He stubbed out the cigarette butt and brushed the ash into the carpet. Mary would never notice, he knew this from his past practice of disposing of fallen ash. It was the smoldering ash that gave him grief, as Mary kept track of the numerous small carpet burns that marked an arc around the front of his chair.

He settled back into the chair once more. *Maybe I should call Isaac by the nickname Pink. No, that's not as good a nickname as Pres.* He would have to think some more on the nickname before he came up with the correct one for Isaac. He wondered, *Why had God made so many different types of people—the whites, the blacks, the Asians, the Indians, and then there were Eskimos and who knew what other kinds of people—in this big world?* Will certainly didn't know. *God made us different, so surely he meant for us to stay different, didn't he? Yes, he wants us to stay separate,* Will answered his own question. *But if he wants us separate and different, why did he mix up our lives as much as he did? Strange, wasn't it?* Then he recalled that the colored people got to America by slave ships and had not come on their own idea. *We brought 'em. Huh, was that God's plan?*

*Then there was that Jap boy who was Frank's friend. Frank brought him home one Thanksgiving to Millersburg, and the two stayed for three days before they caught the Greyhound back to Richmond. The boy was nice . . . what was his name? . . . George something or other.* Will didn't know Japanese people had names like George. But this George spoke just like all Americans. Will guessed that was because he was born in California. Frank showed George all about farming and the barns and the farm tools. George loved learning how to drive the tractor, until he turned it over in the ditch and it had to be pulled out using the neighbor's tractor. Still, George was a nice young man; he had baked a pumpkin pie under Mary's supervision, something even Frank had never tried. *Then one evening he said he saw three . . . now what did he call them? . . . Herbaceous denizens, yes that's it. Yes, herbaceous denizens. I said I didn't think I had them on the farm, then he said they were deer grazing over near the river. He and I just laughed . . . he was funny . . . nice kid. Now the government has him in a camp somewhere out west. Huh, was that right? George didn't seem like a threat to anybody. Besides, he made a good pie.* Will chuckled to himself, then the smile melted and he thought about George in a detention camp with his wife and children.

There were more questions than answers rattling around in Will's head on that hot June day. He paused in his memories and dropped off into a restful nap.

# CHAPTER 12

## *Knoxville*

## *July 3, 1942*

*Dear Daddy, We are having a lot of fun this summer me and Floyd and Gerry. Thank you for re minding me to use capitols and periods.. Granddad and I went to a smokys ball game last Sunday we lost to the Lookouts 7 to 1. The game was good. Those players you saw in the army were not at the game. He took me fishing and I caught two fish and we had for dinner. We are going to have a lemon ade stand on the fourth of july on 17 street. We hope to make a lot of money. Yum yum we can buy cake and candy.*
*Your son Ted Warring* *june 22*

AGAIN FRANK REREAD the letter several times as he did with each missive from Ted. He was grateful to his father for filling in and doing some of the things he missed doing with Ted. He did miss Ted very much; in fact, that was the one continuing worry of his life now that he was in the army. When he was not thinking of Ted, he reflected on his current and emerging role in the army; he was very certain he had made the right choice in volunteering for service, it helped structure his otherwise meaningless life. He had been selected as the leader of his squad of twelve men by the lieutenant who led their platoon of fifty men in the company of 200 led by the captain. He knew the selection criteria for squad leader was arbitrary but suspected he was chosen because of his age and quiet, steady demeanor. He observed the younger lieutenant and tried to imagine himself in that role, a position he hoped to be in by the end of the year. Frank's company was one of four in the battalion of 800 men. He did not let his current leadership position go to his head. As squad leader he saw to it that members of his unit assigned to guard duty kept their assignment; he helped police his floor of the barracks for an orderly appearance that met the sergeant's directives. Frank was beginning to practice in a low-key manner being in a leadership position.

Tomorrow would be another strenuous day with at least one trip through the obstacle course, only this time they must crawl under live machine gun fire a few inches above their heads. If anyone failed to negotiate the course in a given amount of time, the corporal had them repeat the course, and if four or more failed, the entire squad had to redo the trip. He hoped tomorrow would offer a chance to return to the firing range and practice with the M1 rifle. Frank was good at that, very good.

During the pre-breakfast roll call, their platoon was ordered to be ready for a training deployment by 0700. After breakfast they were loaded into trucks with full backpacks and driven to a far point on the post. They unloaded from the trucks and began a double-time trot through the Georgia woods. After a twenty-minute jaunt, the platoon was instructed to march at a normal pace. The troops gasped for breath. After another double-time trot and another normal march, the platoon took a break. Each soldier dropped in his tracks to recover. The squad leaders were called together and given maps that prescribed a route to a target destination where they would be met by a timer and given another map for the next leg of the march. Each squad had its own assignment and intermediate destination points that led to the final common destination.

Frank began reading the ground contours and vegetation markings from the map as he directed the squad's route through the woods and intermittent clearings. There were in fact a series of four connected legs of the reconnaissance mission for each squad, the objective being not to get lost and to attain the final reconnaissance point in as short a time as possible. Frank had little trouble with the map and the route identification, avoiding very steep slopes and at times having the men break into a controlled trot on downhill slopes. They successfully negotiated the first three checkpoints and briefly overshot the final point but recovered in time to be the first squad of the platoon to reach the end point. The men in his squad were elated, and Frank accepted pats on the back and his rear end from the men. From then on he was called the Prophet for his ability to combine information and still see the objective in the distance.

During May and June the world war had taken its final shape as the Pacific theater was afire with Japanese attacks from Burma to Borneo and Australia to the Aleutians. The Germans were advancing across western Egypt toward Alexandria, and the Russians had given up defending the Crimea against the Third Reich. The good news was hard to come by, but some heart could be taken: the British RAF were holding firm defending their island home as they continued their daring day-and-night bomber raids against Bremen and Essen, and the Americans were defeating the Japanese naval force near Midway Island, having sunk four Japanese aircraft carriers. General Eisenhower had also arrived in Britain as the commander of American forces in Europe, and Winston Churchill had survived a no-confidence vote in Parliament, so England continued under the same steadfast leadership as relentless pressure from Nazi Germany showed no signs of abating.

The morning of Saturday, July 4, 1942, dawned with a crystal clear sky that promised another hot day in the continuing heat wave that had seen temperatures reach a hundred degrees on four of the last eight days. Mary had been saving ration stamps and making discrete purchases in order to accumulate supplies to make a large quantity of lemonade. Jerry and Floyd's mothers also contributed part of their precious sugar supply. Jerry's family had provided a card table for the lemonade stand, which would be set up on the sidewalk at the corner of Highland and Seventeenth Street on the right-hand side of the Warring's house. Both Ted and Floyd had provided black umbrellas to open over the stand to give some relief from the relentless rays of the sun. There was a problem, however, in fixing a stand to hold the umbrellas in place. Will proposed they drive a six-foot-long iron reinforcing bar into the ground and then tie one of the umbrellas to the bar. The other umbrella could be held by someone if they were in the sun and hot enough to do so. The reinforcing bar had come from Will's supply of useful junk in the storage room next to the apartment. Floyd and Jerry collaborated on lettering a two-by-three feet sign to announce the stand's operation: Buy Your Cheap Lemon Ade Here, Get It Whil It Lasts.

Immediately after breakfast, Will and Ted climbed into the truck and drove to the ice house on Western Avenue, where they purchased a fifty-pound block of ice. They placed it in the bed of the truck wrapped in burlap feed bags, also taken from the junk storage room, and drove immediately to Highland Avenue. Upon seeing the condition of the block of ice, Mary insisted first on washing it to remove the particles of fiber and dust from its melting surface. The block was placed in a wash tub and broken into large and small pieces, and the first pitcher of lemonade nestled in the center of the ice chips.

By ten o'clock the three young entrepreneurs were in business with umbrella in place and Floyd yelling at the traffic on Seventeenth, waving the sign to announce their new business. Leroy Ames was the first customer of the stand, purchasing two Dixie cups of lemonade for five cents each. "I declare, this is the best lemonade I've had since I left home, maybe the best ever." By noon the salesmen had sold seven cups and saw their wealth grow to thirty-five cents. Mr. Gooch and his teenage daughter Doris, plus three pedestrians walking on Seventeenth Street, comprised the additional customers. Floyd's gesticulations on the street corner had failed to attract a single driver to stop, and he soon tired of the exertion and seemingly futile exercise.

The sun directly overhead signaled lunchtime, and the entrepreneurs had sandwiches along with peanut butter and crackers, all washed down with part of their inventory. Ted secured a second pitcher for the stand as Florabelle and Marie walked down the street and assumed positions alongside the boys.

"Don't you have any cookies to sell?" asked Florabelle.

"No, just the world's best lemonade," came Jerry's confident response. "This is a lemonade stand not a cookie stand."

"You should have cookies; that way people have to buy more lemonade to wash down the cookies," she said knowingly.

"Well we don't," came the slightly agitated response from Ted.

"What does 'w h i l' mean on your sign?" asked Florabelle.

"That's *while*," said Jerry, growing more irritated.

"You misspelled it. 'While' is supposed to have an 'e' at the end of it," she said triumphantly. She picked up the black crayon that Ted had used in lettering the sign and added the 'e' above the word *whil*. "There," she said.

She then walked home and reappeared five minutes later with a plate of chocolate chip cookies, which she plunked down on the table. "Let me sell these, and we should get a whole lot more customers," she offered as she began to add the word cookies to the For Sale sign. She assumed a seat between Jerry and Ted. Neither boy said anything. Floyd and Marie had walked down the street and around the corner to Roberts Grocery on Eighteenth Street to tell customers of the great opportunity available on Highland Avenue. Three customers stopped on their way walking east on Highland and bought four cookies and three cups of lemonade. Ted and Floyd were surprised when Florabelle announced the cookies cost ten cents apiece. She had sold four of them and had almost as much money as they had after a morning's work. Their sense of envy grew when one of her cookie purchasers returned to buy two more and no more lemonade. Florabelle's larder now exceeded theirs.

Leroy returned in midafternoon and, surprised to see the cookies, asked for one as well as another cup of lemonade. Seeing the disgust on Ted's face at the cookie order he amended his request. "Let's see, I have fifteen cents and I'm very thirsty so let me have a half of a cookie and two cups of lemonade." The boys faces erupted in a smile that one might interpret as gloating.

By three o'clock when the thunderhead approached Knoxville from the southwest, Florabelle had seventy-five cents' worth of cookie sales and the three boys, sixty-five cents of lemonade profits. The peal of approaching thunder and the sudden gust of wind brought an abrupt close to the business day. The boys managed to get the card table folded and onto the Warring's porch along with the chairs and wash tub, while the umbrella and reinforcing rod remained in place. Florabelle and Marie also retreated to the porch with the plate of cookies as the rain began to pelt down. The wind soon drove the rain in slanting sheets and sent the business sign flying to the opposite side of Seventeenth Street, and the umbrella, ripped from the reinforcing rod, flew across the street where it was pinned against the side of the Gooche's house. The Warring's porch faced north and turned out to be a safe and dry refuge as the rain approached from behind the house and the children sat with their backs against the front outside wall. Recognizing that the end of their business had been determined by nature, Ted said, "Let's have a snack," and soon the last dozen cookies and quart of lemonade were on the insides of the young business people.

The rain stopped by three thirty, and the sun broke through the dissipating clouds by four. At four thirty the children walked along the steaming sidewalk on Highland to Roberts Grocery, where they purchased three boxes of sparklers and five bags of penny candy. Florabelle, much to the disgust of her male companions, had two of the sparkler boxes and the largest bag of candy plus thirty cents left over. She of course would be required by her mother to divide her loot with Marie, "Because after all, Florabelle, I made the cookies and provided the recipe's ingredients." *Mothers can be so unreasonable at times*, thought Florabelle. The boys had one box of sparklers to divide among the three of them and enough candy for the evening's festivities, they assured themselves.

The sun didn't set until eight thirty, and it was nine thirty before it was dark enough to light the sparklers. Mary, Will, and Leroy sat on the porch steps as the children gathered to start the evening's sparkler celebration. Unbeknownst to the adults, Jerry also had five firecrackers that he had secured from his older brother. Will, with a book of matches, lit each sparkler for the children. The McGruders, parents of the girls, plus Jerry and Floyd's parents joined the celebration on the Warring's porch. First the lit sparklers were waved in wide circles as the fiery sparks wrote arcs in the darkening air. Soon the thing to do was to throw the sparkler up in the air as it reached the end of its short life. The last gasp of each sparkler lit up the evening sky then crashed to the ground in a final cascade of sparks. Leroy joined the fun, and launched one sparkler higher than the rooftop of the houses, it then fell on the Highland Avenue pavement where it died.

Jerry with his last sparkler lit the five firecrackers and tossed them into the street, setting off loud bangs and howls from the neighborhood's dogs. The commotion was immediately recognized by the parents but greatly surprised the children who had had limited contact with firecrackers. The children and dogs both shouted with joy and howled in fright for minutes after the conclusion of the evening's celebration.

After the firecrackers exploded, Mary announced, "I'm going inside; the 'skeeters are beginning to bite. Please come in if you want to get out of their reach," she said to the adults as she entered the screen door into the front hall. Parents of the other children allowed as how the evening was late and they better go home. They cautioned their children to come soon.

With the fireworks expended, the children gathered in the Warring's living room to relive the day's events. Leroy suggested he tell them a story, and they readily agreed, not suspecting his motives. He started by telling them of George Washington's early role in fighting the French and Indian War. The children sat on the floor, as Leroy turned off the room's lights, sat on Will's footstool, and continued telling of George's ventures into the deep, dark forest of western Virginia, with special emphasis on deep and dark. Next he told of rumors among the Indian tribes in the mountains of a headless ghost who had once been the wickedest chief of the Delaware Indians. This chief was so wicked, he ate people he didn't like, especially children who displeased him. And just before he ate them, he let out an awful scream.

As the story proceeded, the tension mounted. George, alone in the forest, heard noises and witnessed strange events that seemed beyond the limit of human experience. He crept over a ridge where he saw a strange, headless visage in the distance hovering over the valley floor, beckoning him to follow. As George crossed a small stream, the image disappeared. George didn't know where it had gone or if it was coming back. As he climbed to the crest of the next ridge, the figure appeared again, beckoning him to continue following. He crept down into the next valley as silently as possible, just like an Indian. All of the children now leaned forward, their bodies tense with their imagination placing them in the valley with George in a search for the headless chief.

"George stood looking into a dense, black forest and heard the snap of a twig. 'Who made that noise?'" After a long pause, a sudden loud "Screeeaaammm" screeched through the downstairs rooms of the house as a face lit by a flashlight appeared in the dark doorway from the entry hall. All of the children screamed, throwing up their arms and hands in a reflexive self-defensive reaction. Will entered the living room from the hall laughing, holding the flashlight under his chin, and the children realized they had been drawn into a ghost story orchestrated by Leroy and Will.

The nervous laughter erupted as they wanted to tell each other how scared they were, and then after Jerry said he knew it was a ghost story all along, they each changed their interpretation of events to "I knew it was a ghost story too."

Mary entered the living room. "What's goin' on in here?" She guessed who was at the bottom of the racket as Will and Leroy laughed loudly. "Lands sakes, you two old men are just big ole boys, aren't you," as she playfully slapped Will and Leroy's shoulders.

Still laughing, Leroy made his way out through the kitchen on his way to his apartment in the back yard and a cold beer from his ice chest. Florabelle, Marie, Jerry, and Floyd all left at the same time and ran to their houses as fast as they could, just in case there was a headless Indian chief on the loose in Knoxville.

# CHAPTER 13

## *Knoxville*

## *Summer 1942*

LETTERS BETWEEN KNOXVILLE and Fort Benning crossed paths as father and son wrote of events on the Fourth of July.

*Dear Daddy,*
*We had a great day on the forth of july. Our stand made some money and we got sparklers and candy and set them off in the dark. It was great and Granny and Granddad and some more adults watched. Then LeRoy told us a ghost story and we were really scared when Granddad made a loud noise. I don't like Florabell she hogged in on our stand and sold cookies. She is a pain but her Mother bakes good cookies. Whenn are you coming home.*
*Love your son Ted Warring* *July 6*

*8 July 1942*

*Dear Son,*

*We are having a very hot summer down here in Georgia. The end of basic training is now in sight; we should be finished by the end of August, and then I will get a leave and come home for a visit before Officers Candidate School starts in September. I don't know the exact schedule yet, but I will let you know as soon as I find out.*

*I hope your lemonade stand was a success on the fourth. We had a parade on that day here on the post, and it was so hot that several men passed out while they were standing at attention. Two men were treated for heat stroke, and they should recover fully by the end of the week. On the fifth we had a lecture on how to avoid heat exhaustion, and the men in my squad said the best way was not to stand at attention for half an hour in the full sun during an army parade. Ha, ha.*

*I am now keeping up very well with the young men in the squad and platoon—so well in fact that I am sometimes one of the fastest through the obstacle course. The course is set up to train us on running, climbing up a rope on a sheer wall, pulling ourselves over the wall and dropping to the ground, and crawling on the ground without sticking your rear end up high enough to catch on the barbed wire or get it shot off by a bullet.*

*Give my love to Granny and Granddad and keep plenty for yourself.*

*Love, Daddy*

Seven weeks later on August 28, Frank placed a long-distance call from the service club to 1702 Highland Avenue. He made the call from one of three phones provided by the USO for such purposes. The calls were limited to one call per soldier per day and could last no more than three minutes. The candlestick model phones consisted of the speaking microphone attached to the top of a vertical stem that rested on a base. The phone's earpiece was in a separate device to be held to the ear and attached to the phone's stem by a short cord. The earpiece when not in use hung on a switch at the side of the stem. When the earpiece was raised, the phone clicked on and signaled the operator that a call was to be made. Often the user picked up the phone in order to position the microphone at a comfortable place in front of the mouth with the earpiece held to the ear with the other hand. The phones were not the newest technology represented by the compact cradle phone, but they did nicely in meeting the soldiers' needs.

The long-distance call process was a marvel of the day: to think you could talk directly to someone in a far-off place from this location in west central Georgia. Frank completed the call first by clicking the arm that held the earpiece and telling the operator the destination city and then the local number in Knoxville. Frank could hear the chain of calls as the operators patched together the call linkages—Columbus to Atlanta, Atlanta to Chattanooga, and Chattanooga to Knoxville—in only about five minutes.

Mary answered the phone held in the wooden cabinet that hung on the wall of first floor hall. She picked up the earpiece from the phone and spoke into the microphone, "Hello, who's this?"

The operator said in a rapid voice, "This is a long-distance call for either Mr. or Mrs. Warring."

"Yes, what do you want?"

"Is this Mrs. Warring?"

"Yes, who's this?"

"Please hang on for a long-distance call."

"Hello," said Mary, "what was that?"

"Mom, it's me calling from Fort Benning," said Frank in a raised voice so she could better hear him.

"Frank's not here now," said Mary.

"No, Mom, this is Frank calling you."

"Frank? Frank is that really you? Lord a mercy . . . Will!" she called loudly to her husband who was smoking a cigarette on the front porch. "It's Frank," she added in the same loud voice.

Will came through the front screen door. "What's the rumpus about?"

"It's Frank on the line calling from somewhere." Turning back to concentrate on the earpiece and microphone, she said, "Frank, where are you? Are you in trouble?"

"No, Mom, I'm calling from Fort Benning to tell you I'm coming home for a leave. We finish basic training next Tuesday, and I'll be home Tuesday night sometime if I can possibly make it."

"Oh, Lord a mercy, he's coming home sometime," she blurted

out to Will. "When you coming?"

"Next Tuesday, Mom, next Tuesday, late in the day or night. I don't know what time I'll get there."

"Lands sakes, Frank, I'll have to get started on baking your favorite cake for your birthday. It's on Friday the eleventh, you know."

"Yes, Mom, I know when my birthday is." Frank chuckled. "I'll be there to eat the cake."

"Oh, Will, he's comin' home for his birthday. Isn't that grand?"

"Mary, can I talk to Frank," asked Will?

"Goodbye, son, here's your dad."

"Hello, Frank, it's good to hear from you."

Frank repeated to his father his travel plans and the uncertainty about his arrival time, including the possibility he would not arrive until Wednesday morning.

"Can we go to the station to wait for Daddy this morning?" asked Ted.

"Well, we don't know when he'll get in," replied Mary.

"We could pack a lunch and wait for him," countered Ted.

"Teddy, I know you are anxious, all of us are, but it could be tonight after we go to bed when he gets here," said Mary. "Granddad talked to your dad, and he wasn't certain whether he could get here today or whether it would be tomorrow. He also said that he was pretty sure he would come by train, but there's an outside chance it would be on the Greyhound."

"Ohhh," lamented Ted.

Mary tried to change the direction of the conversation, "Teddy, it would be best if we waited here. If we go downtown, we might miss him and he would get here to the house and we would be looking all over downtown for him. We don't want to do that, now, do we?"

"No," said Ted dejectedly, "no." With a deep sigh he slumped into the kitchen chair.

"Why don't you go sit on the porch swing after lunch and wait for him to come around the corner," offered Mary as she kissed the top of his head.

The morning went slowly for Ted as he scanned the street from the living-room window. At eleven o'clock, he quit his observation point and moved out to the porch swing. Ted brought his atlas to the porch to study the communities in Georgia between Columbus and Atlanta and tried to imagine where his father might be if he were on the Greyhound. There didn't seem to be an obvious road connecting the two cities, but Ted was certain the driver would know how to get there.

North of Atlanta he knew his father would go through Chattanooga to get to Knoxville, and he found US 41 that went through Calhoun and Dalton. North of Chattanooga he saw that 41 strayed off to the west and didn't come to Knoxville, but US 11 did connect the two cities right through Cleveland, Athens, Sweetwater, and Lenoir City. Ted had ridden to Lenoir City with Granddad and Granny in June to buy flower plants at a nursery. He remembered the small downtown that was smaller than Frankfort but larger than the Forks of Elkhorn. *Any place must be larger than the Forks*, mused Ted.

The Forks was as small as a town could be, and he knew almost everyone who lived there. He had ridden the Little Dinky railroad car into Frankfort with his mother to buy school clothes when he was getting ready for the third grade last summer. He missed his mother so much, sometimes it hurt in the middle of his chest when he thought of her. It hurt so much that at times he wanted to cry; sometimes he did, mostly at night in his bed, but he mustn't cry today *'cause Daddy is coming home*. This would be the best day of his life, at least as far back as he could remember.

He brought his peanut butter and jelly sandwich to the porch and ate it with a glass of milk and two Oreo cookies. After lunch, as he sat on the porch steps, Georgie and David came around the corner and up to the steps.

"Want to play ball?" asked Georgie. He had a tattered baseball glove that appeared to have been brand new twenty years ago and a dirty softball. David carried a fat stick they planned to use for a bat.

"No," said Ted, "I'm waitin' for my dad. He gets home from the army sometime today."

"Oh," said Georgie, "after he gets here do you want to play then?"

"No, I want to stay with him."

"When's he comin'?" asked David.

"Don't know, that's why I'm waitin' here for him. We don't know when he will get here. I hope it's soon. He's coming up from Georgia."

"Where's Georgia?" asked David.

Ted opened his atlas to the map of the eastern United States, and balancing it on his lap said, "We are here," pointing to Knoxville, "and he's coming from here," pointing to Columbus.

"Yeah, but you said he was coming from Georgia, where's that at?" asked David.

"Georgia is the state that Columbus is in; it's all of this place," instructed Ted as he traced his finger around the state boundary.

"You dummy," said Georgie to David, "Georgia is like a state like Knoxville's in Tennessee. That's a state too, that's our state."

"Oh," said David, "I don't like geography and stuff like that."

"I love maps and geography," said Ted. "Look at all these places to go when we get bigger," turning to a map of the US, "there's Chicago, there's Detroit, there's Cleveland, there's—"

"I've been to Cleveland—that's near Chattanooga, my Granny lives there," said Georgie.

"That Cleveland is down here in Tennessee; the other Cleveland is way up here in Ohio. It's a very big city on Lake Erie," Ted said.

"Yeah, you dummy," said David. "Don't you know there's two Clevelands?"

Georgie swung at David with his glove but missed as David ran down the steps to the sidewalk, and the two boys raced toward Eighteenth Street. Georgie caught up to the slower David in the

McGruder's front yard where they rolled in the grass. After a few minutes the boys returned laughing. "Well, do you know if Jerry or Floyd's home? Maybe they want to play," asked Georgie.

"No, I haven't seen 'em today," Ted replied.

The two would-be ball players walked to the sidewalk and then broke into a race heading toward Jerry's house near Eighteenth.

The early afternoon dragged slowly into mid- and then late afternoon approaching suppertime. Mary had made a stew reminiscent of the Burgoo she had often made on the farm in Kentucky, but in Knoxville she lacked the usual squirrel and 'coon meat or whatever "game" meat that was available. Instead she used pork bought with her ration book at the downtown market and seasoned the stew with a lamb bone. Later she added all the chopped vegetables. After four hours of cooking, she removed the bone, shredded the meat, and the stew resembled a thick but tasty chunky stew. This was Will's favorite and reminded him of his mother's and grandmother's cooking on the farm. Cornbread would finish out the meal. Will and Leroy arrived home from work about five o'clock, and the family was eating fifteen minutes later. By six Ted was back in the front porch swing with Will while Leroy sat on the steps smoking.

"Can I bum one of your Luckys?" Will asked Leroy.

"Why sure," came the reply followed by a half-full package of Lucky Strike cigarettes tossed through the air. Next came the book of matches by the same air route. It was a peaceful evening for the first day of September. It had been hot today but noticeably cooler than the weekend. "It was a scorcher," Leroy correctly described the weather. The hot weather and lack of rain had also substantially cut back the number of mosquitoes.

With the cigarettes smoked down to stubs and the butts flicked into the street, the men went back into the house, Will to read the paper and Leroy through the kitchen and out the back door to his apartment to listen to the radio and drink a cold beer.

The paper told of the continuing resistance of the Japanese

following the successful landing of American forces on Guadalcanal in the Solomon Islands in early August. This had been the first aggressive land action taken by the Americans as they tried to stop the Japanese tide in the South Pacific. American fighter planes were now based at Henderson Field on Guadalcanal and had taken part in protecting the American GIs, as well as engaging and driving off Japanese fighter planes. The Japanese troops, in an attempt to retake the island, had suffered significant losses as they resorted to a blind *banzai* charge at American gun emplacements. A charge of this nature had not been seen by Americans since the action by the Confederates against Missionary Ridge at Gettysburg, according to a historian at the University of Virginia.

"The Japs didn't have any better results than did General Lee," was a quote attributed to Professor Silas Protou. A related article described the advance of the Japanese troops across New Guinea as they approached Port Moresby northeast of Australia.

In Russia, the fighting near Stalingrad defined the German's continuing advance toward the east, as the Russian Army was pushed into the city and the Germans entered the suburban ring of demolished villages. The communist government in Moscow announced that Marshal Georgii Zhukov had been appointed as commander of the Stalingrad forces. A final story in the European theater of the war told how the last remnants of the raid by Joint Allied forces had been withdrawn from Dieppe, a port on the northern coast of France.

Six thousand Canadian troops had landed on July 19, and total casualties accounted for about 60 percent of the landing force. Opponents of the Churchill government had referred to the landing as ill conceived. The initial intent of the raid was to test the German response to an invading force and, perhaps, seize and hold on to a port on the continent. Critics in London said the military planners proved they had a lot of work to do before a full-scale invasion would be undertaken.

At nine o'clock the sky was dark when Mary looked onto the porch and found Ted asleep on the swing. She went out and touched his shoulder.

"What," said Ted with a start. Then recognizing that he was on the porch and knowing why he was there, "Is Daddy here?"

"Not yet," said Mary. I thought you might want to go up to bed. I promise to wake you when your dad arrives."

"No, I want to wait here."

Mary went back inside and spoke to Will in the living room. "He was asleep, but wants to stay on the porch."

After a moment Will said, "Why don't we make him a bed on the porch and let him sleep out there. There's nothing to harm him, and I'll sleep in my chair here so I can hear if anything should happen. Remember, we got that old cot in the attic I used to sleep on in the barn during foaling season."

"Lordy, I remember it. Weren't it hard on your back?"

"Sure, but for a night it's all right. Teddy may consider it a special treat to sleep outdoors, especially tonight."

By ten o'clock Ted was asleep on the cot with the pillow from his bed under his head and a sheet underneath his legs, a sheet he probably would not need during the warm overnight cool-down period. The occasional cool breeze that had added to the comfort of the evening continued into the night and into Ted's dream. He and his father sat under a tree on the bank of a stream, Ted recognized as the south fork of the Elkhorn River. The sycamore tree spread out over the water and provided an ideal spot to watch his grandfather and grandmother toss their fishing lines into the slow-moving current. "I didn't know Granny fished," said Ted.

"Oh, she's a good fisherman," said his father.

"There's Mamaw and Papaw too. They're fishing," Ted said pointing upstream as his other grandparents entered his dream.

"Hi, Teddy," came a soft voice from behind him.

He turned to see his mother. "Mommy," Ted gasped and rushed into her warm embracing arms.

"It's so good to see you, dear," said Ted's father as he came and embraced both his wife and son. Ted thought in his dream this was the third time she had visited him in his sleep. In fact that was one of the benefits that he enjoyed in going to sleep each night, that he provided her the opportunity to visit him. There was so much he wanted to tell her about Knoxville and his friends and his school. As the family embraced, Ted's dream melted into a warm sensation of overriding comfort and peace. As Ted's sleep slowly dimmed, he became conscious of the waking world and he realized he was being embraced by a real person. Ted pulled back his head to look into his father's eyes. "Daddy," Ted said aloud as his muffled voice melted in his father's military clad shoulder.

"I'm home," Frank whispered. Father and son embraced for several minutes before Ted pulled his head away and ran his hand over his father's shoulder and felt the tailored uniform material and the single stripe on his upper part of his right arm. "That's my PFC stripe," said Frank. "That means I've completed the first step in becoming a soldier. Here's my sharpshooter insignia—that means your ole dad is pretty good at hitting what he aims at." Frank chuckled. Ted also ran his fingers over his father's short haircut; in the dim light the dark shading of his unshaven face resembled the short stub growing from the top of his head. After Ted finished inspecting his father, Frank said, "We better go inside."

Ted scrambled off the cot and grabbed his pillow as Frank hoisted his duffle bag onto his shoulder and quietly closed the screen door as they entered the front hall. As Frank peered around the corner of the double door into the living room, he set his bag on the floor.

Will roused from his sleep in his stuffed chair. "Well I'll be, you did make it." Rising, he added as he embraced his son, "I was beginin' to think it'd be tomorrow."

"I got into Knoxville about eleven and caught a cab. I didn't know if the street cars were still running. It's good to be home."

"Lands sakes, Frank, you're home," blurted Mary as she suddenly roused from her nap in her comfortable chair. She rushed to him and hugged her son's trim body. "Oh, Frank, it's good to have you home. Have you had supper? Do you need something to eat or drink?"

"I'm fine, Mom, I've been well fed today."

"Just look at you," said Mary stepping back as she continued to grasp his waist. "You look younger than when you left." She too reached her hand up and ran her fingers across the bristly, short hair on his head.

"I'm in better shape, that's for sure," said Frank. "Younger, I don't think so. I'm still the oldest PFC in my outfit—well except for the butcher from Cincinnati. He's thirty-six and in better shape than I am or most of the younger men."

After a moment of enjoying the presence of the reunited family, "OK," Will said, "everybody upstairs and to bed. Granny needs her beauty sleep." Mary swatted Will's backside as he closed the front door and started down the hall for the stairs.

# CHAPTER 14

## *Knoxville*

## *End of Summer 1942*

THE DAY AFTER Labor Day, Frank walked Ted to the first day of classes at Van Gilder. Mary had registered Ted the previous week and secured a place for him in Miss Simpson's fourth grade class. Ted knew that Jerry and Floyd would be in the class and assumed all of the rest of his friends from the third grade would be there as well. Frank walked down the hall of the school and noticed the giggling, excited students as greetings were exchanged between friends who had not seen each other over the summer break. New students, often accompanied by a parent, stood silently by the side of the hall waiting for instructions to proceed to their room. Teachers standing in the hall by their room doors made certain there was no running. Ted led his father into the fourth grade room and to the teacher in front of the class. "This is my father. He's in the army," Ted said to Miss Simpson.

"Nice to meet you. We need to begin class very soon," she said coolly.

"Oh, yes, Ted just wanted me to see where he'll be going to school this year; I'm only home for a week's leave."

"That's nice," said Miss Simpson as she glanced around the class room. Frank recalled Ted's comment in one of his letters about Miss Simpson not being liked by the students; Frank began to experience some of the signals she was sending to her class and realized it was not a warm, welcoming message. "Thank you so much for coming," said Miss Simpson as she extended a hand for a quick handshake with Frank and in so doing dismissed him from the class.

Frank bent and whispered in Ted's ear a good-bye until after the half day of class was over. "I'll see you at home for lunch."

"Bye, Dad," murmured Ted as his father left the room. His father's appearance in the classroom had not gone as Ted had envisioned. The other students didn't get to really see his uniform and his sharpshooter's badge—that was the important thing his father had accomplished—but now no one else knew but Ted. He would just have to tell Jerry and Floyd about it, and maybe Georgie and David and Dicky and Roger Berger and . . .

As Frank left the school and began walking to Highland Avenue, he recalled the feeling of dread he had experienced as he walked into his first day of classes in seventh grade, the first year of junior high school. He had heard all of the stories of how the upperclassmen would stuff little kids in their lockers and close the door leaving them helpless until a passerby took mercy and let them out. After seeing the size of the lockers, Frank concluded that anyone stuffing him into the tiny space would have to perform amputations in order to eliminate the legs and, probably, arms from the victim. His anxiety subsided somewhat until he had his first encounter with the male teachers in gym and shop class. The teachers were very direct and told the students what to expect in their class. Frank just wasn't used to male teachers, having had only women teachers to that point.

It was at the semester break that his parents decided to send him to the Millersburg Military Academy located in their home town. The transition was difficult at first since Frank had only begun to get comfortable with the rigors of a large school. "Getting comfortable" was probably not the most accurate description of his reaction, for Frank had developed a very lackadaisical attitude about school to match that of his friends, and it was that attitude that spurred Will and Mary to make the decision to send him to military school. The rigors of public school had been nothing compared to life in the academy, where he lived in the dorm with only an occasional weekend pass to return to the nearby farm. Fortunately the parents of one of Frank's closest friends also took the same remedy in addressing the attitude of their son, and the two boys suffered through the spring semester before getting the summer off. The semester, although rough especially at the beginning, had a remarkable effect on Frank for his attitude toward his studies, and life in general changed as he began to develop a sense of pride in his academic accomplishments and mastery of military life that required acceptance of personal discipline and responsibility for his actions. At thirteen Frank was starting to grow up, something his parents regarded as a reward for their schooling decision.

The leave went fast for Frank, Ted, and the grandparents. On Saturday the three generations of Warring men sat in the stands and watched the University of Tennessee football team practice as they prepared for their fall schedule of games that would begin in the middle of the month. The 1941 season and now extending into 1942 would mark the second time Coach Neyland had been called away from his football coaching position at the university to active military service. He had spent the 1935 season serving in the Panama Canal Zone, and he was now in Burma following his promotion to brigadier general.

In his career at Tennessee thus far, Coach Neyland had developed, arguably, the most accomplished football program in the country. In his second tour of service at the University from '38 through the '40 season, UT had been a dominating power; in fact, in '38 his team was designated the undefeated national champion with a victory in the Orange Bowl, and in the '39 season his team was not scored on until its loss in the Rose Bowl at the end of the season when its starting tailback was hurt.

Neyland's defensive genius showed through the preparation of his team. Under the current coach, the university's team continued to dominate the Southeastern Conference. The single-wing offensive formation offered many running options for the backfield and occasional passes to the ends, but it was on defense where the team still shone brightest. Will and Frank, on the other hand, due to their roots in Kentucky did not have particularly strong feelings for the Tennessee team; in fact, if truth be known, they really disliked the team since Kentucky had been regularly defeated by the Volunteers.. They did respect the UT team, but they kept no secrets when it came to admitting they wished them a terrible season, especially during the final game against Kentucky.

After watching an hour of the practice, the men and boy picked up their fishing poles from Will's truck and spent the remainder of the pleasant afternoon on the banks of the river below Shields-Watkins Field watching the slow current provide ample hiding places for the fish that refused to bite the bait they offered. Will offered the only reason needed for the lack of success, "I guess the fish have had their fill of worms for the season; maybe they want shrimp now." The lack of fish did not detract from their feeling that the day had been an entirely joyful one for the Warring men.

Late Sunday afternoon, Ted, Jerry, and Floyd sat on the front porch steps wondering what to do after their game of "ball," where they took turns hitting the tattered baseball into the weeds of the vacant lot on Laurel Avenue. Frank and Mary sat on the porch swing, Frank reading the *News Sentinel* and Mary crocheting.

Leroy emerged from around the corner on Seventeenth Street and walked up to the porch steps. "Did you boys see any of those snipes go by?"

"No," said Floyd.

After a long, reflective pause Jerry squinted as he shaded his eyes and looked up at Leroy who stood casually peering around the Highland Avenue street scene. "What's a snipe look like?"

"Oh, it's a furry, kind of bushy little fellow about so big," said Leroy, holding his hands about eight inches apart. "They hardly ever come out in the open so you can see 'em, but I just saw a pair in the back yard, and they was headed down the sidewalk on Seventeenth . . . they was headed this way. I thought you may have seen 'em," Leroy added, still peering under the bushes. "The University is doing some research on 'em, I've heard, and they will pay a reward if someone catches a pair of 'em. They especially want the females—they are larger and bushier than the males, don't you know. So I thought I had a nice reward when I seen them two, but they are awfully sneaky and they hide in the darnedest places."

"Can we help?" asked Ted.

And Jerry added simultaneously, "Yeah . . ."

"Sure, I'll split the ten-dollar reward with you and give the one who actually catches the little critters, ah . . . four dollars."

"Wow," said Floyd, stunned by the sum of money offered as a reward.

"It works best if you get sticks and beat the bushes and get 'em on the run and one of you hold a big sack to catch 'em in when you get 'em cornered, you see."

"I'll get a grocery sack," said Ted as he ran into the front hall slamming the screen door behind him.

Jerry and Floyd ran to get sticks from the Gooche's yard across the street.

"Now, Leroy, don't you fool the boys thataway," said Mary with a twinkle in her eye.

"Oh, it's good exercise," said Leroy in a muffled voice as Ted reappeared on the porch with an A&P bag that was intended to be used for collection of garbage.

"Teddy, don't tear the bag. After you get through with it, I need it back in the kitchen," said Mary with a stifled grin.

The hunting party was soon gathered on the walk in front of the house when Leroy shouted, "There goes one now into the McGruder's yard." The boys took off in hot pursuit of the reward they were already counting. Leroy ambled after them and directed their search for the elusive critter on down Highland Avenue toward Eighteenth.

"Lordy, that Leroy is just a kid at heart. I wish his family could move here and give him a decent home life. He misses 'em somethin' awful," said Mary.

"Yeah," added Frank, "I bet he drives his wife crazy with his antics. He must be a holy terror with his own kids."

After more than thirty minutes, a bedraggled hunting party came around the corner of Seventeenth and onto the porch steps where the exhausted boys flopped down.

"You boys been running?" asked Mary.

"Yes'sum," said Jerry, "Leroy kept seeing them snipes up ahead, but we never could catch 'em. We went over to Clinch and Nineteenth and all over, and we couldn't get 'em."

"Did any of you actually see them?" asked Frank.

"I think I did . . . somethin' out of the corner of my eye, I think . . . yeah I saw 'em," announced Ted.

"Yeah, me too," said Floyd, "I think I seen 'em go under a car."

"They didn't go under a car," said Jerry in a reproachful voice.

"Yes they did. I think I seen 'em," reasserted Floyd.

Leroy came ambling around the corner and joined the boys on the steps, "Yes sir, we gave a good chase, but they just were too smart and too fast for us," he explained. "The boys gave 'em a good run for their money, but the snipes won."

Will came out the porch door having awakened from his afternoon nap, stretched, and overheard the word *snipes*. He knew nothing of the hunt that had just ended and mused to no one in particular, "I remember as a child being sent on a wild-goose chase on the farm looking for snipes that were stealing chicken eggs. We hunted all over and of course never found any."

"Why didn't you find 'em?" asked Ted.

"'Cause, well, they don't exist. They're make believe, kinda like the Easter bunny or Santa," explained Will.

"Yes, they do to exist. Ask Leroy," said Floyd. "He seen 'em all over the neighborhood."

"Oh, I see, you been chasing 'em with Leroy. He sees a lot of things no one else can see, especially little animals," said Will. "Yes sir, that Leroy is some kind of hunter," added Will as he broke into laughter and walked back inside the house. The front porch party could hear his prolonged laughter as he returned to the living room.

"Maybe we'll have better luck next time," said Leroy as he also went through the front door with a serious frown on his face. A few seconds later the laughter from inside the house erupted again from Will and this time Leroy joining in.

Ted and Jerry looked at each other and thought about the hunt they had just conducted, and they considered the possibilities. They knew they had been had by Leroy.

"We need to think of some way to get even with Leroy," Jerry whispered, and Ted nodded in agreement. Floyd, who still believed in Santa Claus, had no misgivings about the seriousness of the hunting experience; Will's comments had flown over his head without the slightest bit of recognition. He planned to tell his parents about the hunt at supper and how he planned to continue to search for snipes so he could earn the reward money for himself.

On Wednesday morning, September 16, Frank walked Ted to school in the company of Jerry and Floyd. On the sidewalk leading to the school door, Frank said good-bye to Ted, and they hugged briefly as two girls in his class walked by and through the school doorway. Frank had insisted that Ted go to school today, the day he returned to Fort Benning, rather than miss a day in class. Frank's unconvincing argument included the fact that Will would be working and only Mary would accompany him to the train. Ted was certain he should go as well, but Frank reminded him of the seriousness of his studies and the need to "start the year right." Nancy Griffin and Susan McIntyre waited for Ted inside the door and asked about his father.

"He's leaving for the army training camp again today. He's

going to be an officer," said Ted somewhat forlornly. The girls were impressed, asked questions about the training, which Ted answered as best he could using his imagination and what he understood from his father's comments about the OCS program. The three walked with into the classroom; the interest the girls had shown improved Ted's outlook immeasurably on the departure of his father.

Mary and Frank left for the train terminal immediately after he returned to Highland Avenue from Van Gilder. This time the only tears were a few shed by Mary who cried when any of her children left. The other children, all older than Frank, lived so far away that good-byes said to them were very rare and very stressful.

# CHAPTER 15

## *Knoxville*

## *Fall 1942*

*20 September 1942*

*Dear Son,*

*I arrived back at Fort Benning Wednesday evening after taking the Greyhound from Macon. I had missed the bus that ran directly from Atlanta to Columbus but was able to make connections through Macon, a very nice-looking little town. If everything works out as I expect, I'll be home about January fifteenth. Cross your fingers and wish me luck.*

*We are in a very special training program. Besides training to be an officer, our class includes Negro officer candidates as well. General Omar Bradley is commandant of the infantry school and has directed that all officers train together. This is the first time that Negroes and whites have been together as equals in the army. It should be an interesting experiment. They have separated the races in the barracks, but in training we all are expected to do the same things. Our class has about two hundred men, and the major on the first day warned us that we can expect between 15 and 30 percent of our class not to be here when we finish. I don't think you have learned about percentages in arithmetic yet, but the percentages I quoted means that between thirty and sixty men out of the two hundred men won't graduate as officers. It will be a tough program, but I fully expect to be one of the graduates.*

*I hope your school is going well. I have decided to pay you twenty-five cents for every A that you earn on your report card. If you do as well as I believe you can, you may be wealthy by the end of the fourth grade, assuming you save your money, of course. I also hope that you continue to read the newspaper and work on your scrapbook. That is a good way for you to learn about the world we live in. This war won't last forever, and before you know it, you will be out of high school and ready to strike out on your own.*

*Give my love to Granny and Granddad and keep plenty for yourself.*

*Love, Dad*

TWENTY FIVE CENTS for every A. *Golly!* thought Ted, *that could be a lot of money, 'cause I get a report card every six weeks. That could be about, uh . . . a dollar for every four As when school's out next spring . . . gee whiz . . . dollars.*

The part of the letter that talked about Ted going out on his own after high school didn't sound appealing; he was happy right where he was living on Highland Avenue and going to Van Gilder. He could not imagine wanting to leave the home he now knew, much less graduate from high school. In fact, he couldn't even comprehend attending high school. Right now he was in the fourth grade and that was the extent of his plan making.

Ted pasted the envelope he had received into his scrapbook and then inserted his father's letter for safe keeping. He then pulled out the recent news articles describing the war that he had cut from the paper and pasted those in as well. The articles told of fighting that continued on Guadalcanal as the Japanese made a futile attempt to recapture Henderson Field and push the Americans into the sea. On the island of New Guinea, the Americans had reinforced the Australians, and together they had successfully beaten back the Japanese attempt to seize Port Moresby. In Russia the city of Stalingrad was now surrounded by German forces, with the Russian army fighting a desperate delaying battle. Ted examined the maps with arrows drawn to show troop movements and imagined the army's moving in an orderly fashion as they marched into battle. Ted's image of battles reflected more of a medieval manner of fighting than the reality of the mechanized movement of soldiers and tanks fighting at close range as aircraft and artillery delivered a barrage of lethal arsenal on the enemy and occasionally on the heads of their fellow soldiers.

Ted's scrapbook contained blank pages where he pasted his collection. The blank pages resembled the same type of paper that his fourth grade teacher provided the class for art work. So Ted frequently drew pictures of battles, almost always showing a Japanese or German plane going down in flames in an otherwise clear blue sky. He was at a loss for how to show the actual ground battle except to reproduce explosions that threw large quantities of earth in the air, replicating the pictures he often saw in the News Sentinel. The colorful crayon drawings helped him imagine the glory of war but not the horror.

The remainder of the month of September and October passed uneventfully for Ted as he and his classmates adjusted to the fourth grade and their new teacher, Miss Simpson. She was a stern-looking individual who seldom smiled and gave every indication that she did not really enjoy everyday life, especially when dealing with nine- and ten-year-old children. She did acknowledge, when she confronted her circumstances, that she was glad her charges were only nine rather than the twelve-, thirteen-, or fourteen-year-olds; those were the ones who were experiencing rapid growth and the effects of "raging hormones" that accompany puberty. In her humble opinion, that was the period *when children should be confined in isolation and only allowed to emerge into society when they could be conversed with, about the age of sixteen or maybe fifteen, at the earliest.*

Miss Simpson was aware of the opinion the students had of her, and in fact she relished it. She wanted to keep very tight control over the students, although at times she admitted she did overplay her hand a tad. But all in all, she wanted to teach them everything she could and not be their best friend. She was convinced that a disciplined student who paid attention learned more. She did occasionally let her hair down, like when she gave a ride to school for those students she saw walking up the Seventeenth Street hill on their way to Van Gilder. Under those circumstances she conversed easily with the passenger until they reached the school door. Those opportunities worked best with a single student or a limited number of students; otherwise, with the entire class, she made sure she did not undo any of the strict teacher-student relationships.

After the relatively uneventful and non-holiday Columbus Day that occurred on Sunday the eleventh of October, the next real obstacle to class stability was Halloween. One of the girls in the class, Susan McIntyre, was having a party at her house, and all of her classmates were invited. Miss Simpson did know Susan McIntyre's mother through the PTA; Della McIntyre had been the president during the past year. In fact, during the recess break on the last Tuesday morning in October, the principal's office had informed her of a call from Della that she must remember to return during her lunch break.

Miss Simpson had noticed the level of excitement rise as the last day of the month approached. This year Halloween occurred on Saturday; at least she could take some comfort in the fact that it did not occur on a school day. She prepared herself for the student's lack of attention on Friday the 30th and knew there would be constant whispering by all the students, giggling among the girls, and sudden loud outbursts from the boys. As far as she could determine, the dominant costumes were to be soldiers and bums among the boys and nurses and fairy princesses among the girls, with perhaps a Shirley Temple dress-up in the mix as well.

"Let's put a moustache on your upper lip," suggested Mary.

"That would be great," said Ted. "How you gonna do that?"

"Well, I thought of getting a woolly worm from the garden and then gluing it to your upper lip."

"Ugh," said Ted, "it would wiggle and tickle all night and drive me crazy."

"Oh, we would stick a pin in it to kill it first, then glue it on."

"Double ugh! That means I would have wooly worm blood on me," Ted blurted out as he instinctively swiped the back of his hand across his mouth. He was sure his grandmother was teasing him but he pretended to take her suggestion seriously; he knew she enjoyed the give and take between them as much as he did.

Mary finally broke into prolonged laughter as she pulled from her apron pocket a small glass vial of mascara. She had never used mascara for its intended use around her eyes but had read in the *Saturday Evening Post* stories of painted ladies that used it liberally to enhance their allure to men. The whole notion of going to that amount of trouble to attract men seemed unimaginable and completely unnecessary to Mary, but nonetheless she understood the general idea of the liquid and gingerly opened the bottle. By turning the cap and removing it, she discovered an attached stem with a brush circling its end. First she drew the brush across the back of her left hand to discover it left a trail of thick powdery liquid. "Ah, this will work fine."

Ted, who had viewed the experiment with some trepidation, extended his neck and stuck out his lower jaw. Mary put the brush back into the vial and got a full load of the liquid on its bristles and then drew it across Ted's upper lip on the left side of his face.

"Eee-ou, that tickles," said Ted, jerking away from the brush. His sudden movement gave an accidentally rakish downward turn to the short moustache on half of his face.

Mary broke into prolonged laughter and she instinctively covered her mouth with the back of her hand. "Teddy, hold still," she said. Now with his eyes closed, he tensed his whole body as he jutted his neck forward for a second time. Mary deftly applied mascara to the right side of his face and a little more to the left side. She leaned back to admire her work as Ted held his frozen pose, eyes closed and neck and jaw extended. "There," she said with a level of satisfaction admiring her handy work, "I think that will do fine. Just remember not to wipe your mouth. If you use a napkin, kinda dab at your mouth; don't take a big swipe."

Ted slowly opened his eyes to stare at a reflection of his face in the hand mirror held by Mary. He was surprised and pleased at the change in his appearance. "What do ya think?" asked Mary.

Mary lowered the mirror and Ted began to laugh. "It's great."

Ten minutes later Ted descended the stairs and stood in front of his grandfather. "This is my army uniform," he said.

Will admired the blue denim shirt with stripes sown on the upper part of each sleeve, a knotted dark green tie around the neck that hung three inches below his belted waist, last year's Sunday-best gray trousers with a vertical yellow stripe stitched down the outside of each leg, and this year's Sunday shoes polished brighter than they had been since the first day they were worn. His face bore the rakish moustache, with slicked back and combed hair under an army hat given him by his father. "Yes sir," said Will, "you're a soldier, sure 'nough. I especially like that wooly worm under your nose."

"That's not a worm; that's what Granny wanted to glue on. This here is mask-rare-ah."

"Do tell," said Will. "I would never know it was not real if you hadn't told me. You look very slick. Now, if there are some wild dames at this party tonight, you steer clear of them and don't let them catch you in a room by yourself."

"Ah, Granddad," exclaimed Ted as his cheeks added a light shade of pink.

Mary, having reached the first floor, stepped into the living room. "Don't he look nice?" she asked Will while looking at Ted in profile.

Will immediately burst into laughter.

"He don't look funny, Will. Now, you stop that laughing."

Will continued as he looked at Mary and not at Ted. "Looks like you grew a moustache as well," he sputtered between breaths.

"What're you talking about, old man?" she said with a mockingly straight face.

"Mary, look in the mirror."

Mary turned and strode into the hall to stare at her known face in the mirror that was built into the combination hat rack and clothes tree that stood by the front door. She saw her image broken and spotted by the old mirror that lacked some of its silver backing. Something was wrong though, and she moved closer in the dim light of the hall to see a smeared moustache rubbed into the right side of her upper lip. "Well, I'll be. How did that happen?"

Ted, now standing in the hall along with Will said, "You had it on the back of your hand and then you brushed it on your face."

Ted, Jerry, and Floyd walked to Susan's house on Forest Avenue near Fifteenth Street. A tall, dark figure stood in the shadows of the front yard just inside the gate at the sidewalk. Light was provided by the streetlight six doors west on Forest and the porch light, which cast a glow behind the solemn figure. "Welcome, young lads, it's very *gould* to see you," came the soft, firm voice with emphasis on the word *gould*; a sinister chuckle bubbled to the surface of the shrouded figure, and a long arm with an extended long finger pointed toward the front door. "Please go into my secret chamber; we have many surprises for you, some are even pleasant, others . . . well, you'll see."

"OK," said Floyd as the soldier and two bums laughed nervously and scurried past the stranger, up the steps, and through the front door. Floyd looked over his shoulder to make certain they were not followed by the stranger. Inside the door they were met by Susan, dressed as a princess with a tiara, and her mother, who shocked Ted with her abbreviated black outfit with a short skirt the length of his summer short pants and black fishnet stockings with high heel shoes adorning her very long legs. Ted had never seen a mature woman dressed in such an outfit, and *the legs, the legs, oh my*. The warm greeting on the inside of the house offset the weird greeting they had had in the front yard. Nancy Griffith stood nearby, and Ted was surprised by her fairy outfit that doubled as a ballerina's tutu when Nancy took ballet lessons.

Ted had trouble taking his eyes off Nancy; she looked very special to him in that stiff horizontal skirt and dancing slippers. The girls and boys slowly split into their separate groups, girls in one and boys in the other, although eyes stole frequent glances at members of the "other" group.

Several games followed after all invited guests had arrived. There was a secret vote by ballot for the best-dressed costume for girls and boys. Nancy won for her tutu-fairy outfit, and Roger Berger won for his mad scientist get-up, which included a lab coat, stethoscope, and circular mirror worn on a strap around his head. Next was a wild, noisy game of musical chairs in the family's dining room. Because the number of guests exceeded the number of chairs, everyone was divided into groups of eight, and the four winners, including Ted and Jerry, then had a playoff that determined Jerry as the grand winner amidst cheers and screams of gleeful enjoyment.

As the noise began to subside, a door previously closed slowly began to open with a sound of un-oiled hinges, a looong squeeeaaak that silenced the guests. The sound was very reminiscent of the door-opening sequence of the radio show *Inner Sanctum* broadcast on Saturday nights. The interior of the room beyond the door was dark, and no one was visible until a pair of long fingers slowly crept into view and grasped the frame of the door. A pause followed before a head slowly came into view, with long, unkempt dark hair, a pointed nose with warts, and beady eyes below bushy eyebrows. A tall, conical, black hat topped the head.

"It's the wicked witch of the west!" shrieked Beverly Goodman, who was dressed as a junior-size witch. Nervous giggles and uncomfortable laughter erupted from the guests as Susan's mother stood at the back of the observers with a broad grin on her face.

"Welcome, children, to my secret chamber . . . I have many interesting things to show you," said the witch in her best sinister-sounding voice, a voice made more believable to the nine-year-olds by the *Wizard of Oz* movie many had seen or heard about. "Won't you please come into my chamber and see and feel for yourself my delights? Please form a line of a boy and girl together and come in two at a time. Igor will tell you when to enter. He, he, he." The tall stranger from the front yard stepped forward and helped line up the guests in a boy-girl arrangement. The first two students entered the darkened room, and the door partially closed. The hushed students held their breaths until a squeal erupted from the room and nervous laughter burst from the group. Couple after couple entered the room with similar noises of surprise coming from the room. After several couples had entered, Ted realized they exited from another door into the adjoining dining room and stood around nervously laughing and gesturing.

To Ted's surprise and delight, he entered the room with Nancy Griffith and felt her stiff tutu brush against his leg and heard the rustle of the fabric as they tiptoed into the shadows. In the darkened space they were welcomed by the witch who led them to a long table. "Please place your fingers into my bowls," she said. Nancy and Ted hesitantly stuck their fingers into the first dimly lit bowl and felt rather slimy round objects. "My collection of eyeballs," said the witch.

"Eeek!" said Nancy and quickly withdrew her hand.

"You'll notice on the back of the eyeball is a slight indention; that's where the optic nerve attaches," came further news from the witch. Ted's hand on first mention of eyeballs started an involuntary withdrawal from the dish, but he overcame his reaction and felt again. He could feel the rough spot, but he couldn't quite guess the real identity of the objects. He knew, or rather hoped, they were not real eyeballs.

The next bowl emerged from the shadows, and their hands felt another slimy object, this time much larger and more slippery. "My liver collection," came the proud words from the witch and accompanied by a soft chuckle.

"Eeek," again came Nancy's response.

"And here's a lively treat. This time they felt again a larger object and again slimy, but this object was a little lumpier and firmer under the slippery surface than the last liver. "My heart collection."

"Oooooh," Nancy squealed as she jumped back from the table.

"And my final treat, brains from one of my visitors from last year." This time Ted felt a strange rounded object a little larger than half of a softball but with a many-indentured surface, modeling into an uneven surface, again with a slimy touch. Nancy tentatively stuck her fingers into the bowl until she came in contact with the object and then quickly withdrew them. "They were such smart children, He, he, he." Ted and Nancy were ushered into the dining room where the other survivors of the witch's chamber of treats were gathered.

"Here's a towel to wipe your hands," said Susan's mother.

"Ted, you were so brave in there," said Nancy squeezing his arm.

Ted turned a bright shade of red and mumbled unintelligibly, "Ah." Any other formulation of words completely escaped his brain as a pleasant confusion momentarily engulfed him.

The children now thoroughly integrated by sex retold their reaction to the chamber, often with exaggerated gestures. After Floyd wondered aloud if the objects were real, several boys laughed and one punched his shoulder claiming they knew they were fake all the time even if the unsaid truth was that when they felt them they were unsure. The girls mostly giggled when they were not telling of their reaction to the slimy objects. Susan stood at the back of the group with a broad smile on her face, a smile based on knowledge of the truth.

With all of the class talking and mingling in the dining room, the exit door from the witch's chamber opened again and the witch entered the room. "I'm so glad you enjoyed my treats," she said as she slowly bent her body at the waist and removed her hat, wig, and mask. When she stood erect the class screamed almost in perfect unison, "Miss Simpson!" Laughter erupted again with Miss Simpson and Susan's parents joining in. "I'm a friend of Della McIntyre, and she asked me if I wanted to join your party, and I said yes if I could wear a disguise." Miss Simpson then pulled a tray from her chamber to reveal four bowls containing oiled grapes, calves' liver, the heart of a cow, and a head of cauliflower, again with a generous dose of cooking oil poured over the top.

"I had to go downtown to find the heart at Market Square," explained Miss Simpson.

"It's real?" came the near unanimous response from the boys as they crowded around the bowls, some poking the organ again. Roger Berger picked it up and pretended to take a bite.

"Ooough," came the response from both girls and boys. Miss Simpson now laughing retired to the kitchen for coffee with the senior McIntyres as the younger guests had cake, cookies, and ice cream while some still got a closer look at the four bowls. A louder noise was created when two boys started playing toss with the heart only to have the kitchen door open and the game stop when Miss Simpson stuck her head into the room and gave a slight shaking of her head. She did not smile and the heart was returned to the bowl.

# CHAPTER 16

## *Fort Benning*

## *Fall 1942*

*Dear Daddy. It is Sunday November 8 and I am getting over a bad cold. I wish you were here. We had a swell time at a party at Susans house on Haloween night. Every body got scared with the witch and her scary stuff, I knew it was fake but I did not tell on her to Jerry and Floyd and Nancy and every body. The witch was our teacher Miss Simpson and she wore a disguise. I like Nancy a lot. She is nice and she dances on her toes and does ballet. She gave a dance at a school asembly. She was very good. Jerry and I got even with Leroy for the snipe trick he played on us. We had a fishing line tied to a nail and rosin and we stuck the nail under Leroys window and rubbed the rosin on the line and made a funny sound. Kind of spooky. Leroy could not tell who made the sound and where it came from. He looked all over and could not find us. We were in the bushs. It was at night and very dark. He said he got very scared and wanted a gun to chase away the ghosts making the sound. But he did not have a gun, I guess.*
*Love Ted Warring*

THE SEVENTEEN-WEEK course that Frank had entered for Officer Candidate School would promote graduates to the rank of second lieutenant in the infantry, armor, or artillery branches of a ground fighting division. Frank would likely choose infantry if he had a choice and would be placed in command of a platoon of fifty men. If things worked out as he hoped, he could expect more responsibility in the future, perhaps leading four platoons in a company of about two hundred men. Frank knew he shouldn't contemplate the future rank as much as concentrate on the present school; he needed to learn as much as it had to offer. The majority of his training was taking place at the main post at Fort Benning and not in the post's outlying facilities at Sand Hill and Harmony Church where he had spent time in basic training. About half of the training involved building physical stamina, similar to the training he had endured in the basic training program during the summer months. Because he was building on his recent exercise program, the physical part of the training was much easier, and despite his advanced age compared to most of the rest of the school's students, he often excelled at the physical challenges. Commanders of the OCS had set down specified time and distance requirements that were to be achieved in running and marching, as well as time requirements for completion of obstacle courses.

There was also a repeat of training in infantry weapons, including all the weapons they would be expected to command in the field, from use of concentrated rifle fire to machine guns and mortars. Next was introduction to the tank: its operation, weapons, and the combined tactics of tanks and ground soldiers. Finally, an introduction to artillery and the power, accuracy, and range of field pieces to support infantry operations was provided. Tactics were a basic part of the program, stressing the assimilation of the three integral operations into an arsenal of weapons tied together by effective ground and radio communications. It struck Frank that the approach to infantry tactics was based on the fighting situation that confronted soldiers in the Great War, or the First World War as it was beginning to be called now that the current maelstrom in Europe and Asia was being labeled as the Second World War. *What a pity they didn't get it right during and after the first try at fighting a world war; now my generation has to go through it again in both Europe and Asia.*

By early November, training had expanded to include students taking command of a platoon of fifty fellow students to achieve certain objectives in the field, sometimes under mock combat conditions. Training commanders assigned field objectives for the exercises delivered through simulated briefings similar to those the students would receive in future combat situations. The experience gave students an opportunity to lead and allowed instructors to judge their ability to react and improvise solutions. Frank did well in the command exercises, especially those involving marches and movement of troops across a terrain of unknown ground obstacles. Even when Frank was not in command of the student exercise, the student in charge often kept him close as an advisor; his classmates were rapidly learning of his ability to understand and interpret complex situations, especially students in their early twenties without any previous military training, which described most of the class.

The three themes of the training program emphasized on the opening day were rigorous physical training, strict discipline, and efficient organization, requirements set down by General Bradley.

Thursday, November 19, was an unusually warm afternoon in west-central Georgia as the students rested following completion of a timed fifteen-mile run made up of five three-mile segments. Although the daytime temperature in central Georgia could be quite variable in the fall, today's high of ninety degrees was unusually warm and produced prodigious amounts of sweat by all participants. Frank had reached the end of the run near the front of the pack and reached the finish line at the same time as a tall, black fellow student. The two finishers slumped into the grass in the shade of an oak tree and concentrated on breathing the moist air that promised thunder showers during the evening. "Golly, that was a stretch," mumbled Frank's companion. "I haven't done that much running since football practice."

"Where did you play ball?" asked Frank between breaths.

"At the University of Illinois in Urbana," came the reply. "I finished in '36. I'm one of the old guys."

"You may be the old guy among the colored soldiers, but I've got you beat by four years or so," replied Frank.

"Really, you're thirty-two?" asked the lanky colored student as he leaned forward on one elbow.

"Actually, thirty-three as of September."

"Well I'll be. I thought you were about my age or a year younger. You compete very well for an old-timer." Frank's companion returned to a prone position in the soft grass.

"Yeah, for an old guy . . . I went through basic training last summer, and that shook up my old bones and got them into a little better shape."

"Your name's Frank, I believe," said his companion.

"Yes, and you are Henry, right?"

"Yes, Henry Boudreau." The two roused themselves from their prone positions and shook hands for the first time.

"Boudreau, you related to Lou Boudreau the ball player?"

"No." Henry laughed. "Wrong color. But he was at Illinois when I was there . . . he was two years behind me. He played both baseball and basketball until he signed with the Cleveland Indians and that stopped his college playing days after his sophomore year."

"I played basketball in high school and then retired," said Frank. "I decided I was too small for college ball. I went out for football in high school for two days until I realized we were supposed to start running into each other, and I decided my 120 pounds wouldn't get me very far, so I sat in the stands as a spectator."

"Where did you play basketball?"

"I was a guard in at Millersburg Military Institute; we played very small schools and not always very well, but we did compete even if we lost most of our games."

"Sounds like my high school football team. We were one and eight in my senior year. I was a walk-on in college and grew several inches my freshman year and was on the junior varsity squad. Then I got promoted to the varsity team in my last two years and played a lot in my last year. But I had my fill of getting beat up and was glad to finish my career without a serious injury."

"I guess we together are the old boys of this junior officer's class," said Frank stretching out on his back in the shady grass and staring at the overhead leaves and small patches of blue sky peeping through the dense foliage. "I went to Eastern Kentucky State Teachers College for two years, but the Depression made me drop out in '30 and then I got married that same spring and that gave me another set of things to think about, mainly making a living."

"So, you've been married for . . . twelve years?" asked Henry.

"Well . . . yes." Frank avoided the obvious answer that he had lost his wife almost a year ago. He didn't want to confide in every stranger he met about his family life. The loss was still too hard to talk about.

"Do you have children?"

"We have one boy, he's . . . nine now, yes, nine. He's in the fourth grade in Knoxville, living with my parents until the war is over. Then we'll start new, either there or back in Kentucky." After a pause Frank asked, "What are you going to do after the war?"

"Well I have a law degree and plan to get a job, maybe in government or with a private firm. A fellow named Cassius Brown has offered me a place in his office, but I don't know what I'll do. He's on the Southside."

"Southside?" asked Frank.

"Yes Southside, Chicago. A lot of colored folks live on the Southside. And a lot of them get into trouble. There are a lot of black businesses there, as well, and when you have trouble and business combined, it can be a pretty good living for a lawyer. But first I need to survive the war." After a pause, "What do you think we're going to be getting into besides a hell of a fight?"

"That's the big deal, nobody knows for sure. It looks like we are going to have to invade Europe . . . my best guess is France, although Belgium is close to England and could be a target. Now that Eisenhower and Patton have landed in Morocco, we are beating the tail off the Germans and the Vichy in North Africa. And since the British have pushed the Germans out of Egypt, things are looking up, at least in North Africa . . . so I guess Europe is next. Maybe we could invade from North Africa to Italy, Spain, or France . . . now there's a possibility as well."

"Huh, I wonder what it would be like for an American Negro soldier to fight in Africa for the United States, kind of a homecoming," Henry said with a chuckle.

"I suppose it could be considered that," smiled Frank. "But weren't you folks from farther south than Morocco?"

"I guess so, but the truth is, we don't know where we came from, just Africa. But you're right, not Morocco. When they picked us up on the west coast off Guinea or Angola, they didn't keep very good records."

"No, they certainly didn't, and as I recall, they didn't inquire if your ancestors wanted to get on the boat," mused Frank.

"No, they didn't ask us," said Henry no longer smiling.

The two men enjoyed the opportunity to simply relax and carry on a surprisingly candid conversation. When they took time to consider the conversation, both men realized they may have found a person of the "other" race with whom they could, apparently, converse openly.

At supper the white and Negro students usually sat at separate tables, white or Negro, with only occasional mixing. Tonight Frank asked if he could join Henry and his friends at their table. "Please," replied Henry. He introduced the other five Negro students, most of whom Frank could already identify by first name. Henry was aware the conversation had hit a lull with the arrival of Frank and said, "I was telling these boys that we may go into Europe and fight the Germans."

"I can speak some German," offered Jesse White, a light-skin student, after swallowing a mouthful of meatloaf. "Maybe I can lead the invasion," stuffing in another large bite.

"No shit," said Shelby Young, "if you lead the invasion I ain't goin'. Where'd you learn to speak German from, and why would any colored man want to speak it?"

Swallowing after a pause for chewing, "My grandmother was from Lingen, a small German town near the Dutch border. She had a son with my grandfather who was, of course, colored, and that son was my father. Then my grandfather went to California in 1918, and he was never heard from again. He was probably murdered out there, 'cause he had promised to send for my grandmother, but that didn't happen. My Nanny raised my father, and she taught me some German words when I came along, and then I took German in college at Wilberforce."

"Well, I'll be," said Shelby. "A black German, whoever would've guessed?" The six men laughed.

"Nanny was a tough, determined old girl; the Teutonic people are known for being stern without any foolishness, and there wasn't nothin' that she would let beat her. She fought all of her life, and she taught my father to fight as well," offered Jesse. "That's particularly important if you are a black in Massachusetts."

"I thought she was German not that 'too' stuff," countered Shelby.

"Well, the Teutonic tribe settled in Germany a long time ago about the time the Romans were ruling Europe."

"You mean white people had tribes too? I thought only us blacks had tribes. Is there nothing the whites won't steal from us?" asked a playfully oblique Shelby.

With that last comment, Jesse took an ineffectual swipe at Shelby with his napkin and the laughter continued. Jesse added, "I tell you, if those German troops are anything like my Nanny, we are in for one hellava fight." The laughter stopped.

Monday, November 23, found fifty of the officer candidates crouched in a ditch about five miles from the main post. In front of the ditch were dense woods, and at the rear of the troops was a gravel road paralleling the ditch. The student commander for the exercise, nicknamed Louey Lou, had received a briefing on their objective, and he had gathered three students acting as squad leaders into a huddle in the ditch with the remainder of the students huddled as close as the ditch's terrain allowed. Frank was one of the three squad leaders.

"We got three targets in these woods, so I am dividing the men into three squads with you three guys as their leaders. We are each going to proceed independently to find one of the first set of targets and fire on it till the evaluator waves a flag."

"The evaluator, probably a sergeant or corporal, is in a bunker below the target, so don't fire too low or we may get a very bad score." There was a soft chuckle from those within hearing distance.

"After we hit our target, we proceed southeast and rendezvous at point 37.5 on the field maps. There we engage another target or targets, we are not certain how many there will be, and there will be live fire at 1.5 meters over our heads, that's about four-and-a-half feet, so stay down for God's sake in that final assault.

"The two flanking squads will now separate from the center by a hundred yards; stay in the ditch, and I will give a hand signal to move out together. We are to stay low and move as silently as possible through the woods.

"Frank you take fifteen men to the right, Jamison you go left with fifteen, and the rest stay in the center with Randy and me. Randy is the squad leader in the center. Any questions?"

"I assume we are to have no radio contact during this exercise?" asked Frank.

"Right, radio silence, but we have three radios, and each of the three squads will take one, but we break radio silence only in case of a dire emergency. Any more questions? OK, get set up on the right and left."

Frank moved about 120 yards to his right, taking the fifteen men on the right hand side of the group. There he repeated the instructions for his men to make certain they knew the battle plan. "Also watch out for trip wires on booby traps," he warned. The hand signal was waved by Louey Lou, and the right-hand squad moved ahead into the woods, the soldiers stooping down and walking as quietly as possible. Frank had appointed two scouts, Shelby Young and the youngest student, Ralph Emerson; the scouts preceded the squad by fifty feet into the dense grove of hardwoods and underbrush. Three men trailed the squad to protect its rear, while the remaining ten made up the core unit.

The hardwood trees with their attendant undergrowth and piled-up leaves soon gave way to a dense grove of southern pines with a carpet of brown pine needles. Frank signaled the scouts to return to the group. In a hushed voice he showed the men how by periodically getting on the ground and viewing under the tree branches that a much longer distance could be seen than from the height of about four feet, their bent-over positions.

The scouts returned to their positions, and the squad carefully moved ahead at a reduced pace. Off to the left the men heard a distant bang followed by a siren. *Someone probably hit a booby trap wire and set off the fake mine device*, thought Frank. Just then Shelby gave a hand signal to halt, and Frank moved forward to get his report. "There's a wire running between those trees," whispered Shelby.

"Mark the wire with a flag in the middle and its ends," said Frank, "and keep on the lookout, they may come in clusters." The squad continued creeping forward. After five minutes, the silence was broken by another mine-device explosion to the left. Frank's squad found two more trip wires, and each were marked in turn and avoided by the men.

Thirty minutes into the trek, the squad had reached a high point along a sharp ridge. In the woods on the opposite side of the narrow valley they faced, one of the men spotted a manmade object hidden in the trees. "That could be the target," whispered Frank. We are exposed if we cross directly down the hill in front of us. Shelby you take eight men and cross the creek to the right behind those rocks and then work your way back toward the objective. The rest will go with me to the left and cross just around the bend in the creek. We then approach the objective from two directions, and if it is the target, we lay down fire from a spread position from both the right and left on my signal. Before firing, take cover wherever you can behind trees or rocks or a ground depression. Remember, shoot only at the target. Let's go."

After crossing the creek, the two groups approached the structure and observed a row of barely visible targets above the edge of a concrete bunker. Frank signaled Shelby that the structure was the target and the men fanned out, staying low and securing firing positions. Frank sent one of his best marksmen farther to the left and up the hill to gain slightly higher ground and a better view of the row of targets as the squad fanned out into an arc facing the bunker. Frank raised his hand and caught the attention of Shelby before dropping it. Fifteen guns immediately shredded the November air and a barrage struck the concrete bunker shattering the five clay targets. Almost immediately a flag attached to a rod was extended above the bunker.

"Move out," signaled Frank, and the squad circled past the bunker and reassembled before proceeding to the top of the hill and down the other side, moving silently along a bearing Frank determined from his field map. In the distance they heard two distinct rounds of rifle fire as the two other teams apparently fired at their preliminary targets.

The hour walk brought the right-hand team to the rendezvous point. Seeing that no other troops had yet arrived, Frank sent out three scouts to locate and observe the objectives that lay ahead. After five minutes, Frank heard the snap of a twig and observed troops from the center group arriving within fifteen feet to their left. Lou and Randy crawled to Frank. "Seen the left-hand squad?"

"No," replied Frank. "We've heard explosions and gunfire but haven't seen 'em."

"We set off a trip wire, and the judges took five of our guys away as casualties, and the same thing happened to the left 'cause Jamison broke silence and said he lost a bunch of his men. So combined we got 'bout thirty-five men. That should be enough."

"I've sent out three scouts to try and pick up the forward targets. They went into this sector," Frank said pointing at the map.

"Good, I'll send three to their left and see what they find."

Then Lou and Randy crawled to the left to Randy's squad.

The thought struck Frank that if they were in real combat and had just lost soldiers that the words from the commander, "that should be enough," was rather cavalier. Shouldn't the commander have felt the actual loss of soldiers, either wounded or dead? It seemed the impact on the commander should have been greater, but then again, in combat maybe that attitude of accepting death was part of the price they faced in fighting a real enemy who was trying his best to kill them. Frank's final thought during his brief reverie was to acknowledge that they were playing a sophisticated war game to prepare them for the real thing, fighting and dying; no one was going to die today. He sensed that the emotional impact of death on the leader or the troops could not in the least be adequately replicated in these war games. The officers would have to cope with that as it happened in the coming battles in Europe.

Twenty minutes later the left-hand squad still had not made an appearance at the rendezvous point, so Frank joined Lou and Randy in the center to discuss their options. They plotted the reports of the six scouts who had now returned with information on the location of five clustered targets. They found that the targets were in an approximate zigzag pattern about four hundred feet in their front. "We have to take out the three closest targets and then the two set to the rear. There's that open field between us and them, with little cover except a depression running parallel to the targets. Without Jamison's squad we are down to the twenty-eight men I counted," said Lou. "Do we think that is enough?"

"Yes," said Frank, "speed is important, and I think we should go ahead."

"I guess we could go with ten men in the center and nine on the right and left," the commander said tentatively.

"We have one submachine gun. How about putting down a smokescreen in the center and running the submachine and five rifles into the center along the ditch opening fire first on the center target to draw the enemy fire straight ahead. We continue with the smoke to the right and left sides and slip half the rifles to each side and open fire at once, aiming at both the forward and rear targets at the same time."

"Should you break silence and find out where the fuck Jamison's squad is at?" asked Randy.

"I don't think so. We are on the target, and this is especially the time for silence since we are supposed to surprise them," stated the commander.

"I agree," said Frank.

"OK, Randy, you stay in the middle with the submachine gun and three more rifles, and Frank and I will divide the men to the right and left. We all have smoke canisters; we will all lob the canisters into the center to cover your advance, then, Randy, take your position in the middle and open fire and continue to lay down a cover smoke shield on the right and left so we can get in close position on their flanks before we open fire."

"Remember to watch for trip wires; they are likely to try that again or maybe other booby traps," warned Frank.

"Move out," said the commander.

The mock attack was completed as outlined and the twenty-eight soldiers assembled in a clearing behind the "destroyed" targets. "Well, looky there," said Randy in a mocking voice, "here comes Johnny Come Lately." Jamison and the remains of his squad walked through the trees into the clearing. "Where you been?" continued Randy.

"We kinda got lost," said Jamison with his crumpled field map still grasped in his left hand.

"Kinda," blurted Randy. "You—"

"Hold your tongue," Lou said looking at Randy. Turning to Jamison, "You have, what . . . eight men. Did you lose some to the booby traps?"

"Yeah, the judges hit us hard and took 'em as casualties."

"Too bad. Okay, let's form up and head to the pickup point," ordered Lou.

"Don't let Jamison lead the way. I want to get back to the post in time for dinner," cracked Randy without a smile.

At dinner that night, Shelby Young told of the right-hand squad's successful negotiation of the day's attack and his role. "Yes sir, we took out those Germans or Japs or whoever they were. We got 'em clean the first time."

"I was a casualty in the left squad," said Henry Boudreau. "Anderson was to my right and set off the trap, and two judges walked in and pointed at eight of us as either dead or wounded. I think we were bunched too close together, so after being wounded or killed we got a ride back to post early . . . We had some coffee and donuts like any good wounded soldier would do," and the supper group laughed.

"Did the corpses drink coffee too? inquired Shelby."

"Absolutely, and had donuts."

"It's a good thing your wounds will heal overnight, 'cause we are going in for a debriefing tomorrow morning. Maybe they'll give you a purple heart, or somethin'," offered Jesse White with a straight face.

Shelby stirring his coffee added, "Poor Jamison. He lost half his troops and then got the rest lost in the woods. I bet he's in for a special debriefin'."

"You kiddin'? He looks for all the world like he's goin' to make colonel, maybe even general. I think he shows promise as a real leader. That fella's going somewhere." The laughter grew louder as Jesse offered a mock salute.

"Maybe not where he wants to go, though." The last comment continued the laughter as the group pushed back from the table and moved toward the door.

Later that evening in the barracks, "Frank, you some kinda Nigger lover?" asked the burly blond-haired student standing at the foot of Frank's bunk.

"Gene, that's a strange question," replied Frank as he lowered the book he had been reading.

"Well, strange maybe to you, but you seem to get along with them boys pretty well," replied his inquisitor as he withdrew his hands from his pockets.

"We are all in the same army, if you hadn't noticed."

"That don't mean we are all the same. The coloreds have got their place, and it ain't leading troops in battle."

"General Bradley would disagree with you; he's the one who ordered us to train together."

"That don't cut the mustard with me and some of the other guys. We know where they belong, in the kitchen ordering around pots and pans, that's what they're good for. God made us separate, and he wants us to keep it that way."

"You know what God wants do you? Well, I've heard General Bradley's orders, and I have not heard God change them."

"God marked us at birth, and some got a big brain and some a pig-size little brain. We all know they ain't too smart, and if you get too friendly they get uppity and stuff and start to thinking they is as good as us."

"You're mistaken," said Frank. "We all don't know that," Frank said with an emphasis on the word we. "I'm sure you believe that, but I don't accept that simple view."

"Let me tell you a few things about my simple view," blustered Gene Tulley with emphasis on "simple view" and pointing a finger at Frank. "We lost the war over them Niggers, and they been givin' us big problems ever since." His finger jabbed the air. "They're a shiftless bunch of lazy bastards that won't work a full day if they can avoid it."

"You ever work in the fields with Coloreds?" asked Frank. "I have, and I've found some of 'em could out-work me without breaking a sweat."

"That's not the point. My daddy is a banker in Pulaski, and he knows all about them Niggers in Giles County and he won't lend them a dime 'cause he knows they don't have a dime to their name. And he's on the school board and he knows that money spent on their schools is a waste, so he helps keep 'em in their place by not lettin' them get big ideas." Gene's voice rose in pitch and volume as he blurted his last comment.

Several other students were attracted to the heated conversation between Frank and Gene.

"Well, Gene, it seems to me that if you keep your thumb on Colored people, you are going to get what you want: don't educate them and then blame them for being uneducated."

"The point is they can't learn even with the best schools, and they is meant by God to serve as a servant race . . . my God you're dense," shouted Gene.

Frank put his feet on the floor, rose with his hands at his side, and stepped toward the end of the bunk. "Gene, did you know that Henry Boudreau is an attorney with two college degrees? He had the good fortune to be from Illinois where he got an education. Did you know that most of the Negro officer students here have been to college and that they are trying very hard to fight for this country and give up their lives, if necessary, just like you and me."

"They is subhuman. They should be sent back to where they come from—"

Frank interrupted, "And I would trust them under any circumstance just like I would trust you."

Gene's face had turned a menacingly bright pink color as his fists clinched, and he moved toward Frank. The two students standing immediately behind Gene grabbed his arms and restrained his forward progress.

"Cool it, youse guys," barked Jim Yablonski, the student holding Gene's left arm. Gene shook his head, shrugged the intruding hands from his arms, turned walking between the two students, and stomped out of the barracks.

"Oohwhee," said Jim, "you both got some strong ideas."

Frank stood still watching Gene leave the room, "Well, if there's one thing I sure don't like, it's putting people in a pigeon hole without knowing what you're talking about."

"Well, I would avoid gettin' in a fight with old Gene. He's one strong son of a bitch," said Jim. "He played for Mississippi State or some school like that for a couple of years, and he has pushed a lot of people around. I'd keep my eye on him if I was you."

"Thanks for the advice, but I'm going to defend myself if I have to."

"I understand, I'm just tellin' you about him. I figure if you two fight, you'll defend yourself all the way to the infirmary."

"I'm surprised he didn't bring up the Jews as long as he was going after the Darkies," said Stanley Rosen. "I'm from Memphis, and I know his father has a reputation in the state and has been linked with the Ku Klux Klan. My father's on the state board of the Civil Liberties Union, and they are fighting a constant battle with the likes of Gene Tulley Senior."

"What kinda union is that?" asked Yablonski.

"It's to protect our rights under the Constitution. That means Coloreds and Polacks like you and Jews like me and even Christians like ole Frank," smiled Stanley, "and even Gene, not that he needs much protection."

"This war is going to change a lot of things," said Frank as he resumed his reclined position on his bunk.

"You think so?" asked Stanley in a tone of bewilderment.

"We are going to beat the Germans and their totalitarian state, mark my words. Then the soldiers are coming home and everything'll change."

"I don't buy that," said Stanley. "You know there are still lynchings of Darkies going on, and they aren't all in the South, and they lynched a Jew in Georgia a few years ago."

"I don't know nothing about lynchings, but I don't think things will change either," said Jim. "My dad has worked in the Pittsburgh mills for twenty years, and his union is constantly fighting for money. My grandpapa was killed in a riot years ago for the same reason. He was killed by a policeman. Things won't change: Polacks will still be Polacks working the mills."

"We'll see," said Frank with an upturning tone to his optimistic voice.

"I like your sense of optimism and hope you're right," Stanley muttered as the conversation ended and he headed for the washroom.

*Isn't that odd*, mused Frank as he interlaced his fingers on top of the book lying on his stomach. *So many different kinds of Americans willing to fight for our country. Our country, that's the collective "our." The foreigners, the bigots, the Negros, and Jews all willing to fight. The Negroes and Jews could easily say "your" country, but they believe in the "our" part of it. That's amazing after what they've been through, especially the Negroes. I'll have to think about that some more.* Frank's mind then jumped to another unrelated thought, or was it unrelated?

As a child his grandmother on his father's side, Big M, always came for Sunday dinner, and there was a time he recalled when she had been to an evangelist's tent meeting with a young preacher who must have been one hell raiser. *I must have been about ten or so, and after dinner she started talking about the Jews and how they were going to hell unless they became Christians. Then after she left, I felt funny about the way she got so mad when she talked about Jews. It didn't seem right. I asked Daddy about it, and he explained that Big M had her very fixed and hard opinions and that we should not take her word as the gospel. I remember he used the word "gospel." He said we should make up our own minds about people.* His father's advice rested easy on the mind of Frank as a boy. At a young age, he sensed when people's judgment was blinded by hatred or other closed-minded reactions, and now as an adult he had begun to take offense at their attitudes. Now he realized that he was reacting to the very dogmatic type of people who knew all the answers to all of life's questions and never stopped to question their own beliefs. With that, he raised his book once again and began to read *Trees of Heaven,* the first novel by the Kentucky poet Jesse Stuart.

"I heard you had a little set-to in your barracks the other night," said Henry.

"Yeah." Frank and Henry were walking alone toward the service club.

"What happened?"

"Well the true colors of Gene Tulley became very clear . . . It seems he has some strong feelings about you folks."

"That's not news to me. We don't expect to get respect from any white man when we first meet him, especially down South, and I'll tell you the North isn't much better."

Frank paused and stared at Henry. "You always assume the worst?"

"Absolutely. We've been educated our whole life to watch our backside and to watch the backs of our fellows. That's just the way things are."

"My God," said Frank, "what a way to live. I guess I never thought of it in those terms, but I'm not surprised though," as he started walking again.

"Why were you so surprised?" asked Henry.

"I don't know, maybe it's because I tend to withhold judgment when I meet someone . . . someone for the first time. I hadn't thought of it in those terms, but I guess that's the way I am."

"Life doesn't work like that when we Colored folks meet a white person; we expect to be put down, kept in our place. But there are a few exceptions, like you, for example, and a teacher I had for constitutional law at Chicago. He was a Jew from New York City, and he was a very straight talker and good legal thinker. He was a very good teacher. And with you I knew right off that you were OK as far as an army buddy is concerned, but I wouldn't want you marrying my sister." Both Henry and Frank broke into a laugh.

After gaining his breath, Frank said in a soft voice as if thinking aloud, "The other night after the incident with Gene, I realized that all Americans, whether white, black, red or yellow, or the foreign new-comers, we are all in this war together. Lord only knows the whites should be ready to fight harder than anyone else since we seem to run things and arguably have more to lose than anyone else, but I don't detect any difference in the soldiers here."

"Frank, it's our home as much as it's yours or Gene's, despite what he believes, and right or wrong I think everyone should be willing to give up something for their home when called on." They reached the service club door, entered, picked up a beer, and sat in the corner of the large lounge in easy chairs with a nickel bag of potato chips on the table between them.

Henry picked up the thread of their conversation. "In law school I read some of Hitler's writings in *Mein Kampf*. . . That man is a scary hombre, and to think the German people actually put him in charge." Shaking his head, he continued, "He believes in the master race of the Aryans, and he has identified the Jews and Gypsies as his first round of targets. And he doesn't think much of the Slavs, so he invaded Russia. He actually seems to take seriously this master race shit. Now it doesn't take much imagination to figure out what he would do to Negroes if he was in control in this country. My God, if you think slavery was bad eighty or ninety years ago, it wouldn't compare to what he would do to us."

Frank added, "I had an encounter with a Nazi-type sympathizer in this country about a year ago. It's surprising to me how gullible he was in believing the most outrageous claptrap characterizations about different people. He was willing to accept the notion that the Jews were responsible for the Depression, and he thought Hitler had some good ideas."

"Yeah," said Henry, "I'm glad we have the Constitution and at least the promise of an improved life. Under Hitler the non-Aryan people of Europe have no chance. Our Constitution hasn't always protected us, but I see a better day ahead once this war is over."

"I agree," said Frank, "I think things will change in the future, it'll be slow and tough but they will change."

"I agree in the idea of change, but what we need is for the change to make things better. I'm glad you're optimistic. That makes me feel good knowing that you believe it. Most Colored, especially the older folks, don't."

"The war is going a little better than it was just a year ago.

Hitler's a long way from being whipped, but those Russian soldiers are fighting for their home even if it's run by the communists. With those long supply lines the Germans are going to find themselves in a bind like Napoleon," Frank injected. "The longer the Russians hold out, the worse for the Germans."

"I haven't figured out the communists and the Russians yet," said Henry. "They're a totalitarian state and I don't know that I would trust them any more than Hitler, Goering, and their henchmen. You remember just a few years ago, Stalin and Hitler were in the same bed together when they divided up Poland. That was before Hitler turned on Stalin. Man, this world is a scary place today," Henry concluded. "But, everything said and done, I'd rather be here with a gun in my hand than, say in 1860. You talk about scary times, Lord what a mess we had in the country then, and it's gotten some better for us Negroes but we still have a long, long way to go."

"We have to make sure we keep our democracy here in America and not let either the communists or fascists get control."

"I agree," said Henry. "Even though we have a long way to go for equal justice, we have a better chance in America than anywhere else; us colored folks, that is." A dry, sardonic laugh bubbled from his mouth.

Walking back toward the student barracks, now in silence, Henry broke the reverie, "I'm looking forward to having children like you someday. I want to help teach them about the country and how to get along without being pushed down and made to feel inferior. You know I've been married, but I lost my wife very early in our marriage before we even thought about kids."

"Really, I'm so sorry to hear that." Frank paused stunned by the news. "Well, we have something else in common besides being the old geezers in the class." After a long pause, "My wife died during the birth of our second child. I lost both at the same time. The child was stillborn, and my wife died of a major infection. We thought the hospital would be a needless expense so she tried having the baby at home, and then she developed an infection and there was nothing the doctor could do to save her. We called an ambulance to take her to the hospital, but she died just after she got there."

"Oh, golly, that's so sad. I'm sorry for you and your son." They walked on and Henry continued, "My wife died after we were married three months . . . when the house we were living in caught fire. I was at school studying."

"That's terrible," said Frank. "I didn't realize you'd been married."

"That's a real tough deal. I guess you and I are both starting over with life after our losses," said Henry.

"I know I am," said Frank, "and that's part of why I'm here. I just didn't know what to do with myself, so I brought Teddy, my boy, to Knoxville with me to live with my parents. I had to leave him when I left for the service last spring, and I guess I feel a little guilty, but I think I made the right decision. He's doing well in his new home, and I think I'm succeeding here—not that I really want the war, but it's on us now and we have no choice but to fight."

"You talk about not knowing what to do with yourself, I felt the same way. God we were happy, my wife and me. We had those three months together, and then she was ripped from my life. I have dreams about the fire that consumed her, and think if I'd only been there rather than at school, she would be alive. I dropped out of school after the fire and didn't go back until two years ago. The Department head understood about my circumstances and let me have the time off, then I graduated in the spring of '41 and passed the Illinois bar early this year."

"That's a real accomplishment. I was just an English major for my two years of school and didn't really know what I would do with the degree."

After a long pause Henry said, "You know if you finish your degree, you might consider law because I've found that English is a good background for the law. That's what my degree was in at Urbana. All lawyers have to know how to read and write; that's essential. A lot of the rest is remembering the legal structure and then the cases that help shape the law to our everyday world."

"Hmm," mused Frank. "I hadn't considered law. I guess first I have to concentrate on winning this war though, and then I'll see what the next stage in life has for me."

"Well, don't win the war single-handed; let some of the rest of us help." Henry smiled.

After another pause in the conversation, Frank asked, "It still hurts a great deal to think about Ellen; that was just a year ago when she left . . . Do you still miss your wife? Does it get any easier?"

"No, I don't think so, at least not for me . . . not yet. It hurts every night when I go to bed and when I wake up in the morning. Now I say a prayer for her and ask God to protect her and give her peace. I used to damn God for taking her from me . . . that was right after her death. Then I realized that I was being selfish and thinking only of myself. I finally started to accept the words of my pastor that Eleanor was in a better place now, in the loving arms of Jesus, and she was better off. I really had trouble believing that. I guess I do now, but it hurts. I don't know, maybe accepting his explanation was better for me, but I can't quit thinking of her and what we both missed . . . Shit, it's so hard," Henry said wiping his eyes. "Excuse my language, but—"

"No need to apologize." In the dark of the night the two men shook hands and stared into the other's eyes as they understood the profound losses and now a profound bond they shared.

# CHAPTER 17

## *Knoxville*

## *Early February 1943*

*1 February 1943*

*Dear Son,*

*By the time you receive this letter, I will have been sworn in as a second lieutenant in the United States Army. TA DUM. The other good news is that I'm coming home for a leave next week. It will be very good to see you, Granny, and Granddad. I am looking forward to some home-cooked meals for a change.*

*I am bringing with me a fellow officer. His parents are in the process of moving to Knoxville from Chicago. Chicago is a very large city in Illinois. In fact, there are more people living in Chicago than live in the entire state of Tennessee. His parents do not have a place yet for Henry, my friend, to visit so he will stay with us. He is a Negro officer whom I am sure you will enjoy meeting, and I know he wants to meet you. I will write Granny and Granddad about fixing up a bed for Henry in the storeroom on the second floor. We should arrive in Knoxville on the 17th of February. His last name is Boudreau, just like the Cleveland ballplayer.*

*Give my love to Granny and Granddad and keep plenty for yourself.*

*Love, Dad*

"LANDS SAKE, WILL, did you read this about Frank bringing home a Nig . . . a Negro student . . . ah . . . an officer to stay in our house?" asked Mary, her cheeks turning red as Frank's letter slipped from her fingers onto the kitchen table. "What are we going to do?"

"Well, let's see, we can introduce ourselves and then—"

"Will, be serious. What are we going to do?"

"I don't know exactly. We've never had a Negro stay in our house before. I'm not sure what we do."

"Oh, that's Henry Boudreau," offered Ted. "He has the same last name as Lou, and—"

"Do you know about this?" Mary asked in a sharp voice.

"Yes'sum, I forgot to tell you. Daddy sent me a letter last week, and I kinda forgot to show it to you," said Ted looking down at his afternoon snack, a half-eaten apple.

"And who's this Lou fellow? Is he coming too?"

"I don't think so. He's a baseball player for the Indians. They're in the American League and—"

"Fiddlesticks, I don't care a hoot about baseball players, but Will . . ." Mary stared at her husband.

"Mary, let's go in the living room and talk about this. Ted, you goin' outside to play with Jerry and . . . what's his name?"

"Floyd. No he's got the flu or somethin', and his mother says he's too sick to play."

"You stay away from the flu if that's what he's got. Now, Will . . ." Mary was already walking into the hall talking to Will as Ted finished his apple and launched the spent apple core toward the paper garbage bag by the refrigerator. He was practicing his long basketball shot as the apple core bounced off the back side of the paper garbage bag, toppling it and spilling the top layer of contents onto the kitchen floor.

"Oops," said Ted as he went to his hands and knees and picked up most of the spilled garbage and returned it to the bag. The wet coffee grounds presented a problem as Ted tried unsuccessfully to scoop them with his fingers. Wiping his hands on his pants, he then grabbed his jacket and headed for the front door. At the door into the living room he said, "Granny, I spilled some coffee grounds, and I can't get them all up . . ."

"Oh, for heaven's sake, Teddy, leave it alone. I'll clean it up in a minute," she said sharply as she turned back to face Will.

The front door closed softly as Ted slipped onto the front porch aware his Grandmother was agitated but uncertain of the cause. He knew it had something to do with Henry's visit. He was glad to be out of the house.

"Mary, I think you should talk to the new temporary preacher at church, what's his name, Askew or something, and see what he says," advised Will. "You know we have always taught our children to be tolerant of others, and maybe he can help you sort out these questions."

"Bein' tolerant is one thing, but having them in your home, that's another thing. And you say help *me*, why not you too? You got any questions?" she asked with an edge to her voice.

"Well, I . . . Okay I'll go with you to see him if you want."

"I certainly do want," said Mary as she walked resolutely back down the hall to the kitchen.

Things were very quiet at the dinner table that night. Mary had a stern look on her face, one that Ted was unaccustomed to seeing. Finally Will spoke, "It's very quiet around the table now that Leroy has moved out with his family comin' to town."

"Yeah, he had a lot of good stories. Where'd he move to? I forgot," Ted asked.

"He rented a little house across the river. There're some houses in the Island Home neighborhood that service men rented out while they are away training. Sometimes their wives go with them and live on or near the base to be near their husbands so they rent the house . . . don't you see."

"That means we could have gone to Georgia with Daddy and lived in Columbus while he was at Fort Ben—"

"Don't be silly, Teddy," Mary interrupted. "Your granddad has to work here, so he can't go off following your father, now if your moth—. Eat your beans, Teddy." Mary abruptly stopped talking.

After Ted had left the table with a chocolate chip cookie for dessert, Will said, "Don't be too hard on the boy."

"I'm sorry, it's just that this idea of Frank's is so disturbing to me. How can we sleep under the same roof with him?" Mary's soft voice came in sharp contrast now that she reflected on her attitude during dinner.

"It wasn't so long ago that our grandparents had Negro slaves in the same house with them night and day," said Will.

"But that was different," protested Mary.

"It was, but I'm not certain how much different it was. I'm sure there were some slaves my granddad Archer didn't want in the house, but the household slaves were good people; they were a part of the family. They didn't eat together, but they ate the same food and slept under the same roof."

"These are different times," Mary interjected.

"Yes, they are different, but people are still people, and there are good people and others I would just as soon kick in the ass and never have to bother with. But I do bother with some of them at work. There are a couple of real bastards down at Fulton's, as well as some really swell people."

"Will, don't use those words, at least around the house."

"Mary, you're right. This is a different time, but we have to trust Frank. He's still our son, and he knows what he's doin'. Now you told him to pray on his problems before he left for the service, and maybe you . . . ah . . . and I ought to do the same thing."

"Will, you're just saying that? You haven't prayed for years, have you?"

"Well, let's see . . ."

"Now, don't lie," chided Mary as she softly slapped the back of his hand. "If you lie to God, you will pay a big price in heaven or wherever he sends you."

Will smiling said, "You think I may not make it to paradise with you?"

"I'm sure he has his eye on you all the time, you old goat." Mary patted his hand once again and stacked the dinner dishes to carry to the kitchen. "You think it will be all right?" she asked from the kitchen door.

"Mary, I'm sure we will live through Lieutenant Boudreau's visit just fine."

Mary faced the kitchen sink as she ran hot water into the Vel flakes that burst into suds for the evening's dishes. Will came up behind her and circled her waist with his arms. "Let's see if that old preacher fellow, Askew, can help us straighten this thing out," he said as he nuzzled the back of Mary's neck.

"You're right, he's an old one. They brought him out of retirement till we can get a replacement for Doctor Rodgers," said Mary. "Old man, don't you go nibbling at my neck," Mary said in a mockingly stern voice as she hunched her shoulders. Will made soft growling sounds. "You go sit in the living room and try and behave yourself for the evening, if you can."

"Will you join me later?" asked Will.

"If you are a good boy, I may sit with you, but remember you need to behave yourself." Will smiled as he walked down the hall knowing that Mary's storm was showing signs of clearing up and promising her usual sunny days ahead.

Reverend Askew was a slender gray-haired man, probably over seventy years old. He reminded some parishioners of a sparrow as he moved quickly from task to task or subject to subject if you engaged him in casual conversation. Everyone regarded him as a short-term substitute minister until a replacement could be found for Dr. Rodgers who had died a month earlier from a heart attack. Reverend Askew had come out of retirement, "to help out in the most unfortunate of circumstances for a church." After sermons delivered the last two weeks, members of the search committee were redoubling their efforts to find a permanent pastor.

"Please come in," he said crisply as he saw Mary and Will standing at the door to his church study. A smile flickered across his face as he waved them toward two chairs opposite the large mahogany desk. He sat abruptly in his desk chair and leaned back eliciting a prolonged squeak from the chair's coiled spring. "Mr. and Mrs. Warren, what can I do for you?" he asked as he leaned forward causing a second loud squeak. He straightened a pile of folders on his desk as Mary answered.

"It's Warring, not Warren," started Mary. "Well, we have a problem with our son and—"

"Is he in trouble with the law?" queried the Reverend.

"Why, no, he's an officer in the army, and he's coming home for a leave and—"

"Is he fooling around with a woman and have her in a family way?" he asked with his tongue circling his thin lips.

"If you let me finish, I'll tell you," she said sharply.

"Hmm," replied the Reverend leaning back in his chair with his lips now tightly pursed after Mary's crisp reply.

Mary waited for the squeak to subside. "He's bringing home a fellow officer to stay for a visit—"

"Oh Lord, don't tell me he's an apostate . . ."

"I don't know what you mean. He's a good son and the friend is a Negro, for heaven's sakes," said Mary. "If you would only listen," she added with an exasperated edge to her voice.

The reverend's eyebrows shot up as he dropped the folders on the desk. "Well, that won't do if this Nigro wants to stay in your house. You mean overnight? I wouldn't let him stay, if that is your question. After all, you run a good Christian home, I'm sure, and it wouldn't do to bring in such a blight."

"What are you talking about?" asked Will abruptly. "What's a good Christian home have to do with a guest who is a good Christian army officer, and what's this about a blight?"

"Well, you said he was a Nigro, that's what."

"Reverend Askew, we come here to ask your opinion based on your understandin' of biblical teachin', what to do about having a Negro officer as a guest. Mary was just a little uneasy about it. She's not used to the idea."

"No, she shouldn't be used to it. The Bible doesn't talk about Nigroes. They were all in Africa when our Lord brought his message to our people in Palestine; no sir, the Bible doesn't speak to the question."

"What about the Good Samaritan story where a Samaritan helped the stranger by the side of the road?" asked Mary.

"He wasn't a Nigro," said the Reverend triumphantly, folding together his fingers on the desktop. "God made us separate and intends for us to stay that way," and another long squeak erupted from his chair as he rocked back and then forward.

"I don't remember seeing that or hearing any preacher tell about that in the Bible," mumbled Will.

"You see there is the larger Christian community to consider. What would your neighbors think if you have a Nigro in your home? Have you thought of that? What would you do to your neighbor's property value, for instance. There's no telling what damage you could do. Now, I have this four-plex apartment building. What could I rent the units for if you had Nigros living next door?"

"We're not exactly suggesting the young man move in with us; he's a guest for a few nights, for God's sake," blurted Will.

Mary patted the back of his hand. "Don't take the Lord's name in vain," she said softly.

"You came here for my studied opinion and guidance, and I have given you the results of my years of religious studies and thoughts on the problems of society and the tricky problems of applying our Lord's Word to the problems we face today." Again the prolonged squeak as he leaned back and then forward. "You see, we in the religious world think about these things all the time; that's why you hire us as your ministers. Now, the Lord didn't have to face the problems of the modern age, before the motor car and all these conveniences we have nowadays. He wasn't spoiled by such things as you are. He led a pure life in a wonderfully peaceful place, and he had time to walk and think on subjects, you see."

"Now, you're talking about that peaceful place and time where they hung Jesus from the cross and executed him for what he believed," said Will, his face turning red.

"That was later when the Jews turned on him. You see, they were misled and didn't take time to understand his teachings.

We've been trying to convert them ever since and show them the error of their way, yes sir. You know the Roth family in our church, I think they may have been Jews sometime back in their past before they were converted. You notice Mr. Roth's nose . . . If you get at the right angle and study him, he looks a little Jewish, maybe a great grandfa—"

"I've had as much guidance as I can take." Will rose abruptly and headed for the door. "Thank you, Mr. Askew," he said turning to look at the shocked face of the reverend and then turning again to exit the office.

"Thank you," said Mary over her shoulder as she hurried out the door in pursuit of her husband.

"I look forward to seeing you at church on Sunday," the reverend called after the retreating couple.

The church's temporary spiritual leader sat in his chair staring through the open door, then he clasped his hands in prayer as he lifted his face toward the ceiling, and with closed eyes, "Dear God and Jesus our Lord and your son, forgive that misguided Christian family, the Warrens"—he opened his eyes slightly to peek in a folder on his desk and elevating his chin once more—"that's Mary and William, and show them the error of their way before their time comes to meet you. And don't let them spread their heinous ideas about hosting Nigros around their neighborhood. Amen."

*What will these poor misguided people come up with next? Making Nigros equal to us?* Another loud squeak punctuated the air. *It's so hard spreading the true Word of God among these uneducated people in Tennessee. Give me strength.*

The trolley car ride back up the Clinch Avenue hill occurred in silence. Mary and Will sat on the seat made of wooden slats. At Seventeenth Street the car turned right up the final grade to Highland Avenue at the top of the hill where they exited the car. After climbing the porch steps and entering the front hall, Will helped Mary shed her wool winter coat that he then hung on the tree stand by the door along with his fleece-lined denim winter jacket.

"It's startin' to get cold. I'd better light the grates and check the hot water heater to make sure the pilot is lit," he said as he walked down the hall through the kitchen and down the cellar steps.

Mary sat in her comfortable chair. *Well, that didn't help much. That Reverend Askew, I just don't know what to make of him. It was so simple when I was a girl. I just knew that whatever the minister said was right and that he knew things I didn't know and I didn't need to second-guess him, but now . . . Lordy, what do I make of him? Did the wrong man get into the ministry, or am I just too old to believe? Jesus taught us to love, not to hate and mistrust each other. Even if the Negroes weren't around in Judea like he said, what difference does that make? The Chinese weren't there either and the English weren't there and I don't remember any mention of the French in the Bible. Tell me, Lord, what difference does that make?*

*When I was a girl, we didn't have to worry about the Negroes; they lived in their houses and we lived in ours. They were close, but you knew each had their own part of town. Winchester wasn't big, but we knew how to get along. They had their school and churches, and we had ours. Mama Mae came every day and helped Momma fix the meals and do the laundry and help with the cleaning. We didn't have any problems with her. She got paid, and we gave her clothes for her family that we had outgrown or got tired of. She was pleased to get our hand-me-down things. Her daughter moved up north and went to college and is a teacher now, I guess. Let's see, she's my age; she must be a grandmother. I wonder whatever happened to Betty. She was so pleasant, but she wanted to get ahead in life. I guess she didn't like life in Winchester. At the time Betty left, Momma said she was uppity for leaving Mama Mae who was getting old. Momma assumed Betty would replace Mama Mae and continue coming to help in our house. Maybe things weren't so good, after all, for Negroes in Winchester. Maybe that's why Betty went up North.* Many conflicting ideas about Mama Mae and Betty fought for expression in Mary's mind as her teenage years replayed in her memory.

*Oh, there was that time when Lydia Peterson came over, and she giggled and said Mama Mae was a "Licorice Nigger" because she was so dark, almost black. And Daddy overheard her and told me later that Lydia was a very disrespectful person and that no one deserved that kind of name. He said nobody on this earth has ever picked who their parents would be or the color of their skin before they were born, and that we are all God's children and I should remember that and show everybody respect . . . Funny how certain things stick in your memory, and what he said has always stuck with me . . . But I guess I almost forgot those words till now. Daddy was such a kind and patient man. Frank favors him, he favors him a lot more than he does Will's side. Maybe Daddy should have been a minister. He would certainly know what to tell me now. Maybe he did tell me, maybe he did.*

She was now more at ease looking out the front window as snowflakes started to fall. Mary loved to watch snow fall and settle on the earth. Her memories melted into silence as a distant clunk emerged from the basement, and she knew Will was working on the hot water heater. She felt warm and safe and loved. Then the snow started to fall more heavily.

# CHAPTER 18

## *Knoxville*

## *Late February 1943*

MARY PLACED A pan of water on the stove's back burner. "Now you say Henry and his folks are coming to dinner tomorrow night?" She placed her hands on her hips.

"Yes, ma'am." Frank sat down at the kitchen table sensing he was about to be questioned again about the invitation he had extended to his friend.

Mary stood in the center of her domain looking at her son. "Now, you say his parents just moved here from Chicago and he didn't know that they had room for him until the day before you left Georgia?"

"Yes, ma'am."

"Now that doesn't sound like a very close family if you ask me," she stated.

"Mom, Henry's dad works in the physics lab at the University of Chicago, and the Government has just decided to move a bunch of people from there into a place they are calling Oak Ridge, just west of Knoxville."

"Now, is this going to be a Colored project?"

"No, Mom. No it's a secret project the Government is building. It's got something to do with the war effort. The US Army Corps of Engineers is in charge of building it."

"And they're using Negro labor to build it?"

"No, Henry's dad is a science technician working in physics, and he and a large staff are apparently being moved down here."

"Well, if I was a swearin' person I would say somethin' nasty about picking 'Nowhere, Tennessee,' to build a secret . . . you call it fizz something?"

"Physics is a theoretical study of mathematics. You've heard of Einstein? Well, he's a leading physicist and—"

"Is he coming too?"

"I don't know, Mom, it's a secret. I do know that the people in Anderson County are fighting mad. There are a bunch of folks that have been evicted from their property, and the Government is in the process of fencing in the area and putting in guard houses so they can protect the secrecy of the project."

"Laws, your dad has had an earful from one of Fulton's workers. They took his daddy's land and gave him four weeks to clear off the land. I guess that's all part of the secret project. It just don't make sense to do it in Anderson County, whatever it is," she said with certainty as she placed peeled potatoes into the boiling water.

"Mom, maybe the government picked Anderson County because it's isolated and they can protect the secrets better there than other places," suggested Frank.

"Maybe so, but aren't there isolated places in Illinois or Indiana or up North somewhere?"

"I'm sure there are, and I don't know why they picked Oak Ridge, but they did, and Henry's family is living in temporary quarters. He was allowed to visit and stay with them because he's a military officer and the authorities can trust him to keep secret whatever he sees there."

"Uh huh, so he's staying with his folks while he's up here; that was mighty convenient timing for us. Frank, you know I've been having a hard time gettin' used to the idea of having Negroes in my house overnight."

"Yes'sum, I know."

"Well now, I have got to get used to having them over for dinner and cookin' for them folks. Are there more comin' like Henry's brother or sister that you forgot to tell me about?"

"No, Mom, just the three of them." Frank should have known that trying to treat Henry as an equal would be a trying job because the people in the South had such fixed ideas, but he never considered that his mother would have such worries. *Well she hasn't said no*, and he knew, *she'll be alright once she gets organized.*

"What does a Negro scientist and his wife from Chicago like to eat for supper?" she asked with her hands back on her hips.

Frank knew this was her real question, to figure out how to cook dinner and be the hostess for people she had never met and probably never would have met if the choice had been hers to make. "Mom, I expect they are regular folks and would be glad to eat whatever you serve," Frank offered.

"Uh huh, do you think a roast would be OK?"

"That would be perfect."

"Mashed potatoes, stewed tomatoes, and creamed corn I put up last summer?"

"Perfect."

"And some dinner rolls?"

"Yes, all that sounds terrific."

"And lemon meringue pie?"

"Yes, is that with a graham cracker crust?"

"Of course, how else would I make it?"

Frank stood and embraced his mother. "That all sounds delicious, Mom."

Will entered the kitchen, paused at the door, and sensing a serious discussion was in progress turned as if to return to the living room when . . .

"Will, Frank tells me Henry's father is a scientist and the government has moved him to Anderson County. You know that Ethridge fellow at work you was tellin' me about? Well his father must have had his land taken for this science project."

Will turned looking at Mary and then Frank who had returned to the table. "That so? Huh, maybe that explains it." Sitting at the table, he continued, "Tommy Ethridge was fit to be tied, and he said his father was getting' out and loadin' his shotgun, but the sheriff got to him first before he could hurt the 'govamint people,' as he called them. But Tommy said they didn't ask him for any permission to go on his land or nothin'. His dad and his neighbors live up in a place called Bear Creek Valley, or somethin' similar to that, and the Army Corps of Engineers just took a large piece of the county for themselves. The owners were given two weeks to clear off their land 'cause it weren't theirs any more. It was the govamint's. Yes sir, those folks that got kicked off their land are hotter than a beehive after the bear stole their comb. To make matters worse, the folks in Anderson County are still getting used to the idea that they lost property to the TVA dam project up at Norris. Yes sir, they feel picked on, that's for sure." Will chuckled. "Now what's Henry's dad got to do with this science project?"

"I don't know, and Henry wouldn't tell even if he knew, which he probably doesn't," Frank replied. "It's a big secret. Seems like a group of scientists are being moved to a place they are calling Oak Ridge for a secret project. Henry's dad worked at the physics lab at the University of Chicago before the move."

"That's funny that they would move a Negro family from Chicago to a place in Tennessee. Where are all these people goin' to live, I wonder."

"Don't know, Dad. The few that are here now are in temporary housing. Maybe they will build houses on the Oak Ridge property," Frank speculated.

"While you two are settling the problems of Anderson County, you can just keep talking and go down to Market Square and see if you can buy us a nice roast for tomorrow night. And look at the apples and potatoes. Maybe we will have stewed apples instead of the tomatoes. And I need two pounds of nice potatoes; the ones from Idaho are good if you can get 'em."

"Frank, you got all that?" asked Will.

"I think so," as he repeated Mary's order. "Let's see if Teddy wants to go with us," as the men left the kitchen.

"Now, get a nice roast if they have any, you hear, and take

all of our ration books, cause you may need 'em," Mary added to her instructions.

The following morning, Frank and his father were doing additional grocery buying at Robert's on Eighteenth Street. "Our trip up here was a real eye opener for me," Frank said to his father as they exited the store. "Henry and I took the Greyhound from Columbus to Atlanta and then caught the Southern to Knoxville."

"Why do you say it was an eye opener?" asked Will as he lit a Camel cigarette.

"I got to experience some of the indignities that Negroes have been going through for a long, long time. I say *experience*, although it was no more than a sample. But I didn't like it one bit. On the bus we sat together in the Colored section at the back. The driver in Columbus knew better than to challenge me on where I sat, but in Macon we changed drivers, and the new guy tried to get me to move up front with the 'nice folks,' as he said. But I wouldn't budge, and he didn't seem to think it was necessary to try and force me since I was in the back. Now if the situation had been reversed and Henry sat with me in front, there would have been all hell to pay. The driver would have called the sheriff or the Macon police. And it wouldn't make one bit of difference to those rednecks if Henry was wearing a U S Army uniform and was a general." Father and son turned the corner from Eighteenth to Highland and started the walk up the slight grade to 1702.

"In Atlanta we got tickets on what they call the Royal Palm—that's the Southern Railroad train that carries folks from Detroit to Miami and back again. We got the northbound, and they put Henry in a Colored car behind the engine and made me sit in the white coaches in the middle of the train. Since there were MPs at the Atlanta terminal and our tickets had assigned seats, well, I couldn't fight those bastards."

Will was taken aback by the new belligerent attitude exhibited by Frank. "Keepin' apart the white's and Coloreds seems to bother you a lot more than when you left this summer," Will observed. "Were you lookin' for a fight with the police or someone?"

"Maybe so, I'm not sure. It's just that after I trained with the colored troops, they have become real people, as capable as any white soldier on the post. I've been close to Henry and his mates all fall, and those rules that people set just don't seem right; in fact, I know they're not right. Most all of us at OCS, that's both white and Negro students, got along fine in training. There were just a few narrow-minded bastards who tried to insist that we keep some degree of separation, but most of 'em didn't do anything but get booted out of the class. Thank God the post's command staff followed Bradley's orders."

"Who's Bradley?" Will asked as he flicked off the long ash on his cigarette.

"He's the general who set up the school. He's over in north Africa now with Eisenhower."

"Oh, yes," said Will, "I've heard that name. He's the head of our army in Africa, I think."

"Yeah, we think Ike is going to gather his command staff now and prepare to invade Europe, either across the Mediterranean to Italy or France or maybe across the English Channel to France or Belgium."

"I don't know what happened to the French in this war. They folded quick to the Germans in '40 and almost caught all the English at . . . what was that city?"

"Dunkirk."

"Yeah, that's it. When Willard was in the Great War, the French held up better than this time. For somebody my age, I just can't figure out what's happenin' in Europe. They've been doing nothing but fightin' or gettin' ready to fight most of my life. I swear they can't seem to get along with each other at all. Now twice, their wars have gotten so big we have to go in and help stop it. They better figure out a better way to live after this one is over, that's all I can say."

Will flicked the cigarette butt into the street, and the two men climbed the steps and entered the house. Frank carried the groceries into the kitchen and placed the bag on the counter. "Where should I put these things?"

"I'll do it," Mary said.

"Whooee, that roast smells good," Frank said as he opened the oven door and let the aroma fill the kitchen.

The back door closed with a bang as Ted walked into the kitchen. "Oops, sorry for the door. What smells good?"

"Lands sakes, Teddy, what've you been doing? You look like you've been playing in the pig sty," Mary exclaimed looking at her grandson.

"Oh, we're playing in the dirt pile down at the hospital, and—"

"Ted, go upstairs and take off your clothes and have a bath. We have company coming in half an hour," Frank instructed his son.

"Oh, I'm not that dirty," Ted said as he glanced down at the front of his jacket and began brushing off the dirt.

"Not in my kitchen," said Mary with a crisp tone.

"Teddy, upstairs," said Frank.

"Yes, sir," as Ted dropped his jacket on the chair at the table.

"And hang up your jacket in the hall," Mary added.

Ted picked up his jacket and headed for the front hall.

"Sometimes that boy is nothin' but—"

"A boy," Frank added the last word to her statement.

"Yes, I guess so," she agreed as she picked up the broom by the back door to sweep up the remains of Ted's entrance into the kitchen.

"I'm going to tell him to put on his Sunday trousers and a clean shirt," said Frank as he followed his son up stairs.

"I better tell Will to spruce up a bit before they get here," Mary mumbled as she left the kitchen.

At six o'clock a US Army Jeep stopped at the curb, and the driver turned off the motor and headlights. The twilight hour deepened the vehicle's olive-green color into an olive-black shade. Three occupants got out. The two passengers stamped their feet to make certain they had feeling in them after the long cold ride. "Jeeps are not made for comfort," Henry stated the obvious as he checked the house number and motioned for his parents to precede him up the porch steps at 1702 Highland Avenue. Two men, heavily bundled against the cold air, walked briskly down Highland toward Eighteenth Street and observed the family as Henry rang the front door bell.

Will opened the front door with Frank looking over his shoulder. "Welcome," said Will.

"It's as cold as Chicago down here in warm Tennessee," said Henry as he shook Will's hand and followed his parents into the home's front hall. "I'm Henry Boudreau," he said to Will and warmly grasped Frank's outstretched hand.

"I'm Will, Frank's father," he said as he shook hands with the older man.

"This is my mother, Mary, and father, Cyrus," Henry introduced his parents.

"And this is my Mary," Will said as Mary came down the hall from the kitchen.

"How're you all doin'?" asked Mary with the tinge of a smile crossing her face.

"We're still warming up after that cold ride; that Jeep is kind of drafty," Henry explained.

"In an army Jeep," asked Mary?

Henry explained they were allowed to drive the vehicle off the military compound as long as he, an army officer, did the driving. "We were glad to get it, though, despite the cold draft that came from everywhere."

"Laws, yes," said Mary Boudreau, "Cyrus and I sat as close as possible in the backseat to preserve our body heat." All laughed, the older four did so rather nervously.

After an awkward pause where nothing was said and seemed ten times longer than it actually was, Will extended a hand toward the living room. "Let's go sit down," he said. They walked through the open double door off the hall.

Mary and Cyrus sat on the horse-hair divan as Mary and Will dropped into their customary seats and Henry and Frank backed up to the gas grate. Henry shivered as he warmed his hands behind his back.

"Was it a hard drive into town?" asked Frank.

"Not too bad," answered Henry. "A bit long, but that couldn't be helped considering that we were starting out in the sticks."

After a short pause, Will mused, "Now bein' out in the sticks, I just can't get it through my head why you science folks are out there in the country," as he reached for his cigarettes and then dropped the package when Mary cleared her throat. "Mary doesn't like for me to smoke in the house anymore," he added dropping his voice with a slight smile crossing his face.

"I'm not supposed to discuss what we're doing," came the soft but clear voice of Cyrus. "The Army Corps of Engineers have put in a tight clamp on all information about our project and I just can't discuss it."

"Well, knowing Tennesseans, I guess the news will get out sooner or later."

"As long as it doesn't start with me that's all right," Cyrus smiled. "But I think you'll find it very hard to find out anything about it."

"I do know that there're a bunch of folks out in Anderson County that are up in arms over the Corps coming in and taking their land. Some were given two weeks to clear out of their property," Will continued.

"Yes, I've heard a little about that, but by and large we are kept apart from the community, and we don't have that firsthand involvement with the local folks. We have temporary housing, and the army feeds us and takes care of most of our needs," explained Cyrus, "all in our project area."

"All our needs except warm weather." Mary Boudreau laughed. "We left Chicago in a hurry, and the major who was helping us make arrangements said it would be warm in Tennessee, so we left our good winter coats—and I might add heavy winter coats—up there, and it's been nothing but cold, cold since we got here. It turns out the major was from Minnesota, not Tennessee."

The laughter this time was more relaxed as the guests settled into the Warring home. A thump was heard from the hall, and Frank knew it was Teddy landing at the bottom of the stairs. Teddy poked his head around the corner of the door to the hall and was greeted by smiles as he was introduced to the Boudreau family.

"I call him Ted," said Frank, "and his grandmother calls him Teddy." He was used to responding to the two names since the older grandparents were slow to use his new name. He then sat on a footstool to the side of the divan wearing his Sunday pants, shirt, and shoes. He noticed that Mr. Boudreau had a ring of neatly trimmed whiskers, mostly black with a few white sprinkled in, circling his mouth with a rather dark complexion and a thin frame for his shoulders and long legs; Mrs. Boudreau had a somewhat lighter complexion with freckles covering her cheeks and was rounder and a little broader than her husband. He had never seen a Negro with freckles. Both of the older Boudreaus wore glasses; Mr. Boudreau's were rather thick. Henry, his father's pal, was taller than his father by several inches, but both Henry and his father looked very smart in their army uniforms. The adult men were discussing something about how different Tennessee was from Illinois, but Ted had not caught the first part of the conversation and was not following their discussion. Mrs. Boudreau and his grandmother were discussing something about their families, he thought.

"I had best see to supper," Mary said as she rose and headed for the hall. "I still have a few things to do, not much though."

Mary Boudreau immediately stood and started to follow. "Can I help?"

"Well there's not much to do . . ." Their conversation dwindled to unintelligible words as the two women walked down the hall toward the kitchen.

Ted pulled his box from under the divan with a sheet of folded paper and read his handwriting. Also in the box were pennies, marbles, and several red and black game pieces that had belonged to a long-lost checker board. He sat on the floor and started purposely flipping the pennies and reading the side they landed on and made notations on the paper.

"Cyrus, would you enjoy a little taste of hard cider?" asked Will.

"Why, yes, a taste would be nice if you join me."

"Of course," said Will as he disappeared into the hall and returned carrying four small glasses and a dark brown glass bottle. "Just a little sip to help our digestion, not that Mary's cookin' needs help, but"

"Dad, you don't have to justify a little hooch once in a while." Frank laughed, and the four men joined in the joke and began sipping the golden liquid.

"You know one of the corpsmen out at the camp brought in a jar of clear liquid that turned out to be the strongest hard liquor that I've ever tasted. I had a little drink and my head ached for two days after that." Cyrus laughed.

"I see what you mean by the corps taking care of your needs," Frank remarked, smiling.

"Well, that need doesn't need tending to anymore." Cyrus continued laughing.

"Pop, I think you participated in a federal felony by drinking moonshine," Henry observed with a sly smile turning up the corners of his mouth.

"Oh, I may have, but my defense would be that I was an innocent and a thirsty bystander and my son the lawyer would get me excused from any guilt."

"Don't be too confident; I may be the prosecutor in the case."

"My, my, this younger generation has no respect for their elders." Changing the subject Cyrus added, "Young man, what're you doing with those pennies?"

Ted looked up from his prone position on the floor, sensing that attention had switched to him. "Oh, I'm pretending that the people in this place are having an election and I flip the pennies to see how they vote for either heads or tails," explained Ted. After a brief pause he continued as he sat up, "You see, I've drawn this county or country and it's got these mountains and rivers and cities, and I have drawn lines to divide it and then there are people living in these areas that vote and I am conducting the election now to see who wins." Ted was slightly out of breath after the long explanation. He held up the sheet of paper to show Cyrus the pencil outline of the imaginary geography he had described. Two columns of numbers lined the margin of the page as he handed the sheet to Cyrus who had extended his hand for a better look at the paper.

"Well, look at this. What's the name of that city?"

"That's Georgetown," said Ted settling next to Cyrus on the divan, "and this is Frankfort and this is Willville named for my grandfather," Ted added a little sheepishly. This was the first time he had explained his game and he didn't know how the adults would react.

"That's wonderful!" exclaimed Cyrus. "You've got the rivers draining the mountains and running into the sea . . . Who's ahead in the election?"

"The heads are losing. They're the Democrats, that's who I want to win, and the tails are the Republicans, and they are ahead so far two hundred and fifteen to two hundred and two."

"That's a very close election," Cyrus observed.

"Yes, sir, the heads have been catching up, and I've got about one hundred votes to go before it's over."

"My, my, that's exciting. You have a fertile imagination, young man. I'm like you, I hope the Democrats win as well. I was a Republican voting for Mr. Lincoln's party until '32, then I switched to Mr. Roosevelt."

"I see," Ted mumbled as he didn't really understand the full meaning of Cyrus's comment. He took the sheet of paper and returned to the stool but did not return to the coin-flipping election.

"I feel honored," said Will, "having a town named for me. My name will go down in history now." Ted led the laughter this time. Ted was a little embarrassed at the attention he had had but felt better since Mr. Boudreau seemed interested in his game.

"Good food." Cyrus sighed as he and his six companions each eased their empty plates toward the center of the table as an unintended signal that their appetites were sated.

"Best since we left Chicago. No, best since I can't remember when," added Mary Boudreau. "Let me help." She stood and collected the plates on her side of the table while Mary did the same on her side. As the women disappeared into the kitchen, Mary Boudreau said, "Wait till you see what's coming next."

"More?" asked the incredulous Cyrus.

Mary soon entered the dining room holding the lemon meringue pie. The peaks of the meringue topping were a golden brown surrounded by the glistening white topping; the brown crust showed through the Pyrex pie plate.

The dining room was filled with *oohs* and *aahs* as Mary Boudreau followed with the green glass dessert plates.

"Oh my," said Cyrus as the first bite of the bright yellow pie dissolved in his mouth, "this is good. Have you thought of starting a restaurant, Mrs. Warring?"

"Lordy no, this is just farm cookin' moved to the city. We lived on a farm for the first . . . let's see . . . ," counting on her fingers, "I guess thirty-seven years, then we moved down here. Farm work was gettin' hard on Will."

"Now, Mary, you know that wasn't the whole reason," Will countered. "The Depression helped push us off the land. My brother Willard is still on the farm, and he's six years younger than me."

"Yes, the Depression changed a lot of things for us also," Cyrus said. "I had got a job in the University of Chicago physics lab in '28 and was laid off in '30 for a few months and then got called back to work. You can't imagine how relieved I was to have a job.

I was the only one in my family to be working for several years. The University had this new president, Hutchins, he's still there of course, and he changed the whole direction of the institution. He emphasized academics and deemphasized other things—"

"Like football. Hutchins disbanded their team and took Chicago out of the conference," inserted Henry. "I was on the Illinois team when we played 'em in '35. We lost that year, but in '36 my senior year we won eighteen to seven, and I scored one of our touchdowns." The mock puffery displayed by Henry was obvious to the adults as he raised a fist to honor his performance. "That was my only score during my brief, but spectacular, career," he added.

"All I've got to say about your career in football is," Cyrus broke in, "praise the Lord you don't have to try and earn a living playing the game. If you did, you would be on the street or selling programs outside Soldier Field."

Ted and the others enjoyed the amusing give and take between father and son as Henry concluded, "You missed seeing my best performances. Of course they were during our team practices, but I made some spectacular catches before every game."

After the chuckling subsided, Mary asked, "Have you folks always lived in Chicago?"

"I was born and raised in St. Louis then moved to Chicago when I got out of high school," Mary Boudreau explained as she placed her elbows on the table and gestured with her hands. "My Aunt Margarite lived there on the Southside, and I lived with her and got a job at a public library branch near the University and then I met Cyrus and"—gesturing with her open palms—"well you can guess what happened next." Laughing, she continued, "We've been married ever since and have three boys: Henry, Harvey, and Homer."

"And their names all start with aitch," mused Mary.

"That's a tradition in Cyrus's family," responded Mary Boudreau.

Cyrus spoke, again calmly, clearly, and smoothly, "When my family came out of Louisiana, there were three brothers who escaped north in '63 before the end of the war. They went to Chicago, and Uncles Horace and Harvey—wait, I guess they were my great uncles—well, anyway, they joined the Union Army, and my grandfather Henry stayed in Chicago and started a small business. My grandfather was raised in the plantation house and could read and write, while his brothers worked in the fields and had had no education except what they picked up from Henry. Horace was killed in the war in a battle on the Mississippi River—I think they called it Fort Pillow, or something like that—that was during one of the raids by Nathan Forrest. So despite Horace's misfortune, my father named three of his first sons Henry, Horace, and Harvey, and my uncle Harvey did the same with his three sons, Harvey, Horace, and Henry. So we had three Harveys, Horaces, and Henrys, and Boudreaus all over the Southside. When I was born as the fourth boy, my mother put her foot down and insisted I be named for her father, so I'm a Cyrus."

"Did your grandfather like Louisiana or Chicago better?" asked Ted. "I want to go to Chicago someday. It's a big city."

"I'm certain my grandfather liked Chicago much better, because in Louisiana he was a slave and—"

"Oh, I didn't know that," said Ted softly, feeling ashamed as if he had committed a social error.

"That's all right, I'm sure you haven't studied that yet in school, and most of us old folks who did study it have forgotten most everything. But I remember because it was so important to my family. Teddy, you see I'm not ashamed of the fact that I'm the grandson of a slave; there's nothing I can do about that, it just happens to be part of my heritage. What I have to worry about is what I do while I'm on this earth, and I hope that when the good Lord calls my name, I'll be rewarded in heaven. But"—Cyrus smiled—"I'm willing to wait for a long time before I find out my fate after my name's called."

Ted felt better. "Was your grandmother a slave too?"

"Yes. My grandfather, we called him Pappy—"

Ted smiled at the name.

"—he went back to Louisiana in '65. That was 1865, after the war and Mr. Lincoln had set us free. He went to the plantation where he had been raised, and all his people were already gone. He heard they had gone to Baton Rouge just about twenty miles away. So he went there and found Colette, and they went North and were married. I remember her . . . We called her Gramer, that was our version of saying *grandmother* in French." Cyrus chuckled.

"Was she from France—or French?" Ted continued.

"No, she actually had been born in Martinique—that's a French island colony in the Caribbean—and they shipped some of their slaves to New Orleans where the master of the plantation bought her and her mother and brought them to the plantation where she met Pappy. She always spoke with a French accent, even when she was in her nineties. She died in '35."

"Oh, Cyrus, I didn't think I was going to get you started on your whole family history," Mary Boudreau said as she squeezed his hand.

"I'm sorry, I just got carried away."

"You know, what's interesting is that we can sit here, descendants of both slaves and masters, and enjoy each other's company and share a meal. Some things have changed for the better over the years," observed Frank.

"Yes, things certainly have changed, but oh so slowly," commented Cyrus. "So slowly."

"I think things will change after this war is over, change for the better," Frank continued.

"I wish I could be optimistic," said Cyrus, "but, I just don't know. It seems like it takes a whole generation to get a little step of change. I don't see a lot of improvement for the Negroes here in the South, and in the North it's like a thin veneer of attitude that, I think, doesn't run very deep."

"I think your comment on generational change is correct," said Frank, "and our generation," gesturing to include Henry, "will be in charge after the war. I just can't see the same attitudes continuing. Then we have Ted and his mates following along behind us to pick up the ball in the . . . seventies and eighties."

"You have a way of giving us hope," said Cyrus. "I hope you're right, and I hope I live to see some of that Promised Land that our preachers keep talking about. Maybe it won't all be in the hereafter."

"Pop, I see the big pivot point for change after this war to be whether the Negroes and other Colored people will be given full protection and rights under the Constitution," Henry observed. "If that starts to occur, change could snowball throughout society. If the courts don't respond, then we will be stuck with these Jim Crow laws for a very long time."

"Do you honestly believe that the courts can change the way people feel?" asked Mary Boudreau.

"Mom, yes, up to a point. After a while there could be real change that would occur after the generational change occurs and your generation dies off and the following generations take control, like Frank said. The new generation will grow up under a new way of looking at people and maybe recognize we're all Americans."

"My sakes, I've got to die before it happens." Mary Boudreau laughed with a strained expression on her face.

"I was just using you as an example, Mom," said Henry. "I mean most everybody over forty or fifty will probably be gone or else sitting in a rocking chair by the time the new court decisions take effect, if they ever happen."

"Well, I'm glad it's all right if I live a while longer," Henry's mother said with a less strained chuckle.

Ted was completely lost in the conversation. Even though she didn't completely follow the discussion, Mary did marvel at the nimbleness of the minds of her son, Henry and Cyrus. She recognized the value of education in their lives and recognized the limitations placed on her by her lack of schooling beyond high school. Things were different then; girls simply didn't need more education after high school. After all, high school equipped her to teach for a year in a rural grammar school before she married;

that was enough for her. But Teddy, that was another story. He must go to college, and Frank must also finish his college work.

"I hate to break up a fine evening, but I'm afraid there may be a little snow this evening and I don't like the idea of a long drive out in the country in a Jeep," Henry said as the conversation lulled.

"Is the Jeep good when you drive in snow?" Will asked.

"It's supposed to be. It has four-wheel drive, but I haven't driven it yet in snow, especially going up and down hills. We didn't get any snow in Georgia to practice on," he said, smiling.

"Let me help with the dishes," Mary Boudreau said as she picked up dessert plates and headed for the kitchen.

"Now, that's all right I can do 'em," said Mary as she followed Mrs. Boudreau into the kitchen.

"No, I insist," came the other Mary's reply.

The men stood and stretched and slowly made their way to the living room. "Teddy," called his grandmother, "the garbage needs to go out tonight."

"Yes, ma'am," said Teddy as he ran to the front hall, grabbed his jacket, and then ran to the kitchen.

"Just a minute, son," said Mary Boudreau as she finished scraping the plates into the open brown paper garbage bag. "There. Anything else to go in here?" she asked Mary.

"No, but, Teddy, hold the bottom of the bag with your hand in case something wet soaks through," said Mary.

"Yes ma'am." Ted liked having jobs to do, especially when there was company, and he felt like he was doing something necessary to be part of the world of the grownups. After dropping the bag in the garbage can and replacing the bent lid, he walked back across the yard and entered the kitchen door. Mrs. Boudreau seemed to be crying, but she turned her head as he came in and he couldn't be certain.

"Thank you, Teddy, now you go in the living room with the men," his granny said. Ted again thought he detected a break in his grandmother's voice as if she too were crying. He was puzzled as he walked back down the hall to the coat rack and then into the front room to stand in front of the fire.

Both Marys sniffled as Mary washed and Mary Boudreau dried the evening's dishes and stacked them on the kitchen table. "When you all were talking about the generations at the table, I thought about how important it was for Frank and Teddy to get a college education," said Mary, "and then the premonition hit me that Frank should go to college if he comes back from the war. I almost cried then. I'm ashamed of myself and I'm sorry I asked you about Henry, and if you worry, it made you cry too."

"Don't be ashamed. I worry about him every day. I also have two more boys in the service; one is in the Navy somewhere in the Pacific, and our youngest is in boot camp in Texas right now. I worry all the time, but I try not to cry when Cyrus is around. He's so sensitive he just can't bear to think about losing any of his boys. I try to be brave for him, but when I'm alone . . . sometimes I'm just a mess"—Mary Boudreau laughed through the tears—"just a mess."

Mary dried her hands on a dish towel and hugged Mary Boudreau as she returned the embrace, and the Marys shed more tears; they shared the unspoken truth: they were both mothers with children in peril.

"I didn't know you had more boys in the service. My other boys are too old to be drafted. Frank is our youngest, and he's so special 'cause he's with us now and we get to help raise Teddy."

The two women parted, wiping eyes with the backs of their hands. "You're lucky to have a grandchild close. My girl has my grandchildren, but they're up in Wisconsin and I don't see them very often. Coming down to Tennessee has helped me take my mind off the boys a little bit 'cause there's so much to do right now. I just hope this war gets over real soon and all survive and life gets back to normal, if that's ever going to be possible."

As the Boudreaus donned their coats in preparation to leave, the two officers embraced. "Good luck up at Knox," Frank said to Henry. "I hope things work out for you in those Sherman tanks. Fort Knox is just south of Louisville, and you should be able to have a little more night life up there than in Columbus, but be careful of those clubs."

"You're telling someone from Chicago to be careful of night clubs, especially Negro clubs. Why, Louisville will seem tame compared to Chi-town."

"I guess you're right," Frank replied, chuckling, "I forgot for a moment about you being from Chicago. But be careful, it's still a Southern town in many ways."

"I'll survive." Henry added, "Good luck with your teaching back at Benning and watch out for the green recruits when you get to the grenade-throwing department." Henry laughed.

"It's a shame you fellows are being sent in opposite directions, north to Kentucky and south to Georgia," Cyrus said.

"That's the army for you," Frank observed as he was embraced by Mary Boudreau and as Mary hugged Henry. The older men shook hands all around, and the Boudreau family hurriedly exited through the front door into the cold night.

"Drive carefully, y'all," Will called out. "I hate for people to drive on a night like this. It feels like there's snow in the air." He hurriedly closed the door.

At ten o'clock Mary and Ted knelt beside his bed as he said his customary night-time prayers, except at the end he added, "And bless Henry and Mr. and Mrs. Boudreau, amen." As Mary reached for support of the bed to steady herself in rising from her knees, Ted asked, "Were you and Mrs. Boudreau crying tonight?"

Mary sank back down on her knees. "Yes, it's such a sad time for mothers these days; we have a lot to worry about."

"Are you worried about Daddy?" asked Ted.

"Sometimes I do, but not often," Mary added somewhat insincerely as she knew she did worry every day, but she didn't want to bring Teddy into her circle of grief.

Ted extended his arms part way around her shoulders with a hug and comforting squeeze. "I do too," he whispered in her ear. "I get afraid at night and I try to think of Mommy and not cry, but it's hard. Daddy may get in the war where the Japs and Germans are shooting real bullets at him, and I get scared. Sometimes I want to cry, but I try not to."

"Teddy" was all that Mary could enunciate as she returned the hug and cried harder. She realized that Ted was not immune from the fears that plagued the adults in the family, and her efforts to protect him from his father's risks were ineffective.

To accurately describe winter weather in Tennessee, the ups and downs of a yoyo come to mind with the temperature driven below freezing for several days by winds from Canada to the high point of the yoyo as southern gulf breezes push afternoon highs into the sixties. During the last week of February, the thermometer hit sixty-five degrees as Will and Mary sat in the Saturday noontime sun on their front porch steps. Marie McGruder was pushing her older sister down the sidewalk toward Eighteenth Street on a scooter contraption made of boards attached to two pair of roller skates. Florabelle screamed with pleasure.

"I guess Frank's back at Fort Benning already this mornin'. I wonder what he's doin'," Mary mumbled as she stared through the bright light at the dull winter colors along Highland Avenue. "I don't have the slightest idea of what any soldiers do when they're trainin'. Maybe they march all the time." She shaded her eyes from the sun's rays.

"I guess he's gettin' ready to start teachin' the new recruits. Frank said they're havin' a new class arrive on Monday," Will answered the rhetorical question.

"Do you think he's goin' to be all right? I get to worryin' so that I scare myself."

"Mary, all we can do is wait and pray and take care of Teddy like we said we would. Things will happen in the war, some men will die, more will be wounded, and most will come through unhurt." Will's arm circled her waist and he pulled her tightly against his side.

"Teddy worries about his dad too. He told me last week when we said his prayers. He doesn't show it, but he does."

"I'm not surprised. He's a fine boy and will be a fine man like his father."

"And his grandfather," Mary added as she brushed his whiskered chin. "You haven't shaved yet today."

"I get Saturdays off from shavin'. I let my skin get well on Saturdays so it can undergo the razor during the week."

"Poor ole man," Mary added as she rubbed his chin, a wry smile turning up the corners of her mouth.

"Ain't this the darnedest weather you ever seen?" came the voice to the left of their walk as two neighborhood men walked toward Seventeenth Street.

"Hello, Bill, Dicky. You boys out for a stroll in the sun?" Will asked.

"Got to go down to the post office this morning to look for a package," Bill answered.

"I'm just goin' along for the ride," Dicky added.

The two men paused at the foot of the Warring's walk as Bill put his hands on his hips and looked around at the street, turning to Will and Mary. "We was walking down the street the other night, Sunday it was a week ago, that really cold night, and we seen your army guests arrive," Bill observed. "They friends of your boy?"

"Yes," said Will, "Henry has just graduated from the officer's school like Frank, and they're both second lieutenants now."

"I didn't know they was any Nigger officers," said Bill. "I thought they was all cooks and tater peelers." He and Dicky laughed.

Will's relaxed demeanor shifted instantly as he sat very erect, and the arm circling Mary returned to his side. "There will be a lot of Negro officers before this war is over," he said in a flat voice.

Bill, not noticing the change in Will's attitude, said, "Well, I hope they stay in the Nigger units and don't try an' boss around the white soldiers." Bill chuckled as he glanced at Dicky and he got a reinforcing laugh. "That'll be the day when they think they can do that," he added with a continuing laugh. "That Nigger boy that was here, he was a big 'un, wasn't he? The better to hit with a stray bullet." Bill raised his hand like he was holding a pistol and pulling the trigger.

Both Bill and Dicky laughed heartily as Will and Mary stood, Will pointing his finger said in a cool, hard voice, "You God Damned hypocrite. You are standing there making fun of a young man who's willing to go die for you two just like my Frank is doin'. Why should Colored soldiers want to protect you?" Now in a rising volume, "You son of a bi—"

"Now, Will, don't get so excited," said Mary as she pulled Will's arm to prevent him from going down the steps.

The frozen smiles on the faces of Bill and Dicky slowly melted as the men stared open-mouthed at Will. "I didn't mean—"

"Oh, yes, you did," Will screamed, and Mary pulled harder turning Will and forcing him to take a stumbling step onto the porch.

"Will, they're not worth you havin' a heart attack over. Come on inside."

Will glared over his shoulder at the two stunned neighbors as Dickey took a step toward Seventeenth in his escape from Will.

"Go on and get out of here," Will shouted, stumbling again as Mary pulled him inside the house.

Mary closed the door. "Will, look at you, you are redder than an apple. Go sit down in the living room."

"Did you hear those bastards? Did you hear them?"

"Yes, Will, I was right by you."

"The nerve they have." Will swung his arm in an effort to strike at the memory of Bill's comments. "I swear, I can't abide by those people anymore, I just can't abide—"

"Please, Will, sit down and calm down; you're still bright red."

Will stumbled trying to catch his balance, which he failed to do. He fell onto the footstool in front of his chair. He made a sound as air was rapidly forced from his chest. He gasped for a breath and slumped to the floor. "Will!" cried Mary as she knelt by his shoulder, and her hands grasped his face. "Will. Will, can you breathe?"

"Yes," came the gasping response followed by several deep labored breaths, and then the two sat in silence as he slowly regained a nearly normal breathing rhythm. "I do believe I knocked the breath out of me," came the halting words as Will straightened his legs to a more comfortable posture. "I got kinda dizzy; that's what made me fall."

Ted, who had been upstairs listening to his radio when he heard loud shouting from the street and then the first floor of the house, stuck his head around the corner of the hall doorway. "What happened?" he asked in a shaky voice. "Is Granddad all right?"

"Yes, Teddy, I think he's all right now. I think God just flew into Granddad's head, and I think he just woke him up. I think God woke me up too," Mary said as she stroked the thinning brown and gray hair from her lover's forehead.

# PART 3

*Attack*

# PART 3

*June 20, 1944 to January 1, 1945*

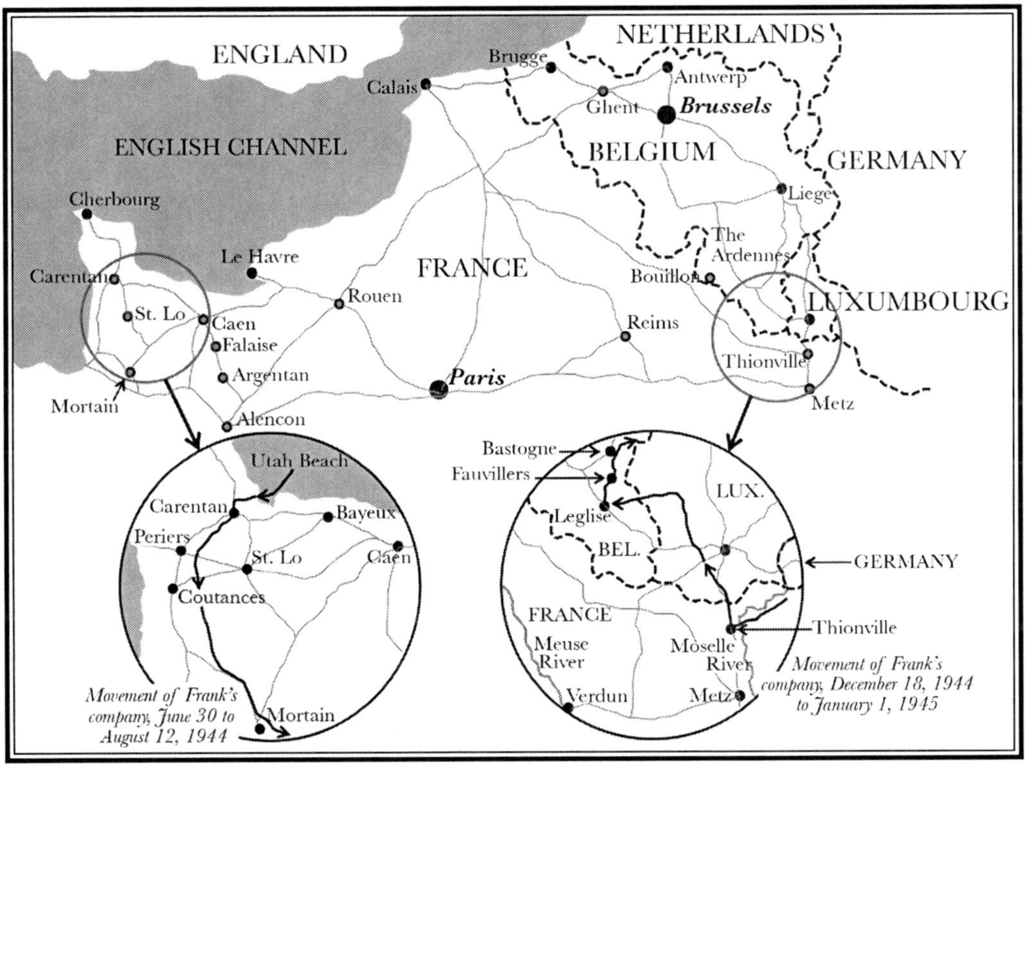

# CHAPTER 19

## *Knoxville*

### *Winter 1943 to Winter 1944*

ON WEDNESDAY, FEBRUARY 24, Frank received an envelope from 1702 Highland Avenue containing two letters.

*Dear Daddy,*
*GrandDad got sick last Saturday and the doctor came and said he is all right now. He has a bruse on his stumick but says he is fine. Bill and Mr. Gross from down the street said some things about Henry and Mr and Mrs Boudreau that were not nice. Granny heard them and she was mad at them but she had to get Granddad in the house when he was red in the face. Granny did not yell at them like Granddad did. The doctor said Granddad would be ok if he behaves himself. I hope so. I will try and make granddad comfortabal. How is the army? Good I hope.*
*Love Ted*

*Monday, Feb. 22, 1943*

*Dear Frank,*

*Don't worry about Dad. He is fine now. He had a little problem last Saturday when he got very mad at Bill and Dickie Gross from down the street about the comments they made about Henry and his folks coming to our house. Dad said some things when he was mad and got very red in the face, and I finally got him in the house. He was dizzy and fell in the living room. Mr. Gooch from across the street came over to see what all the yelling was about, and he looked at Dad and said we should call Doctor White, which I did, and he came and said Dad needs to calm down and he may have broken a rib when he fell. He is all right now but still sore in the chest.*

*He will stay home from work the rest of the week and rest as he is not feeling entirely well. Teddy is fine. He helped me pick up Dad and get him in a chair after he fell. Doctor White says he has high blood pressure and must relax. Mr. Gooch staid late talking to Dad, and he was very calm when he went to bed and looks fine this morning. Mr. Gooch teaches at the University, and he gave Dad some poems and Bible verses. Dad has been reading them this morning and says he feels like a new man. He must be, because I don't remember him reading the bible before. I don't think he's new yet, but he may be working on it.*

*Mr. Gooch said all soldiers like you should remember the 23rd and 121st Psalms when you go into a battle: they will give you strength to live. I read them and think they would help if you actually have to fight. Do you have a Bible, or should I send you one? I am writing to you because I don't know how to call on the phone to Fort Benning, it is so big, so I decided to write you a letter. That way I can take my time and remember to tell you all that happened. Take care of yourself and don't worry. Daddy is all right. Teddy will add a letter to you in this envelope as well.*

*Your Loving Mother*

Frank did worry and received a week-long pass to attend to personal matters. He travelled home for five days and was satisfied after that time that he could do no more for his father in Knoxville and so returned to his assigned post at Fort Benning as part of the instructional team for new recruits.

While in Knoxville he did become aware of his father's calm countenance. When he arrived, he found Will in an unusually relaxed state. Frank assumed Will was going through a brief period of overcompensating for his violent outburst for fear that a subsequent event could cause another period of high blood pressure, or worse, a heart attack or stroke. But day by day Frank became convinced that the change in attitude and mannerisms was genuine. This did not mean that at some point Will might not revert to his former self, but for the foreseeable future, Frank was convinced his father had changed. *He was mellower, yes that was a good way of describing him now, mellower.* Will would never have been described as a violent man, but as Mary said, he could be provoked, and sometimes mightily provoked.

Frank remembered several incidents as a boy when Will flew into a brief outburst that transformed his usual calm, thoughtful approach to life to one of outright rage. Those had been frightening events. There was the time Frank and the neighbor Collins boy set a haystack on fire when they were experimenting with smoking corn silks out in the east field. Then the time he jumped into Stoner's Creek that bordered the farm. Frank was six or seven, and he wanted to try swimming in the rain-swollen creek, something he was sure he could do based on his ability to swim across the normally placid waters.

He was pulled from the stream by his older brother Caleb, sputtering and gasping for breath. Caleb had to explain to his parents why Frank looked like a "drowned rat" when they appeared at the supper table. Will had spanked him there at the table in front of everybody and sent him to his room. Mary told him later that Will was scared and frightened for Frank's safety and Frank should try and understand and listen to his father's advice. Frank was too sore to be very forgiving, but he did try and listen from that point on. His father had made an impression on him, an impression on more than his rear end.

As a young man of nineteen, Frank tried to pattern his own actions after those of his father. This didn't happen until Frank went away to college and lived apart from his parents for months at a time. While patterning himself after his father, he did try and avoid the rare violent outbursts: he had been successful so far. On second thought he now realized he probably had a somewhat different personality than his father and he probably wouldn't be capable of such actions.

Now, Uncle Willard was a different kind of person. They said he took after his father in being very "chippy," or thin skinned, at times and would get out of sorts with people and become very mad. Frank remembered several incidents when Will and Willard's families both lived on the farm in adjoining houses. Once Willard got mad and turned very red in the face, and Mary said that if he didn't calm down, steam would start erupting from his ears. Everybody laughed at the comment except Uncle Willard, and he stomped off to the barn.

Will was Willard's older brother, and he was the one known in the town as the peacemaker in the family. If the feed store or bank had a problem, they preferred to deal with Will when Willard was not present. Will always said that part of Willard's problem may have been due to his fighting in France in the Great War.

Frank's reverie paused. *I wonder what combat does to a person, aside from getting hurt or killed, of course. What effect does it have on the actions of the survivors, their approach to life, their personal relations? Huh.*

The rest of 1943 passed uneventfully for the Warring family compared to the degree of change they had experienced in 1941 and '42. Will's health seemed very stable as Doctor White measured his blood pressure every three months and encouraged him to continue his new outlook on life, the one with less stress and more laughter.

Frank continued in his new role as instructor of green infantry soldiers in their initial boot-camp training program. Many of the graduates of the basic soldiering school were temporarily released back to civilian life to help fill the serious void in the manufacturing labor force that resulted from the patriotic rush of men to military service after Pearl Harbor and the parallel need for a drastic increase in employment brought on by increased military production.

The return to civilian life was generally regarded as a temporary period. The nation braced for the inevitable, a sustained surge in the military that would occur when the US invaded continental Europe. Many Americans were now serving in the Pacific, but many more of the new soldiers were being stockpiled in America for the European campaign.

During two trips home for a one-week leave in April and October, Frank and Ted plotted conflict hotspots around the world on maps in the atlas. There were finally decisive victories by the US on Guadalcanal, a retaking of Rangoon in Burma by British forces, and the Aleutian Islands were reclaimed by US and Canadian units from the invading Japanese army. The hard-won success in Asia was the realization of a strategy to stop the outward spread of Japanese domination and to start rolling back the tide and eliminate Japan's access to the vital oil and natural resources it had seized in southeast Asia. In north Africa, the British successfully stopped the final German thrust in Egypt at El Alamein and began a relentless drive west clearing Egypt and through Libya, while the US forces under Eisenhower pushed east from Morocco. The combined British and US forces then joined to complete the German defeat in bloody fighting in Tunisia. The Allies then turned their focus on the European mainland and invaded and captured Sicily in July and August and invaded the Italian boot in early September. Meanwhile the Royal Air Force continued to attack German cities during the night with Americans bombing occurring during the daylight hours. The Russian army had finally stopped Germany's eastern and southeastern advances against Stalingrad, Leningrad, and Moscow. The eastern front had begun a slow westward retreat as Germany found it increasingly difficult to hold, much less advance their nine-hundred-mile field of engagement that stretched from the Baltic Sea in the north to the Crimean peninsula in the south. Like Napoleon, Hitler was over extended and learning the hard way what it meant to invade the vast reaches of Russia.

Ted had drawn a simplified outline map of Europe so many

times that he could now do it from memory as he played imaginary games of invading armies and wars that pushed a make-believe battle line back and forth across the continent.

Will and Leroy also faced major tasks in helping to refit Fulton's plant to cast brass shells for medium artillery and tank munitions. They worked daily with industrial engineers as new machinery was installed, tested, put into production, and then maintained in double shift operations. Production was increased substantially. The plant also began to hire both women and Negroes into the labor force as the rank of the white male labor force was thinned by the call to war. One of the Negroes hired was Isaac. The plant needed a full-time plumber to maintain piping to the numerous machines that used water in the manufacture of brass shell casings. He was also used to help run electrical conduits that carried power to the same machines. On numerous occasions, Will, Leroy, and Isaac had to work during late nights and on weekends to maintain the plant's equipment. Management was unwilling to shut down the facility between six in the morning and eight at night, thus shifting maintenance to the deep hours of the night.

Mary asked Will if she should apply for a job at the plant, and he rejected the idea without any discussion. Mary at first was upset by the rejection, since she knew that she could do the work if other women were doing it. On the other hand, she really didn't want to change her routine because they didn't need the income that she would earn, and she had her days filled with keeping Will and Ted fed, dressed in clean clothes, and the household in some semblance of order. She knew if she began working, something would have to give and probably all of her current tasks would suffer to some degree. But still, she wanted Will to take her interest in work more seriously. Will, for his part, knew that most of the plant's working women were doing it because their husbands, sons, or fathers who under normal times supplied the families' income were now engaged in the low-paying task of defending their country. He knew Mary could do the work, but he just couldn't bring himself to imagine a home without her present all the time and tending to management of the family. He knew how indispensable she was in that role, although he never told her so.

Frank sat in the living room at 1702 Highland Avenue and stretched his legs to receive the full warmth of the grate's fire. The late January day in 1944 required extra warmth as the ten-degree weather outside cooled the interior of the house, especially near windows and outside doors. Ted brought his atlas into the room and opened it on the floor in front of the fire. Father and son were soon on their knees looking at the atlas page showing northern France, Belgium, the Netherlands, and the western border region of Germany. The southern coast of England was visible at the top of the map across the English Channel from France.

"Eisenhower is setting up his army bases here in southern England, and the Germans are over here in France on the mainland with their troops dug into defensive positions," Frank said tracing his finger across the map. "Everybody is guessing where Ike will land his troops. It could be here in Normandy, in Dieppe, in Calais, or maybe even in Belgium. You see it is a short hop across the channel to land at several different places."

"Couldn't they land at all of them at the same time?" Ted asked squinting at his father with his best scholarly gaze. Ted had watched Mr. Gooch who used the same quizzical affectation when he talked to Will about the war and when peaceful times might return.

"Well I guess they could invade all of them, but they would have a better chance of success by concentrating their forces in one place in order to gain a solid foothold and then drive the Germans back into Germany over here on the east border of France. They also may not have enough boats to land at that many places at the same time."

"Oh, I see," mused Ted rubbing his chin. "What's this little place lux?"

"That's Luxembourg. It's a very small country caught between the big countries. It has been invaded a number of times over the years, but they don't try and fight back so they aren't destroyed as the invaders pass through their country. They just do the best they can and try and get along with whoever has occupied them.

"And here's Switzerland down here," Frank said as his finger moved to the bottom of the map. "They are a larger version of Luxembourg. They don't have an army and they usually don't get invaded because they are in the mountains and not in the path of armies as they go back and forth between Germany and France."

"Oh, I see," replied Ted. Frank smiled down at the top of his son's head as he pored over the map. He recognized Ted's new studious pose. With Ted living under the grandparents' roof, Frank had little doubt that he would be influenced by good people.

Mary sat in her chair with her knitting needles moving expertly back and forth across the sleeve of a new sweater emerging from the ball of maroon yarn. Although her eyes focused only on the knitting, her ears and mind were aware of the father-and-son scene before her. Will read the evening paper as he sat in his chair; he would eat supper and then leave for one of the late-night work sessions at the plant.

"Frank do you have something to tell us?" asked Mary as she emptied the Ball jar of canned tomatoes into the sauce pan; they were to be part of the evening meal. The pork chops sizzled slowly in the large skillet on the back burner.

"Yes." Frank smiled. "You are a hard one to hide things from. In fact, you always were. Remember the time when I wanted to buy that old Model T and—"

"But these days," interrupted Mary, "things are a lot more serious. Is it about your service?"

"Yes." His smile faded as he studied his hands resting on the kitchen table.

"Are you going overseas?"

"Yes."

"When?"

"In two weeks," he said looking at his mother.

"So this is your last trip home before you go."

"Yes."

"Do you have to go?" Mary moved toward the table.

"Yes, I'm going with the last troops I helped train. We are to become part of the 4th Infantry Division. I'm not certain what army we'll become part of; that final decision hasn't been made as far as I know."

"Oh my," said Mary. She wiped the remnants of tomato juice from her hands onto her apron as she sat opposite her son. "Of course you don't know how long you'll be gone?"

"No, I suppose till the war is over."

"Oh my . . . Do you know what you and your division will be doing?"

"Well, we're trained as infantry and I suppose we'll see some combat service, but in a time of war, events have a way of dictating how the men will be used, and we just can't say for certain what'll happen. We'll probably have a million soldiers over there before this is over, and less than half of those will see actual fighting."

Mary's eyes filled with tears and she wept silently. Tears ran down her cheeks as Frank rose and knelt beside his mother's chair and extended his arm around her shaking shoulders. The length of time that she cried seemed interminable to him; he deeply regretted being the cause of the pain she was suffering.

After a pause she said, "It seems like all I want to do these days is cry. I'm so glad your brothers are too old to be in the service. But there's poor Mary Boudreau: she has three sons in the fighting. And Inez Brown at church, she has four and, one is missin' in action out on one of those Pacific islands. Lordy, how can we live through this hideous time? Why did it have to happen now?"

Frank had no answer to her questions. Mary wiped her eyes on her apron, kissed Frank on the cheek, rose, and walked to the stove. Facing the back door she asked, "When are you goin' to tell Teddy?"

"Tonight . . . when he goes to bed. Tomorrow afternoon I thought we could go down to Alumni Gym and see the basketball game. Kentucky is coming into town to play Tennessee. Maybe on Sunday we could go see a picture show downtown. I'm not sure what's on, but there's usually something he would enjoy seeing."

"It'll be hard on him. He worries about you," she said as she knelt to pull another pan from the cupboard shelf. She stood and dabbed her nose and reddening eyes with a tissue she took from her pocket.

"I'll talk to him about that as well. The worst part of worrying about me is that if worry takes over, it can really harm you. Remember when Roosevelt said, 'We have nothing to fear but fear itself,' he was trying to get people to look at ways to get out of the depression and to not let fear infect each person's attitude."

Mary cored and sliced several apples as Frank talked, then deposited them in the pan with a little water. She planned to make applesauce. Turning to face Frank she observed, "That was a little different during the Depression . . . or maybe a lot different. Back then you could do somethin' on your own to plant a garden or to move in with relatives to save money, this is different.

"I know you're tryin' to ease my mind, but there's no doubt that you're goin' to war and there's nuthin' I can do about it but worry."

She wiped her hands and dabbed at her nose again with the tissue then added a dash of salt to the apples, "That's what mothers are good for, lovin' their children and worryin' about them when they're in trouble.

"This is not the Depression. I can't write Mr. Hitler a letter and tell him to stop bein' a bad man, and I can't grow enough vegetables to make any difference. I'm helpless. This is something you'll learn about with Teddy. Right now we're takin' over his care for you, and we're so thankful to have that chance, but later on after you come back you'll be a parent again and have all the worry every day as he grows up."

She adjusted the heat under the apples and tomatoes. "I don't mean you aren't a good parent now, but as children get older they got different problems that you haven't gone through yet, but you will and you'll do fine at it when the time comes and you'll worry like a parent does."

Mary paused again, then, "Today standing here in Knoxville during this war I'm just so mad . . . I'm damn mad, pardon that word, but I'm so mad at all these leaders in the world leadin' their countries around and fightin' and killin' each other." She waved the wooden spoon grasped tightly in her hand. "I'm just sick to death and I don't understand why they do it. Why don't they let us live in peace?" The spoon slipped from her hand and clattered on the counter top before hitting the floor.

Mary stood staring out the window in the back door. A bright red cardinal landed on the post that held the clothes line then hopped to the ground and began pecking at unseen objects in the frozen grass. Frank circled his arms around his mother, and she turned to bury her face in his sweater. "Mom you know if there was some way to change things I would do so, but I'm as helpless as you. I've trained myself as well as I can, but I don't know what's going to happen. I'll try as hard as I humanly can to come back and continue living my life. I have a lot to look forward to, I'm over the deep trouble I was in two years ago. The army has been a godsend for me to get my head on straight again." He paused as she took a deep breath to fight back tears. "I'm so fortunate to have you and Dad as the best parents anybody could hope for."

Leaning back from Frank's tight embrace, she said, "Imagine that, God sent you to the army to clear up your head. I'll have to think on that and see if I agree. Seems to me the army gets young men ready to die. That may be too harsh, but that's the way I feel."

"What would happen if we didn't have an army?" Frank asked.

"I don't know. We've always had one and we send men off to die every twenty years or so. Your daddy was thinking about enlisting in '98 for the war with Spain, but it was over in a matter of months before he could get himself together to go, so he didn't go. Do me one big favor when you are over there. Don't be a hero like that Gary Cooper soldier, what's his name?"

"Sergeant York?"

"Yes, and do me a second favor when you see that Mr. Hitler:

tell him that if he comes here I'll take my butcher knife and cut a few choice parts off him and make a stew and throw it to the pigs. There, you tell him that."

Frank burst into laughter. Mary thought of more choice things she would like to say and do to the chief scoundrel in the world conflict, but she didn't use that kind of language aloud, so she kept those thoughts to herself. "I guess we'll get through this like your daddy says. But, Frank, always know that I will pray for you every night, and I'll worry about you every day till you come home."

Frank and Mary embraced in a mighty hug that lifted her off her feet.

The conversation with Ted was not easy for Ted or Frank. Both cried, although for different reasons: Ted for fear he would lose his last parent, and Frank as a parent grieving with his child and recognizing that he was the cause of Ted's pain. As with Mary, Frank said he did not know what would happen in Europe and he may be assigned to stay in England, but inside he doubted he would be so fortunate. As an eleven-year-old fifth grader, Ted reacted as an older child might with a greater understanding of why his father was going, but as a child he still feared the unknown and that the war could take his father's life.

On Tuesday, March 14, 1944, the family took the all-too-familiar early morning trolley ride down Seventeenth and then Clinch Avenue on their way to the train station to see Frank off. This morning was very different because each one knew of the potential consequences of his departure. Without the dread of his death being spoken aloud, Frank said he would return as soon as he could and asked that they write so he could keep in touch with the ones that meant so much to him. Tears fell in abundance among all members of the tightly woven family. Will was not able to express his feelings at his son's departure, but Frank had no doubt about his father's love for him.

Will could not bring himself to say that he knew why Frank had to go, for he feared that if he said the words aloud they could cast a spell on his son's life. Mary knew she might be sacrificing a son to a war she simply did not understand. She could not, or would not, grasp the fact that America's future freedom might be at stake, she saw the war as the reason for the deprivation of her son's presence and his placement in the devil's hands.

She knew, as sure as she breathed, that the devil was one and the same as that Mr. Hitler.

Ted felt he must be brave for his dad during his departure, but try as hard as he could, he could not hold back the tears as he said good-bye. Ted had often recalled that he did not see his mother alive again after she told him to go over to the Kostigan's house on that late November morning three years ago; now he only saw her in his dreams. Ted so wanted his father to be real in his life and not a fading memory. He knew he desperately needed him.

Frank boarded the southbound train as the 4$^{th}$ Division assembled at Fort Benning before being sent by train to New York City, their port of embarkation for the overseas passage.

# CHAPTER 20

## *England*

## *Spring 1944*

*17 April 1944*

*Dear Son,*

*It has been an eventful month, full of travel and seeing many new sights. We took a very long train ride from Fort Benning to New Jersey, where we spent two nights, and then to New York City, where we went directly from the train and boarded our transport ship. Our ship happened to be a luxury liner, the Queen Mary. It is a new ship only about ten years old and has been refitted to carry as many soldiers as possible. The Queen Mary is a very fast ship. We traveled alone rather than with other ships in a convoy because she is so fast, she can outrun the German ships—and did so in the very rough seas that we went through. Many of our soldiers on board, including me, got seasick and had some uncomfortable times. There were 12,000 men on the ship, and we made the crossing in just six days. Not only is our ship fast, it is also very big, about 1,000 feet long. This is more than three football fields in length. Our route took us on the north side of Ireland, and we docked near Glasgow, Scotland, at a port called Greenoch. Greenoch is in the Firth of Clyde, which is a narrow inlet off the North Atlantic. We then took an English train south and have been installed in a camp at Bristol, England, near the west coast.*

*I hope you are studying hard and enjoying school. And I hope it has finally warmed up after that bad winter in Knoxville. I will write again soon and tell you about England. Give my love to Granny and Granddad and keep plenty for yourself.*

*Love, Dad*

TED WAS EXTREMELY anxious to read the letter upon its arrival, and in tearing open the envelope he ripped through the return address. Mary helped him piece the envelope together so they could write down Frank's address. Mary was equally anxious to read Frank's missive and did so as soon as Ted had finished. They immediately pulled out the atlas and found the port city Greenoch, but with a different spelling, then they found Glasgow and Bristol.

"I wonder what Scotland looks like," mused Mary. "I remember seeing pictures of men wearing skirts over there," she said with a chuckle, "and I think it gets pretty cold up there. You would think they would wear long pants, and heavy ones at that."

Ted laughed as well. "They play those bagpipes too."

"Yes, yes, I heard them played at a church service and I guess the player wasn't too good cause he screeched something awful and everybody in the audience just looked at each other to see if anybody knew if he was playing right. After church Wilmer Palmer said he was a terrible player and that he had heard them played in New York at a fireman's funeral and the sound was right movin', but I guess you really have to know how to do it so it doesn't screech. Let's go get some lunch."

"Yeah, there's a baseball tryout at 1:00 down at Tyson Park, and Jerry and I are going to go try to get on a team."

Two weeks later a second letter arrived at 1702 Highland Avenue.

*30 April 1944*

*Dear Son,*

*The city of Bristol is an old city like almost every city in England.*

*(A heavy black line made by the censor marked out the next sentence.) I'm certain you can find both of those places in your atlas. Our camp is also on land that had been farmed up until very recently before the war started in '39. The earth still has that certain aroma of farming about it. There is also a farm next to our billet, and I can smell the animals as they graze, and it is very nice since it reminds me of our farm in Millersburg. The country around here is very much like the farm land in Bourbon and Nicholas counties in Kentucky, with some rolling hills and pasture and crop fields with numerous small streams with tillable flat land in the valleys. Be sure and tell Granddad about the land. He will be interested because of our farm in Millersburg.*

*One thing that I am still getting used to is the way people drive in England. In America drivers stay on the right side of the road, and over here they drive on the left-hand side. We asked a taxi driver why they drive on the wrong side of the road, and he laughed and said all Americans ask that, and he tells them that it's the Americans and French that drive on the wrong side; the English drive on the correct side. He was a very jolly fellow as they say over here and told us a lot about how to drive through the roundabouts that are very common here. The center of Bristol has been badly damaged by German bombs, so it doesn't look its best, and we have not spent much time down there.*

*We had a two-day pass, and another officer and I took the bus to Bath and walked around that city. It is very, very different from any place I've seen in America. They have very stately row houses built in the 1700s in the Georgian architectural style. One group is built in a half-circle called the Royal Crescent and another group is built in a circle they call the Circus and then there are additional row houses built on the street that connects the crescent and circus. It would be a fine place to live if we were Englishmen and could afford to have one of them.*

*We also saw in Bath an old Roman public bath. I guess that's where the city got its name as a place for public baths. The "bath" was built in the days when most people did not have baths in their home and came to this public building to bathe in large pools. Some of the baths also had a steam bath. That sounds strange to us in America but it was a very normal thing to do in those old days. The Romans ran the government here in southern England for four hundred years starting shortly after the birth of Jesus. Think of how long ago that was and how long they ruled England. Our country is about 160 years old and won't be 400 years until 2184. By then you and I both will be forgotten, as will many generations of our children and grandchildren. It is amazing how old this place is. You can ask Granddad and Granny about this, but I believe we are descended from Englishmen who sailed to America in the 1600s or 1700s. When our ancestors came, they may have sailed from Bristol because it is a very old and important port for ships, and most of those ships that went to America started here.*

*I need to get to sleep now. We have to get up very early in the morning. Tomorrow we are going to practice what is called an amphibious landing, where we go out to sea for a short distance and then come ashore from a boat that is in shallow water near a beach. Give my love to Granny and Granddad and keep plenty for yourself.*

*Love, Dad*

# CHAPTER 21

## *Knoxville*

## *Spring 1944*

LILY LAKE ARRANGED two stacks of twenty-seven ditto-copied worksheets on her desk in preparation for tomorrow's class. She had a stack for the arithmetic and counting exercise and another stack containing new words for spelling. She knew several of her students were having difficulty with both study areas, and she resolved to spend more time with those five or six students during the afternoon. All but one of those having difficulty were boys, and she accepted the fact that young girls at seven or eight seemed to do better in their studies than boys. But then again, her brightest student was Aaron Smith, the son of a postman. She believed that boys in general were a little less able to apply themselves to book work and were more at home on the playground chasing each other or hitting or kicking a ball. Her ideas about differences in children had been formed during her own education and her brief experience in teaching in the classroom.

Lily closed the door to her second grade classroom and walked down the hall to the lunchroom, where a school committee would meet to discuss plans for the year-end assembly and play-day festival. She had been told that this was one of several events during the year where the Parents Teachers Association collected money for special school projects. Lily had been at Van Gilder for only three weeks since accepting a second grade teaching job replacing Mrs. Langston who had taken a leave of absence for the birth of her baby. There were rules that prevented teachers from working after they showed visible signs of pregnancy. Lily had returned to Knoxville as an employee of the school district. She had received a degree from UT in education in '37 but had not visited Knoxville since she left the day after graduation. Still, she felt at home teaching at an elementary school located on a hill next to and above the university campus on Cumberland Avenue. The neighborhood that she now taught in was the same one she had often walked through during her college days. She felt exceptionally fortunate.

She pushed open the lunchroom door and saw a table occupied by a cluster of women all talking amiably in a relaxed atmosphere; several were sipping from cups of coffee. Lily introduced herself to the first two women she encountered, Mary Warring and Anne Shields. She knew, or at least had met, the five other teachers but made a point of meeting the parents. She was heartened to meet Marilyn Smith, mother of Aaron, her best student.

Miss Evelyn Crosby entered the room, and all of those present knew the meeting was about to begin. Evelyn, the school's principal, along with Mary was the only person considered to be a senior citizen. After greeting each woman individually, "Thank you all for coming and agreeing to serve on the committee," began Miss Crosby. "Several of you have served before, so this shouldn't take too long to organize. For the sake of those new to our school-closing festivities, we have a final assembly where we hand out awards and announce that the students have been promoted to the next grade. This promotion ceremony is not necessary as far as the school board is concerned, but I think it adds a sense of accomplishment for the students to have mastered the year of study and to be recognized as a member of the next grade level. After the assembly we have a fair that provides for the sale of good things to eat as well as some student crafts. This is what we use to earn money for the PTA. We also have games for children to play."

Lily sensed Miss Crosby had given this speech numerous times during her tenure at Van Gilder and obviously had the day's events already planned out in her head. After answering several questions from the new mothers on the committee, Miss Crosby appointed Lily to serve with three other women, one teacher and two parents, on a refreshment committee that would assemble goods to sell at the fair. After completing other assignments, Miss Cosby closed the full meeting and encouraged the committees to begin work. Mary, Marilyn Smith, Rebecca Ambrose, and Lily gathered at a remote table to begin planning for the refreshment sale. Marilyn began, "Last year we sent home with each student a sheet for the mothers to sign up for baking cookies, pies, cakes, and whatever else they think is good to eat. But it's really just a nice bake sale like we have had at church."

"Last year as I recall," said Mary, "we did a real good business with sellin' coffee, to the adults, and those lemon cupcakes of yours, Marilyn."

"Yes, that's right, I'd a forgotten if you hadn't reminded me. I think we sold all four dozen of those cupcakes. Well, I'll sign up to do those again. Although I'll have to check coupons to see how much sugar and flour I can get."

"I'm new in town," said Lily, "having just replaced Evelyn Langston. She's out on maternity leave, and I'm still living at the Y until I find an apartment to rent, so I don't have access to a kitchen. Would it be all right if I do the office work of printing out the signup sheets for the students to take home?"

"Lands sakes, yes," said Marilyn and Mary almost simultaneously, they then chuckled at the unintended harmony of their response. "The teachers on the committee usually have their hands full with our children, so we don't expect them to do much of any baking; we leave that to the parents," Marilyn added.

"Well, I really like to bake, but just can't, considering my circumstances," Lily replied.

"Tell you what we could do," offered Mary, "you could come to my house on the Saturday before the sale, and we can bake up a storm together. You could do your recipes, and I'll do my chocolate chip cookies."

"That's a deal." said Lily, smiling. "Now I'll get my mother to send a couple of recipes and my ration book. I forgot to bring it with me."

"Yes, your book will help. Those ration books really cut down on the amount of sugar we have for baking, so the sale will be a little sparse, like last year," reminisced Marilyn. "We pretty near sold out of everything. I think those fig bars were the hardest to get rid of; maybe we won't get those this year."

"I think Agnes brought those and she still has a sixth grader, so we will probably get some more this year," offered Mary.

After ten more minutes of conversation, the small committee agreed that Lily and Rebecca would work with the school secretary on the notice to be sent home with the students and Marilyn and Mary would help tabulate the response to the notice and compare baking plans of the parents. They would be on the lookout to make certain there wasn't going to be too much of one type of goody and not enough of another; if necessary, calls would be made to the mothers to get them to adjust their baking plans to even out the inventory. As they walked out of the lunchroom, Mary spoke to Lily, "Did you say you are staying at the Y downtown?"

"Yes, it was the nicest and safest place I could find on such short notice. I just moved over here from Nashville and don't have any relatives right in Knoxville, so I have to get a place to live. My aunt lives in Bristol and another in Elizabethton, but they aren't close enough. So far, it seems there aren't many places available in Knoxville right now, and there's not any construction going on so I'm not sure what I'll do. I'll try again this Saturday and see if I can find anything on a streetcar line or within walking distance of the school."

"You know we had a fellow stayin' out in a small apartment in a little buildin' on the back of our lot, and he's now moved to a house across the river. But that little apartment wouldn't do for a lady; it only has part of a bathroom and no kitchen. He ate with us and he wasn't very particular about just having a toilet, but . . . I don't think it would work for you."

"Where do you live?" inquired Lily.

"At the corner of Highland and Seventeenth," Mary replied.

"Oh, I'm so sorry. That would be ideal because that's where I now get off the streetcar and then I walk down Highland to school. You think your place wouldn't be nice enough for me? I can live pretty ruggedly; I was a girl scout." Lily chuckled.

Mary laughed. "Oh, I don't know."

"Could I at least stop by there and look when I walk up to the car line on my way home?"

"Certainly," said Mary. "In fact, if you're ready now we can walk together."

"Oh good, let me get my coat and purse."

Mary and Lily walked from Fourteenth Street to Seventeenth, crossed the street and then turned into the walk and up the porch steps at 1702 Highland Avenue. "This is very nice," said Lily upon entering the front door. "It reminds me of my parent's home in Nashville. They live on Shelby Avenue across the river from downtown. It's about the same distance from their downtown as you are from Gay Street."

"Let's go back this way," said Mary heading for the dining room. "I've never been to Nashville."

As they entered the kitchen, "It's a nice city, but I wanted to move out of town now that I was starting to teach."

They walked out the back door and across the yard, and Mary opened the door to the apartment. "It's pretty dusty; no one's been here for a while and the heat hasn't been on."

Lily saw the Spartan furnishings of the room and the makeshift bathroom with the curtain drawn open on the toilet partition in the far corner of the room. "He slept upstairs in a cozy little bedroom; that's probably the nicest part of the apartment. But he had this table and two chairs, a small divan, and a stuffed chair. Oh, and he had a radio and seemed to get along fine, but he was a man and wasn't used to too much comfort. He would take his bath on the weekend in our bathroom and of course eat with us in the dining room, so he was happy. But I just have trouble seeing a young lady livin' here."

"Well," said Lily, "it is a little rustic. Let me keep on looking and see if something else turns up. But this is certainly a good location on the car line and close to school." She paused looking around the room and stroking her hand through her hair.

"I'd be glad to have you here, but this is a lot rustic." Mary chuckled. "You can probably find somethin' better."

The women walked back through the house and to the front porch. Lily extended her hand, and Mary took it and then gave her a hug as well. "Somethin'll turn up," she said with a positive tone.

As they exchanged their goodbyes, Ted came up the Highland Avenue sidewalk and turned into the front steps and paused. He was surprised to see a young woman talking to his grandmother. "This is Teddy," said Mary. "He's my fifth grader. His father is over in England in the army now."

"Hello, Teddy," said Lily as she extended her hand.

"It's Ted," he responded softly almost under his breath and took Lily's hand.

"Oh lands, I forget sometimes to call him Ted. I'm so used to Teddy."

*You forget all of the time*, thought Ted and smiled at the stranger. There was something slightly familiar about the woman.

"Miss Lake is the second grade teacher at Van Gilder," Mary added.

"Oh, yes," said Ted, "I've seen you in the hall. I thought you looked familiar."

"Your grandmother and I are on a PTA committee, and we met this afternoon to work on the final school-day festival in May," Lily added as she descended the steps. Walking backward along Seventeenth facing Mary, she said, "I'll think about the apartment and be here for certain on that last Saturday for our baking day."

"That'll be grand," Mary said smiling at the young woman. "We'll have fun that day."

---

On Friday morning, the fifth of May, Mary handed Teddy an envelope addressed to Miss Lake. "You be sure and give this to her, and don't forget. Promise?"

"Yes'sum," Ted responded as he picked up his lunch bag, books and headed for the front door where Jerry was waiting on the porch steps. "I've got to deliver this to the second grade teacher," he said to his friend as he waved the envelope.

"Are they putting you back to the second grade?" Jerry teased.

"Naw, she's on a PTA committee with Granny. I guess it's about baking stuff for the fair we have at the end of the year."

Jerry grabbed the envelope and raced ahead crossing Seventeenth Street. A car screeched to a stop narrowly missing the laughing boy. The driver honked at Jerry and yelled through his open window, "Watch it you damn kid, I almost killed you." Jerry shaken by the close call stood on the curb, and Ted grabbed back the envelope as he reached the east side of the street. This time Ted stuck it in his pocket.

"Did you see that old man try and run me down?" blurted Jerry.

"I saw you run in front of him after you stole my envelope," replied Ted.

"No, I knew all the time he was there, and I think he speeded up to hit me."

"No, he had to slam on his brakes or he would have made you a hood ornament on his Hudson." Ted laughed. Jerry took a swipe at Ted, but Ted dodged the effort and started running east on Highland with Jerry in hot pursuit. Both boys reached the school door at the same time, laughing and sweating on the early, humid May morning. As they entered the door and started walking down the hall, Miss Lake came out of her room.

"Hi, Ted," she said.

"Oh, hi, Miss Lake, I have a note for you from Granny," Ted said, blushing slightly.

"Thank you." Lily slid the envelope into her skirt pocket; she would read it at lunch.

---

At four that afternoon, Lily climbed the porch stairs at 1702 Highland for the second time and rang the doorbell.

"Hi," said Ted as he opened the door. "Granny said you were coming. She's upstairs; I'll call her."

Mary came puffing down the stairs and then along the hall to the living room where Lily and Ted stood looking at an old photograph hanging on the wall. "This is some grandmother, I think. I'm not too sure, but . . . ," Ted stumbled in his explanation.

"That's my mother," said Mary, entering the room, "and your great grandmother. I wish you would get that straight. Her name was Mary Gardner, that's before she married my daddy, Chester Wright." Mary was proud of her heritage and would give a lot more information to anyone that even hinted at the slightest interest. But this afternoon was different: she had another message to deliver. "Lily," as she embraced the young woman, "have a seat. Have you found a place to live yet?"

"No," replied Lily, "I'm on a waiting list at two places, but they weren't too encouraging about getting an apartment very soon."

"Well, how about this: we have a spare room upstairs and would love to have you as a boarder. That way you would have access to the bathroom, and that room has a washbasin built in like the one in our room. I don't know why they put those basins in the bedrooms , but they do come in handy. The Gooches across the street have basins in every single bedroom, don't you know. But anyway, do you think that would work?"

"Oh my, I'm a little stunned that you would go out of your way for me like this, but—"

"Let me show you the room before you decide anything for certain," said Mary, rising.

Mary led Lily up the stairs with Ted at the rear.

"Here we are," Mary said opening the door into the room. "We have a large closet over here and there's the sink and you look down on Seventeenth Street from these two windows."

Lily saw a three-quarter-size bed with a bedside table and lamp, a clothes tree, dresser, and two chairs separated by a small table and lamp arranged by the east facing windows. One of the chairs had padded seat and back cushions in bright red corduroy. The windows had curtains tied back at the midpoint of the sash; the curtains were of a mixed blue and green print complimenting the colors of the bedspread. "This is lovely," said Lily, opening the closet door, "absolutely lovely." The light blue walls and area rug in the center of the room completed the room's décor.

"Granddad and I carried all the stuff that was in here down to the apartment out back," said Ted. "There was furniture and some boxes and other junk in here that we took down there; that place is now a mess," he said chuckling.

"We'll deal with that next week," said Mary. "Come across the hall, here's the bathroom."

It didn't take long for the deal to be agreed on between the companionable women. As Lily prepared to leave, they stood by the front door. "I'll give my notice to the manager at the Y and move my clothes here on Sunday if you're sure that's all right."

"Oh, yes. In fact, you call out here Sunday afternoon, and Will can bring the truck down to get you so you don't have to lug your suitcases on the trolley."

"I don't want to put him out any," said Lily.

"He won't mind at all," reassured Mary.

"All right," said Lily, then after pausing, "actually I have boxes of books and pictures that I brought from home and maybe we can get them in the truck as well." The women hugged.

"I'm sure he can get everything in that ole truck."

# CHAPTER 22

## *Knoxville*

## *May 1944*

AS FRANK OPENED the thick envelope, a pictured fluttered to the floor. Picking it up, he saw Ted and his parents standing on the front porch steps at 1702 Highland Avenue. Ted, squinting at the camera, was in the middle of the Kodak image with his arms draped around the shoulders of his grandparents; he stood about four inches taller than his grandmother and about even with his grandfather. The angle of the shot placed Ted's knees at the bottom of the image and seemed to place Ted slightly behind Will. Then it dawned on Frank, they were not standing on the same stair tread. Ted was probably on the top step, his grandmother one step down, and his grandfather two steps down. Bright sunlight highlighted the right side of their bodies and faces, and broad smiles washed over the faces of Ted and Mary. Will had put on his most dignified pose. He even had his right hand tucked into his shirt placket at the top of his belly, à la Napoleon Bonaparte. Frank would have to remember to kid Will about the pomposity of the pose; Will would probably allude to the need to uphold the dignity of the family in sending a picture to France, the home of Bonaparte. Frank put the picture in his wallet for safekeeping.

*Dear Dad,* *May 7, 1944*
*Thank you for the swell letter from England. Granddad joked and said he was going to take me to Bristol and I asked when could we go and he said any day now. Then he said it was Bristol in Tennessee*

*and I said oh Granddad that's not fair I thought you ment England and he said it was a joke but he may take me anyway on Saturday.*

*We have a new lady that is going to live with us. She moved in today. She is Miss Lily Lake she teaches the second grade at Van Gilder and is very nice. Granddad and I cleaned out the room where we had all of those boxes stored and we fixed up the room real nice and she likes it. She is a new teacher and can not find a nother place to live. Granny said the place out back where Leroy lived was not nice enough for her so she had us clean the store room so Miss Lake can use our bathroom. I know you like to get letters and I have asked her to be your pen pal and she said she would like that and is going to put a letter in this one to you.*

*Pensive won the Ky derby this year. Granddad and I listened to it on the radio and he was betting on Stir up and he came in 3. Granddad said he always loses the derby. The horses wait and see who he wants to bet on and then they decide on another horse to win he said it is a consperency (I do not think I spelled that right) against him.*

*I hope your Bristol is nice and you have a good time there and stay there for a long time.*
*Love Ted*

*May 8, 1944*

*Dear Lieutenant Warring,*

*I believe Ted has told you about my new living arrangements here with him and your parents. I feel very fortunate to get the room since I have not found another accommodation in the city on a trolley line or in the Van Gilder neighborhood. I hope I won't be a burden to your family, especially since they are doing such a kind favor for me.*

*Ted suggested that I write to you, which I am very pleased to do. If at any time you have trouble finding time to respond to my letters, I will certainly understand your position over there during the war. Ted tells me you are in the Bristol area, and I am sure it is quite lovely there. I was fortunate to visit England in 1937 for three weeks and enjoyed it very much. Of course, that was before the war and a much safer time to be there. We spent a week in London and then travelled around to Cambridge, Nottingham, Oxford, Brighton, and Bath, which Ted said you have also visited. If you get a chance, you might try and visit an ancient ruin, I believe the oldest in Britain, called Stonehenge and is not very far from Bath.*

*Ted and your mother said they hoped that you get to spend the war in England, and that is certainly my wish for you as well. I wish you the best during these troubled times.*

*Best regards, Lily Lake*

Frank read the two letters with heightened interest. Having a young woman in the house would probably be good for Teddy since she is a teacher and she might be able to provide the kind of help with studying that he had hoped to give him. But then again, he realized he was jumping to conclusions. Why did he assume she was young? She may be in her forties or fifties and white haired and more like Mary, a grandmother type. Well, no matter her personal circumstances, Frank hoped her presence would help stimulate and guide Ted in his school work. That would be a great contribution while he was away.

On the morning of May 8, the Warring family had its first test of the new living arrangements with Miss Lake now residing on Highland Avenue. There was the understanding about the bathroom schedule, that Will and Mary would go first, Lily next, and Ted last, unless Will's schedule changed, which it could do on any given day. When that happened they would have to be polite and still accommodate everybody, albeit in a difference sequence. Lately Will had spent late nights at the plant and got up about eleven o'clock in the morning, much to his chagrin since he was by nature a morning person. On this Monday morning, Will and Mary did make the first bathroom round followed by Lily and then Ted. Lily was the first to leave for Van Gilder so she could get to the building far enough ahead of her students to prepare for the day by arranging her desk with the requisite piles of work sheets she intended to hand out to her charges.

At breakfast she had been early also and helped Mary prepare Will's breakfast and set out a bowl and spoon for Ted. *I think she's right handy in the kitchen*, Mary mused. *She's not goin' to be a burden at all.* The whole week, in fact, passed uneventfully as did the next, as the family absorbed Lily easily into their routine.

On Saturday morning, May 20, Mary and Lily began working in the kitchen at midmorning to cook for the upcoming school-ending assembly and fair. With the oven warming, Mary started mixing the ingredients for the chocolate chip cookies as Lily, sitting at the table, studied her recipes received from Nashville.

"Do you think chocolate drop cookies would go over with the kids?" she asked Mary.

"Anything that has chocolate in it will sell," Mary replied, chuckling.

"I have another recipe for a cinnamon cookie, and if we can find the little red-hot drops at Roberts, then I could decorate the cookies and add a little something extra to them."

"Well, that sounds grand to me. I like cinnamon, and the chance to have a dessert that's not chocolate would be wonderful, as long as it's not a fig cookie."

Ted sauntered into the kitchen and slumped into a chair and began looking at Lily's recipes that she was reading across the table from him. "What's a cin . . . Is that a Cincinnati cookie?" he asked.

"No, cinnamon," Lily replied.

"Oh, I was trying to read it upside down."

"I thought you and Jerry and Floyd were going over to the school to play ball," Mary said from the counter.

"Naw, Jerry got in trouble. He sassed his mother and she's making him wash the windows on the outside on the first floor, so he can't go till she's satisfied. Then Florabelle wanted to go too so

I don't want to go now."

"Is Florabelle the girl down the street?" inquired Lily as she looked at Ted and engaged him in a conversation, something that was coming very easy for both of them now.

"Yes, and she's a hog when it comes to getting her to try and play in the field. All she wants to do is hit the ball, and she won't chase it when she's not at bat. She's a pain to play with."

"And she's a girl," inserted Lily.

"Yeah, she's a girl." Recognizing how his admission sounded, "Now all girls ain't, er . . . aren't bad. Susan can play real well, and she can catch good, as good or better than Floyd," Ted added.

"Is Susan in your grade?" asked Lily with a smile.

"Sure . . . and she's nice, but she's tall too," he added sensing there was an ulterior motive to Lily's probing question. It seemed to him that all women, and now even girls in his class, were always hinting at love or something else that was kind of mushy, something that he didn't think he wanted to think about. He knew that Barbara Hightower was sweet on him, but he thought she was a pain in the neck, kind of like Florabelle. Barbara would hit him sometimes on the arm or chase him on the playground, and once passed him a note. She sat behind him in class, and he could sense her presence even when he tried to ignore her. But she was persistent, that was a word he had learned recently when his teacher said he was persistent in studying geography and drawing maps even when he was supposed to be doing arithmetic.

"Ted's sweet on another little girl. What's her name . . . Nancy?" asked Mary.

Ted's face turned red as he rose and mumbled turning toward the door, "Aw she's OK, I guess."

"Ted, could you do me a favor?" asked Lily.

"Sure," said Ted turning and welcoming a change in the conversation's subject.

"Would you run over to Roberts' Grocery and see if they have any of those little heart shaped, red hot candies? You know, the ones that have the strong cinnamon flavor?"

"Sure."

"Then when you get back, you can help me decorate the cinnamon cookies. Let me get some money from my purse and my ration card if you need it." Lily was on her feet and going up stairs as Ted stuck his finger in his grandmother's batter and then in his mouth.

"I hope your fingers are clean for a change, but the oven will bake out any germs—I hope."

"That's real good," as he bit into a chocolate morsel and a piece of pecan buried in the soft dough.

By lunchtime, Lily was rolling her dough into one-inch balls and Ted was inserting three cinnamon candies into the center of each. As the dough baked, the cookies flattened and rose at the same time as they spread, melting the candies and leaving the red spots somewhere on the top surface of each cookie, but not in a constant pattern.

"That smells good," offered Ted as he peeked inside the oven.

"Don't open the door; you'll let out the heat," Lily spoke up from the sink as she washed her mixing bowl and utensils. "They'll be ready in three minutes. See the clock, when the minute hand reaches twenty-seven, you can take them out, but not before."

"Yes'sum," said Ted as he sat at the table and stared at the clock.

"Have you ever played tennis?" Lily asked as she dried the mixing bowl.

"Oh sure, Jerry and I have hit the ball around the court a lot. I use Dad's old wood racquet. It has a brace and it's not warped at all. It's kind of like a small baseball bat."

"Do you know the rules of tennis?"

"Well, no, I guess not. We just hit that little ball over the net as hard as we can."

"Would you like to learn?"

"Sure," said Ted.

"After the cookies are done and we've had lunch, let's go down to the university's courts and I'll show you the rules and see how well you stroke the ball."

"Stroke the ball? Jerry and I, we hit that little sucker. Sometimes it goes over the fence that's around the court."

"Hitting the ball over the fence in tennis is not exactly a home run, you know. You get no points for that." Ted laughed while Lily continued, "Tennis is as much about where you hit the ball as well as how hard you hit it, so let's have a little fun this afternoon."

"They teach tennis in college?"

"Yes. The list of different subjects you can take in college is almost endless. After you get oriented at the end of the first or second year, you pick a major and then concentrate in the subject area and study it in detail." Lily washed the egg-beater blades and large spoons. "Now, some students come into college knowing what they want to study, but most of us take a little longer to decide since college is a big change from high school."

"Yeah, and I don't even know what high school is like," offered Ted. "I got to finish grade school then junior high school and then go to high school. I'll never get to college. I'll never get out of school."

"Poor boy," moaned Lily in mock sympathy. "You still have a lot of time to find out about what you will do in life." Lily smiled at her ease in talking to Ted, so much easier than talking to her younger sister, June. Was that because he was a boy? *Funny, maybe being an older sister closes June's ears to me. At fourteen she's going through a rough patch. I don't think it would ever be hard to talk to Ted.*

"I want to play baseball in the summer and football in the fall and basketball in the winter," Ted said with casual confidence.

Lily rolled her eyes and realized Ted was years away from understanding about the value of time and schooling, but then at eleven, there was no rush. She knew it didn't do any good to try and push the development of students; it will come in its own time, or rather their time.

"Oh my, look at the clock!" Lily exclaimed. "It's time, Ted. Grab two pot holders and open the oven door slowly and lean back so you don't get the heat in your face . . . Now lift out the sheet . . . Let's see the bottoms of the cookies." Lifting one with a spatula, "They're perfect. Now use the spatula to scoop the cookies onto the wax paper . . . that's right." As Ted worked on the cookie sheet, Lily closed the oven door and turned off the range. "Yes we'll go down and play a set of tennis. I think you'll find it a lot of fun when you know the rules."

Mary sat at the kitchen table with a slight smile on her face as she knitted and listened. *Lily certainly does know a lot about how to talk to Ted. I bet she's a good teacher, and she'll make a good mother someday. I wonder why a girl like her is not married.*

The end of the school year arrived on schedule without any disasters, including the school fair that was determined a success measured by how fast the bake sale sold out all of the donated desserts. The last week of May, Lily caught the Greyhound to Nashville to spend Memorial Day weekend with her parents and middle sister, who had just graduated from East High School, and June, who would enter the ninth grade in September. She returned the first week of June and enrolled in an education class at the University. She continued to be very comfortable in her new surroundings. Being within walking distance of the campus added to her feeling of being at home.

On June 10, Lily received a letter from Frank.

*28 May 1944*

*Dear Miss Lake,*

*It was very nice to receive your letter, and I look forward to further correspondence as time permits between my efforts to win this war, ha, ha, and your efforts to teach small children. I add the laughter since things seem to be very disorganized at times over here while our plans are worked out, but I guess directing the location and movements of a million soldiers must be a daunting task, so I have decided not to complain. I would like to set one ground rule for our letter writing. Let's drop the formal titles and you call me Frank, or any name you prefer, and I'll call you Lily. There, can you stand to live with that level of familiarity?*

*We are still training for (a heavy black line marked out the remainder of the line and the next two lines of the letter), although that can change at a moment's notice. I can't say any more on that subject lest the censors begin to exercise their right to wield the mighty black pen, or maybe it's red, who knows.*

*We have not had time to get to Stonehenge, although the native Brits say it can be a wonderful excursion especially on a clear night with a full moon. I'm not certain what is supposed to happen when the moon comes out, maybe the spirits rise from the earth and dance among the stones. It's a mystery that I will not be able to witness.*

*We did get to walk on the Exmoor moors, and that was quite interesting with the grasses and winds and wild flowers. It's easy to see how it might become very mysterious in the gloom and rain of winter, and one could easily get lost if they strayed from the path. Fascinating countryside here in England.*

*Well, enough of the travel log. I must hit the hay, as we Americans say, or better yet, the cot. One other thing, if you have any friends or other acquaintances who would like to write letters to soldiers, I have added a list with the names of three men in my unit who do not receive mail for one reason or another, and I know they would appreciate a letter from time to time from the States as well as a timely box of cookies. That sounds good. You can add my name on the cookie list as well. Please pass that word on to Mom. Thanks.*

*Warm regards,*

*Frank (formerly known as Lieutenant Franklin Edward Warring)*

*What an engaging letter,* thought Lily as she reread her first letter from Frank. *He certainly seems to be a very nice person and doesn't take things too seriously. I guess we better get busy on the cookie baking again; I'll tell Mary in the morning,* as she snapped off the bedside light and prepared to sleep. *Let's see, maybe some of the unmarried teachers at school. I'll ask, and . . . Oh, maybe June would like to write. I'll ask her too.*

# CHAPTER 23

## *Normandy*

## *July 1944*

AT NOON ON June 30, 1944, Frank and his platoon of fifty one men were packed into three tarp-covered troop trucks with no room to spare. A fourth truck for equipment completed their immediate entourage. The vehicles began a slow lumbering trip over the gouged beach toward high ground that rose up to a grass covered low ridge facing Utah Beach in Normandy. The beach had been the landing site of the US 4$^{th}$ Infantry Division on June 6, D-Day, twenty-four days earlier.

Remnants of the invasion were visible everywhere: demolished tanks, half-tracks, tank destroyers, jeeps, and artillery pieces made up the bulk of the identifiable scrap metal on the beach. Five hundred feet off shore were several destroyed LSTs and other vessels grounded and listing in the waves. The wreckage bore witness to the fierce, initial resistance thrown at the invading Americans by the German defenders. All the human casualties of the landing force had long ago been taken to hospitals for treatment or recovered for burial by the division's morgue unit.

Frank's platoon and one thousand other troops constituted a reinforcing battalion that had been landed to replace men in the 4$^{th}$ Infantry Division lost in the invasion and the subsequent drive toward Germany. Frank realized that the notion of a "drive toward Germany" was a trite phrase he had read in the papers in England that hid the reality of the fierce fighting that he feared lay ahead for his men. There would be nothing leisurely about this drive.

The 4th Division after landing on June 6, had swept west off Utah beach and linked up with the combined 82nd and 101st Airborne Division troops who had parachuted behind enemy lines on the night of June 5, and seized the village of Sainte-Mère-Église. German field commanders had devised a strategy to retake the village and then drive east to push the American force back to the beach. But before their initiative could begin, the combined paratroopers and 4th Division troops struck the Germans, deadening the effects of the planned counterattack. In the American thrust, they captured senior German field commanders, thus adding to the confusion among the Third Reich's chain of command following the invasion.

The once pretty village was now pitted and scarred by mortar shells and rifle fire, visible results of its capture by the airborne troops and its subsequent defense. It lay as a crossroads on the main road between Saint-Lô and the northern port city Cherbourg. With the successful defense of Sainte-Mère-Église, the combined US troops continued to drive west to the coast across the Cotentin Peninsula and then north to liberate Cherbourg, which they did on the twenty-seventh of June. Having secured a port, they then pivoted to the south and were in the process of clearing German forces entirely from the remainder of the peninsula. The new line of battle now taking shape at the peninsula's south end had the combined 4th and 1st Divisions that had linked up to form a growing wall with the Canadian and British troops that hoped to push rapidly east across France.

The 1st Division had gone ashore at Omaha Beach, east of Utah. Compared to Utah Beach, Omaha had been a near disaster because the slowly sloping sea floor that swept toward the open channel left a long stretch of water too shallow for LST landing craft to get close to the beach and too deep for many of the soldiers and heavy pieces of equipment to successfully cross. The slow progress toward shore hampered by high tide and heavy waves provided ample opportunity for German gunners occupying the bluffs adjoining the beach to lay down a deadly fire on the advancing Americans. The sheer weight of the attacking force had, however, overcome the defenders, and the 1st Division seized control of Omaha at the end of the first day but at a dear price in men's lives; many men did not live through their first and only day of combat.

The rain began to fall as the trucks bearing Frank's men passed through the village of Sainte-Mère-Église. The four-truck entourage had joined a long string of vehicles and motorized equipment moving south toward the front. South of the village of Carentan, the convoy moved to the side of the road and halted as military police raced along the road leading a string of jeeps and troop trucks to the south.

"That must be the brass going to set up HQ so they can tell us where the hell we are supposed to go fight," remarked Sergeant Johnson, who sat on the side bench in the first truck with Frank and the A Squad.

"You'll find out soon enough," responded Sergeant St. John. Twenty-eight-year-old Sergeant Alcie St. John was a Southern-born boy from Montgomery, Alabama, with a reputation for being a staunch Baptist because he did not swear, did not chase the young women of Britain during their brief encampment there, and did not smoke or drink. Despite these eccentricities, the Sarge—or as Frank called him, the Saint—was respected by his men for his calm and sensible handling of both men and tactical situations.

The Saint had spent four months in Italy with the 5th Army pushing the Germans from the US landing site at Salerno north to Cassino. As the only veteran with actual combat experience in the platoon, Frank had learned to value the Saint's advice during their four months of training in England. The Saint was the leader of the A Squad. Frank's three other squad leaders were Sergeants Dupuy, Garrison, and Johnson, called Frenchy, Fran, and AJ by Frank.

Before the convoy could resume its southward trek, a string of northbound trucks passed, bearing men from the 101st Airborne Division. To a person they looked dazed or asleep. They sat in their open trucks oblivious to the mist and darkening sky. Unshaven and battered, they were wasted soldiers. Frank's men observed their countrymen in silence as they realized the men of the 101st were a prophetic omen of their future. The silence grew heavy.

When the road cleared, the convoy resumed its slow travel to the south and then west as the trucks turned toward the town of Periers. The countryside was defined by a unique formation of distinctive earthen hedgerows about six feet high that seemed to enclose every agricultural field. Trees and dense undergrowth grew from the sides and tops of the hedgerows bordering both sides of the road. Tree limbs formed an almost continuous canopy over the road. Except for the earthen mounds, the tree canopy reminded Frank of the similar tree canopy over country roads in the Bluegrass between Frankfort and Lexington. But he couldn't dwell on home now. A jostling bump in the road shattered his recollection and he returned to the present moment in France and the bitter prospects that lay ahead.

Openings in the hedgerows revealed enclosed crop fields and pastures of several acres. At some places, the hedgerows had been crudely ripped open by explosions or heavy equipment, revealing signs of intense recent fighting. Frank had heard in England during their training exercises that ingenious American mechanics had welded extra steel plates to the front of tanks converting them into make-do earth movers capable of plowing through the hedgerows, thus opening them for attack. Perhaps these openings had been gouged by such innovative maneuvers.

As the dark afternoon fell into the blackness of night, the trucks came to a halt and the men clambered onto the damp ground, formed up, and started marching south through the continuing mist. After an hour they reached the edge of a headquarters encampment and were instructed to set up sleeping tents for the night. Hot food was available in the camp's mess tent, a welcome relief from the cold unwelcoming French weather.

Frank also found two letters waiting for him.

*Dear Dad,* *June 1, 1944*

*I have made the team in baseball, yeah, yeah. I play second base for the Cubs and Jerry plays right field on the Giants. We are in a Kiwanis league with the Braves, Reds, Pirates, Giants, and Dodgers. We did not have enough players for the Cardinals and Phillies. I wanted to get on the Reds but I got picked first by the Cubs so I guess I will stay there and play as good as I can. We won our first game with the Reds and then lost to the Giants so we are 1 and 1 as they say on the sports page. I have two hits, five strike outs and three walks and some more outs too. The Smokies are third in the Southern Association and Granddad and Lily and Granny and I have been to a game with the Lookouts and it was fun. I had a weenie on a bun, they call it a redhot, and a Hires root beer that's the best.*

*Lily asked me if I would like for her to read my letters and help me with periods and capitals and spelling and things like that and I said yes that would make me feel better about writing since I known sometimes I make mistakes that I should not make. She is real nice with her corrections or improvements as she calls them.*

*I hope you are safe and staying out of fighting over there wherever you are.*

*Your Loving Son, Ted*

*June 2, 1944*

*Dear Frank,*

*Yes, I believe we can drop the formal greetings in letters since I am living in your house and getting to know your loving family quite well. I have fallen in love with Ted, but alas, you should not worry as a parent. I do believe I am too old to wait for him since I will be thirty-seven by the time he reaches twenty-one. But seriously, he is a lovely boy, and ALL BOY at that, with baseball, a grimy hat, and dirty jeans, not to mention those foul tennis shoes he wears. Mary says it's time to learn to hold our noses as he passes through this phase and that all her boys, including a soldier in Europe, did so successfully without getting stuck permanently in the dirty, smelly phase. Sound familiar?*

*Ted and I have played several games of tennis; I am teaching him the rules of the game. He shows some promise, but your old racquet is awfully heavy for him. He could improve his game with a lighter-weight model, but that can wait until he shows a real love for the game. Right now and through July, his attention will be drawn to King Baseball.*

*I have enrolled in a summer class at UT, and I am either working on a master's degree or just taking continuing education classes. Neither I nor my advisor has decided yet which course I am pursuing. The whole education administration seems a little arbitrary if you ask me, but the university is not asking me.*

*Mary sent a big box of cookies last Thursday. I hope they find you before long and that you and the other men enjoy them. I have given out all the names of your men that you said would like to have pen pals; my kid sister is one of the "pals." She has the name of Corporal Henson, the boy from Central City, Kentucky. I do hope all of you are safe. I include you and your men in my prayers at night.*

*With affection, Lily*

*So, Lily is twenty-eight . . . no, twenty-seven. I wonder why she isn't married. Maybe she was and her husband was killed in the war. Hum, probably not. Then again, maybe she is not a raving beauty but more on the plain side, but who knows . . . It's hard to tell what Ted's batting average is, but as long as he has fun, that's the important thing. He certainly won't be a pro player like he wants to be, not with inheriting my ordinary athletic skills . . . I wonder what Lily looks like. Should I ask her to send a picture? No, that might spoil any illusions I may come up with over here, and right now illusions about girls or women at home are a useful distraction. Anyway, I guess she's a woman and not a girl.*

After reading the letters, the gloomy spell cast by the French countryside was easier to bear.

---

By sunrise the camp was fully awake with food already served to Frank's unit and other platoons, which had formed up again and were marching south to take up positions along the line of attack. By 10:30 AM they had been led to their position and Frank was briefed on the day's planned incursion into the German line. Frank's platoon and those to the right and left were to form the right, or west flank, of the probe to the south. He was informed that tank support would not be available to his platoon; the tanks would be concentrated in the center of the attack. The larger strategy was to strike south toward Periers and break through the German line, or failing a breakthrough, to turn the Germans to the east toward Saint-Lô.

The platoon's first day of combat proved to be a harsh taste of the reality of war. Two men were killed and five wounded, requiring evacuation to the field hospital near Sainte-Mère-Église. Three of the wounded men would return in a day after medical attention. The other two wounded soldiers were taken to a hospital in England for long-term care; they did not return. The casualties had occurred as his men attempted their first attack in the hedgerow environment. In the initial encounter of the day, Frank's rifle platoon was ordered to take the enclosed field to the right of a narrow country lane. A second rifle platoon was to take the field on the left side. Part of a light weapon platoon with 60mm mortars and machine guns also supported the two rifle units. Frank and his fellow platoon officer, Lieutenant Gary Rosen, conferred behind an earth and log barrier thrown across the lane.

Both platoons faced hedgerows ringing their respective targets with German machine gun emplacements in the far corners of the fields. An unknown number of German infantrymen were also placed at unknown locations along the far sides of the enclosing hedgerows, thus adding to the enemy's firepower. From their covered position, the enemy could rake the entire field with a deadly spray of fire. Another German gun emplacement had been thrown up behind a temporary mound of earth pushed across the lane at the far end of the fields. That position blocked any attempt to circle around the hedgerows along the lane. The setting was ideal for defense and hellish for an attacking army.

Frank, Gary, the Saint, Frenchy, AJ, and three other sergeants conferred in the lane. They knew their options for attack were to go over the top of the hedgerows, which could be deadly for their troops, knock down the hedgerow if they could devise a way to blow a gap in the six foot wall of earth, or finally, eliminate the enemy's lane-blocking guns and attempt to encircle the fields. It was decided that the platoon's first objective was to eliminate the lane-blocking machine-gun emplacement located behind the earthen barrier some three hundred feet in the distance.

In the meantime, both the attacking platoons and the defending Germans had set up mortar fire that was zeroing in on their foe's positions. As the men conferred, a Jeep drove rapidly south toward the platoons, and an American major stepped smartly from the vehicle and asked abruptly, "Who's in charge here?"

"I am," said Frank from his prone position, "the second platoon."

"And I am," responded Rosen, "third platoon."

"What are you doing in the dirt? Get up and lead your men," snapped the major.

"We think it's better to lead from down here," answered Frank.

"You are leaders and you can't lead from a ditch sitting on your ass," snapped the major.

"I beg to differ," said Frank. "Why don't you come down here and we can talk."

"Nonsense, stand up," came the reply as a mortar shell landed on the side of the hedgerow twenty feet in front of the Jeep. The Jeep driver dove to the ground, and the major found himself in the dirt along with his junior officers. "I see . . . ," he said and dusted the dirt from his crisp uniform. "How are you going to advance?"

"First, we're going to try and out flank them," said Frank.

"Right," said the major, "but don't rule out a charge, and remember we are counting on you men to keep pace with the rest of the line. We've got to push the Krauts out of these hedgerows." The major ordered the driver to turn the Jeep around, and when he had accomplished that from a position hunched over the steering wheel, the major jumped into the passenger seat and they sped north to safety.

"What kind of chicken-shit officer was that?" blurted Rosen. "'Remember to charge.' Wasn't that helpful now? Where did he get his training, on the back of a box of Wheaties? He could get men killed if they don't send him back to England. That son of a bit . . . ," Rosen's complaints were muffled by a series of mortar shells landing to the left, and he buried his face in the Normandy dirt.

After conferring more, the officers zeroed in on eliminating the road barricade as the first step in their plan of attack. The Saint suggested that a one-man sneak attack along the top of the hedgerow berm with fire to distract the enemy would be worth trying before a full frontal assault on the road barricade. Because the men were not battle tested yet, he volunteered to demonstrate his idea. The Saint stuffed grenades in his pockets and, running close to the ground, broke for the hedgerow and secured a position on the top of the berm. He then began crawling at a very slow pace along its top toward the mortar position. His pace of inching toward the enemy guns was faster than a snail but slower than a meandering stroll.

To occupy the attention of the enemy blocking the lane, the two platoons kept up a steady fire from behind their barrier and from the roadside ditches. The machine guns concentrated on the lane barricade, and the mortars were used to fire at the fields as well as taking shots at the barricade. If detected, the Saint had few options for escape. If he rolled into the field on the back side of the hedgerow and away from the lane, he would be exposed to fire from Germans in the far corners of that field. His only option was to proceed undetected until he could launch a surprise attack on the lane barricade.

At one point he must have caused a disturbance in the undergrowth, as an alert German saw a suspicious movement in the tangle of weeds, briars, and bramble. A blast of gunfire ripped into the ground two feet in front of the Saint and then sprayed the ground for another five feet farther away from his position. He froze. He knew binoculars were scanning the top of the hedgerow. This position was somewhat akin to deer hunting in the Alabama woods, where the deer might sense the presence of a human, but in Alabama the deer did not have guns; he was in the middle of a reciprocal life-and-death struggle.

After remaining motionless for what seemed like an eternity, the Saint continued to inch forward, being even more careful to avoid movement in the brush. The German gunner had evidently satisfied himself that he had been mistaken in firing at the hedgerow. He probably reasoned that the movement he saw out of the corner of his eye was caused by a squirrel or bird taking flight. To divert the Germans from looking at the hedgerow, Frank ordered two men to alternately take a quick jump toward the hedgerow, fire, and drop to the ground before the German machine guns could respond. This done, the enemy returned fire as Frank, Rosen, and the men hugged the ground.

At a yard past the back edge of the German lane barricade, the Saint reached the cover provided by a dense mass of undergrowth between two tree trunks. Studying the height of the brush and the space below the overhanging branches, he estimated he had a window of three feet to throw his grenades through. They had to be thrown high enough to go over the brush and yet not bounce off the tree limbs and fall back toward him. This would be a challenge, but not unlike some basketball shots he had tried in high school. As a somewhat shorter player, he was often confronted with the raised hands of a taller player that he had to shoot over but then not go so high or hard that he missed the goal and backboard.

He decided not to think about all of the missed and misjudged goals as he pulled the pins from two grenades and lobbed them in quick succession over the brush. He hugged the ground for cover on their release and the two almost simultaneous explosions. The first grenade found a clear path through the hedgerow growth and bounced twice on the road before it rolled and exploded. The second clipped the overhanging branch and spun lazily through the air exploding a foot from the ground. The Saint released himself from his safe ground position, rolled to his right into a kneeling position on his right knee with his left foot firmly planted for support of the Thompson as it spat out the contents of the first magazine. The hedgerow to his rear now afforded protection from the German machine gunner behind him who now realized he had, in fact, spotted the enemy but failed to eliminate the threat.

The surprise attack stunned the Germans in the lane as the Thompson sprayed the gray clad troops. Having expended his first magazine, the Saint slammed a second into the gun and prepared to continue to rake the German position. He did not need to fire again. Three soldiers lay dead, two more wounded lay writhing in shock on the dusty road, and the final four, all officers who had stood twenty feet behind the barricade, had their hands raised in surrender.

At the sound of the exploding grenades and the burst of fire from the Thompson, men from the two platoons charged at a full run from the ditches and barricades and soon joined the Saint in disarming the captives. The captives were marched to the rear, the wounded tended to by medical corpsmen, and later that afternoon the dead were recovered for burial by a morgue unit.

Having cleared the lane blockage, the platoon assumed firing positions along the hedgerows to the right and left, popping up and firing into the remaining enemy gun emplacements and then diving for cover before return fire. The light weapon's platoon was also used to good advantage as they zeroed in their mortar fire to pick off several enemy firing positions. But at this rate the battle may extend into the night, not an acceptable option.

At 1300 hours Frank received word that a single Sherman tank was approaching from the north to assist in their assault. When sighted, jubilation among the rifle platoons soared as the tank had a dozer blade welded to its front end. Frank, Gary, and the tank commander conferred, then the tank surged forward and began gouging a hole in the hedgerow barrier. The earth was ripped apart as it gave way to the ferocity of the tank's forward thrusts. Frank and his men formed up behind the mobile steel shield as it barreled into the now open field with its machine gun and cannon blasting observed German hiding positions. Frank's rifle platoon stayed behind the tank as long as possible, but as they moved farther into the field, they were exposed to enemy fire and forced to take cover in the dense grass and to return fire at the German positions. The final frenzy of the attack saw the green troops hurl themselves across the field, resulting in their casualties, the capture a dozen Germans and winning the ground. The Sherman pulled out of the field, moved east, and led Gary Rosen's platoon in taking the second field to the east.

In the afternoon Frank's and Gary's platoons joined three other platoons all operating under Captain Cooper. The company surged through, around and over a heavily wooded terrain, and pushed the stubborn enemy slowly south. Although the American command had assumed the quality of the German forces would be inferior to the crack Panzer units the Wehrmacht had used to invade France, the low countries, Poland, and Russia, Frank's first taste of battle convinced him they still faced a potent enemy, one to be respected. His platoon had suffered casualties at the expense of moving one quarter of a mile south. If this was to be a typical result of fighting, it promised to be a tough, slow trip to Periers, eight miles distant. Could they survive the four hundred miles to Germany?

# CHAPTER 24

## *Operation Cobra, Normandy*

## *July 1944*

By JULY 20, Frank's platoon had lost half of the men that came by truck from Utah Beach to the front line on June 30. Twenty were wounded and four dead; two of the deaths were believed to be from friendly fire that occurred during the frenzy of a fire fight. Captain Cooper was wounded and out of action, along with two of the five lieutenant platoon leaders including Rosen. Frank had escaped the enemy's fire. Similarly, the devastated 82$^{nd}$ and the remainder of the 101$^{st}$ Airborne Division troops had been withdrawn to England to recover from severe losses and integrate replacement troops as they trained for the next airborne jump into the war zone. The remains of Cooper's company were withdrawn from battle for two days of rest at a camp outside Carentan. Frank, now temporarily leading the decimated company, brought the survivors into camp and received new recruits to be incorporated into the depleted platoons and squads. Frank had given the temporary command of his platoon to the Saint. Frenchy and AJ had been evacuated to England for treatment of wounds, but each promised to return as soon as possible. Neither officer would return to the fighting. Frenchy was shipped to the states minus his left lower arm and hand. AJ died on the operating table and was buried in the American cemetery in Cambridge, north of London. Before the fighting ended, AJ would be joined by 3,800 of his countrymen.

Frank checked on mail and found two letters but no cookies from Knoxville. He knew letters could get through the morass of war, but as for cookies, that remained to be seen. He was encouraged that each of the men named on the list he had sent to Lily now received letters. Corporal Henson was especially pleased; he now had a girl in Nashville who cared enough about him to write. The fact that she was only fourteen didn't bother him.

"What's her name?" asked Frank.

"It's June Lake," said Henson. "Ain't that a pretty name? Thank you, Lieutenant, for setting up her as my pen pal. You know, Central City's not too far from Nashville. Maybe I can visit her after this war is over and thank her for writing me."

"That would be a good idea. Do you have paper to write her a letter?"

"Yes, sir, I got some from the chaplain, and an envelope too. Now, he's a real nice fella."

"Yes, you can trust chaplains to have your best interest in mind. Now, generals, well they may be a different thing altogether," said Frank with a straight face.

"Yes, sir," smiled Henson, "we got to look out for the generals." Frank laughed. "But, now, the captains and lieutenants, there're on our side, I mean us rifle toters' side." Henson laughed and his dark eyes sparkled. "You know I really was glad to get to go in the army last winter. It got me off that farm where I was living, or where the county put me. As soon as I was eighteen years old, I joined up. And I got to see some of the country, and now the world, bein' over here in France now."

"Were you living with your family on the farm?"

"Oh, no. My daddy was a tenant farmer in Muhlenberg County, near Central City, and he did some strip minin' too, and then . . . he got caught in a bad blast of dynamite when they was clearin' some rock to get to the coal." Henson's face was now very somber. "He was half buried in big rock pieces. At his funeral they kept his coffin closed, but Momma looked like she was already dead on the inside. It was as if she wanted to crawl in his coffin with him. She never did get right in her mind after he died. The county sent us to the poor farm, but then she took the flu and died in the winter, and the county sent me to the Cudliffe farm and sent my little brother and sister to some other homes in Central City and Greenville. The Cudliffes, they made out as how I was through the eighth grade, it was time for me to work full-time on the farm. So that's what I done for the last four years, and that's why I left them Cudliffes as soon as I could. I guess it's because of where I come from that I was so glad to get to go to Fort Benning." A slight smile brought life back into his eyes. "Most of that basic training was easy as pie after comin' off the farm. When you chop weeds and bale hay and walk to town, well, it weren't nothin' to do the army exercises and go for long walks with gear on our backs. And getting to learn about rifles and grenades and bayonets was all very interesting. Oh, you know the best part was the money and the food. I could spend money in Columbus, and they had good food and all you could eat. I've grown an inch taller since January, and they had to give me bigger boots." Henson laughed aloud. "Aw shucks, Lieutenant, here I am talking off your arm, just jabberin' away. My friends in the squad all say I'm a jabberbox, and I guess I am," he continued, laughing.

"I see we not only fed you well, but I know you earned that promotion to corporal. We're all proud of you and the way you took control of the squad when you were ambushed. You've developed into a real trustworthy man in your squad and platoon."

"Why, thank you very much, Lieutenant. Those are real kind words."

"Well, they're the truth."

"Thank you. I best go catch up with my buddies so I can get a decent place to sleep tonight." The lanky corporal ambled off with long strides, clutching June's letter in his hand.

As Frank watched the boy walk away, the thought occurred to him of how many of his men came from very different backgrounds. Yet they were all equal when they entered battle. Henson's life had been harder on him before he entered the military, in stark contrast to Frank's boyhood in Millersburg. While he didn't come from wealth, he did have an education and loving, nurturing parents. Yet Henson with his underprivileged life was bound to be a fine man when he got home; that is, if he survived the war.

Frank found a quiet spot and sat down to read his mail.

*Dear Dad* *June 30, 1944*

*Granny got sick two weeks ago but is feeling better now. She was in the hospital for four nights, and the doctor let her come home because she was strong and causing trouble in the hospital. Granddad said they were glad to see her go. She stays up all day now, not like when she was sick when she would stay in bed. Lily does the cooking now, and I help. I know how to cook hot breakfasts and make Campbell soup and grilled cheese and hamburgers, I think.*

*The Cubs have now won eight games and lost seven. We are tied for third spot. I play some at 2nd base and some at left field. Coach wants me to try pitching but I told him I don't know how to throw a curve ball and he said that was ok since no one else in the league knows how. So I will try pitching and see if I can help from walking the other team's batters. We practice tonight and play tomorrow night. Nobody likes to practice. We all like to play.*

*How is the war coming along? I read the papers sometime with Granddad and sometimes with Lily. We read about Normandy and the awful time you soldiers had over there. I hope you are all right.*

*Love Ted*

*June 30, 1944*

*Dear Frank,*

*As Ted has told you, Mary was sick. She had a case of pneumonia, and as a precaution she spent four nights at Fort Sanders. She was not a happy patient and apparently tried to improve the operation of the fourth floor nursing staff and the dinner food, which did not win her any friends. They are shorthanded, with people in the service, and*

*I think she just didn't feel well and took out her miseries on the staff. But now she is feeling much, much better and has a sunny disposition and only a slight cough. When she came home, Ted and I fixed her old-fashion chicken-noodle soup by boiling real chicken bones, and that did wonders for her. My grandmother swears chicken-noodle soup will cure most ills for people if they eat enough of it. She may be right, because Mary perked up very fast. She also had a good dose of medicine at the hospital, which may have reinforced the effects of the soup.*

*Our eating habits have changed some now since I am doing most of the cooking. I don't fix a lot of fried foods. We baked a chicken on Sunday. Ted said it looked like a small Thanksgiving turkey, and I think he was right. Will brought home a beef tongue that we baked, and it was very good. He said Mary was not terribly fond of tongue but he prevailed on her to try some, and she seemed to enjoy it. Will announced last night he may go to the market and get some brains to fix with eggs. I have absolutely no idea how to cook brains. When he told Mary, she threw a pillow at him and he ducked into the hall and about had a fit laughing.*

*My course at the university is getting boring, and thank goodness I am over half way through with it. I can't wait for it to end.*

*I hope you and your men are continuing to be safe and well. Everything is fine here: we just had a little scare with Mary for a few days.*

*With affection, Lily*

Frank couldn't help but laugh aloud at Lily's description of his mother in the hospital and the tussle over the dinner menu. Somehow he didn't worry about his mother now that Lily was living in the house. Was he fooling himself with a false sense of comfort about the conditions in Knoxville? He wasn't certain, but the one thing he did know was that if she wasn't there in the house, and Will and Ted were caring for Mary alone, then he would have a lot of worrying to do. In any case there was nothing he could do from his post in France. *It's not like I can run home for a quick leave like when I went home for Dad's high blood pressure attack. Nope, I'm stuck here, but I'm not going to worry about Mom; I think she's in good hands now that Lily's there.*

During July the line of attack had moved slowly, and at times painfully so, to the south with the town of Saint-Lô having finally been taken after a bloody struggle by the 1st Division on July 13. The 4th Division's progress toward Periers had been less successful, as the front was still two miles north of the town. Except for the town of Saint-Lô, the road connecting Saint-Lô and Periers was still under German control. Daylight hours saw little activity along the road, as frequent American attacks by P-47 fighters rendered it useless. But at night the Germans were able to use it to their advantage for moving troops and equipment parallel to the line of battle.

The two days of rest at Carentan saw a new company commander arrive, Captain Henry Schmidt. With his arrival, Frank returned to his platoon, and the Saint to his squad. In briefing the platoon leaders about the next phase of the attack, Schmidt described what Central Command had named it, Operation Cobra. There was to be a massive aerial and artillery assault parallel to the front along the road between Saint-Lô and Periers, followed by a troop surge to punch through the damaged German defenses.

The aerial bombardment was to be at a scale not previously seen in the campaign in northwest France. July 24 was the kickoff day for the Cobra bombardment and troop surge to coincide with the cessation of bombing. Cobra was patterned after British General Montgomery's Operation Goodwood that had used massive bombing support in mid-July to soften the enemy before attacking east of the coastal city of Caen at the eastern end of the Allied Normandy invasion line. Montgomery had been satisfied with modest ground gains to the east as he continued to tie down major portions of German Panzer divisions on the western front.

General Eisenhower, according to Schmidt, intended to have

Bradley and his 1st Army follow the Cobra bombardment with an all-out assault west of Saint-Lô to break through the German defenses. The 4th Division, including Frank's men, was to become part of the newly designated 3d Army under the command of General George Patton. Patton was now on the ground in France, preparing to take active control of the army on August 1. Once in operation, the 3d Army would fight alongside the 1st Army and join in the all-out surge between Saint-Lô and Periers. Captain Schmidt, in describing the designation of Patton's role in the 3d Army, reminded his junior officers that Patton's nickname was Old Blood and Guts, a name he had earned on the battlefield in North Africa and Italy.

The morning of the twenty-fourth dawned with rain and clouds in the forecast, and word was passed down the chain of command that Cobra would be moved back one day, with the bombardment and ground attack now to occur on the twenty-fifth. Frank and his platoon occupied a hilltop position on the twenty-fifth along with a forward air controller who had direct connection to the Tactical Air Command center. When Cobra began, the initial wave of P47s and dive bombers darted in precision over the front line, dropping bomb after bomb in an aerial dance of death. Dive bombers seemed to plunge straight toward the ground with a precision release of weapons directly on their intended target, miraculously swooping into a near vertical climb to fly away from both enemy fire and the explosion of their dropped munitions.

The twenty-minute-long softening-up period was but a prelude to the main act, as the sky seemed to darken with the high altitude B-17 bombers approaching from the northeast. The roar of the planes and the cascading waves of explosions they set off were as awe inspiring as it was dreadful, as Frank realized there were men like himself trying to survive under the rain of death. German anti-aircraft guns began firing at the bombers, and ground observers soon saw several bombers start a tumbling fall to earth, leaving a trail of white and then black smoke in the blue sky. The aerial gnats of the Army Air Force, unarmed Piper Cubs, were soon flying overhead as slow speed, low-altitude artillery observers, spotting the location of tell-tale smoke reports from German anti-aircraft guns. Their positions were radioed to the silencing accuracy of the American artillery gunneries positioned north of Frank's platoon.

The wave after wave of B-17s continued for an hour to pummel the front line along the highway. Pushed by a south breeze, the dust and smoke set off by the havoc began drifting north into the American line. The B-17s were followed by an equally massive onslaught by B-26s, as the aerial bombardment continued unabated. Frank could look to the northeast and see the train of bombers continuing to snake across the French sky toward their delivery line in front of the American troops.

As minutes passed, the bomb cargos dropped by the B-26s seemed to be drifting north along with the dust and smoke, as the sound of exploding bombs grew louder and came closer and closer to the 1st and 4th Division troops. The line of scarred earth created by the bombardment was definitely widening toward the American troops. Soon the sound of the exploding bombs was too close, and troops were taking the best cover they could; men dove into foxholes and under trucks, or just hugged the ground as the scythe of death was turned on them.

The forward air controllers screamed into their radios, but they could not call back bombs already released. The concussions of the bombs were devastating as they fell among American soldiers. The ground heaved around the bomb craters, and thrusts of the explosions sent shockwaves sideways, as well as straight up and all angles in between. Those souls hit by bombs were instantly obliterated; those some distance from the crater and on the ground surface suffered one or more of head injuries, concussions, broken bones, lost limbs, or permanent deafness. Those lucky enough to be in foxholes but too close to the crater would emerge with blood coming from their nose and ears, as the earth saved them from instant death but inflicted lingering physical and psychological injuries that would take time to heal, if they ever did.

Frank's platoon was too near the bombs to escape being hit. Not as badly as some units, but bad enough, considering one death or maiming was too much. The medics swarmed over the scene as the heavy bombers flew southwest before turning north to return to their bases in England. Frank's platoon had two deaths of the total 111 American troops killed that day by friendly fire and eight of the almost 500 injured troops that required evacuation.

To Frank's surprise, the American artillery had picked up the bombardment as the B-26s departed. Then the B-17s that had landed in Britain returned for a second bombing run, followed by the heavily armed P-47 fighters as bombing of German positions continued into the afternoon. Frank's entire platoon pitched in to tend to the dead and, more so, care for the wounded. Frank received a message from his radioman. He was now in command of the company of 200 men, or at least in command of all those who were still battle ready. Captain Schmidt was killed when the division command center took direct hits from the American aircraft. In addition to the field officer casualties, the Americans suffered a great loss in the death of their chief of the Army Ground Forces, General Lesley McNair. The General had come to a forward position to observe the intense bombardment. Frank received a field promotion to the rank of captain from his new immediate superior officer, Major Wychek. Frank stared at the message and, for the first time, imagined that he in fact may not survive the war. He had, of course, understood that possibility as a soldier fighting in a war, but the real essence of that probability had not seeped into his being. It was now there, and he could do nothing about it.

By midafternoon the bombardment ended, and despite the devastation among the American troops, the order came down to advance south. Frank briefed his platoon leaders, and the company formed up and prepared to move south into battle, leaving their dead and wounded in the hands of the medical corpsmen.

The first mile of the company's movement into the bombed

area brought them into a different landscape, one with tree trunks of varying heights, but with few limbs and only scattered, torn remnants of leaves. The ground had lost half its green vegetation and was littered with plants that had thrived across the landscape only hours before. The troops passed a number of enemy bodies, wrecked gun emplacements, and destroyed vehicles. Some of the dead soldiers were recognizable only because of the remnants of uniform still clinging to the bloodied bodies. They passed a small farm with destroyed buildings, and Frank said a prayer for the occupants and hoped they weren't at home when the bombing started. As his platoon marched south, they entered an open field. There were remnants of demolished hedgerows around the oblong pasture; large gaps had been blown in the hedgerows, in other places the earth barriers remained as short mounds emerging from the ground.

Frank walked on the eastern edge of the cratered field where he came across piles of body parts, a casual scattering of recently living and breathing beings that had been ripped and wrenched to pieces in the horrific blasts: arms, legs, torsos, feet, shoulders, and parts of heads. All showed signs of the tearing and severing; there were few intact bodies. American bombs had made a direct hit on a cluster of men. Perhaps they had been officers, perhaps enlisted or drafted grunts; it was hard to tell, death was a somber equalizer of rank. A brown sheen covered patches of the green debris near the body parts. Frank stumbled and fell to the ground catching his body with outstretched palms. As he drew up his left knee to stand he looked at his palms and saw that the brown sheen was blood layered on the pulverized green leaves and grasses. Frank looked at his entangled right foot and saw that he had stumbled over a partially covered lower human torso that still had both legs and feet intact, except for the toes on one bare foot. Frank's right boot had been grabbed by the entrails of the dead soldier; the guts wrapped around his leather-covered ankle. Frank sank to his knees and in an involuntary gesture to the gruesome scene vomited the limited contents of his stomach into the grass, adding his waste to the corruption.

As he recovered, he rose and stumbled on through the human debris now with a throbbing head that threatened to blind his eyes to the gory scene. He had the bitter taste of bile in his mouth, an apt companion that day with death. At the edge of the field, his company came upon more dead soldiers and dead horses that had been used to pull heavy German field artillery that lay nearby in crumpled, tangled heaps of steel. Farther along they passed bodies of Charolais cattle ripped apart by the blasts. The cattle were probably animals the Germans had confiscated as food for their troops; now they would rot as scars of the bombardment while nature slowly healed the landscape from man's brutal intrusion. The humans, horses, and cattle would feed the scavengers of the air and ground for days to come. Frank didn't think long about the feasting that would occur; he rejected the devastating sights that he so wanted to get away from. He and his troops trudged through the shattered world, hoping the effort and the time spent walking would help erase the memory of carnage left behind.

As he walked, a flicker of a remembered phrase passed across his consciousness, something about unleashing the "mad hounds of war that ravaged the countryside." *What was that line . . . was it part of a verse . . . who wrote it?* He could not recall. Was it from one of his college literature classes, high school senior English? No memory, too long ago. Now he wasn't certain if he had heard the phrase or just made up that analogy.

Most of the live German soldiers found that day were so stunned they seemed to welcome being captured and removed from this field of hell. Those who bothered to think about the situation reasoned that prison camp would be a vast improvement over what they had survived. Many who had bought into Hitler's Aryan race dictum had now ceased to care. They marched in a docile column north under a scant American guard. They were not going to try to escape or cause trouble; they wanted peace and quiet, warm food, and a place to sleep other than the unforgiving ground mattress and bedsprings of rock. Frank could feel no special pity for them, but still, they were a piteous lot.

There were some pockets of German resistance, but these were quickly surrounded and held at bay until they surrendered or were wiped out. The Americans this day were not prone to show much mercy to an enemy who resisted. During the afternoon, Frank's men corralled sixty-four prisoners and pinned down two other pockets of resistance who were added in short order to the count of German dead. Tanks and tank destroyers joined the attack in the sector by 1500 hours, and the pace of the advance increased. Troops using bazookas were also in action, as numerous Tiger tanks were destroyed. The German Tiger tanks with thicker armament and heavier cannons were superior to the American Shermans in one-on-one combat. Advantages accrued to the Shermans included their superior number and the ability of maintenance crews to repair damaged units, often with field adaptations, to keep them in the battle.

As Frank's company approached the road between Saint-Lô and Periers, German artillery opened up on them, forcing a retreat to the north side of the road where they dug into the fresh earth so recently tilled by the B-17s and B-26s. Digging was easy in this location, and they would spend the night watching for a German counterattack that did not materialize.

In concert with troops to the right and left, tanks, supporting artillery, and almost immediate on-call response from P-47s, Frank's men crossed the road the following day, July 26, and secured high ground five miles to the south for the night's vigil. They had come into contact with the dreaded Panzer Lehr troops and their Tiger tanks, but the air cover provided by P-47s had a remarkable effect on the Germans, as they backed off from a major encounter. The American superiority in the air was proving to Frank, and every other junior field officer whether American or German, the invaluable contribution that could be made in the heat of battle by the efficient and vicious striking power of P-47s and P51D Mustang fighters.

Frank realized that coordination between ground troops and

aircraft was one component of the war that had not been taught during the infantry training regimens at Benning. And although coordination with the tankers and artillerymen had been superficially taught, it had not been emphasized as a valuable tool; he was now learning the true value of coordinating air and ground mechanized units for the success of the lightly armed, ground-bound infantry.

About noon on the twenty-seventh, Frank and the companies to the right and left learned their scouts had lost contact with the opposing Germans, and artillery shells were no longer being fired at their positions. The American 8th Infantry then approached from the rear and poured into the void and swung west and then northwest to cut off German units that were now becoming separated from their main force; they became individual targets to be corralled or attacked. Radio communications soon came down that the 1st Division had achieved a complete breakthrough of the German defenses west of Saint-Lô, and there appeared to be a general withdrawal underway by the German army in the midst of a very unstable situation for them. Scouting probes were sent forward and radioed back that the enemy had taken up positions three miles to the south but gave signs of continuing their retreat with protection by rear guard units; air reconnaissance confirmed the retreat as well. By 1500 that afternoon, Frank and the company commanders in his battalion were summoned to an immediate meeting at the new Third Army Command Central at the crossroads village, Carentan.

When they arrived at the village, they were ushered into one of four large tents, and after a wait of more than thirty minutes, a parade of officers walked smartly into the enclosure. At the sight of the lieutenant and brigadier Generals entering the tent, colonels and majors who directed the Third Army's three corps and their constituent, seven divisions snapped to attention. This reaction caught Frank and other company-level officers by surprise as they also stood to salute. *My God, it's Patton himself. Look at that . . . And he actually wears pistols, and three stars on his helmet, I'll be damned.* Frank was both surprised and amused at the general's appearance with all of the trappings of his rank. The reaction of Patton's support cadre of officers spoke to the respect they willingly paid him and probably confirmed the rumors that Patton was a spit-and-polish kind of officer who expected all officers to take on the mantle of command as they exercised control over their subordinates. Frank, with a two-day growth of black beard darkening his face knew full well that there was a place for the polish of commanders, but it was not in the foxholes.

Returning the salute, Patton said, "As you were," and the officers sat in unison with absolute silence in the enclosure. Muffled motor noises from the outside could be heard, but no one was listening to them.

"You, as part of the 4th Division, Third Corps of the Third Army, will be an integral part of our campaign to strike Germany. The First Corps will be sent west into Brittany to clear Germans out of the ports of Saint-Malo, Brest, and Lorient. The Second Corps and you, the Third Corps, will represent the dagger that will strike to the east. We expect to move fast during this campaign—and let me emphasize fast—to take advantage of the collapse of the German wall of infantry and armor that is in progress now. Our day-to-day strategy will develop as we go and as we find opportunities to kill the enemy. One thing that will represent a hallmark of this campaign to aid in our attaining speed on the ground will be the incorporation of close cover by armed air support that will be capable of spotting and hitting the enemy should they try and attack our flanks. You must get accustomed to including air cover in your planning for specific maneuvers. Air controllers will be assigned down to the company level and coordinate through the Nineteenth Tactical Air Command of the Ninth Air Force. Finally, the armored units should lead the spearheads with the infantry following up to clean out the pockets and handle prisoners.

"And another thing, when we meet the enemy, we kill him if he fights. We will show him no mercy. He has killed thousands of your comrades in North Africa, Italy, and Normandy, and he must die. If your company officers in leading your men against the enemy find him shooting at you, and when you get within two hundred yards of him and he wishes to surrender—oh no! The bastard will die! You kill him." Patton spoke these words with considerable vehemence.

An officer standing behind Patton on his right side stepped forward and spoke confidentially in the general's ear as be bent to listen. Patton then lifted his head. "This applies to you men leading the corps, divisions, regiments, on down to you company commanders there in the back. We will become known to the German army as killers. We are going to advance and keep on advancing. Understood?"

"Yes, sir," snapped the response from the assembled officers.

"We have three tables set up at the rear; one each for the brigades in the division. You will assemble at those tables for the next stage of briefing. Good luck. I'll see you on the road and in Germany." With that, the general saluted the men and strode from the tent as the officers stood and returned his salute. The officers inside the tent heard the distinct sounds of revving motors as they pictured Patton and his staff leaving the command center and heading for Paris; although, in fact, they would have to wait for the Third Army to lead the way.

In the hastily convened staff meeting that followed, Frank and his fellow company officers were briefed on the next steps in the logistics of moving the Third Corps, consisting of the 1st and 4th Divisions, at speed across France in concert with the Second Corps and First Army on their left wing. Attention was to be given to controlling key crossroads as they travelled, since retreating Germans, whether ahead or trailing behind the Americans, would use the same roads to return to Germany. The Third Army was going to trap as many of the enemy as possible before they could complete their retreat; if enough could be caught, then Hitler may have to sue for peace. That was the big picture: catch the Germans before they could get away and then see what the madman of Berlin would do.

Due to the late hour, Frank and his fellow officers bunked down almost immediately after enjoying a hot meal at the officer's mess. Now they knew that the command staff did not eat C- or K-rations, and based on this knowledge they predicted none of the command staff would lose weight during the war. Frank had time to write two letters that evening.

*27 July, 1944*

*Dear Ted,*

*This will be a quick note to say hi to you, Granny, Granddad, and Lily. The weather here is finally starting to look a little like summer. We had a real bad patch of weather in June with rain, and cool, foggy days and nights. I'm not certain what is considered normal over here, but the summer weather we had when we arrived wasn't normal as far as I was concerned.*

*We have been in the hedgerow country where over the centuries the farmers have built up earth berms along the edge of their fields that are covered with trees, rocks, and dense vegetation so that they become a type of fence to keep the animals in or to clearly mark the limits of their crop fields.*

*I got a chance to be in a briefing today with General Patton. You will read about him soon in the paper, I'm certain. Remember before I left, we read about him when he fought in North Africa and Italy. He is a very polished-looking individual, and he wears pistols sometimes, as he did in our briefing. It was all very interesting.*

*I must close. I'm in good health so don't worry about me. Some of my men came down with colds and influenza, but I escaped the illness. Give my love to Granny and Granddad and keep plenty for yourself.*

*Love, Dad*

*27 July 1944*

*Dear Lily,*

*Thanks for arranging the cookie shipment. I am carrying four boxes to the troops in my company, and they will be greatly appreciated, many thanks. And based on the delicious aroma coming from the boxes, I would encourage you and Mom to keep up the good work. I hope this is not putting too great a strain on your sugar rations. Also, all of the soldiers on my list in the last letter are now getting letters from home. That's very much appreciated as well. I believe all of them have written responses by now. I don't expect great feats of literary brilliance coming from them, but the thoughtfulness of the people you selected is certainly heartwarming for the men. No matter how they try to say it, I can assure you they are very grateful for the letters, especially knowing somebody is thinking about them. They are no longer isolated, and I can tell you from firsthand observations that the feeling of isolation over here can be deadly for any of the soldiers, and I don't mean deadly in a casual sense, but a literal sense.*

*I forgot to mention in the letter to Ted that I am now a captain with a promotion a few days ago. There is no glamour or glory associated with a battlefield appointment, at least in my estimation, but I will nonetheless try and do whatever I am assigned.*

*Keep the letters and cookies coming.*

*Warm Regards, Frank*

*P.S. I'm glad you and Ted are hitting the tennis courts. Maybe in August after baseball season ends, you can continue. Frank*

# CHAPTER 25

## *Hill 317, Mortain, France*

## *Early August 1944*

IN THE HEAT of summer Frank found his company at the heart of a strategic plan that Patton had referred to as finding opportunities to destroy the enemy. This opportunity had occurred because in the first few days of August, Hitler had not accepted the fact that his army was hopelessly beaten in Normandy. Instead, the Fuhrer visualized a counterattack using his depleted men and supplies against a superior attacking army. If he had listened to his army command staff, he would have been told that the attack was an unnecessary and perhaps foolish attempt that would only deplete faster the dwindling German war-making resources. Those resources were quickly becoming defense resources, and as everyone but Hitler saw, the next chapter of the war foretold the allies marching into Germany from the west with the Russians coming from the east. But Hitler dreamed another vision of victory.

By August 6, Frank's company was forty-five miles southeast of Coutances in the southern reaches of Normandy just east of the village of Mortain and dug into defensive positions on a rocky ridge that dominated the landscape. Their position on Hill 317 offered them an excellent view in all directions of the compass. His men had been prepositioned in a defensive location on the fifth after word came down from command center that a German counterattack was expected to strike at the heart of the Third Army with an attempt to break through and drive west to reach the coast at the Gulf of Saint-Malo on the English Channel.

If successful, a thrust of that type would split the Americans in half. Top American generals were counting on men of the Third Corps to hold the Germans in place, including the area centered on the village of Mortain, while the First Army under Bradley on the north and the remainder of the Third Army under Patton on the south raced east to close a trap around and behind the Panzer spearhead. Pre-knowledge of the attack was based on intercepted German messages, but did not include the exact time of the incursion. The predawn hours of August 7 provided the answer to the attack-time question, as two Panzer divisions thrust forward without the typical pre-softening of enemy defenses by artillery. Despite the advanced intercepted warning, the stealth of the attack caught unprepared the American battalion's command post, resulting in it being overrun and personnel being captured, including the commanding officer.

The sudden German thrust then drove west through to Mortain surrounding Frank's company that by now included remnants from two other companies. The isolated men on the ridge retreated farther up to a higher elevation and dug fox holes and trenches as deep as they could into the rocky soil. With the loss of the commander, Frank was now on his own for the upcoming encounter, as the 700 Americans were threatened by Panzer units. Frank's forward observers knew during the still-dark morning hours of the eighth that the Germans had filtered into their sector. They heard the telltale sounds of the feared Tiger tanks prowling in the darkness at the base of the ridge. The tank traffic near the ridge was dispersed, as American artillery drove them back from the immediate area using pre-tested map coordinates for nighttime firing.

As the sky lightened at 0630 that morning, the opening salvo of the German shelling hit the ridgeline and then increased. Second Lieutenant Alcie St. John, now commander of Bravo Company, took a communication team to a precarious position at the peak of the ridge. The sparse nature of the vegetation on the ridge top made them visible to keen enemy observers in the surrounding countryside, and the Saint knew he was in a race with time as he called out the first coordinates of a German battery that had opened fire in their direction. As German shells exploded fifty yards short of the top of the ridge, a radio message came from the American battery, "They're on their way," as shells screamed in from behind and to the left of the observers and erased the German battery.

The early successful marksmanship continued as the Saint spotted the puffs of smoke from German 88mm cannons and tanks and guided American return artillery fire to hit the enemy. As Frank joined the ridge-top activity, the shooting gallery atmosphere struck him as an apt metaphor that he related to the Saint, which elicited a mumbled response from him: "Shooting gallery is right as long as we beat them to the punch with our fire; otherwise, we are a set of statistics for the Third Army,"

"Seems like they are asking for a pack of needless trouble attacking us here," said Frank as they reflexively ducked a German shell screaming over their heads and into the German's forces located at the base of the ridge behind them.

"I pray you are right," responded the Saint, as he focused his glasses on the enemy battery that had just tried to part their hair. The Saint's coordinate sightings were passed to Private Eddie Peters at his right side, and he in turn gave them to radioman Robert Bray, who was in constant conversation with the 34$^{th}$ Field Artillery Battalion positioned to their rear.

Frank, looking through his binoculars, warned, "At three o'clock there's movement in the grove of trees beyond the creek and stone wall."

"Got it," said the Saint as the message relaying continued. After the incoming shells fell short of the target, the Saint gave adjusted coordinates that struck close enough to the target to immobilize it.

"I just got off the horn with Colonel Wells," said Frank. "He and the command staff consider this counterattack to be a big mistake by Hitler. They think he is directing this battle himself based on our radio intercepts. We have Adolph the World War I Corporal running the show on the battlefield. We don't know what they are likely to do next with that maniac in charge."

The Saint barked another set of coordinates as a string of three shells fell to their left and one hundred yards short, then, "We are the finger in the German dike right now. They sure are breathing down our neck, but we couldn't have a better position to fight from, especially with backup artillery."

Frank opened his mouth wide to try and shake the concussive effects of the last blasts. "I've set up two other spotters scanning the left and right rear positions. Those quadrants are pretty quiet for the time being, but they can heat up at a minute's notice. Do you need relief yet?"

"No," said the Saint with a mocking laugh, "it's not like there's a quiet place on this hillside to take a break. I'll just keep my finger on the gun, God willing," the Saint said as he jerked to the right to identify a suspicious movement. "It would help if you would send Crawford up to help scan the countryside. He has good eyes."

"Right," said Frank as he crawled to the left to find Crawford and check on the next spotter team.

Through the remaining daylight, the attacks on the ridge continued as responding Americans shot up enemy troop concentrations, field artillery pieces, and tanks. The view from the ridge allowed for the sighting of tank and troop movements for several miles around the American's perimeter. Spotters continued to call in coordinates for aircraft to rain havoc on the distant targets and artillery on the closer targets that raised an imminent danger for the isolated Americans. The contest continued through the night and the next day.

On the next day, the ninth, Frank and the Saint observed a startling maneuver. On a nearby country lane, meandering toward their hill, they sighted Germen troops riding bicycles into battle with rifles strapped on their backs. American artillery soon broke up the ride through the countryside.

On the tenth, "Rations are gone, and we have the last two chickens and some potatoes and apples we borrowed from that stone barn near the edge of the rise," Sergeant Bills explained, pointing northeast along the ridge. "We can cook up some kind of stew but it ain't much. I don't think there's a thing left to eat on this ridge since we dug up those turnips. Some of the boys ate them straight out of the ground and now they got the scours real bad. We just ain't used to these fancy raw French vegetables."

"Do the best you can," said Frank, "we are supposed to get a food drop this morning."

"I hope it's better than yesterday's; all the parachutes drifted behind the Kraut's line, and they got the meals," gruffed Bills.

"I know," was Frank's unconsoling reply.

A few minutes after 1000 hours, a series of parachutes were spotted dropping from the bottom of the overhead cloud sheath and descending over the ridge. To avoid enemy fire, the delivering plane flew high in the sky, and once again the slight southwest breeze began to gently push the descending food farther and farther northeast, tantalizing the troops, until all but the first of the ten chutes dropped into the waiting hands of German infantrymen. Amidst a cover of small arms fire, the hungry American soldiers retrieved only one chute.

"Get on the phone and tell the center they missed us again, to the northeast," Frank barked to the radioman at his shoulder. "At least we have some rations. Whoever would have thought that K-rations would be considered a delicacy." Frank stared down as the Americans scurried to retrieve the dropped bundle and return to cover as enemy fire picked up.

"See to it that the rations are distributed around the hill as far as they will go," barked Frank to a lieutenant huddled to his right as incoming shells tore into the hillside twenty yards behind and below them; considerable dust, grit, and small rocks pelted their helmets and shoulders as they hugged the side of the foxhole. "Each man gets one food packet, whether its breakfast, supper, or dinner. If there are any left over, we save them for tomorrow."

"Yes, sir." The hunched-over lieutenant ran along the trench and then duck-walked into a crawl as he moved out of the trench to the east.

Medic, PFC Owens crawled up to Frank. "We are out of morphine, have a few units of penicillin, no more splints, and some bandages and a few tourniquets."

"See if there were any medical supplies in that last chute, and if not we'll have to make do. You'll have to make up splints from a wrapped bayonet or anything else that's stiff."

"OK. We used up our last of the fence slats last night; I'll see if we can scrounge any more. We have about a hundred wounded who have gone back on duty and twenty-eight who can't fight, and we need to get them out ASAP."

"I know you're doing the best you can under the circumstances. The 35th Division is trying to get through to us. Are the forty-one bodies isolated from the troops?"

"As much as possible, considering the conditions," the corpsman replied.

With a growling stomach at 1500 hours, Frank made his way along the ridge and then worked his way to a lower elevation to check on his right flank. "Sergeant Sokolowski, where's Lieutenant Kroner?"

"He was just hauled to the aid station. He got hit in neck about ten minutes ago by rock fragments, bleeding pretty bad. Stay low, sir, they got us zeroed in pretty good with machine guns," came the sergeant's warning. "I think Kroner will make it back, but I'm not sure," added the sergeant. A spray of machine-gun fire ripped across the rocky face of the ground behind their crouched position. "It's a machine-gun nest just off to the right," pointing to a rock outcropping below and to the right. "I have a feeling they are going to charge us any minute. There's a lot of movement in those trenches at the base of the hill."

"Do you have a radio?" asked Frank.

"No, sir, the radio got busted up when Stanley went down."

"We need to get artillery on that rock outcrop."

"Here they come!" shouted PFC Robinson as the Germans suddenly rose en masse from the rocks and began charging uphill, firing from belt level. The twelve men in the trench opened fire. Frank grabbed a BAR leaning against a rock and fired the automatic rifle, emptying the first magazine and inserting a second. The hail of bullets fired by the advancing enemy struck wildly at the ground and rocks that sheltered the twelve Americans; the charging Germans had no time to aim their fire. "Stay low," shouted Sokolowski to his men, knowing each troop was an essential asset. The Germans continued coming though; their number was reduced by falling bodies. Still they surged forward, countless men darting from rock to ground back to rock across the rugged slope, firing as they ran. They had no place to stop and hide: they were in the open. Bodies started piling up, some tumbling back down the hill.

The third magazine was emptied, and Frank slammed in another and fired. The Germans dropped, but more kept coming. Ten feet away now, some were hit in the back by their own machine gun fire, but on they came. The first German reached the American shield of rocks and was cut down by fire as he tried to force his way between the boulders. More were on the edge of the rocks; bedlam broke out with shouting and concussive blasts below the American position as troops from both sides zeroed in on the heat of the battle. Frank lost awareness of the situation as he fired at those in his immediate apron of space. He heard loud shouting among the cacophony of firing, but the Germans kept coming. The magazine in the BAR was empty, and he used the gun as a club against a frantic young German on the threshold of the granite shield. The rifle found its target on the side of the German's head, knocking off his helmet and stunning his senses. He slumped forward as Sokolowski placed a bullet in his now bare head.

The rush and noise blasted away all time and place, as the combatants' world dwindled to the three feet in front of them and each second lasted a lifetime. More explosions, more shouting.

Frank swung his rifle club, again hitting another German boy in the rib cage, sending him to the ground, his helmet and rifle flying to the side. Frank swung again, and the rifle butt struck the left side of his head with a deadly thud, distorting the shape of his skull. Frank jabbed his rifle club into the boy's unprotected chest and watched the terror in his eyes fade as life seeped from the crushed skull and death triumphed. Frank was wide eyed and looking desperately for the next German to club, but there weren't any. The rocky approach up the hill was littered by what seemed to be hundreds of Germans; a few were wounded and moving, but most lay still, deadly still. A few ran back down the hill to the safety of their line.

A hand yanked Frank down from his standing posture to a safer place behind the rocks. Additional explosions ripped the rocks below their position as American artillery, called in by the Saint, devastated the German machine gun position and the surrounding area. Sokolowski, a large burly man, cuffed Frank on the shoulder and said in a slurred voice, "Niche schwinging, Cap'an."

Frank blinked and looked at the blood smeared face of the Sergeant. "You've been hit."

"Oh, I t'ought 'ere was somethin' funny goin' on . . . ," his speech slurred again as he slumped against the rock, and his eyes glazed as the first effects of shock settled in. Medics were already in the rocks with the troops.

"Doc, the sergeant needs help over here!" Frank shouted.

A young corpsman knelt beside the stunned sergeant. "I think he'll make it." The corpsman tended the wound left by a bullet that ripped off part of the Sergeant's cheek. "You okay, sir?" he asked Frank as he tended to Sokolowski.

"Yes, I think so. Do you see any blood?" asked Frank, dazed and uncertain.

"No, sir."

"Then I guess I'm OK," he reassured the boy doc.

"That was a bad fight, wasn't it, sir?" as he applied pressure to the bandage on the unconscious sergeant's face.

"Yes . . . that was." Frank closed his eyes, leaned against the rock behind him, and sat still for a period of time, probably not more than two minutes, but they were quiet minutes as his heart rate slowed from its rapid pumping and the ringing in his ears subsided. Frank opened his eyes and found the face of the young German with the caved-in skull sprawled across the rocks and staring at him with unseeing eyes . . . cold, blue eyes. A still, moist trickle of blood oozing from the left nostril and the left corner of the youth's mouth glistened in the bright ray of sunlight that suddenly bathed the hillside.

Frank rose and took three steps to start his climb back up the hill. He looked at his feet so he would make no misstep on the uneven ground, and there in a crevice between two rocks was the body of a gray and white pigeon. The body was intact and had probably been killed by the concussive blast of an artillery shell. The cooling, crumpled body lay on its back with its feet jutting into the air and its head stuck down into the crevice. Frank knelt, pulled the bird up to a level position on its belly, stroked its feathers three times, then picked up a flat rock to span across the crevice covering the lifeless creature and providing a measure of privacy in its tomb.

He stooped as he walked back through the rocks to start up the hill. As he left the safety of the rock-shielded entrenchment, he came face to face with the blank eyes of Corporal Henson. The boy soldier leaned against a large rock and stared into the sky from a blood smeared, ashen face. Frank stopped and grasped his hand firmly then pulled the limp boy into a hard embrace. The lanky young soldier's face melted and tears began flowing from eyes and nose, his body shook violently, uncontrollably. "Come back up the hill with me for a rest," Frank said as he pulled away from Henson. The corporal turned and stumbled ahead with a quaking body. Frank picked up the rifle left behind and followed up the hill; the private was oblivious of the long, wet stain that marked the inside of his left trouser leg and the splattered blood that soaked the front of his uniform. They began their climb through the rocks past dead German soldiers.

Henson and Frank passed six 4th Division troopers climbing down the hill into position behind the rocks, as two dead and seven wounded Americans were carried and led by the medics back to the aid station. Now there were nine men at this position where there had been twelve. The bodies of the dead Germans on the immediate perimeter of the rocky shield were also retrieved and placed near the growing morgue of the American dead on the back side of the ridge.

*This is getting pretty fucking bad.* Frank made his way back up the hill, making certain he kept a low profile. He placed Henson in the hands of a medic and told the boy doc, "He's in shock. Keep him busy, find something useful for him to do." Frank then made the rounds among the troops along the ridge to assess their strength and positioning.

As darkness settled, he replayed in his mind the afternoon's deadly skirmish and realized how close they had come to being overrun. This time they repelled the charge and won the hand-to-hand combat, but how long could it go on? He remembered swinging the rifle during the final fighting, his thoughts invaded by the faces of the frantic young German boys he had dropped with his club. They were about half his age and would never have the opportunity to grow up and live a full life. Frank realized he had experienced a stark reality of combat. It was one thing to fight from a distance—to drop bombs, to fire a howitzer, to fire a rifle at a distant enemy, perhaps you hit and killed humans, perhaps you missed with all of your efforts. But in the hand-to-hand combat, there was no denying his role in the death of two human beings, two boys. One could live with the pangs of responsibility of death at a distance, but in the hand-to-hand conflict you couldn't escape the reality, the personal touch, the sensation of the rifle club coming in contact with the enemy's body, caving-in and crushing the skull. *In a life-or-death situation, you just can't feel sorry for the enemy, you can't . . . Do I feel sorrow for the Germans? Yes, shit yes . . . Am I a part of the mad hounds of war? Fuck it, yes.* Frank shivered in the warm night and shook his head, knowing he was trying to justify the brutality he had participated in. He took no comfort from his reasoning. He looked at his hands; they weren't shaking. Was he getting used to the killing? He hoped not, he truly hoped not, as the image of the cold, blue eyes reemerged. "Lord, am I doing what I'm supposed to do? Am I on the path? Lord, tell me."

The Germans continued their dogged attacks, and the Americans continued their equally determined defense. Men on both sides were killed and wounded. More German troop and tank thrusts were repelled on the tenth and early on the eleventh of August as the exhausted, hungry, and thirsty American observers, radiomen, and infantrymen held firm. At night, they could often hear the threatening sounds of tanks moving around the base and lower reaches of the ridge; by daylight they had retreated to spots hidden from the hilltop observers.

At 0300 in the still, dark hours of the eleventh, enemy mortar and artillery fire grew very heavy. Frank's men were married to the earth in their foxholes and behind rocks. They were out of food and getting perilously low on small-arms ammunition and mortar shells. By midday on the eleventh, amidst heavy return fire by American artillery, word came to the ridge that the Germans were finally showing signs of withdrawing across the width of their twenty-mile-wide phalanx; the Americans had held. Food and relief was promised for the ridge-top soldiers before the end of the day.

The Germans, however, did not follow the scripts of conventional warfare; they continued to attack the encircled Hill 317 for another twenty-four hours despite their imminent withdrawal. Casualties on the ridge became serious as Frank worked the radio directly to the command staff of the 35th Division. Despite the casualties, the lack of food, and dwindling ammunition, the company held on to the hill. On the morning of the twelfth, the relief division finally broke through the thinning German lines to the west of the ridge and moved into position to allow Frank's exhausted warriors to withdraw. Of the 700 men who were initially isolated on Hill 317, Frank brought 400 hungry, thirsty, dirty, smelly men through the battle, relatively unharmed. Three hundred of his men, however, were killed or wounded.

Frank's company was withdrawn from the field on the afternoon of the twelfth, and they were told they had two-and-a-half days of food, showers, sleep, clean clothes, and letter-writing time at a refitting base near the village Mayenne. This was an all-too brief a period to try and recover their equilibrium after spending a week in hell on earth. But Patton was pushing on to the east, and they were not going to be left behind by the action. They were needed.

At Mayenne the second batch of cookies from Knoxville caught up with the troops and Frank's men had the pleasure of gorging themselves on "home baked" goods after so recently suffering from gnawing hunger.

On their third night, Frank wrote two letters in the peace and quiet of a large troop tent. He tried in vain to construct a letter to Ted. What could he tell him? He didn't want to describe the threat of death he faced, and he couldn't tell him where they were. He was left with a limited array of news, for his real news was all about the war. The letter to Lily was different. She was an adult, and he could tell her more of the way war was affecting him, or could he? Should he bear his soul to a stranger he had never met?

Frank reread the letter to Lily and was stunned at its tone and his state of mind. Maybe his writing rant was a way of breaking the inner tension he felt. He lay back on his cot and prayed, *God, please give me the strength to find my way through this hell. Give me the wisdom to take care of my men and to not forget that everyone in this war is a human worthy of your love and forgiveness.* As he lay in the quiet, Frank thought about his prayer. It had a strange collection of requests, asking for strength and wisdom and remembering that the Germans were humans. Did he include Hitler in his prayer as one of the Germans? Was Hitler a German worth preserving?

He certainly included the two German boys on Hill 317. *I'm so confused. Maybe tomorrow things will be clearer. I hope Lily won't think I've gone over the edge when she gets this letter.* Then he wondered how to sign the letter and if he should even send it. Maybe he should throw it away and write her at his next break. *What the hell*, he signed it and placed the letters by his bed to be mailed in the morning. He rapidly slipped into a deep sleep.

After rousing awake and remembering where he was, he eased back to sleep and entered a world of peace and calm. The summer breeze rippled the surface of the East Fork of the Elkhorn River and fluttered the leaves of the sycamore, walnut, and maple trees lining the bank. He sat in the dappled shade with Ellen, her arm entwined in his, they held hands. Four children splashed in the shallows of the stream nearby, sometimes running across the limestone shelf-bottom of the stream, sometimes splashing each other, and always laughing. Four children, there was Teddy and three girls. "Those are my three angels," said Ellen, as if she read Frank's mind.

"Three angels?" asked Frank.

"Yes, three angels. We're very lucky."

"If they're angels, does that make Teddy a devil?" Frank smiled.

"No, of course not. He's just not an angel; he's a boy." Ellen laughed.

"Oh," said Frank, "Oh . . . Oh . . . ," the image dissolved as Frank jerked awake, unable to sleep again. In the predawn morning hours, he remembered Ellen's visit and their surprisingly large family that would never be.

The afternoon of the fifteenth found Frank and his men in the backs of troop trucks, moving east toward the recently captured city of Alençon. Frank and two corporals evaluated the quality of the farmland they passed. Several herds of black cattle were given high grades as were the fields of alfalfa and ripening wheat. Near the village of Javron, the men were awestruck by the bright, yellow field that seemed to stretch out of sight toward a distant tree line at the horizon.

"What's that crop?" asked Frank as the truck bounced across a hole in the pavement jostling the troops.

"Damned if I know. I mean, I don't know, sir," offered twenty-year-old Corporal Simmons as he hastily corrected his air of familiarity with a senior officer.

The lack of protocol didn't bother Frank one iota, because he knew who was in command. The men knew as well, and he saw no need to lay onto the shoulders of enlisted men an added concern to prevent them from talking freely to him. In the midst of battle he knew there was no time for the niceties of protocol. "Simmons, you can talk to me as you would your brother."

"Oh, no, sir, I won't talk to you like I do to that little twerp," Simmons said, laughing. "We give each other no quarter, even if he is two inches taller than me. My parents give him the size and me the brains." He continued laughing, but then his smile melted. "He's over in the Pacific in the marines . . . Last I heard, he was fighting on some God-forsaken little island called Saipan. I'm awful scared for him; he's only eighteen."

"That field back there that you fellows were asking about," came the voice from the sergeant on Frank's left, "that's mustard, I'm pretty sure."

"Mustard," said Simmons. "Mustard, I ain't seen any of that in Missouri. It's real purty though, isn't it?"

"They got a lot of mustard in France," said the sergeant. "Sometimes it's brown, and there is this type called poupon—my dad's a food broker in Baltimore, and he imports the stuff. Or he used to till the war started. I could go on and on about mustard and tell you more than you ever want to know."

"Please continue," said Frank. "You have a captive audience."

"Well in the eighteen hundreds there was this guy named Poupon and another named Gray, and they lived in a city called Dijon and they got together and . . ."

Frank lost the thread of the mustard discourse, but he loved sitting in the truck and driving through the country without being shot at. *Maybe after the war, of course God willing, I can come back here and see what a peaceful France is like. Yeah, I'll bring Ted and we'll explore all over Europe and just take our sweet time. Yeah, that's what we'll do. That's a swell idea even if I do say so myself.*

Thinking of Ted jogged his memory. *I've got letters.* He smiled as he pulled the envelope from his pocket and began to read in spite of the bouncing, heaving truck ride.

*Dear Dad,* *July 30*
*I am sorry we have not heard from you I guess you are busy fighting the war. I hope everything is ok. We read in the Sentinel that the Germans are retreating. Yeah for our side.*

*Jerry down the street broke his ankle sliding into second base in a game with the Reds. He said it hurts pretty bad (Lily says she thinks it is badly) and he has a cast and uses crutches. All of his team wrote their names on his cast and said funny things. I asked him if I could write on his cast and he said no and then his mother talked to him and he said he guessed it was ok but don't make it very big. So I signed my whole name and he said that wasn't fair my name is Ted and not Edward Franklin Warring but it was too late to erase it. HA HA, I guess I showed him. The Cubs came in fourth place we won 13 and lost 15. I got to pitch some and the coach told me to practice and I could pitch a lot more next year when I am 12. I like pitching it puts you in the middle of every play and I like that.*

*Granny says I need new tennis shoes and a pair of oxfords for church. My shoes now are getting tight and the tennis shoes have a few holes, one goes all of the way through so I guess she is right. We are going shopping at Millers or Thom McAns I guess on Saturday. I will get to see the bones in my feet on the shoe x-ray machine when Granny checks the shoe size, that's always fun to wiggle the bones in my toes.*
*Love Ted*

*July 30, 1944*

*Dear Frank,*

*Your mother has recovered completely; she has a slight cough at night, but it does not slow her down. As Ted mentioned, his baseball season is over, as is my class, so I hope we will start playing tennis again next week.*

*The kitchen crisis that I wrote about last time has cooled down now that Mary is back in the kitchen. She made it clear that there will be no brains in her kitchen but that she might tolerate a tongue once in a while if Will behaves himself. I enjoy your parents so much. They have a way of respecting each other, and it is a very good marriage, not like some of the ones in my family. When Mary made the statement about the brains not being in the kitchen, Will started to make a crack about brains, implying human brains in the head of the cook. She started to chase him with a frying pan, and he almost collapsed in the living room laughing so hard.*

*Please take care of yourself and your men as well as you can. Mary and Ted invited me to join Ted's bedtime prayers, and I have. It is very touching to listen to him pray for you.*

*With Affection, Lily*

After laughing at Lily's description of his parents, he had a catch in his throat with her closing comment about Ted. He stared out the back of the truck at the Normandy countryside near Alençon as it disappeared into the western horizon.

The trucks continued east, and in the early afternoon then turned north to the southern fringe of the city of Argentan, where they were held in a camp as reserves for the Third Army's push north in an attempt to close the trap on German units fleeing to the east. These were the same German units that had been locked into battle at Mortain. With the Third pushing north and the combined Canadian, British, and American forces pushing south, the Allies were attempting to close what had become known as the Falaise Pocket and trap a significant contingent of Germans in central Normandy. The desperate defense put up by the German military partially succeeded, as the pocket was closed and then reopened for a matter of hours on the eighteenth and nineteenth before it was finally sealed for good. This effectively ended the war in Normandy and central France. Subsequently a large number of captives were ushered north to holding camps before being shipped to England and America. With the fall of Falaise, the all-out race between Germans and the allies to reach Germany had begun.

# CHAPTER 26

## *Knoxville*

## *August 25, 1944*

MARY DETECTED A slow ebbing of Lily's enthusiasm for daily life as the summer wore on. The change was subtle, and Mary was unsure if she correctly interpreted Lily's mood. Perhaps Lily had been very happy to find a place to live, and in her first months everything about living with the family was new and interesting, but Mary didn't think that was the cause of Lily's current outlook on life. No, if she was a judge of people, *Somethin' was eatin' at Lily*. Lily's decline seemed to become more sharply defined as August neared an end and the Labor Day holiday rapidly approached to be followed by the beginning of a new school year.

On August 25, Lily returned from a day spent setting up her second grade classroom at Van Gilder. At four o'clock she placed a call to Nashville, telling Mary she would reimburse the Warrings for the long-distance call after the phone bill was received. Lily spoke into the mouthpiece attached to the wall phone in the hall. "I see, then it will be over. That's the last chance he has to delay . . . OK, I'll come home tomorrow . . . I'm so glad it's over. You just can't imagine how hard this has been . . . I know, it's been hard on both of us. Yes, I'll be home tomorrow. Good-bye, Mama. Thank you for everything you've done"—there was a catch in her voice as her throat tightened—"and for everything you're still doing . . . Yes . . . Bye." She hung the ear piece on the phone's switch and leaned against the wall and closed her eyes.

Mary, walking from the living room into the hall, saw Lily,

eyes closed and her hands folded at her mouth. Mary enclosed the young hands in hers. "Is everything all right, dear?"

Lily's eyes opened with a ring of moisture circling each. "Yes, I think it will be all right now," she whispered.

Mary kissed her cheek and looked into her eyes. "Good, I will listen if you want to tell me about it, but that's up to you," she said in a return whisper. "Sometimes it helps to talk, and sometimes it doesn't."

"I know, thank you," she gave Mary a brief, strong hug.

The two women walked side-by-side down the hall and into the kitchen, each with an arm around the waist of the other.

Lily sat at the table and traced the pattern of the wood grain in the surface of the well-worn piece of furniture.

Watching her, Mary commented, "This was my mother's table. She gave it to Will and me when we set up housekeeping. It's seen a lot of meals and heard a lot of tales told over the years; it's a good thing it can't talk, 'cause it might never shut up."

A wry smile crossed Lily's face. "I was just thinking about a table I have in Nashville. It's in storage . . . I don't need it now. It was given to me by my grandmother in '37 when I got married."

Mary seemed stunned by the simple statement. "You've been married . . . not that you aren't, I mean . . ."

"Yes, I was married in a July wedding in '37 just after I graduated from UT, and we then went on a honeymoon to England and France . . . I can't describe how happy I was then . . . My whole life was neatly laid out before me. It was like I was living a fairy tale; I was the princess, and I had won prince charming."

"Oh, my." Mary pulled her chair up to Lily and grasped her hands. "Did he die in the war?"

"No, nothing that honorable. I guess sometimes I wish he had, and then I would have a good reason to have a broken heart. No"—she let out a sigh—"he didn't die in the war . . . You see, we met in high school at a local chamber of commerce leadership conference in '33. I had no idea what was happening at the conference; I was from East High School, and we were all novices when it came to such things as civic affairs.

"And there was this boy from a private school, and he spoke very well and took over the students leadership role all by himself. He was so self-confident, I was very impressed. And then I went to college here in Knoxville, and I saw him again at a conference down at Sewanee when I was a junior, and he remembered me after three years, at least he said he did. But I remembered him.

Lily chuckled. "Have you ever seen a man that you thought was gorgeous?" Looking into Mary's eyes she continued, "Well that was my first impression of Chance when I was in high school, and that's why I guess I remembered him so well; he was so good looking." Tears came to her eyes. "We talked a lot that first year, and then I went again to the same conference the next year, and he was there. We went for walks, and somehow we always wound up walking alone, and I thought I was the luckiest girl on the face of the earth when he devoted all of his attention to me. He was just overpowering. And we kissed and held hands and on the last night, he became very amorous and after our conference wrap-up meeting we went for a walk in the dark and he said he had a car and he wanted to sit in it . . . and I agreed . . . but he wanted to do more than kiss, and I said no, and he persisted and I wound up slapping him, and we left the conference separately.

"By that, I mean I felt estranged. It was a terrible feeling but I got over it slowly. Then three months later in my final semester he called, out of the blue, and said I had been right to slap him. He said my slap changed his life and he realized what he had done to our relationship, and he wanted a chance to correct it. So I invited him to our sorority's spring dance, and he behaved very well and we kissed and walked, as well as danced, of course. He was such a good dancer. Oh my, could he glide and move me around the floor; it was like being led by a strong cloud. Smooth and fast or smooth and slow, depending on the music, but always smooth . . .

"He proposed in May, and I accepted. His parents had to have the wedding date at the end of July—that's the time that fit their busy schedule—and I agreed. When I met his parents, I knew they had money and a lot of it, I guessed. His father worked at First National, and Chance had finished at Vanderbilt and was set to go to work for the bank. His career was set, and so was our future. There would be a home in Belle Meade someday, but first we would have an apartment on West End as we got established."

"Hi," said Ted as he banged open the back screen door and walked into the kitchen. His first notion was to sit at the table and ask "What's for supper?" but upon seeing Mary and Lily hand in hand having a serious conversation said, "Err, I'll be up in my room listening to the radio." He passed through the kitchen to the hall and up the stairs.

Lily's eyes followed him. "I love Ted so much. He's going to be a very good man, and he's OK now, as a matter of fact, as a kid." She laughed amid new tears.

"Will and I are very lucky to have the chance to help raise Teddy. You're right; he's a good boy and will be a good man like his father."

"I've enjoyed writing to Frank. He seems to be a very perceptive person."

"Yes, even as a child Frank seemed to care about others, and Will used to say he was afraid Frank would want to become a minister, but he never really had that kinda callin'."

"Oh, I think it takes a special kind of person to be a minister, but you can be a good person and still not be a minister."

"Yes," said Mary as she rose. "I better put on some supper before the hungry troops start pounding on the walls. We can finish talkin' after supper if you like."

"Thank you, I think I like," Lily said with a grin as she played on Mary's words, "Yes, I like."

Dinner that night was tasty pork chops with yams, green beans, and sliced tomatoes, but the meal passed with a minimum of chitchat, much quieter than usual. Ted did try to start a conversation about the Cincinnati Reds, but there were few comments from the other diners, and he soon caught the mood of the evening and assumed correctly that it was an echo of the conversation he had interrupted in the late afternoon.

At eight o'clock with the dishes done and the garbage taken out, Ted went upstairs to read, Will read the paper in the living room, and Lily and Mary went to the kitchen and sat again at the table.

"Well, there's not a lot to tell about after we married," Lily picked up the earlier conversation. "We moved into our apartment, and Chance worked downtown. He didn't want me to teach, although I did my student teaching and got my certificate. I guess I wanted to prove, at least to myself, that I had accomplished something and could have taught if I had wanted to. I was content to try and settle into a life as a wife for a promising young bank executive and, hopefully, a mother. I did get pregnant near the end of '37, and we were looking forward to a baby probably in August, although the due date was something of a mystery to me and seemed like the doctor was guessing. I had morning sickness, and at the end of March I started to feel very bad, and one day I started to hemorrhage.

"My mother took me to the doctor, who became concerned. He said things weren't progressing as they should, and so I went into the hospital. Then on April 1 I lost the baby. They wouldn't tell me whether it was a little girl or boy; I think they knew, but Chance wouldn't let them tell me. I recovered slowly, but things seemed to have changed between us. There wasn't the same spark that we had enjoyed before the baby. My mother said that was normal for things to settle down for the long run after the honeymoon period. She said Chance and I had a whole lifetime to be together. I thought she was right, and she probably was right for most couples, but not for Chance. You see, he had a reputation that my high school girl friend had told me about years ago. He was known as a, well, a tom cat, if you know what I mean."

"Yes, I know," said Mary.

"That particular tom cat was a boy who was always on the prowl looking for a girl who was willing to . . . frolic with him."

"Yes, I know about frolicking," Mary said. "I warned my two

girls about that very thing."

"My friend said there was a girl at the private girl's school where she went who had disappeared for a year, supposedly to live with her grandparents, but Alice said that the rumor was she was in Iowa having a baby, and she would come home after the adoption.

"Chance was supposed to be the daddy, according to Alice. I of course thought he had ended those days in high school, or at least in college. But it seems he didn't. His new girlfriend worked at the branch bank in Madison, and she got pregnant and started making noise about getting married.

"The bank fired her and they tried to secretly hush it up and pay her to move away, but she called me on the phone. That was the worst day of my life. It was at Christmas time in '38. I thought I was going to die standing there in my living room with a telephone in my hand. I couldn't believe it. I couldn't talk—I just listened to her. She hung up, and then I thought she must be wrong, that for some reason she was striking at my husband through me. What had he done to her that so upset her and made her spread lies like that? I had convinced myself that was the truth until Chance came home and I mentioned her name and that she had called, and before I could say anything else, he turned as white as a sheet and said he was so sorry for what he had done. Then I froze; again I was speechless. I couldn't breathe, and I knew I was going to die, I just knew it. I don't think I will ever experience a pain like that again. I don't think it's possible for it to happen again . . . After that we separated, but he said he wanted to get back together, so we had dinner at restaurants and talked and he would come to the apartment and said he wanted to stay, but I wasn't ready.

"My friends told me that Chance was on the loose again and had been seen with other women. Then in '39 he said he wanted a divorce; he had found someone else. I agreed . . . I was numb by that time. It seems like all feeling had drained out of me. That's when his parents got involved and said it wouldn't look good for Chance to divorce so soon after marriage, and they said we should try again to patch things up. Chance's mother would invite me to her teas at the country club and try and involve me in her circle of friends as her daughter-in-law—as if that title was supposed to mean something to me in the absence of a real marriage. He did move back into the apartment, but things weren't right. That uneasy period lasted off and on for more than two years, and his mother said we weren't trying hard enough. She told me she had had a similar incident with Chance's father and that she had learned to live with him with all of his warts—that's what she called them, his warts." Lily gave a scoffing chuckle and rapped her hand on the table while shaking her head slowly from side to side.

"She supposed her husband had had several girlfriends, but she ignored the situation and went right along with the marriage as if nothing was wrong. I told her I couldn't live a lie like that, and she became incensed and told Chance I was hopeless and that she knew he had married below his station in life. When I heard her say that, I went into hysterics—laughing and crying. To think that girls brought up in a country-club home would allow their husbands to roam the bedrooms of Nashville as if it were a sign of good breeding; I was beside myself to get out of the marriage. I had to get away from that family. Everything they represented seemed so hollow, so shallow. Chance had become as an adult just what the parents wanted, someone as shallow as they were.

"You know, the funniest thing about the whole marriage was that his last name was Love. I guess he was trying to live up to that name and spread his love wherever he could." Lily let out a muffled, sardonic laugh and a deeply felt lament. "For a time I was happy as Lily Love. That seemed like such a perfect name, but it turned sour on me, really sour."

Mary placed her left hand on Lily's right hand.

"Chance started divorce proceedings at the end of '42, and we are just now having the final decree. I have to catch the bus in the morning and sign the papers, and we will be through with each other, once and for all."

Lily sat slumped in the kitchen chair, deflated, staring at her left hand as she placed it on top of Mary's left hand; she seemed to be looking at the ring that was no longer on her finger.

Mary placed her right hand on Lily's left and held on tightly; the layered hands matched the bonding of their souls. They sat for several minutes, both looking at the hands as their thoughts replayed Lily's story. They heard Ted thumping down the stairs and sticking his head around the corner of the doorway as Lily looked up into his eyes.

"Good night, I'm sleepy." He disappeared back up the stairs.

Mary rose. "I'll see to his prayers."

Lily also stood and followed her upstairs. The two women joined Ted at his bedside, kneeling. "Now I lay me down to sleep, I pray the Lord my soul to keep, if I should die before I wake, I pray the Lord my soul to take. Bless Mommy and Daddy and Granny and Granddad, and Mamaw and Papaw, and . . . bless Lily . . . and make her happy again. Amen."

Lily pulled Ted into her arms and held him tightly for a very long time. Ted felt comforted having her embrace. He didn't understand why she held on to him for so long, but he was willing to let her hold him if it helped her. Lily released Ted and kissed his cheek; she stood and left the room with tears falling feely as she closed the door to her room.

Two days later Lily returned from Nashville, and she and Ted started school again at Van Gilder the day after Labor Day. Ted was immediately struck by the happy carefree aura that now surrounded Lily. It seemed the world had been lifted from her shoulders, and she was as happy as she had been when she first moved into Highland Avenue. *Ha, I guess my prayer worked. She should have come to me sooner*. He chuckled and congratulated himself for solving Lily's problem, whatever it had been. Life was still simple for Ted.

# CHAPTER 27

## *Knoxville*

## *End of August 1944*

TED AND LILY walked into the kitchen after a rousing tennis match that Lily won but Ted had, for the first time, put up a stiff defense before losing.

"You did really well today. It won't be long before I have to chase the balls that go over the fence," she teased as she pulled a string of very dark, brown, damp hair from her eyes and over her wet brow. In making the comment, she reminded Ted he was the one who hit the balls over the fence and then had to chase after them.

"Yeah, sometimes the balls hit on the top of my racquet, and then they go all over the place. It's the backhand that I can't hit very good." He paused and hooked the big toe of his left foot in the heel of his right tennis shoe and started pushing it off his foot.

"There's mail in the front hall," said Mary as the sweaty athletes passed through her clean kitchen. "Teddy, don't leave those smelly shoes in here," she said as he successfully kicked off his right tennis shoe. "And don't you two sit on my furniture in the living room until you get cleaned up," she said in a loud voice as Lily and Ted passed through the dining room. "And dried off," she said to herself.

Ted tore open the envelope from his father, and with the admonition of his grandmother still ringing in his ears sprawled on the living room floor and read.

*15 August 1944*

*Dear Son,*

*I am glad your baseball season was a good one. Finishing in fourth place is not bad, and your team will probably do better next year. How did you hit, and did your team keep batting averages for the players? When I was your age, I didn't get to play in an organized league like you did this summer. How is that old glove of yours holding up? As I recall it was getting pretty beat up the last time I saw it. Maybe at Christmas you'll find a new one under the tree.*

*We had a cool rainy spell after we landed in France. It lasted for several weeks, and now it is hot and promises to get hotter. I guess by the time you get this, you will be getting ready to start school. This is your last year at Van Gilder; it's hard to believe you are getting that old. There may be new students in your class you can make friends with.*

*I can't say anything about our location except we are in France and things are going well. The countryside we have passed is beautiful, with many crops that have been planted despite the war. There is not a lot of livestock on the farms since the Germans helped themselves to the cattle, pigs, and chickens. The poor farmers, they will have to start over with new animals after the war. We saw fields of a very bright yellow flowered crop that turned out to be mustard plants.*

*Please write me soon and tell me about school this year. Oh, and tell Granny and Lily that I appreciate the cookies as do the men in my company. We had a cookie feast yesterday. Give my love to Granny and Granddad and keep plenty for yourself.*

*Love, Dad*

Lily opened her letter at the same time and read as she stood in the hall doorway.

*15 August 1944*

*Dear Lily,*

*It has been awhile since I wrote. I do wish I could write more often, but wartime is not conducive to a timely rhythm of correspondence. It's hard to know where to start. I hope I won't burden you too much with my thoughts, but I need to talk to someone. I trust you will use your discretion and tell Ted and my parents the parts of this letter that you believe they can stand. I apologize for putting you in this situation since we have never met face to face, but I just need to talk, or in this case write, to someone and place my trust in that person to guard and filter the letter so that I won't worry my loved ones unnecessarily. (My, that was a long and involved sentence.) Seriously, if I am placing too great of a burden on your shoulders, please write and tell me. I do believe we are friends now, having met through letters, or as one of my English professors called it, an epistolary friendship. (I hope that is the correct form of the word, after all it's been fourteen years since I sat in Professor Wilbur's class.)*

Realizing that this was a different kind of letter than she anticipated and observing its length, Lily excused herself saying she needed to take a bath and "get decent" for dinner. She walked from the living room up the stairs to her room. She didn't want to read the letter if front of Ted and then have him ask if he could read it as was their custom to exchange letters between themselves before passing them to Mary and Will. She would have to think of a way to keep the letter from them without raising suspicions on their part about her motive. She continued reading the letter, sitting on the edge of her bed.

*When I get a few days away from the fighting, as yesterday and today, I am stunned at the brutal acts that men inflict on each other while in battle. It is gruesome at times, and I confess I participate equally in the pursuit of victory with any inhumane means, because*

*I know the consequences of losing; the inhumanity will not end if we lose the war. The odd thing is that, now that I think about it, I'm not sure it will end if we win, but that's another story. In this war I can't do anything but follow the plan of attack laid out for me; my men depend on me. We are actors on the stage carrying out the war directed by generals. It is a tragedy in the making for all participants on both sides. I guess Shakespearian in scope, or maybe that metaphor does not do it justice. No, Will S. didn't comprehend the acts we are capable of today. In moving up to our most recent position, we did pass through a village where the people turned out to welcome us. They hopped in our Jeeps, on the tanks, and kissed our men. Now, this was both women and men doing the kissing and cheering. That was a shock to get kissed by a scraggly toothed old guy with rough whiskers. But they were so grateful that we had liberated them, I guess some good is resulting from our barbarity, but those instances are few and far between, so far.*

*I have lost many men including Corporal Henson, the young soldier who had become the pen pal of your sister. He was just a great young man and he so appreciated June's letters. He was talking about how he would write her when he got home and go thank her in person. He said his parents were dead, and he had lived with a family until he was old enough to run away and enlist. I guess the family that took him in expected a lot of work on their farm for his room and board. He had only made it through the eighth grade when he had to drop out of school. Such a loss, he had great potential. He was in a state of shock after a hand-to-hand fight. I'm not sure if it was shell shock that I heard about in the First War, but he went back into the fight too soon and lost concern for himself and stood up at the wrong time to fire at the enemy. After the war he wanted to go back to high school and then try college. He was killed on 10 August. Such a loss. So sad.*

*I'm so afraid I will get used to death, that it will become commonplace. I just can't let that happen. It is quite a dilemma to both cause and witness death in the run of a typical day—that's a laugh; in war a typical day involves causing death, but it is no laughing matter. I wonder a lot about all the soldiers over here that are in support roles for the soldiers on the front line; they typically don't witness death and only indirectly support it by doing their jobs. Don't get me wrong, their jobs are necessary for the front-line troops to fight, but they don't have the same stake in the war that the front liners do. So everybody's war experience will be different; some of us have a lot more invested than others.*

*I've got to turn out the light soon and get some sleep. I have read over the letter and realize that I have rambled on terribly, and I apologize for burdening you with these poorly structured thoughts, but it is hard to get a decent perspective on what we are doing. History will have to do that. Thank you for listening.*

*Your conflicted, epistolary friend and soldier, Frank*

"I played a lot better today, didn't I, Lily?" asked Ted as they ate the evening meal.

"You certainly did. You may become a real Bill Tilden or a, ah Budge . . . what's his name?" replied Lily.

"Don," said Ted.

"Oh, yes, a real Don Budge, before you're done."

"I don't know about that. It won't happen if I can't hit a backhand," Ted interjected.

"That'll come with practice."

"Is being a Don Bug something to be proud about?" asked Mary.

"That's Budge." Ted laughed. "He's a tennis player, and a good one."

"Oh, I wondered why you wanted to be a bug," Mary said with a straight face. Everyone else laughed.

"Dad said in his letter that I might get a new baseball glove for Christmas," said Ted. "That would be swell. I hope it's a Bobby Doerr."

"A what?" asked Mary.

"A Bobby Doerr glove. He's a second baseman for the Red

Sox. He's a real good fielder, and he can hit too. He and Boudreau are leading the league in hitting this year, and it's a real close race. And another thing, I like Ted Williams too and they're on the same team and they hate the Yankees and so do I. I can't wait till Williams comes back from the war."

"I didn't know they had Negroes playing major baseball. I guess that's all right though," Mary observed.

"They don't," said Ted.

"Well you said that Boudreau did something, and I thought that he was a Negro like Henry."

"No," said Will, "they don't let Blacks play, but they have some very good players in the Negro Leagues, and maybe after the war things will ease up. Ted and I saw that game at Brewer's Park here last Saturday between the Grays and the Chattanooga Choo Choos, I tell you, I think those boys could beat the Smokies if they got a chance. We saw Isaac and his son Isaac and grandson Isaac at the game." Will couldn't help but laugh at the repetition of the name, then more seriously, "but they're good ball players."

"There must be Negro Boudreaus and white Boudreaus. They came from Louisiana," Ted said to Lily.

"Oh," she said not following the conversation except the fact that Negroes were not playing in the big leagues. "So you want a Bobby Doerr glove."

"Yeah, Bobby Doerr, that would be swell." Ted started eating another ear of corn. Lily smiled at Ted's eating style as he held the buttered ear at the ends of the cob with both hands and then started at one end and mowed the kernels into his mouth as the ear slid across his working mouth. By the end of the ear, he had a mouthful of corn and buttered lips. He chewed before starting on the next passage of the ear across his face.

"You certainly do have a way with an ear of corn." Lily laughed as Ted finally laid the half-eaten ear on his plate.

"Murff—"

"Don't talk with a full mouth," came Mary's expected reply as Ted swallowed and took a long drink of iced tea.

"I learned how to eat corn by watching Granddad," he said as he wiped his hands on his pants and beamed at his Grandfather.

"Yes, indeed," said Will as he placed his second stripped ear on his plate, "I've taught this boy the fine art of dining, farm style," he winked slyly at Ted.

"Yes, and if you notice after dinner you both leave a ring of corn on the floor around your chairs. Laws, you would think they were eating popcorn," said Mary looking at Lily as they all laughed. After a pause, "I read Frank's letter to Ted. Was there anything interesting in his letter to you? I mean, it's your letter and I don't want to pry, but I just thought—"

"Oh, no," said Lily, "it was like the one to Ted. It seems he can't say much about what he's doing, so he commented about the countryside." Lily took a drink of tea and a deep breath as she hoped her face had not betrayed her subterfuge about the letter. She really had not fully digested Frank's letter and the burden that came with it by giving her a license to shield his family. She was not at all certain how she should proceed from here; she had to think more about the situation.

# CHAPTER 28

## *Paris to Basse-Ham, France*

## *August to Early October 1944*

"WHOEE, WHOEVER THOUGHT I'd be walking down the 'Champs de Lisses,'" bellowed Lieutenant Rodgers. "What was this Lisses guy the champion of, anyway?"

Frank and the Saint laughed as the three officers strolled along the remarkably wide sidewalk under the continuous row of chestnut trees. "He was probably a champion bicycle rider," offered the Saint, "one of those hard-pedaling Frenchmen."

Just then four people walking in the opposite direction stopped the service men and immediately started shaking hands and kissing their left and right cheeks in warm greetings.

A distinguished gentleman wearing a well-worn gray suit spoke clearly and with a great sense of dignity said, "On est si content de voir les Américains qui se prominent ici, dans la plus belle rue du monde. Bienvenus à Paris!"

"Let's see," said the Saint, "he said how glad he was to see Americans walking the . . . no, on our most beautiful street in the world, welcome to Paris."

A slightly overweight matronly woman repeated to each American, "Merci, merci, merci," as she planted wet kisses on their cheeks.

Two much younger women, perhaps relatives of the older couple, erupted into enthusiastic welcomes of their own. The youngest woman with blond hair tucked behind a red and blue scarf spoke passionately, "J'adore les Américains et je déteste ces horribles racailles allemandes, qui sont une abomination de la race humaine. Vive la France, vive l'Amérique."

"Ah, she said she loves us and hates the abominable Germans, something like that, and long live France and long live America."

The dark haired older of the young women planted kisses on the cheeks of Lieutenant Rodgers, and he responded by a long kiss on her mouth, which she returned gleefully as he bent her backwards in a long embrace, her long right arm was extended gracefully over her head as she added flair to the moment.

All the spectators howled with laughter as the couple straightened. "I'm in love, amore, amore," shouted Rodgers, and the laughter continued to ricochet down the avenue. A group of spectators sitting at small tables in an adjacent sidewalk café turned to observe the sidewalk frivolity and joined in the celebration with applause.

The young blond woman, perhaps in her early twenties, said haltingly in English spoken with a heavy Gallic accent, "It is our great honor to welcome all to Paris. We are grateful so for your giving us freedom. Merci, merci." With this she kissed each officer on both cheeks, and Rodgers again took the liberty of acknowledging her welcome with his special knee-bending kiss and embrace. The laughter sparked anew as the elderly gentleman stepped forward and mockingly wagged his index finger at Rodgers as he laughed and stepped between the young woman and the amorous officer. "Je dois protéger l'honneur de ma petite-fille, même si c'est de l'armée américaine adorable."

"What did he say?" stammered Rodgers, "What?"

"He say he must . . . ah protect me from . . . ah you," the young woman said between gulps as she gasped for breath between her bursts of laughter; the old man's laugh was a long, low guffaw issued from deep in his chest.

Rodgers dropped to one knee and clasped his hands together as he looked pleadingly into the yellowed eyes of the old gentleman who laughed and pulled off Rogers's hat and ruffled his hair. He then again waggled his finger at the officer. "No, no."

Rodgers rose, and with more handshakes all around, the older couple began to take steps to continue their walk in the opposite direction from the officers; the patrons in the café slowly returned their attention to their conversations, coffee, skimpy pastries, and equally skimpy newspapers. The young, blond woman rapidly scribbled on a scrap of paper pulled from her pocket and stuffed it in Lieutenant Rodgers breast pocket. "That is my address if you care to write me." she smiled and placed a polite kiss on his cheek as she adjusted her scarf and hurried to catch up with her grandparents and sister, then turning and waving good-bye as she stepped off the curb.

Rodgers, with a big smile on his face and his arms outstretched, stood transfixed, staring after the French family who crossed the intersecting street. "I'm in love. I swear I'm in love. I've found my true love for eternity."

The Saint laughed. "Well, what's the name of your one and only love?"

"Beats me."

"Why don't you look on the piece of paper in your pocket," suggested Frank.

Rodgers tore into his pocket and turned the paper right side up. "Meme Angeline," he said longingly, once again looking down the avenue at the family as their figures continued to diminish in size. "I love girls with two names. Meme Angeline, Meme Angeline."

"That's Miss Angeline, or maybe in English that's Angel, I'm not certain. I only had two years of French in high school," said the Saint, "but her first name is not meme."

"Oh, well, I still love her," said Rodgers glancing back over his shoulder. "I love girls with one first name, especially in France."

Frank had to attend to several problems as he collected all the men in his company. Most had overindulged during their two-day pass in Paris. Some complained about the lousy accommodations—lousy being a literal description of at least one infested hotel. Some also had to be retrieved from the military police for their association with less-than-civil activities. It was Labor Day in

America but a full "army day" in France, which meant it ran for twenty-four hours, although in the current climate there was no one to fight during the daylight or nighttime hours.

The Germans were in full flight toward the east to protect their motherland, or was it fatherland; Frank couldn't remember the Germanic phrase used for their home. Many of his young soldiers were suffering from too much wine and champagne; champagne, that was Seven-Up with alcohol and bubbles, according to the eighteen- and nineteen-year-olds unaccustomed to the sneaky power of wine.

The unenthusiastic lot of soldiers was trucked to the village of Meaux, twenty miles east of Paris, where they entered a newly arranged encampment and picked up replacements to fill out their compliment of 215 men. As the eighty-one new soldiers were incorporated into the company, Frank took pains to have the platoon and squad leaders spend time with the green infantrymen and integrate them into the units as well as could be expected. The only way to be certain they were integrated was to experience battle, where it became abundantly clear for the need to fight as a unit and not as individuals.

Frank hoped all his men would survive their first few days of fighting; if they did, they were automatically considered veterans by the troops who had fought in Mortain and Periers. His two-and-a-half month history in combat had taught him that if a soldier survived his first day of hard fighting, his odds of surviving rose fast. The total turnover in the company now approached 130 troops or well over 50 percent of the fellows who had fought at Periers. That realization was sobering as he read through the list of those killed and the larger number wounded and removed from the front for medical care. Most casualties had been under twenty-two years old and many just eighteen, *boys,* he said to himself, *boys.* He closed his roster and called together his platoon and squad leaders to discuss the next leg of their journey east.

The rapid movement of the Allied force to the east had exhausted much of the available gasoline, resulting in a sudden slowdown to the forward progress of the armored units and, thus, the crawl of the liberation armies toward Germany. The command structure was confident the slowdown was temporary and that their advance would continue with the opening of the port of Antwerp and the overtime efforts put in by the Red Ball Express, the trucking operation that to a great extent depended on skilled American Negro soldier drivers. The military success of the Allies and their rapid advance across France had outrun the resupply depots operating from the beaches and ports of Normandy. While the Allies' supply line had grown long, the German's had shortened as they regrouped on or near home soil.

Men in Frank's company anxiously discussed the end of the war and their return home. They had a chance to beat the odds of the typical infantryman fighting in Europe during this war, which was to return home without being wounded or shipped home in a pine box. Many of their predecessors had not achieved this distinction. Frank heard the discussions and did not point out that the dead were buried in France or wherever they fell and that the allies had not yet entered Germany that still stood behind the Siegfried Line, a line of fortifications stretching from Switzerland on the south to the lowlands of Netherlands on the north.

But to even the pessimistic or the cautious analysts, the end of the war did indeed seem inevitable in early September. Some thought it imminent; others who were more cautious placed it before the end of the year. The signs of a collapse in Germany were many. The combined American, Canadian, and British force had driven across France from its landing in Normandy. An American and French army had landed in Marseilles and driven north up the Rhone River valley, maneuvered around Switzerland, and now occupied the eastern front in central France facing the German border south of Patton's Third Army.

In the east the Russian Army had pushed the Germans from southern Russia, eastern Poland, and the Baltic states of Latvia, Lithuania, and Estonia and had captured Romania. The Germans had withdrawn from Greece and were in retreat on the Balkan

Peninsula. Things were indeed looking good for an autumn end of the war. General Bradley had a hold placed on winter clothes for the army, preferring instead to ship from the ports as much ammunition, equipment, and fuel as possible to the front lines to hasten the war's end. Winter clothes would be held at the ports and then returned to the states.

As troop trucks pulled out of Sedan, a village in the eastern Champagne region, they approached the Belgium border and the village of Bouillon. Barely two miles into Belgium, the road began to descend into the valley of the Semois River, a stream, Frank observed, that was not much wider than the Elkhorn back at the Forks. Descending the hill, they could see Bouillon nestled in the back-to-back horseshoe bends of the wandering stream that had carved its valley from the rolling countryside. The center of town was located in the second of the horseshoe bends below the ruins of an ancient castle that dominated a slim ridge that once protected the town from its lofty perch. The uniformly gray stone buildings provided a continuous harmony to the town's setting. *If the hills were a little higher and the river a little bit bigger, this would be like Frankfort,* Frank thought as he felt comfortable entering the community over the bridge into the heart of Bouillon. Dogs began to bark and chase the trucks, then the children came out waving and yelling and started to run at the same speed as the slow-moving vehicles. The pace of the trucks slowed to a cautious roll along the cobblestone street. Shopkeepers came to their doorways to observe the disturbance, followed by customers and residents who came from stores, homes, and side streets, and within minutes the trucks were surrounded by shouting and cheering Belgians. Just like the enthusiastic welcome the troops had received in rolling through eastern Normandy and the Champagne region, the Belgians were beside themselves to greet and welcome the American liberators. The days of German tyranny were over. Finally the trucks ground to a halt, and to avoid the welcoming crowd from climbing in the trucks, the soldiers climbed to the ground and were mobbed by hugs, kisses, handshakes, and slaps on the back as the joyous crowd pressed in on the troops. Many in the older generation were crying as they remembered too well the German occupation twenty years earlier and, by comparison, knew the one that had just ended was a much worse experience. They prayed silently that, God willing, they would not see the Germans as rulers of Belgium again in their lifetime.

As the spontaneous celebration wore on, the town mayor, complete with the official sash of his office stretched diagonally across his round chest and matching belly, worked his way through the trucks, offering his official welcome to every soldier he could lay his hands on. Frank was given kisses of welcome on each cheek as his men joined in the cheers at the display of the mayor's official welcome. Then the barrel of beer appeared along with bottles of wine, and the celebration gave signs of setting in for the duration of the day and nighttime hours.

Major Carey worked his way through the crowd and found Frank saying, "We better get this show back on the road; we still have Germans to fight."

Frank knew the major was right and had his final swig of dark beer as he swung onto the tailgate of his truck and called to his men to return. The process of unraveling the soldiers from the crowd took some time, but progress was made and the liberation cavalcade began its slow roll again led by Major Carey standing in his jeep waving and shaking hands. The soldiers did the same from sides of trucks before the vehicles started to climb up out of the river valley heading for the border region in eastern Belgium and Luxembourg. As the trucks wound their way up the escarpment, each man had his own version of the welcoming experience; the feeling of goodwill elated the men and gave them a grateful reward for the sacrifice they were making.

The truck caravan moved east through the southern Belgium countryside, meandering near Bastogne and then stopping in the village of Houffalize. Welcoming of the troops in Houffalize was muted since the Germans occupied a hillside a mile east of the village; there was still work for the Americans to do as far as the village residents were concerned. During the waning hours of the afternoon, his company moved east and dug in to their temporary position; all were confident they would be on the move at sunrise. During the night, rain started to fall along with mortar shells launched by the Germans from positions behind the ridge they occupied. By 0400 hours a chill breeze picked up as the weather turned very uncomfortable for an early September morning. If the soldiers had been at home, they would have recognized football weather, but in Belgium it was damned uncomfortable in their wet clothes and boots.

Frank and his fellow captains and their command majors listened to a briefing that outlined the next phase of the Allied offensive.

"SHEAF Command has evaluated several options for moving ahead. Our biggest limitation, as I think you all know, is the lack of fuel. To remedy this we have to open Antwerp to shipping so we can reduce the length of our supply line across France. Instead of moving supplies from Normandy, we need to go a few hours north to the border region, and that means Antwerp is the key. Now we already control Antwerp but not the shipping lanes, so it's useless till we get the Germans out of the Westerschelde waterway here in the Netherlands that provides a sea lane from the English Channel to the docks at Antwerp." Colonel Kuralski pointed at the map of the German borderlands with the Netherlands, Belgium, and Luxembourg spread on the large table. Frank recognized that Antwerp was the major port at the north end of the borderlands. "In addition to freeing the waterways, our second, and equally important goal, is to cross the Rhine River into the heart of Germany. Command has determined to do this.

"Montgomery's up here in north-central Belgium, and he will be provided the lion's share of the available fuel to drive across the Netherlands to Arnhem in Germany on the east side of the Rhine. His mission has been named Market Garden. If we take Arnhem, we also achieve a crossing of the Rhine, and there's only flat land between there and Berlin, very few places for the

Germans to set up a defensive line. Montgomery has a complex plan to strike from his position here in Belgium near the village of Geel into Holland and through these Dutch cities lined up to the northeast, Eindhoven, Grave, Nijmegen, and then into Arnhem. Airborne troops, the 101st, 82nd, Polish, and British units, will drop into each of the cities ahead of Montgomery and secure the key bridges and allow Montgomery to drive straight up this route. Ike is betting that Monty can pull off this maneuver and end the war sooner than later. And that's what we all want."

The colonel then answered several questions regarding the close logistics required for the Market Garden offensive to succeed. There was some concern whether the British could pull off the maneuver of coordinating ground and air attacks after their limited success with Montgomery's Operation Goodwood in Normandy in attacking east from Caen. For Market Garden it became apparent to all that success depended on incredibly close timing of the troop drop and the thrust of the British armor from city to city along the route.

"Now while we are placing a lot of our eggs in Monty's basket, we are going to keep pressure on the line in Belgium, Luxembourg, and south in Saarland and Alsace-Lorraine and move the line east wherever we can. We are looking for the weak spots. Our limitation will be the lack of significant tank support; they just won't have the gas to charge ahead like they want to. And believe me, Patton is upset with this Market Garden plan, but that's Ike's decision so we'll do our part."

The briefing also told the officers of the redesignation of the Allied command structure. Bradley had been moved up to command the Twelfth Army Group, which included the First Army, now under Hodges, and Patton's Third Army. The First and Third armies were still fighting side by side along the western German border, with the First in Belgium and Luxembourg and the Third along the line from Luxembourg south to Nancy, the heart of the Lorraine region of France. Frank learned the Brigade to which his company belonged was to be moved to a point just northeast of Thionville, France, nine miles below the French-Luxembourg border and facing the Saarland region of Germany, so Houffalize proved to be only a temporary stop on their liberation cavalcade.

During the nighttime hours of September 7, replacement troops arrived in Houffalize by truck; the same trucks bore Frank's Brigade south across the small heartland of Luxembourg, through its capital, and into France at sunrise. The troop trucks rolled through Thionville in the early hours of daylight, turned east, and moved into their new positions and dug into the wet ground 500 yards northeast of the village Basse-Ham. Their rapid digging produced individual foxholes, as well as a set of command bunkers interconnected by deep trenches. Based on experience in Normandy, the American troops expected to find that the German bunkers had walls and roofs fortified with timbers and the roofs also covered with soil. The German trenches and bunkers were built for defense; the American foxholes, simply dug into the earth, were intended to be very temporary, and less care went into their engineering and construction. The Americans were destined to spend more time in their temporary holes than they expected on September 9.

The companies to Frank's left were positioned along the southeast bank of the Moselle River and for about five hundred yards farther to the southeast. Frank's men covered the road, Route N 153, leading northeast from Thionville paralleling the Moselle to the German border at the village of Apach. German troops were crowded into the French villages, farm fields, and wood lots in between. An American artillery battery was set up to the southwest of Basse-Ham as support for the foot soldiers. The battalion command post, a Sherman tank depot, and several self-propelled anti-tank guns also occupied the field some two hundred yards west of the artillery on the winding Thionville road.

Before dawn on September 9, eight Shermans pulled onto the N 153 and started northeast through Basse-Ham and stopped abreast of Frank's men. The American artillery had begun firing into the German positions an hour before dawn and continued into the dawn hour, ceasing at 0730 when the tanks thrust into forward gear followed closely by the infantry on foot. The American line from the Moselle to the southeast was in motion attacking the German front. Off to the right another tank column thrust forward across a field as a second point on the American spear. By 0900 the American advance had ground to a halt in the N153 corridor, as well-placed German machine guns and infantry fired from protected positions strung along a tree line that provided ample firing positions for their infantry and hidden tanks. The enemy's gun placement meant that every foot of the field of attack was raked from at least two positions, making cover for the troops in the flat terrain almost nonexistent. Close support from fighter aircraft was called in to rake the German positions as the battle raged, but with little apparent impact on the entrenched enemy. Sporadic firing from German artillery was deadly, but short lived due to attacks carried out by American aircraft. German mortar and tank fire was another matter, as its initial firing left little trace; its points of origin were difficult to locate in the woods. The American troops felt an utter sense of helplessness as they were stranded in a field of fire.

As the sun set on the twelfth, the American line had moved barely two hundred yards slightly northeast, and new foxholes had been dug. The Germans remained in the same fortified positions as when the day started. The opposing troops were now within easy rifle-firing distance of each other.

During the night hours, the Shermans were refitted with fuel and shells and the disabled tanks retrieved; mechanics and welders began working to return them to fighting condition. Heavy rain also returned, turning the fields into potential quagmires for heavy equipment. When the ground was observed, it looked wet, but when walked across, the soldier's boots were soon covered with a thick layer of dead-weight mud, slowing the rate of progress for even the stoutest of men. Conditions required that effective tank activity be confined to paved roads for the time being; otherwise they would become hopelessly bogged down in the plowed fields. On the morning of the thirteenth, the infantry fired from their buried positions without hope of advancing. Mortar, artillery, and tank fire from both sides tried to blast the opponent into retreat, but both sides proved to be equally insensitive to the loss of life, and they continued to fight, wound, and kill. Aircraft were silent due to the low-hanging clouds and frequent showers; all of the action took place on the ground that day.

And so the battle raged northeast of Thionville through September into early October, as the Americans made sporadic advances much as a palsied man jerked forward in a halting gait when trying to walk. At times one part of the body would be in the lead—feet, hips, shoulders, or arms. Other times an unexpected part would thrust forward—the head, upper legs or torso. Small, halting, uncoordinated steps were taken by the Americans as the Germans fought to protect their homeland. When required to finally retreat, the Germans moved under the cover of darkness to the rear into newly built fortifications. Often they planted mine fields in the approaches and inside their vacated bunkers, mines the Americans learned the hard way had to be dealt with first before general attacks resumed. The Americans almost always fought from uncovered positions but benefitted from an endless supply of munitions, equipment and, most of all, men; young men, most without the benefit of combat experience.

The simple command from the Allied Command Center was a single word: attack. There was no particular strategy involved in the command to attack. It meant that the troops rushed into battle always going forward, never retreating. Eisenhower, Bradley, and Patton still believed that the surrender of Germany was within a month or so if the men kept attacking, kept the pressure on, until the Germans cracked one final time. The junior officers in the field fighting with their men did not now share that belief, as they saw the price being paid in lives every day of the continuous battle. The Germans gave no sign of caving in to American pressure.

After three-and-a-half weeks of constant fighting, Frank's

battered company was pulled from the line and trucked to Thionville for a period of rest and recuperation. As in the two days following the battle for hill 317 at Mortain, the essentials for the troops were dealt with first: eating hot food, showering, shaving, sleeping on something other than the ground, and donning clean clothes. Incorporation of replacement troops into the platoons and squads of the company was the next critical step. A personal step in the R and R days was the attention paid to correspondence. Frank received two letters and a very large box of broken cookies. Despite the appearance, he was amazed at the speed with which the pieces and crumbs were devoured by his men. He placed the box in the mess tent, and it was empty after the first evening meal.

*Dear Dad,* *September 15, 1944*
*School has started and I am doing fine so far. Mrs. Cross is our teacher and she is as nice as Miss Thomas was last year. There's a joke in our class that Mrs. Cross is not. Do you get it? Bill Robinson came up with it and everybody laughed. She does not play the saxophone like Miss Thomas either but she is still nice. We had an election for class officers in the sixth grade and Bobby Goldberg was elected president and Joe Smith Vice President. Jerry ran for president but he lost. I voted for him but not many others did I guess.*

*We are playing football this fall. It is called flag football where each player has a flag tucked in their belt and they are tackled when someone pulls out their flag and throws it on the ground. It is a lot of fun. I am an end most of the time when we have the ball and pass rusher when we don't have the ball. Our team is organized by Mr. Teeter who is a new teacher at school. I have never had a man teacher but he only does sports and things like that after school. He says we are going to play basketball this winter. We have a game playing against Beaumont Elementary we are very excited and hope to win. That game is on Saturday. Mr. Teeter says he has two more games set for us but I have forgotten who they are. Mr. Teeter said he played for UT football team about ten years ago and he has leg problems and something else wrong inside his body and can't go in the army like you. He wants to but they won't take him.*

*I hope the war is going well for you and you are safe.*

*Love Ted*

*September 12, 1944*

*Dear Frank, My Epistolary Friend,*

*I love that title. I guess we are the perfect example of epistolary friends. I believe you used the word correctly; in fact, I had to look up the word in the dictionary to get its meaning. It is a form of the word epistle which, again from the dictionary, is a literary composition in the form of a letter. I'll have to remember that word and impress my friends, assuming I can find a way to use it in a conversation.*

*I spent several days in Nashville and took care of some business that had been lingering, and now I am feeling much better. As far as your concern about the tone of your letters, I have given it some thought. Frank, you asked me if I minded having you write me very frank letters about your concerns with fighting and your confrontations with death. Well, aside from the unintended pun that may arise from use of the word frank, I thought a lot about the question and have decided that you may write me whatever you care to, and I will be your sounding board. I hope that is an apt metaphor. That's the very least I can do to assist you. I do not know if I will be able to help you sort out the many meanings of the experience you are undergoing, but the least I can do is to listen and respond if at all possible. At first I was troubled by the notion of keeping your letter from the family, but I will have to find creative ways to read it in private and avoid their questions.*

*I'm so sorry to hear about Corporal Henson's death. When I was home, I told June about it, and she was quite emotionally struck by the fact, even though she had had only two letters from him. It really brought home the cost of the war we have to fight. She had written three letters to him, the last one which was returned during my visit saying the addressee's whereabouts were unknown. I suppose that is standard procedure, but it was a shock for her knowing that he was dead. I guess institutions like the army can't always be sympathetic. When I left to come back to Knoxville, she rode with me on the streetcar to the bus station and said she would like to write to another soldier if you would give her a name. It is a shame that she is growing up now and it has to be during this awful war.*

*I have reread your letter and have a few thoughts on your comments, for whatever they are worth. First, I understand that you have to follow orders even though people die as a result. That is war, is it not? I believe your course of action in following orders is correct, because since you are an officer, the loss-of-life consequences could be even worse if you chose not to follow orders. I am not referring to the obvious problems you would be creating for yourself by being court-martialed, but to the loss of life of more of your men if you were a free actor in the war and not working in harmony with your compatriots. You are right; if you were not the captain of your men, someone else would do the job but probably not as well as you. I think you will be able through your actions to save as many of your men from harm as possible. Such questions as life and death cannot be dealt with in a simple manner.*

*Another thought, with the tone and feelings you expressed in your letter, I do not think there is a chance on God's green earth that you will become accustomed to death as you feared. In fact, I think the war will have the opposite effect on you by making you much more aware of the value of life during the remainder of your years on this earth. I suspect you will become a warrior fighting for the little guy after the war so that he will have a chance to succeed in this world. That would be a swell outcome for those of us who did not fight in Europe or the Pacific.*

*To avoid using another sheet and exceeding the weight limit for the stamp, I will close. I look forward to receiving your next letter. Do take care of yourself as well as your men.*

*With affection, Lily, your epistolary companion*
*(P.S. More cookies are on the way.)*

Frank read Lily's letter and appreciated the thought she had given to her comments. He hadn't considered the fact that through the fighting and killing he might gain a better insight into the value of a life for all people. Perhaps it would have a positive effect on him after the war . . . perhaps. He wrote and posted responses to both Ted and Lily.

# CHAPTER 29

*Sierck-les-Bains, France*

*October 1944*

THE R AND R period this time included three days of training for the combined seasoned veterans and newly arrived infantry soldiers. Experience had taught the American army that street fighting in villages and cities was not always the most effective method of attacking the enemy in an urban setting. Through trial and error a new fighting regimen had been developed. The enemy in defending a town often placed their guns in anticipation of troops attacking through the streets. Guns were placed in the upper floors of buildings and in key locations where they could blast selected street sections and intersections. Instead of the frontal street attack, the Americans were now taught to use tanks, bazookas, or other available weapons to blast a hole in the side of a structure, toss grenades into the hole, then enter the building amidst their automatic rifle fire that raked the interior. The second floor was to be cleared by grenades and fire from the first floor and the basement by the same technique. Instead of then going to the street to attack the next building, the men were taught to blast a hole in the side wall of the attached row structure and repeat the building-clearing techniques. Rather than attacking on the streets, the Americans were taught to fight their way through the buildings one at a time and avoid the open street whenever possible.

Frank and his company practiced the new urban fighting tactic on derelict buildings provided by the local Thionville magistrates, thus the 131 new men in Frank's company of 200 were given a taste of combat and, perhaps, learned lifesaving maneuvers. Time would tell whether the new men would live to see their homes again, and in fact whether any of the men, newcomers or veterans, would survive the war.

The rest period in Thionville allowed Frank to learn about the broader theater of war the Third Army was fighting. The army's left flank near Thionville was grinding slowly and sometimes not moving at all to the east. In the summer of '44, Patton had begun to believe that the army was invincible—until, that is, he faced one of the Germans most heavily fortified emplacements at the city of Metz, thirty miles south of Thionville. Metz was originally protected by a series of forts centered on Fort Driant. The original forts were constructed during the German occupation of Alsace-Lorraine from 1870 to 1918. Then, when the city was seized again by the Germans in 1940, Hitler began pouring more reinforced concrete into Driant, building an impregnable, virtually self-contained fortress above and below ground with chambers connected by a network of underground tunnels. Repeated attacks by the center of the Third Army had proven fruitless against the hardened concrete fortress as Patton continued to throw men and munitions at the fortifications. Through late September and the first two weeks of October, the American assault continued. On several occasions, the Germans called down their own artillery onto the fort to blast away the American troops clambering on the structure as they desperately tried to fight their way inside. For two-and-a-half weeks Patton insisted on throwing his best units against the fortifications to no avail. By the end of Frank's R and R period, Patton had pulled back from the fruitless attacks and was placing his men to attack both north and south of Metz, then combine the attackers east of the city, surrounding and isolating the city and forts. He would then pick off the units in the city one at a time and forego additional attacks on the forts.

Frank also learned additional details about the failure of Montgomery's Market Garden strategy. The British were now bogged down between Nijmegen and Arnhem in the Netherlands after failing to take Arnhem and the crossing over the Rhine River. The Americans blamed the failure of the attack on the British Guards Armored Division for not fighting hard enough to overcome the German obstacles and join forces with the airborne troops dropped in advance of the armor. Montgomery blamed the failure on the Americans, but where the blame rightly fell was of no consequence now, as the British were stopped and dug into defensive positions. The British airborne troops that had been dropped into Germany east of Arnhem had taken control of the bridges over the Rhine, but they were not reached in time by the armored units and were finally obliterated by the enemy. The Westerschelde waterway had not been cleared of Germans, and the Port of Antwerp was still not functioning. So the net benefit of Montgomery's gamble that had had Eisenhower's full support and had gained additional land in the Netherlands, but without the breakthrough that had been needed to end the war. And in failing to clear sea access to Antwerp, the Allies still depended on trucking routes across France for needed supplies. As Frank left Thionville, he heard word that Eisenhower's most recent order to Montgomery from early October had finally been honored, as Montgomery began on October 16 to move against the Germans to clear the Westerschelde. Frank thought, *It seems Montgomery is still chafing from his secondary rank to Eisenhower and demonstrates his independence in ways that irritate our top brass. Bloody British.* he chuckled, *you can't live with them, and you can't live without them.*

The major alignment of the Allied forces was obvious to Frank. He understood that the First Army was focused on pushing from Belgium into Germany at Aachen and then on to Cologne north of the heavily forested area known as the Ardennes. The Third Army was ordered to attack the Saarland region south of the Ardennes. That meant the Ardennes, an extension of the rugged Eifel plateau area in Germany was lightly manned by the allies. The lack of attention to the Luxembourg-German border in the Ardennes would prove to be a costly error for the American senior strategists. The allied planners still had difficulty understanding the military logic and motivating tactics of the chief German strategist, Adolph Hitler.

As Frank's company rejoined the front northeast of Thionville, they were placed on the outer western limits of the village Sierck-les-Bains that sat on the south bank of the Moselle River. The change in tactics by Patton of deferring more attacks on Fort Driant at Metz in favor of attacking north and south of the city had borne some fruit in the army's left flank, as the Germans fighting near the Moselle were forced to cede land at a somewhat faster pace. Frank's company was now fighting west southwest of Sierk-Les-Bains in a wooded valley created by a small stream from the southeast that ran north to its mouth at the Moselle in the heart of the village. Following the first day of the company's return to the fight, the Germans pulled back to defend the high ground on the east side of the wooded valley, thus opening the door for a full attack on the village, which was still believed to be defended by a force of unknown size.

Early on the morning on the eighteenth of October, the fog hung like a blanket over the Moselle's waters and half-way up the valley walls on the south side of the river. The mist obscured the village and adjacent river bank as the reluctant sun broke through the persistent rain clouds and began to consume the mist as the air dried. By 0900 hours the outlines of village structures could be seen by forward observers. American artillery opened on the observed German positions with coordinates provided by forward observers. At 1100, the tanks broke into forward motion and approached the enemy along two roads with infantry units following in their wake. Frank's company was positioned along the Rue Bellevue that ran parallel to and 300 yards south of the Moselle. In this location the cottage-type houses were separated from one another by small yards and resembled the outskirts of any small American town; they were not occupied by Germans. The Americans encountered several machine gun emplacements dug into the sloping hillside that had to be eliminated by the tanks as they worked their way along the road. Frank's ability to direct his men was greatly assisted by the availability of detailed aerial maps prepared from the many reconnaissance flights over the front. The map makers also located fixed German fortifications where they could be observed on the photographs.

Road signs marked the end of the Rue Bellevue where it turned east and intersected with another road that ran to the southwest, parallel to the small stream. From this point, the tanks swung onto the intersecting road; the plan was for the four Shermans to work their way up the road to another cross road where they would move across the stream and link up with Frank's company on the other side of the valley. Frank's infantry company had to work its way across the wooded valley floor toward the road on the other side of the stream and then into the heart of the village led by the tanks. The stream lay about 200 yards in front of the men as Frank ordered scouting parties to be sent to the left and right while the center squad carefully worked its way northeast toward the stream. Trees in the valley were not thick and afforded decent sight lines for observing the enemy. Amid the sound of distant firing on the left from other units moving toward the village, a sudden explosion ripped the air on Frank's immediate right as one of his privates stepped on a mine. "Halt," shouted Frank, "Mines. Keep your position and look at your feet."

A second explosion in front of Frank knocked a corporal from his feet. In falling he set off a second mine which hurled his lifeless body to a resting place in the damp oak leaves. "Everybody look behind you and then walk backwards in your own tracks. Go slow."

Medics moved forward and gingerly pulled the private to a safe place where they began to assess his injuries as a second pair carefully worked their way to the body of the dead corporal. Both men were placed on stretchers within minutes. Frank's men slowly backed out of the mine field as a squad of engineers came forward and began moving gingerly into the woods trying to locate the mines. "Lieutenant, try and figure out how wide the field is;

we either go through it or we go around it," Frank spoke to the leader of the engineers. Two additional mines ripped into life as the experienced team located and discharged the weapons.

"I can't determine a pattern; it looks very random," said the lieutenant. "Sometimes there's some kind of pattern, but not this time. We're going to throw a steel cable into the area and see if we can clear a path." And so the engineers flung a weighted cable out in front of their path and dragged it back across the forest floor as five additional mines were exploded. At times the engineers were on their hands and knees as they probed the ground with their trench knives looking for metal objects buried amid the decaying leaves. Slowly a path fifteen-feet wide was marked through the woods accompanied by more explosions. Engineers nailed signs to trees along the edge of the mine field to warn others of the danger. In talking to the brigade command center, Frank reviewed their situation and learned of the progress of companies on his left and right flanks. It was important to not get too far ahead or behind the flanking companies when sight lines of your comrades were obscured. It was also necessary to check to determine if there was a known risk involved in bunching his men into a fifteen-foot-wide path through the woods. "Move ahead," came the directive from command center. And so the company gingerly moved through the wooded valley following the engineers, wading across the six-foot-wide stream and up the other side of the narrow valley. No enemy gun emplacements were encountered in the woods.

As they emerged from the woods onto a narrow road, Rue du Cardinal Billot, German machine gun fire split the air, and the engineers leading the procession dove for the ground on the verge of the road. Three of their men had been hit. One of their members lay on his back as the last gasps of life escaped his torn body. Frank, lying on the ground behind the engineers, immediately called the tank commander and learned they were only fifty yards away to the south working their way toward the ground-hugging troops. Had it not been for the imminent arrival of the tanks, Frank's men faced dire consequences. They were especially vulnerable because they were still clustered in a thick line along the cleared path. The sound of the tanks now filled the air, as the approximate location for the machine gun was given to the tank commander. The German machine gun had been placed to ambush troops moving along the road; instead Frank's men approached across the valley, right into the face of the enemy. The first tank stopped and raked the ground twenty yards off the road to the northeast. "A little higher up the hill," Frank barked into the radio as the tank's machine gun fired onto a low stone wall. Two other nearby German machine gun emplacements barked into life, striking the ground in front of the engineers.

Frank's men were now in dire peril as the machine gun fire increased, raking the ground and low-hanging limbs spitting dust and bark fragments in the air. The Sherman swung its turret to the right and fired a 75mm shell into the wall in front of the first machine gun, forever silencing it. The explosion sent rock fragments flying in many directions as the Saint and three of his men leaped to their feet and darted in a crouching run behind the cover of the Sherman. The two other machine guns sent fire ripping into the road behind them. The tank turret swung back to the left and sent a second shell in the general direction of the remaining Germans. Amidst the explosion of the tank shell, the Saint and his men broke into the trees and began a crawl up the wooded slope to get a better sighting angle of the enemy guns.

A quick burst from the German guns tore into soldiers lying on the forest floor as other Americans returned fire in the general direction of the hillside and the enemy. The report from the machine gun revealed the gun location to the tank driver and the Sherman sent a third shell into the stone wall to the left of the first destroying the second gun and its crew. An almost simultaneous burst from automatic rifles silenced the third gun as the Saint's circling maneuver paid dividends.

"Hold your position," called Frank as the Saint completed a circle through the woods and gave an all clear signal. An audible sigh of relief came from the sprawled troops who cautiously moved from their prone position to a crouched fighting stance with their rifles at the ready. Frank and several men came to the fallen soldiers when medics came forward along the path. The badly wounded men were tended to and taken to the rear on stretchers along with the dead engineer.

With the all clear signal now understood by the Americans, the lead tank lurched forward and immediately set off a mine buried in the road. The explosion lifted the steel monster a foot in the air before it crashed back to the road with a smoking, gaping hole in the limp left track and a badly damaged driving wheel hanging at an odd angle. The tank crew scrambled from the escape hatch as smoke followed them, billowing into the outside air. A second tank moved in close behind and then ahead of the stricken behemoth. The squad of engineers now had a road surface to examine for mines ahead of the advancing column. The slow walk toward the village began behind the engineers, three working tanks, and the column of soldiers on both sides of the road.

At 1330 the company was in clear sight of the center of the village. Frank's radio sparked to life as the radioman handed him the receiver. "The German line seems to run from the center of the village southeast through the woods and then up the ridge to about the road Rue de Montenach on top of the ridge."

"I see it on the map," responded Frank. "We are on Rue de Saint Georges about a hundred yards from the center of the village. Their front seems to be east of your location, but you are to proceed with caution to the village and engage the enemy there on Lorraine Street and the river bank. Charlie Company will take both sides of Rue de Trier Street. You are to clear the buildings in your sector of the center. Questions?"

"Where is A Company in this action?"

"They are backing you and C Company from the river bank through those Lorraine and Treves streets."

"Got it. No more questions; I'll keep you abreast of our progress."

"Roger, out."

Frank called together his platoon and squad leaders for an impromptu review of the orders and a reminder of the recent building–clearing tactic they had practiced in Thionville. Two platoons were assigned to the north side of Rue de Lorraine and the river bank and two platoons to the south side of the street. The tanks were to move up the street and provide their fire power when needed by the troops. The men on the south side of the street would be adjacent to Charlie Company working along the parallel Rue de Treves. Frank spoke briefly with the commander of Charlie Company and worked out signals for their attack. Frank briefed him on the strategy of fighting through the buildings rather than from the more exposed position of moving up the open street. He was grateful for the advice. As the officers parted, the rain started again in intermittent light and heavy showers pushed by a stiff cold breeze from the northwest.

At 1430, the platoons and tanks swung into position on the southwest side of the village's center, and the tanks fired into the first exposed sidewalls of buildings, opening a gaping hole through which clambered the men spraying the interior with automatic rifle fire. The early going on Rue de Lorraine encountered no German's, but as they crossed a short intersecting street, Germans burst from cellars and attics of side-by-side houses with their arms raised and waving white rags in surrender. *They're just boys. My God, what's Hitler doing sending school boys to war?* Frank pulled aside Sergeant Le Master, "Use your German and question those boys, where are they from, why are they here?"

"Yes, sir." After a moment of hasty conversation, "They say they are from the military academy in Manheim and were drafted into the army in July and sent here to the front in August. They said there are some old men fighting in the north end of the village, and I asked them what they mean by old and they said they were grandfathers some with gray hair. These kids are fifteen and sixteen years old and scared to death."

"Damn. Disarm them and take them to the rear: they're still prisoners if they wear uniforms."

The sergeant and another soldier marched the six uniformed boys west on Lorraine. By 1600 Frank's company along with C Company had cleared the village buildings as far north as Rue de Sierck. In the process, five Germans were killed and twenty-four taken captive. The grandfathers turned out to be veterans of the First World War and were in their mid-forties up to about sixty years old. They were not fighting by choice but by the will of Hitler, who they generally mistrusted. The five German deaths were all senior cadets from the Manheim military academy, according to papers found on their bodies; based on their actions, they were staunch believers in the Third Reich as defined by Hitler. They fought to the death as ordered without taking any American casualties with them. *Hitler must be proud of his young Aryan warriors,* thought Frank.

With the conquest of Sierck-les-Bains, the Americans now occupied an additional half mile of the Moselle River bank north of the ridge currently defended by the Germans. As the sky darkened that gray evening, the weather deteriorated. Rain blew in on an accompanying, unusually cold wind from the north. The company slept that night inside the dry buildings of the village and built fires in fireplaces, wherever possible, to warm their cold bodies and dry out their wet boots, socks, and other pieces of damp clothing. Frank took a few minutes to write two letters to Knoxville.

# CHAPTER 30

## *Knoxville*

### *Late October 1944*

"LANDS SAKES, TEDDY, is that a bruise on your face?" Mary asked as he came into the kitchen and dropped his school books on the kitchen table.

"Yes'sum." Teddy sat at the table.

"Whatever happened?"

"Well, there's this kid from Beaumont, and he and his friend jumped Jerry and me when we were walking home. Jerry hurt his leg when he was kicked, and I got hit in the face and on the arm and back."

"Let me see," said Mary as she pulled up his shirt. "Oh my, let's go upstairs and clean it up."

As they came downstairs from the bathroom, the skin surrounding Ted's eye was showing signs of a darkening bruise.

"Did you have a rough football practice?" asked Lily as she entered the kitchen following her walk home from Van Gilder.

"No, umm . . . I had a little fight," said Ted with his eyes focused on the kitchen floor.

"Fight? That doesn't sound like you."

"Well, Jerry and I were jumped"—he glanced up looking into Lily's eyes, then back to the floor—"by some boys from Beaumont, and they kinda beat us up."

"What were boys from Beaumont doing up here?"

"Well, we beat 'em in football last week, and they wanted to get even, I guess." Ted continued to look at the floor. "One of 'em wasn't even in the game and the other was real big and slow, and we just ran around him all the time. I guess they just wanted to show they were strong or something."

"Well, we'll just see about that," said Mary as she stood in the center of the kitchen, fists clenched on the hips.

"Granny, don't say anything, you'll just . . . you know make things worse and then . . ." He turned with his face reddening as he walked from the kitchen and up the stairs to his room.

"He's had his pride hurt," said Lily. "If word gets out that his grandmother came to school to protect him, it may make matters worse for him. Children are funny that way."

"Well, we can't let him get beat up by those bullies like he did."

"No, Mary, I agree, but—"

The front doorbell rang, cutting off conversation as Mary walked to the front door and admitted Jerry's mother, Gladys. "Come on in. How're you, Gladys?"

"I'm fine. Did Ted get hurt?"

"Yes, some. He'll probably have a black eye," said Mary. "How's Jerry?"

"Oh, he was kicked in the leg pretty hard, but nothing lasting like a broken bone or cut or anything."

"What do you think we should do about it?"

"Why, I don't know. We could let the boys work it out. But if it continues, we'll have to do something, but for now I wouldn't go to the school or anything like that."

"Well, I'm not sure. I just don't like the idea of strange boys coming in the neighborhood and picking on our boys."

"I know," said Gladys. "But Jerry's two older brothers had a few problems that they worked out on their own. I think all boys, or at least a lot of 'em, go through this phase of dealing with bullies."

"I'll talk to Will tonight and see what he thinks. Come on back to the kitchen for a cup of coffee, or do you like tea?"

"I have to get home to start supper, but maybe a quick cup of coffee if you have it made."

"Lands sakes, it won't take but a minute." Mary led Gladys to the kitchen as they began recounting episodes of their older sons' battle scrapes that they survived during their adolescent years.

Will came through the back door into the kitchen with his lunch box in hand.

"Will, we got a problem," Mary announced.

"What's that, my little buttercup?" he said in his best imitation of W. C. Fields, which wasn't very convincing.

"I'm serious, Will. Teddy was jumped by some bullies and got hit and kicked and so did Jerry down the street."

"Oh, where is he now?"

"Upstairs in his room."

"I'll talk to him," said Will as he walked for the stairs.

As Mary worked over the stove flipping the potatoes frying in the cast-iron skillet, Will came back downstairs and into the kitchen. Lily was slicing the very last of the summer's tomatoes at the sink. "Well we talked about how bullies operate and about the friendly art of retribu . . . , what's that word?"

"Retribution," suggested Lily.

"Yes, that's it, retribution. Great word."

"What are you cooking up with that boy?" asked Mary sharply. "I don't want to get him hurt by some big ole boy who is looking for a fight."

"If the big ole boy wants to fight Teddy, Teddy just saying he doesn't want to fight him is not going to stop it from happenin'. We talked about how sometimes you have to call a bully's bluff and kick him in the you-know-what."

"Posterior," suggested Lily.

"Posterior, yes exactly, posterior. That's another great word. I wish I could come up with those words like you do Lily gal. Maybe also he could kick him in the fronterior, if you get the drift of my meaning."

Lily smiled at the name Will often used for her. "I think calling his bluff is a good idea, and even if Ted loses another fight, he just might gain some respect from the bully, causing him to stop picking on him."

"Maybe, but the best way is to kick his ass, er . . . excuse me, posterior," Will corrected himself.

"Now, if this bully is as big as Teddy says, how are you two going to get him ready for another fight? Answer me that," demanded Mary.

"Well, I don't rightly know just yet," said Will. "Mary, don't you remember how we tried to stay out of the spats that our boys had growing up. Remember the Salyers kid who kept chasing Bill in school and tripping him? I don't know what Bill did to him, but he stopped and then they were good friends in high school. And Frank and the Applegate boy didn't get on at all well, and they would fight something awful until they both got their noses broken on that Halloween night. Remember, they took care of things their way and grew up just fine."

"This is different. We're Teddy's caretakers now not his parents, and we owe it to Frank to keep him safe."

"I agree if Teddy is in any real danger, we'll do something ourselves, but so far he's not. Let's give it a week or so and see what happens."

The sun broke through the thinning cloud layer over Knoxville and promised a warm afternoon, not an uncommon event for a chilly, Saturday morning in late October. "Mary, honey, Ted and I have a little chore to do downtown. We'll be home in time for lunch," Will patted his wife's shoulder as he walked across the kitchen to the back door.

"Where you goin' with that sheepish grin all over your face, old man?" she responded wiping her hands on her apron.

Pausing with his hand on the door knob, "Oh, we've got this 'man thing' to do, it won't take too long."

"Somethin' tells me you are up to somethin'," she protested.

"We'll be all right, and back before you know it," Will said over his shoulder as he headed out the door and walked toward his truck.

Ted came bustling past Mary pulling on his sweater. "Teddy, remember you have to rake up the leaves in the front and back yards today. You promised," Mary called to the back side of her grandson.

"Yes'sum," answered Teddy as he raced after his grandfather.

"What's that old man up to?" Mary mused aloud to no one in particular.

Lily sitting at the breakfast table finishing a cup of coffee said, "*A man thing*, that covers a lot of territory, but as long as Will is in charge, I don't think you have too much to worry about for Teddy's sake."

Just than Mary noticed that Jerry ran into the back yard from the alley and climbed into the back of the truck with Ted. "Now there's Jerry gettin' in the truck. My stars, seems like everybody in the neighborhood knows what's happenin' but me, and you . . . Is that right Lily, you are in the dark like me?" Mary asked turning and looking at the young woman with an inquiring glance.

Lily laughed. "I'm in total darkness." She continued chuckling as she stood and put her cup and saucer in the sink and turned on the hot-water faucet. Mary stood with her hands on her hips as she watched Will back the truck into the alley and then roll forward toward Seventeenth Street with the boys rolling to their left and laughing in the bed of the truck.

It was a great adventure for the boys to ride up and down hills without holding on to the sides of the truck and to roll into each other as they turned corners to the right and left, laughing the whole way to Beaumont Street.

Will guided the truck to a stop at the first parking place he could find on Beaumont Street, two doors down the street from Bailey's Gymnasium. The boys jumped from the back of the truck onto the crumbled sidewalk. Will led the way to the gym's front door, checked his watch, and turned the knob entering a new world dominated by a constant hum of rhythmic noise. The three newcomers to the gym saw two sweating, young colored men on the far side of the large room engaged in strenuous exercise, one jumping a rapidly twirling jump rope and the other pounding on a suspended punching bag that swayed with the jabbing fists. An older colored man stood facing the pair of glistening bodies, observing their effort with his back toward the door. He said something to the young man flailing away at the swinging bag, correcting the angle of his blows. The young man looked over his instructor's shoulder and saw the three white faces standing by the door. Will saw his lips moving, but he was too far away to understand his words. The instructor turned and observed Will and the boys and walked over to them.

"Somethin' I can help you gentlemen with?" he said stiffly as he approached Will.

"Yes, my name's Will Warring, and Isaac Johnson said he would meet us here and give these boys a little boxing lesson."

"Do tell . . . Well, he didn't say nothin' to me about it, but if you want to wait for him, ah"—the instructor gestured toward a row of chairs along the wall by the front door—"sit over there, if you want. I'm workin' with these men over here," gesturing toward the two young men who now stood watching the discussion.

Will, Ted, and Jerry sat in the stiff upright wooden chairs and observed the inside of the dark gymnasium as the instructor walked back across the room. Along the far wall were several pieces of exercise paraphernalia, including stands with ropes, bar-bells, and an assortment of round weights held in wall racks. In the center of the room was a boxing ring with sagging ropes enclosing its four sides. The elevated floor of the ring appeared to be covered by a dirty, heavy canvas stretched tightly over a hidden floor structure. Above the ring were four large, round reflectors for four lights that were now turned off. The instructor, a burly man in his late fifties or early sixties, had a substantial belly hanging over the front of his pants that fell in a graceful drape over and around the tops of his shoes. His light-skin complexion was offset by a large bushy mustache of mottled gray whiskers. Equally bushy hair covered his head in a halo of bright, white hair surrounding a large bald spot on the crown of his head. As he instructed the young man at the punching bag, he gestured and showed a surprising agility as he quickly demonstrated a fleeting movement of feet on raised toes, a twisting torso, and jabbing arms. The young man than did his best to mimic the instructor's directions.

Just then the front door opened, and three dark-skinned young men entered and turned to head for a door at the side of the large room with a hand-painted sign over the door, Dressing Room Shower. The tallest of the young men spotted the three white faces and paused before walking ahead to catch up with his mates. As he walked across the room, he scowled and shook his head after seeing Will and the boys.

"Is it OK for us to be here?" asked Ted as he looked up into his grandfather's face.

"Yes, it'll be OK as soon as Isaac gets here," answered Will. Will was now getting more uncomfortable being in the colored part of town.

The front door opened again, and Isaac, Isaac Two, and Isaac Three entered the gym. "How y'all doin'?" said Isaac. "There's my friend Mr. Teddy. How you boys doin'? And what's your friend's name?"

"This is Jerry; he lives down the street, and we're in the same grade. Hi, Three," Ted spoke to the small boy standing between his father and grandfather.

"And you know Two here," said Isaac, patting his large son's shoulder.

"How y'all doin'?" Isaac Two asked in a deep rumbling voice without a trace of the friendly gesture extended by his father.

After more casual conversation, Isaac Two walked over to the instructor and talked to him and gestured toward the two small white boys. The Instructor lowered his head and nodded, apparently agreeing with Two's requests. The Instructor spoke audibly as Two walked back toward the newcomers. "You can have thirty minutes, then we need to get the serious boys in the ring." The instructor walked to the wall, flipped a switch, and the lights over the ring burst into a dazzling glow.

And so for the next thirty minutes, Two gave Ted and Jerry a basic boxing lesson, stressing how to hit, as well as how to avoid being hit, by an opponent. He also showed them a few basic wrestling holds to use when a confrontation with their fists becomes overtaken by more aggressive grabbing and twisting of limbs and torso.

"Yes sir," said Isaac, as he and Will watched activity in the boxing ring, "Two there, he worked up in Detroit city for three years, an' did some boxin' up there an' saw Joe Louis, yes he did." A broad smile spread across Isaac's face as he admired his large, agile son demonstrating a quick dancing move both away and toward an imaginary opponent.

"See there, he's showin' how to get your body movin' in the right direction to make the punch harder . . . to use all your weight, don't you know, and to jab straight away. That really rocks the other guy." Isaac inadvertently moved his feet and swayed with a sympathetic punch as he reflected his son's footwork. "He was fightin' as a welterweight, and the last fight he got knocked out and said he never saw what hit him." Isaac laughed. "He retired with a four and one record. At least he's smart enough to know when to quit." Both older men chuckled.

"My son takes after his momma. See how big his shoulders is? All her people is big, yes sir." Isaac smiled. "He has her attitude too. Seems like all these young men, they got an attitude that I never had, no sir. They gets tired of what the white people does to 'em, and they say things gonna change. Yes sir, that's what they say. My boy says before the Good Lord calls him up to heaven, us Coloreds are gonna be better off. Now my daddy taught me to get along and mind my business and make do with whatever you have. Not these new boys, no sir. See that tall boy over there liftin' the weights? He's real bad 'bout changin' things. Yes sir, real bad. He just got his greetin' letter from the govamint, from Uncle Sam. He goin' in the army in two weeks." Isaac didn't smile as he told Will about the younger generation. Will stood next to his friend and coworker listening and trying to understand the changes that could occur. He just couldn't think of many.

"Well, enough talk 'bout these youngsters." Isaac's stare was fixated on his large son as he danced around the ring with Ted and Jerry doing their best to mimic. During the teaching episode, Three stood on the apron of the ring hanging onto the top rope and also moving his feet, copying his father. Isaac nudged Will. "Look at Three there. He goin' to want to try boxin' in a few years. Hope he works on his studies as much as he wants to fight." Will saw the young boy lift his right leg and swing his body over the bottom rope, entering the ring so he could better copy his father's demonstration.

"Isaac, looks like you got another generation of fighters comin' on," commented the instructor as he ambled to Isaac's side. The three men faced the ring with Isaac in the center.

"Yes sir, believe I do. Clyde, this here is my friend Mister Warring," Isaac said looking at the instructor and then turning to face Will. Will extended his hand and the instructor belatedly reciprocated as they briefly shook hands in front of Isaac. The instructor didn't smile and seemed locked in a dour mood. Two of the young men who had emerged from the dressing room were now busily clanking weights as they worked through a series of exercises on the far side of the room and the tall man worked on the punching bag with strong jabs.

"Isaac, your time is about up; we got some serious boys to work with, me and Two."

"OK, well, we plenty pleased that you let Two teach these boys somethin' 'bout fightin'," Isaac said.

"Yes, we sure are," added Will.

"Well, I hope it did a little good, 'cause they got a good teacher," the instructor ended his conversation with Will and walked toward the ring clapping his hands.

All three boys jumped to the floor of the gym from the ring and continued dancing in make-believe moves as if they were fighting imaginary opponents. Jerry backed into one of the straight back chairs and sent it bouncing to the floor. "Oops, excuse me," he said as Ted continued with uppercuts and jabs dancing all the time. Three also landed several extraordinarily good blows on his airy opponent, and he clasped hands with Ted over their heads as they relished their fighting skills.

"Thank you, Two," Will said with a broad smile, "I don't think they will be good fighters, but maybe they can do a better job of defending themselves now."

"Yeah," said Two with the hint of a smile, "yeah, at least they are better than when they got in the ring." He now had a somewhat larger, but still faint smile.

Will clasped Isaac on the back. "Much obliged, Isaac, much obliged."

The oldest Isaac extended his hand for a firm handshake. "Glad we could help your boys, glad we could help."

Will and the boys rolled into the back yard as Mary pinned a load of washing to the sagging clothesline. Ted and Jerry jumped from the truck and danced across the yard as Jerry then broke into a run into the alley, heading for home. Mary rolled her eyes as Will smiled at his grandson frolicking across the grass with his jabs and uppercuts.

"Teddy, the mailman came and there's a letter for you in the hall. Lily took her letter already from the— Lands sakes, he won't never stop to listen when the mail comes." Mary's pronouncement was to the back of her grandson as he tore into the house at the mention of mail. Ted found the stamped envelope already opened, but the one addressed to him was still sealed. He supposed Lily already had her letter. He plopped on the settee, opened his envelope, and started to read.

*15 October 1944*

*Dear Ted,*

*I'm glad your school has started and you are doing well with your studies. I wish I had had the opportunity to play organized sports like you are doing. The flag football sounds like good fun. But if I were you, I would avoid playing tackle football when you get to high school. I don't think you are going to be built heavy enough to absorb the hits when tackling starts; but then again, maybe you will grow enough and put on some weight so you can play if you want to. When I was a senior in high school I weighed about 125 pounds and was almost six feet, so I was a string bean and certainly not built to play tackle with boys who weighed up to a hundred pounds more. But I'm glad you are having fun. Let me know how your games go.*

*I hope the war is over soon and I can come home. As you have been reading in the paper, we are now in eastern France. I am getting very homesick these days and want to see you and Granny and Granddad and meet Lily and see the hills of west Knoxville again. Tell Granny and Lily that our feet are still cold and wet and getting colder as November approaches. The Lorraine region has crummy weather if you want my opinion. The sun hardly ever shines these days, and it is always wet.*

*Give my love to Granny and Granddad and keep plenty for yourself.*

*Love, Dad*

Lily had retrieved her envelope and taken it to her room as she mumbled something to Mary about getting her dirty clothes for the Saturday washing. She read the letter in the privacy of her room and wondered how to keep its contents from the Warrings.

*15 October 1944*

*Dear Lily,*

*Thank you for letting me be frank in my comments. Actually I have had to live with being Frank all my life, but in prose I am usually a little more guarded in my language and not so frank. But here goes: another frank letter to you, this time I will try to avoid being so negative. As I think about the next line to write in this letter,*

*I do not think I can be positive; the more I think about it the worse it gets. This war stinks and everything associated with it stinks. The things I have to do stink to high heaven. I continue to lose men at an alarming rate. The single command we get from Command Center is attack. No strategy, just attack. British General Montgomery tried a strategic move that you probably read about in the paper, invading through Holland to try and cross the Rhine and get into northern Germany behind the Siegfried Line. That didn't work. Now it is back to attack, attack full time. (The next two sentences were blacked out by the censor's line of heavy India ink.)*

*Now that I have got that off my chest I feel a little better. I still worry about how I will adjust to life after this war. Your comment about how the war might sensitize me to the needs of others—I have forgotten how you put it in your letter and now the letter is gone—maybe you are right, I hope so. At least I hope I will be fit to live in a civilized society. Wait a minute, I'm assuming Knoxville has a civilized society. Well, let me see. I guess if you are educated, a hard worker, white, and a Christian, then Knoxville is pretty civilized. But if you are a Negro or a Jew a Catholic or Japanese or anything other than white, you will have some problems fitting in and joining in all the fruits of the mid-south society. Am I being too critical? It bothers me that we have all kinds of men in our armies from all different sorts of backgrounds who are giving up their lives for America and the Americans. We are just going to have to open up opportunities for our soldiers and for everybody. RIP DOWN THE BARRIERS, I say, tear them to shreds. Let us start over with our democracy and see if we can get it right this time.*

*Oh, Lily, I wish I could come home. I am tired of the killing and maiming of healthy young men in our uniform and in the uniform of our enemy. We thought we had the war won in September, but the Germans had a different thought, or maybe it was that maniac Hitler. I guess his thoughts are the only ones that count now. Any responsible leader of a country would have sued for peace in September, but not Adolph. He must truly be a madman to sacrifice the next generation of his country for what, a bunch of cockamamie ideas. (Is cockamamie spelled correctly? I don't think I have ever used that word before. I have heard it a lot but never written it.) But I digress, getting back to that maniac, he just escapes description. It is impossible to see how the Germans ever gave power to him to run their country.*

*Well, enough of this babbling, but I do feel better after writing you. I hope you can say the same after reading my harangue. I hope your school year is going well and that you are teaching little students to get along with their classmates. That is important.*

*Your epistolary friend, Frank*

*(P.S. I apologize if I have gone overboard with you in letting off some of the steam that has been building up in me. Thank you for being my friend. Also on the separate note, I have given you another soldier's name for June to write. He is from a little coal mining town in Mingo County, West Virginia. He recently lost his dad in a mining accident and his mother died several years ago, so he is feeling very down in the dumps and has nobody to write him. I know he would like to hear from June.)*

After dinner, as Mary and Lily washed and put away the dishes, Lily confided that Frank was using his letters to her as a way of relieving the pressures he felt in leading his men and he was reluctant for the rest of the family to read them, especially Ted. She offered Mary the chance to read the latest one, and after reading it, Mary said maybe Lily should keep them to herself. It was easier worrying about Frank without knowing the details of what he was going through. *The abstract is easier for her to take than the reality,* thought Lily. Lily had more of the reality to deal with.

As Mary lay in bed that night beside the snoring Will and before sleep overcame her, she reflected on the letter. *The war is awful for Frank to have to endure. I'm so sorry he has to do it; he was always a sensitive boy. The little things always bothered him. I always knew he would grow up to be a good man. Dear God in Heaven, please take care of my boy like you have been doin' and keep him safe and take away his worries so he can pay attention to what he is doin' and come home safe to us, amen. I wonder what that epistol word was at the end of his letter. Epistol, it doesn't make much sense. That must be a college word . . . I'm not worried about not knowin' it, I'm sixty-three years old and that is the first time I've read it, so it can't be anything to worry about . . .* Mary slipped into a dreamless sleep.

# CHAPTER 31

## *Belgium*

### *December 1944*

THE 4TH INFANTRY Division continued to push the line of battle closer to the German border as October ended and the calendar lumbered into November. The days of the week or month made no difference to the men on the front line; every day was the same: a day to survive. Survival was what the game was all about now. The disappointment of not ending the war in September, or October at the latest, was very disheartening to the troops, and it seemed fighting and dying would go on forever.

Disappointment among the Allies on the western front was commonplace in the fall of 1944. Among Frank's troops he sensed they often asked each other, whose fault was it that the war was continuing? One of the American generals? Which one? Eisenhower, Patton, Bradley, Hodges? Surely one of them had goofed up, maybe all four. Hey, maybe it was Montgomery? In August and September the Germans were running toward home so fast that the fighting had to stop. But no, the Americans ran out of gas, literally ran out, and had to slow down. Was that the fault of the quartermasters? Yes, that's it, the quartermasters. If only the army had kept moving, they might be heading home now. Damn those generals . . . damn those supply stiffs.

Frank was in a foul mood along with most of his men as the mail was passed out on that gray day in December. He opened the envelope and read the two letters.

*Dear Dad,* *November 5, 1944*

*I hope you are fine. Granny and Lily and some ladies from the Y have knitted you a bunch of socks so you won't be so cold. I hope they fit you. I tried on a pair and my feet got hot so they should work for you too. I went with Granddad and we got boxing lessons from Isaac Two. He had lived in Detroit and knows all about boxing and things like that and fighting. A BULLY from Beaumont school gave me a black eye a few weeks ago and I got even with him after I learned how to box and fight and I hit him real good on the nose and he went away crying. I don't think he will hit me again. I got called into Miss Pritchett's office and Granny was there and so was Lily and the Principal from Beaumont and the BULLY kid and his mother and we talked about the fight and the BULLY kid and his mother left when she started to get mad at him and hit him and that other principal told him to go home till next week. Miss Pritchett gave me a good talking to and I felt bad about getting in trouble until after school when I felt real good.*

*Jerry was hit by another BULLY and he went with me and learned how to box and he beat up his BULLY. His mother did not come to Van Gilder to complain so she was not in the meeting and so Jerry was not there either. We are heroes in our class now and Bobby Goldberg gave us a gold star for beating up the BuLLies. Yea Yea. Nancy Griffith said she liked me a lot. Yea Yea.*

*I hope you stay warm and come home soon.*

*Love Ted*

*November 7, 1944*

*Dear Frank,*

*I have a great story to tell you about your son, who is growing up very fast now. Besides having equaled Mary's height, he is also maturing as a young man, I believe. About two weeks ago he came home from school with a black eye and a tale about how a bully from Beaumont had hit him. His sidekick punched Jerry. Mary was very upset, but*

*Jerry's mother as well as your father cautioned her to wait and see if the boys would work it out without the parents and guardians having to get involved.*

*I'm not real clear about what transpired, but I suspect your father has a hand hidden in the solution that developed; that remains a suspicion, however, as he has kept quiet on the subject. Apparently, Isaac Johnson's son Isaac II, who is called Two, showed Ted and Jerry some fighting or boxing techniques.*

*Then on Wednesday of that week, Ted came home from school with a big smile on his face and cuts on his knuckles, but he wouldn't say much about the cause. Thursday of that week Mary got a call from the school, and she and Ted were called to a meeting in the principal's office the next day to talk about a fight. Ted still remained pretty closed mouthed about the whole affair. I asked Mary if I could attend the meeting, and Miss Pritchett the Principal didn't object, so I sat in the corner and watched.*

*It turned out to be very comical. The mother of the boy that started the fighting came into the office in a huff; she was out for blood. That one of the Van Gilder boys had hit her son was unthinkable. The mousy principal from Beaumont came with her. To make a long story short, the mother, her name was Mable, was put on the defensive when she saw that her son was about three inches taller and much heavier than Ted—her boy had told her Ted was larger—and Ted had been the first to initiate the fighting. Before long she was saying a lot of unfortunate things to her son and then to everyone else within earshot, and she dragged her boy out of the office and was gone. Miss Pritchett could hardly keep a straight face, but she told Ted not to fight and he said, "Yes Ma'am," and she excused him.*

*After he left, both principals, Mary, and I had a very good laugh about the situation. It turns out that the boy Jerry fought didn't bother to complain, and Jerry's role in the whole affair didn't come up at all, even though we were aware of it. I guess it goes to prove that the children can work out their own problems sometime. (Especially with a wise old grandpa, or maybe that's granddad.)*

*Well I've about used up my paper, so I will stop. I hope the socks arrive on time to do some good for your men. We are still knitting and baking, so more will follow soon along with more cookies, I hope. Take care of yourself.*

*Your loyal reporter of juvenile affairs and epistolary friend,*

*With affection, Lily*

Frank couldn't contain his glee at the two letters, then he wondered what he would have done if he had been in Knoxville and had talked with Teddy after the first fight. Would he have shown restraint, or would he have favored action, like Mary? He was uncertain. Now he could see the value in the soft hand shown by Will. *I wonder how that old rascal pulled off getting Teddy together with Isaac's son. He had to do something; it's not like they are bosom buddies or anything. The old rascal.* A faint smile lit up Frank's face. Like Lily, he had his suspicions about his father's invisible hand in the situation. Frank smiled and felt better than he had in quite a while. That is, until the radioman handed him the receiver.

The commanding voice in the radio announced, "Capt'n Warring, you are to pull your men from the line and move west and join the 9th Battalion to go against Apach in the river corridor. Report to Major Djuric. His command post is on the north side of Sierck-les-Bains. Your replacement troops will be there at 1900 hours."

"I know the Sierck-les-Bains area well," replied Frank. "We were just through that village. I'm on the right of Djuric's men now so I'll reach him before I pull anyone back."

The battle line was now about a mile-and-a-half northeast of Sierck-les-Bains and two miles south of the common border point where France, Germany, and Luxembourg meet. The units in the extreme left flank of the Third Army fighting on the south bank of the Moselle had to coordinate with the extreme right flank of the First Army fighting on the river's north bank. The flanking operations of both armies lacked the firepower and resources of the centers of the two armies. The Third was intent on clearing Germans from the Alsace region east of Metz, and the First Army was fighting to keep and expand a foothold in Germany at Aachen north of Luxembourg. But these backwater units on the flanks of the two armies along the Moselle were expected to keep pace as well as they could with the thrusts of the centers of their armies. The German tide was reluctantly giving ground from Holland to Switzerland.

Over the next ten days, the 9th Battalion attacked to the northeast in the river corridor; the Germans stubbornly fell back one step at a time. The fighting through the scrub forest and across farm fields was fierce, with hand-to-hand combat on two separate occasions. The Shermans were initially effective, but air support was not available due to the day after day of hard rain from low-lying clouds. As the rain accumulated, the ground became a quagmire and tanks as an effective participant in the fighting were compromised; they were either stuck in the mud or pulled back out of combat to wait for drying weather. The pavement on the Rue de Ecluse, a rural road paralleling the river, gave way and began to disintegrate from the combined armor traffic and the constant rain.

The level of the Moselle rose up the bank and invaded low-lying areas, backing up into the small feeder streams that normally drained the nearby fields and wood lots. As the water rose, the opposing forces moved southeast to stay out of the flowing water. No one engaged in the fighting could stay dry; thousands of men were drenched as the chilling winds from the northwest continued to blow briskly. Incidents of colds and flu became commonplace as relief units were rushed into action to maintain the pressure on the Germans.

Frank's forlorn company spent two days back in Basse-Ham with thirty-five men in the hospital for flu symptoms and all of the troops drying out and receiving new clothing. One thing the troops said about the quartermaster battalion was that they may not have much gas, but they sure had boots and dry clothes. Not heavy winter clothes, but nonetheless, dry clothes.

On the first of December, Frank's company rejoined the attack amid a heavy snowstorm; Apach fell on the fifth. Germany was now a mile to the north and east. The Saint estimated he could reach it with five or six consecutive swings with his Bobby Jones driver and a Titleist golf ball. That would, of course, require cooperation of the Germans, which was unlikely to happen, so he had to be content with using his "Thompson to fight my way through to the first tee."

American casualties were high, as the battle and weather continued to take a toll on the troops. Cases of pneumonia were found among the troops, and those with the worst symptoms were sent to England for care. The number of trench foot cases also suddenly rose as the rain continued and the air temperatures dropped. The combined semi-frostbite and wet feet brought many men from their foxholes—where their feet were in six inches of water from dusk to dawn—and sent them to the aid station in the rear. Some of the men returned to the front in several days, others required a week or more, and a few lost one or both of their feet to amputation in the face of the spread of deadly gangrene.

In a briefing with Major Djuric, Frank learned that divisions in the First Army in the Ardennes reported an increase in distant sounds coming from the east. Villagers acted worried, as they reminded the troops that the Germans had come through the forest in 1940 and they feared their return. Djuric contacted Third Army Central Command and was informed that intelligence had picked up other signs of activity in the Ardennes, but the top American brass was convinced that an attack by the Germans there would not make military sense, and in any event the Germans were trying to stem the tide at Aachen and in the Alsace-Saar region and didn't have the manpower to spare for an attack in the Ardennes. If a counterattack did occur, it would be north of Aachen.

Another strain of "intelligence" believed that the German force facing the Americans in southern Belgium and Luxembourg was comprised of a "handful of beaten and demoralized troops . . . supported by horse-drawn pieces of artillery." So believed the

American army. The American army was wrong.

Hitler did not conceive of plans like a traditional military officer, and at 0530 on the morning of December 16, he demonstrated his degree of irrational military behavior by attacking through the Ardennes forest once again with a rejuvenated army of superior numbers. Frank learned after the war that Hitler was attempting another counterattack on a much larger scale than the one he had faced at Mortain in early August.

This time Hitler threw virtually his entire reserve strength into the attack with his newest and best equipment. The immediate objective was to cross the Meuse River at the border of Belgium and France and then drive through to Antwerp, splitting the American Army into two parts. In the field of battle, the Germans outnumbered the weary American divisions in the Ardennes—manned by worn-out veterans and numerous untrained replacement troops—by a ten-to-one margin. The line of attack stretched across the Ardennes from Monschau on the north fifty miles south to Echternach, another small German border village.

By 1000 on the sixteenth, Frank was leaning over maps trying to make sense of the latest communications received from the First Army. At 0530 that morning, the sky to the north had erupted with flashes of light cascading through the low overhanging clouds. The flashes were accompanied by the distant roar of heavy artillery. Something was happening in Luxembourg and maybe in Belgium, according to the sketchy reports coming over their radio.

Major Djuric strode into the room of the partially destroyed building in Sierck-les-Bains that was used as his command center. "The latest information is that the attack extends from just north of us about fifty miles into Belgium. It seems to be a full-scale attack with armor and infantry pouring over the border. We don't have maps of those areas, so we are limited in knowing where they are exactly. Have you spotted any signs that they may attack this far south?" All the officers under his command responded that they had seen no preparation and found no evidence of an attack in their sector.

"Well, it all seems to be north of us for now. We just don't know the strength of the attack, but it gives every sign of being a very large one. It's also unknown where these German troops came from. The Army Group Command Center has not changed our orders so far; there's just no word from them yet. For the next twenty-four hours, hold your position where you are and stay alert to report any observed changes in enemy activity. We will meet back here at 1400 hours today."

Stunned by the news, all the officers hopped into jeeps and raced back to their troops on the front line. Frank briefed his platoon and squad leaders with what little news they had, and the men of the company settled in for another cold, wet day and night in a foxhole.

At 1400 hours Major Djuric opened the meeting, "Still no news on whether there's any real penetration of our line. Still no news from Command Center either. I talked to the First Army Center, and they are slowly getting their arms around the situation, but they don't have the picture yet. They've been hit hard, but they don't know how hard. With this stinking weather, we can't get any eyes in the sky yet. I want patrols sent to probe the enemy in our sector to see if the response has changed. I don't want to be caught flatfooted by the Jerries."

The following morning at 0600, Djuric reconvened the conversation about the attack. "There are at least twelve German divisions involved in the attack. Yesterday they made gains, but we held at key points on the roads running west. But today they may break through, and then we'll have to see where they'll go next." The field officers were stunned by the news. Indeed, where had these German troops come from? The eastern front, not likely, and there were no places on the western front that had seen a reduction in forces opposing the Allies.

"Do you think they may be headed to the Channel?" Frank asked.

"That's a possibility, but they have a long way to go. Continue to hold your positions today and be back here in four hours."

Today was starting off like yesterday. *What's going on up there?* thought Frank. A vision of the last day of fighting at Mortain flashed in Frank's mind as he returned to his troops. He knew the desperate situation that some of the American army units may be facing at this very minute, and he knew it wasn't a pretty picture.

"OK, now we know something," started Djuric at 1000 hours, "and it ain't good at all. The Germans have broken through about forty miles north of here up near a place called Malmedy and seem to be running west as fast as they can go. The 101st and 82nd Airborne are being pulled from Reims here in France"—Djuric pointed at the map—"where they are recovering from their drop into the Netherlands to help Montgomery, and they are moving north by trucks not by air. The 101st is headed to a place called Bastogne in Belgium where they are supposed to hold the Germans. The 82nd is going farther west and north. We are being pulled tomorrow, the eighteenth, and heading west. It's a very fluid situation as of now, and our tentative destination is north of Luxembourg City, but that could change." The major then went over the details of their pullback, as the adjoining Battalion to the southwest would expand their position and thin their troops to cover the withdrawal.

"Hodges at the First Army says this is Hitler's last gasp, and the Jerries seem to be doing it up big time. It's all or nothing, and we must make sure it's their last gasp. Here's one thing we can expect, and that's for our troops to strike north and try and cut off their salient that is heading west. That's what we did at Falaise, and I'll bet a million that's what Ike says to do here. The farther west they go, the harder time they have in resupplying their troops and tanks. Now, they may pick up some of our supplies along the way, but I can't imagine we'd have that much to keep them going. There's also some reports that there are Jerries dressed in British and American uniforms that are behind our lines messing up the road signs and spreading confusion among the troops. Now that's unconfirmed, but if we encounter unknown units, we should be wary of their identity until we can confirm they are real Americans."

"One way we were told in radio school to confirm identity was to ask 'em questions that we Americans would know about but the Germans may not know," offered a lieutenant, "like, who's the governor of New York, or who's the—"

"Hell, I don't even know that," a captain on the other side of the table said with a smirk.

"All right then, who plays second base for the Yankees," replied the lieutenant, and a quick burst of laughter circled the table; the officers clearly revealed the stress of the dire situation.

"All right, pipe down," said Djuric, as silence washed over the officers. "That's a good suggestion, but be sure it's a question an American would know the answer to. These Germans in our uniforms all speak American English, so they may not have an accent. Now, when the replacement troops move in tomorrow, you are to march your men back here to Sierck-les-Bains where we will be picked up by trucks. As of now, we are scheduled for a pickup about 1200 tomorrow, but that timing will depend on the replacement troops moving into our sector and the arrival of trucks."

At noon on the seventeenth, as the officers headed back to their units, a vibrant sense of excitement and mission filled the air. They now knew they had to move fast and catch and destroy the German counteroffensive to beat Hitler at his own game. The seemingly senseless banging of the troops against a stiff wall from Basse Ham to the German border was now replaced by the thrill of the hunt in bringing down the enemy and ending the war. The logistics of moving men into and out of the front line, however, didn't meet the initial schedule, and the 9th Battalion didn't get on the road until nearly 1400 hours on the eighteenth. As the truck convoy headed toward Thionville, Frank heard the thump of American artillery from behind him as firing started north of Apach. He imagined that some of the shells were falling on German soil, a very satisfying feeling.

The convoy moved north through the afternoon to the capital city of Luxembourg. They traveled over a well-paved but damaged road and then west and north over a patchwork of local roads threading the small country's hinterland. During the night, they passed into Belgium at Martelange and continued to drive west. A distant rumble of artillery could be heard, and occasional flashes of light reflected off the low-slung clouds.

At dawn they pulled to a stop at Leglise, a small Belgium village fifteen miles southwest of Bastogne. The distant rumble now grew louder, with individual pops of explosions occasionally heard. The light of the new day brought into clear view American troops retreating from the front, walking to the south on both sides of the road. They were remnants of different units that had been routed by the swift German advance. Pockets of American troops had staunchly refused to give in to the overwhelming strength of the German attack and had abruptly slowed their advance for a day and extracted a huge loss in the relentless advance of Panzer divisions.

Most of the American fighters who had stayed in place had now been killed or captured, with a few able to make a strategic withdrawal and stay engaged with the edge of the German salient. These walking, retreating men were the ones who did not fight to hold their position. Many had fled in panic. Now they were a disorganized mixture of infantry, tank crews, engineers, supply quartermasters, and medical personnel. There were enlisted men, draftees, junior officers, all walking south to safety. To a man, the weaponless walkers bore similar facial expressions and body posture; their eyes peering from solemn faces were downcast looking at the road, and a feeling of deep shame seemed to be pushing them to the rear. It was a sad and disheartening sight for the battalion headed to confront the enemy these men were fleeing.

Hitler had attacked a sector of the American line that was lightly defended but also underserved by a road network through the Ardennes. In this weather, control of paved roads was a critical military tactic, and the 101st had seized control of a key crossroads community, Bastogne. American units were at this moment engaged eight miles to the north, trying to break through to relieve the 101st, but so far to no avail. The briefing colonel identified the units in attendance that would move north at dawn and join in the battle for Bastogne; the list included Djuric's battalion.

At Leglise the battalion was instructed to set up a temporary camp in a snow-covered field north of the village, along with untold other units. Pup tents were set up in the field as the men checked their supplies and replenished needed ammunition, mortar shells, C-rations, and water. Heavy clothing was still in short supply; this was partially compensated for by receiving double layers of socks and pants. A mess tent was working around the clock to provide a hot meal for the men, something they might not get a chance to eat again for weeks on end.

Frank attended a briefing session and was told the 101st had moved into the crossroads village of Bastogne and was now surrounded by Germans. So far, the Americans were still in control of the key intersecting roads coming from Germany, fifteen miles to the east. The longer they held, the longer the German advance to the west was slowed, giving American forces time to intercept and turn back this part of the salient. The road blockage at Bastogne stalled the movement of enemy tanks, artillery, and trucks, as well as slowed marching troops.

As the officers gathered around a large folding table to get a close view of the map, Frank noticed on the opposite side of the table several Negro faces in the back row straining to see the map. Frank himself could see little of the map and the area they were to attack, but all units were to get detailed maps as soon as they arrived from the command center of the Third Army. With his concentration on the map disrupted he became aware of a pair of eyes fixed on him as he scanned across the circled solemn faces. *Is that Henry? It certainly looks like him.* The lips below the eyes that stared back at him broke into a slight smile as positive recognition struck both officers. *My God, it's Henry.* Henry nodded in the direction of the back of the command tent and both men made their way in that direction as the briefing ended. Some officers made for the door, and many others stayed pointing at the map and discussing fine points of their planned strategic advance.

"You son of a gun," blurted Frank as the two got within an arm's length of each other, and then in less than military gesture, they hugged with the force of friendship. Both men were struck by the strength of the other's embrace. It was apparent to both that the months of fighting had deprived them of basic need of everyday life and contact with family and friends. Contact with their men mattered during the war, but each officer realized they kept an arm's length distance from those who may lose their life. Fighting caused a shell to grow around each to protect them from grieving too much over the loss of their men. Now the shell was temporarily dissolved.

"Damn, it's good to see you, and all in one piece too," said Henry as they relinquished their hold. "Where've you been?"

"We've been traipsing across France. We landed at Utah Beach on 30 June and moved through the hedgerows and then got stuck at the point of a counterattack at Mortain in early August. Then we moved on to Lorraine near the Luxembourg and German border and have been slugging it out with them up until we were pulled for this bulge of the Germans," Frank responded. "What about you?"

"They trained us for two years at Knox in Kentucky and then in Louisiana, and they finally tested us and said we were highly qualified, which we already knew, and then they finally sent us over. We got into action down south of Metz in a town called Moyenvic, and then we attacked east, leading a column of infantry. We had our first combat at the beginning of November and have been in the thick of things ever since. But everything considered, we're fresh still. I think they sent us overseas because we were the most trained unit in the army, and the brass ran out of reasons not to send us since they needed men so badly. This war has been chewing up a lot of good men, a lot." Henry shook his head as the reality of his casual statement struck home.

"I've lost count of my casualties, but it's well over one hundred percent, about a hundred twenty-five or thirty, I would guess by now. You're right, it's goddamned awful, and I'm very fortunate to still be here."

"You remember the young kid who had a white German grandmother, Jesse White? He went down in a God forsaken little burg called Morville. His tank was hit simultaneously by a Tiger tank and an antitank artillery shell. Just blew the tank to smithereens, He never knew what hit him. Damn, I can't stop thinking about that kid. He was such a good fighter. Nothing escaped him when he was moving in on a target area. But you know what?"—Henry's face brightened—"Shelby is still with me, and he's leading a squad of tanks. He's one hell of a fighter too. His unit is my very best."

For the first time Frank glanced at Henry's sleeve and realized he too was a captain, and one who also took great pride in accomplishments of the men under his command.

"The worst part for me is that I'm having trouble remembering all the names of the good men that have passed through my company. Of the ones that I trained at Benning, there are only three or four of us left and only about sixty that came from England with me." Frank shook his head and stared at the floor. "God, this is an awful place to be. When I stop to think about it . . ."

"Maybe for the time being, not thinking about it is the best way to focus on what we have to do to stay alive and keep as many of our men safe as possible," said Henry.

"Yeah"—an ugly chuckle bubbled up from Frank's throat—"I've thought about that: if we wanted to protect them, we would send them home; instead we have to send them into a fight to kill or be killed. Sometimes I don't think our generals give a damn about the men who are dying; if they do, they sure are keeping it a secret."

"Yeah, but Frank, you know that in a war soldiers are going to die. That's war. The time for negotiation stopped when the fighting began. Our challenge is to win because to lose we would pay too dear a price."

"Yes, yes, I know that's the theory," stammered Frank, "but damn, damn, it still hurts like hell to see a kid you just sent as a messenger back to the CO get blown off the face of the earth, erased, by a lucky Germen shell. Damn."

"Frank, I think you've been fighting too long. Have you considered going back to the rear and getting your head together?"

"I . . . no, I can't do that to the men . . . I can't leave them; they need me."

"Frank, look at me. You need to recognize when you reach that point when you are a greater detriment to the safety of your men than you are a benefit. You need to know that sometimes that happens. You may fall into that slot. If you do, give it up and go back. Promise me you'll do that."

Stunned, Frank looked into Henry's brown-black eyes. It took him several seconds to re-listen to the words just spoken. Was he right? Of course he was. Did they really apply to him? Of course they did. "Yes, yes . . . I'll do that," Frank heard his disembodied voice say from some distant place. *What's happening to me?*

"Come on, let's go get some chow," said Henry as he took Frank's arm, and the two walked from the tent into the biting wind from the northwest that blew a light snowstorm into their faces. If nothing else, the wind and snow snapped Frank's attention back to the reality of the time and day, December 19, as the friends leaned into the wind.

Finding relief from the wind inside the officer's mess, Henry and Frank placed their laden trays on the folding table amidst row on row of tables. No one else sat at their table for eight. "I sure love this fine French cooking." Henry chuckled as he spooned his first taste of hot creamed corn into his mouth.

"Yes, indeed, as long as it's hot food, it's good food." Frank slurped, as juice from his Spam and tomato dish ran down his chin. Wiping his chin on a crisp paper napkin, Frank saw a major walk up behind Henry and then step to the end of the table where both men could see him.

"Attention," he snapped. Henry and Frank were both on their feet in a reflexive response to the one word order, although their attentive posture would have left a drill sergeant in boot camp screaming in their faces.

"You know, captain, there is a colored section over there," the major said to Henry, motioning to the corner of the tent. "Now why don't you move over there and leave this man alone so he can eat his supper."

The fork in Frank's hand slipped to the table, clanged off the side of the metal plate and to the floor. Frank's voice emerged as a deep rumble as he responded, "Sir, we're good friends, we trained together at Benning, and we just met again." Frank's eyes bore into the senior officer.

Henry's mouth opened temporarily, but he closed it as Frank spoke. Staring back at Frank, the major replied, "Well you know that's just fine, but we do have some protocol to uphold in the army over here, and we just need to remember where we came from and what we're going to go home to in a few months." The major's chin protruded, and a slight smile creased his face as his body below his chest seemed to extend forward and his weight shifted to the heels of his boots. Although the mess hall was the scene of a constant movement of men coming in and leaving, movement seemed to freeze as most eyes were fixed on the three standing officers.

"Sir, we ate together at Benning, and we see no difference from those circumstances. We are still officers fighting for our country," Frank replied.

"Now, captain, I don't think you understand the gravity of this sit—"

Henry slammed his fork onto the table and glared at the major. "Sir," he carried out the long pronunciation of the single word, "Sir," repeated again, "General Bradley opened up Officer Candidates School to include both races; he didn't mention anything about segregation of the mess hall. I don't remember General Patton saying anything about segregation in the mess hall either. He personally addressed us in October, and he has thrown us into the heat of the fight south of Metz and we haven't let him down, sir."

The major's mouth hung open as he cleared his throat licked his lips. "You boys know what I mean is we're going home soon. You better not forget the way things are at home."

"Things can always change," snapped Henry.

"It's high time it did. It's been eighty years since Lincoln settled the matter of Negroes; it's time the rest of us caught up with Mr. Lincoln," Frank spoke in a deep, threatening voice.

"Alright, goddammit, you sons of bitches go ahead and have your way over here. Just wait till we get you back home, and we'll see who eats with who," shouted the major. "We'll just see."

"Yes, we will," said Henry, "yes, we will."

In a sharp whisper that only the three combative officers could hear clearly, "Major Compton, you are entirely out of line." The crisp reprimand was uttered by an officer who rose from his seat at a table behind the major. Brigadier General Jacob Kaminski wadded up his napkin and threw it onto the table. The sharp whisper continued, "My God, major, you're bringing up the race issue to divide our men. If you ask me, these officers are both as good of examples of fine young American men that we can find over here. Captain Warring has been through thick and thin and is one of the most effective infantry field officers we have, and Captain Boudreau of the 761st is one of the best tank commanders we have in the Third. Fighting that stupid battle over color stops here, stops today. Come to my tent. I've said enough here in front of everyone," the general closed with a final stabbing whisper. General Kaminski walked briskly to the exit and the major reluctantly followed.

Frank and Henry watched the two disappear into the cold evening and then sat down. "That small minded son of a bi—"

"Now, where were we?" interrupted Henry in a voice that had quickly regained its equilibrium.

Frank realized his mouth was open. He closed it and stared

at Henry, and a smile slowly crossed his face. The smile quickly turned into a chuckle followed by a laugh and then a sound that resembled a howl as he covered his face with his hand trying to stifle his growing mirth. He buried his face in his arms as tears came to his eyes and he snorted requiring use of his coarse napkin to blow his nose. Henry laughed as well but soon regained control of his mirth.

"Frank, we shouldn't be laughing," Henry said as he glanced at the nearby tables.

"I know," said Frank getting his breath, "I know, this is bad form," as he buried his face again and returning laughter shook his shoulders. After a time that seemed interminable to Henry, Frank sat up, straight faced, and took a bite of roll. "Damn, it's cold." Then Frank looked at the surrounding tables. Several faces glared back in response to his gaze. A few other faces were smiling, and one lieutenant gave a thumbs-up signal, but most only looked with noncommittal eyes. As Frank engaged his food again, the surrounding faces returned to their meals.

Frank realized his fork had fallen to the floor, and as he bent to retrieve it, a pair of boots came into his view at the end of the table. "Here's a clean set of tableware," came the voice from a second lieutenant who placed the metal utensils next to Frank's plate.

"Thanks, lieutenant," uttered Frank as he looked onto the rigid, unsmiling face of the junior officer who had already turned to retake his seat behind Henry. Frank could see the young officer talking to two other lieutenants, and all three glared at him. At the initial approach of the lieutenant, Frank looked at his cold face. Henry looked at his hand holding the knife and fork as one would grasp a weapon and had started to react, but the utensils were turned before he could reach out to protect Frank. Henry sat down heavily on his folding chair.

"Everything is cold," repeated Frank as he put a bite of potatoes into his mouth.

"Make up for it with two desserts," suggested Henry.

"What?" said Frank. "Oh Yeah, at least two," as he focused his attention on their conversation.

"Who was the general?" asked Henry.

"That's Kaminski from Patton's staff. I guess he's up here to help organize our pushback on the Nazis. I didn't know that he knew me at all, but I guess since you stand out, he probably recognized your smiling face," Frank said playfully.

"Yeah, sometimes I sure do stand out . . . Unfortunately it's usually for the wrong reasons. But I'm used to it and don't let it bother me too much."

Just then Frank felt a tap on his shoulder, and his immediate reaction was the arrival of another critic of the friend's seating choice. Frank stood and spun saying, "What?"

He looked into the startled eyes of Shelby Young as Henry smiled at his comrade. In a stern voice Shelby said, "What kinda trouble are you two gettin' into over here. I swear you two are always causin' trouble for us good soldiers."

"You son of a gun," said Frank as he threw his arms around Shelby who responded with equal enthusiasm. "Have a seat; we have plenty of empty chairs at our table."

"I don't know if it's safe to be too closely associated with you troublemakers," opined the wise, serious Shelby as he sat down.

"Henry tells me you are doing all right in leading your steel boxes around the battlefield." Frank chuckled.

"I do all right, and I get Henry's butt out of tight scrapes. Some major tells Henry to do something, and ole Henry says 'yes sir'. Then he turns to me and says go do what the major said, and I turn around and there's no one there but me and my tanks, so we have to go do what they commanded Henry to do. The army is one hell of a buck-passing organization." As he spoke Shelby's mocking serious tone slowly melted until he was openly laughing at the end of his practiced speech.

"I think my men have the same complaint," Frank commented. My key man is Lieutenant St. John, I call him the Saint. My God, he's quick and fearless. He'll get medals before this war is over. He sizes up situations in the field in a flash and knows how to handle them. Men such as the Saint and you make us look good." Frank whacked Shelby on the knee with his wadded up napkin. "Make us look good."

"Well, speakin' as a humble officer and soldier, we do what we have to do to make our senior officers excel. Yes sir, that's our role." Shelby gazed at the ceiling with an angelic look on his face. All three officers laughed.

Spotting the familiar face of the Saint moving toward the exit, Frank rose and called to him. "Henry and Shelby, this is Alcie St. John. Meet Henry Boudreau and Shelby Young."

The men shook hands. "We all went through OCS together at Benning," said Frank with a gesture toward Henry and Shelby.

"Nice to meet you." The Saint's lips twisted into a slight smile.

"I hear you are known as the Saint," said Henry with a larger smile. "That's a big name to live up to."

"Yes, Frank stuck me with that name when we got together in England. It's kinda misplaced however. I don't think I qualify at all for bein' one. But, Frank's the boss, and he can call me anything he wants." This time Alcie smiled broadly at Frank.

"I've picked up a few names in this man's army as well, but I ain't sayin' what they are," murmured Shelby as the four sat down laughing.

"Now, we got us a true hero in the 761st, a guy named Warren Crecy; he's a sergeant," Shelby explained, "and we were down at this little place called Mayonnaise or something . . ."

"Moyenvic," said Henry.

"Yeah, that's it, thank you Mr. Captain Lawyer, and Crecy's tank was hit by artillery and knocked out, but Warren was so mad at those Krouts that he got in a jeep with a mounted machine gun and took out a machine gun nest and then got the forward artillery observers who had called in the artillery. And then he got in another working tank and kept firing to protect the foot soldiers around him, and then that second tank ran in some deep mud and lost a tread, and so he gets out and starts to fix the tread.

Then the German infantry moved in and he jumps back in the tank and drives them back with the 50 cal gun in the tank, and the Germans had to withdraw. Man, oh man, we call him the Baddest Man in the 761st. He's a fightin' fool, and the funny thing is that he's this quiet guy that you would never expect somethin' like that from; he sure isn't a boaster."

"Or a big talker, like some people we know," observed Henry provoking greater laughter.

"It's the quiet men who can do some of the worst damage to the enemy." Frank smiled at the Saint as he spoke.

The four officers traded more recollections of their battle experiences, each contributing descriptions of events they could not have imagined two years ago.

"You all know something," murmured Alcie in his Lower Alabama drawl, "this war has taught me that my enemy is in the sight of my gun and all of those men beside me are my buddies." He said looking at Henry and then Shelby.

BANG, Shelby brought his hand down on the table with a loud thud. "Damn right. Let's go fight this Goddamn war and kill some more Germans."

"Oh, Frank, I heard we have a briefing in twenty minutes for our battalion, we are HQed in a stone building just beyond the last mess tent," Alcie said.

"I'll see you two tankers for the last meal if both of us are still here after we get orders."

"I'm glad you didn't call it the last supper," said Shelby as the four headed into the biting wind.

At 1530 hours, Major Djuric opened the briefing outlining their immediate plan of attack. The primary objective was to break through to the 101st Airborne troops surrounded in Bastogne. At last word, the 101st was holding its own. The infantry was to be led by armored units in the breakthrough push. Each individual platoon was to work very closely—those two words "very closely" were emphasized—with a pair of tanks in the assault. Artillery was to give close cover, but because of the miserable weather, no air support could be expected until the clouds cleared or at least rose well above the tops of trees to provide pilots with a descent view of the ground. The Battalion was to leave at daybreak, 20 December, for a forward position at a village called Fauvillers. From there they would push off to the north at 0900 hours and expect to encounter the enemy within a mile of the village.

That night, Frank and Henry sat again at this same table in the mess tent. "This may be our last hot meal for a while," gruffed Frank.

"Yeah, by the way, you look like you've lost a few pounds over here," observed Henry.

"Yes, it's been the steady diet of C-rations and the K-rations. They keep you alive so you can keep fighting, but day-after-day they're hard to take and you lose weight, but you finally have to give in and eat them or starve . . . so we eat them."

"Our food is about the same, but we do get back behind the lines more often than the infantry. We need a constant supply of gas and shells, but I guess we fare a little better than you boys when it comes to eating."

Frank toyed with his spoon in the tin coffee mug. "Did you get to vote in the election."

"No, we were in the thick of it down near Metz. How about you?"

"Nope, we were otherwise engaged during those days with the Germans, but Roosevelt won without us, that's good. I think Lincoln was the last and best good Republican." Frank chuckled.

"Well, considering he was one of the first, I guess they had a short life." Henry also chuckled. "But Teddy did some good things for the country."

"Teddy? Oh, you mean Teddy Roosevelt and not my son. I guess, but I don't know much about him. I will say that Franklin doesn't look at all good in recent pictures. This war has been hard on him, kind of like the rest of us. He's the commander in chief, after all, so I guess he has to share in the hard life . . . Tell me, do you ever get scared of being trapped in that tank of yours?" asked Frank. "Being hit by a shell and burning up."

"I've thought about it, and I've seen it happen to others, but it's not that different from you boys being out in the open and being exposed to machine gun and rifle fire. I guess I rationalize it that we both play a part, and when your time comes, it comes no matter where you are.

"I guess so," replied Frank looking up from his cup. "What are you going to do after the war?"

"Go back to the Southside. I've got nowhere else in particular to go. I've thought about California, but I don't want to be that far away from my parents. I guess my dad has another ten years or so to work, and then they may need someone to look out after them sooner or later. What about you?"

"I'm not certain, except that I'm certain that I'll finish college."

Henry's face suddenly lit up as he leaned forward, "Frank, why don't you think about law as a career? You go ahead and finish at UT or UK or some other U and then go to law school. I know you should go to law school in the state where you want to practice. Now here's a great idea: you come out to Urbana and go to U of I and get a law degree. Then we open a practice in Chicago and you cover the white clients and I'll take care of the Coloreds. How about that? We'll clean up."

"I've been thinking about law ever since you mentioned it in OCS, but I don't know. That's three more years of school. Besides I grew up on a farm and in a town a whole lot smaller than Chicago, I bet Millersburg is even smaller than your smallest neighborhood. I think a small town would be a better fit for me. That could be almost any place in Kentucky or Tennessee."

"OK, OK, listen, we could have an office in the suburbs. Yeah, and I drive out from the city and you drive in from the country. There are a lot of farms in Illinois, and it has good soil, I'm told. Frank, think of it this way, your new school days will be like starting over. You are mature now, you know what you want to do, and you will eat up the curriculum. And according to the stories in Stars and Stripes, they are going to pass a GI Bill to pay for school for veterans. So you could get that young man of yours . . . Ted, and both go to school. Illinois has some very good high schools, especially in Urbana where all the professors live. And while you're in school I could get established on the Southside. Wow, I can see it now, Boudreau and Warring in the city, then out in the sticks we could go by Warring and Boudreau. Yes sir, we could make a difference in this world."

"Why don't you move out to the 'burbs' and live near the office?"

"Frank, my boy, you are talking about Chicago. Just because I live in the north doesn't mean I can live wherever I want. I think the Southside is the best place to live with the people that I serve. For me to move to the burbs would be like moving to the moon; there are some places we are not welcome."

"Oh, I thought it was different up there."

"No, housing in America still has a wall built around it. This is 1944, almost '45, but we are apart when we sleep in America."

"Well, I'll think about law. But you know what, what if your father and mother stay in that Oak Ridge place and he has a long term job and then wants to retire there? You would have to move to Knoxville or someplace close in order to care for them in their old age.

"My parents stay in Tennessee? Never, that's impossible. They are Chicago from the core; I can't see them anywhere but Chicago."

"Well, it may not matter what you can see. Events will take care of them just like us, and we can't predict the future."

"That's for sure, that's for damn sure as we sit here in this little village in Belgium. Whoever could have predicted that? I didn't know where Belgium was for certain until I got here. Sometimes I still wonder where I am now." Henry chuckled. "All I know is what's ahead of me on the road and where I'm supposed to attack next. The army makes being in Europe very simple sometimes."

Henry chuckled.

"In the meantime, we better get to bed. We have an early start in the AM," said Frank as he pushed back from the table.

"Right," replied Henry. The two rose and embraced. "After all we may have a meeting with destiny up the road in Bastogne."

"Make that a rendezvous with destiny," Frank corrected.

"Yeah, that sounds like a movie or something."

"OK, I'll be Clark Gable, and you be, ah . . . Who'll you be?

"I guess. Let's see, we are a little short on leading black movie actors. I'll be Paul Robeson maybe."

"Can you sing?"

"No."

"That's OK, I don't have a moustache and I can't act." Both laughed.

"You keep your head down and maybe I'll see you in Berlin before this is over," said Henry. "We'll have a beer there."

"You do the same, and we'll have that drink." They shook hands and left the mess tent smiling as each went to their unit's encampment.

# CHAPTER 32

*Bastogne Area, Belgium*

*Late December 1944*

BEFORE FIRST LIGHT on the twentieth, the re-manned company was trucked to Fauvillers and then started moving north on foot as part of a battalion force. Frank felt guilty about bringing green troops into his company. The infantry replacements were young men or boys, many eighteen- and nineteen-year-olds with three months of basic training who were then sent overseas with no additional training in the full range of infantry weapons or in useful survival techniques. They had a much greater chance of not making it through their first day of fighting than the more veteran troops; they didn't know what to expect or how to react. But now there was simply no time left to integrate them into the unit or train them. They would have to learn by watching veterans, and with a large measure of luck they may see tomorrow's dawn while still in their foxhole. Every veteran of combat knew the replacements would probably end up quickly on a casualty list. As if they were fodder to satisfy the military dictum of always going into battle with a full complement of troops.

In the Bastogne action, the company control was in Frank's hands as usual, and he entered into the thick of the fight along with all of his men. They were aligned in a pasture; the tall dead grasses that had been lush during the summer heat were now brown blades bent to the ground in thick clumps weighted down by winter's frost and snow. Dirt removed from the fox holes ringed the openings and was now under the accumulating wind-blown drifts of snow. Despite the cold, water pooled in the bottom of foxholes returning the ever-present, debilitating trench foot and frostbitten feet. Belgium was colder and wetter than the weather had been in France east of Basse-Ham.

On the night of December 22, Frank and the Saint shared a large foxhole along with a radioman, Sergeant John Bieleck, and PFC Roger Cohen, who wielded a Browning Automatic Rifle, a deadly but light weapon suited to use by the infantry. Cohen, a stout youth, had the physical build to handle the rigors of firing the BAR. Under the conditions they faced, the company was to hold its position during the night against any German counterattack and in the morning go back on the offensive. Cohen was one of the new replacement troops who had been drafted during the summer following graduation from high school in Cleveland, Ohio. After ninety days of basic training, he had been shipped overseas arriving in Europe at Antwerp just after it was finally placed back in operation as an allied port. Bieleck was a veteran who had joined the company following Mortain; he had the benefit of gaining familiarity with the company personnel in Paris and Bouillon before suffering through his first bitter taste of combat east of Basse-Ham.

"Try and keep your feet out of the water," the Saint said to Cohen. "Stay on the shelf. Do you have an extra pair of socks?"

"No, I sure don't."

Frank fished around in his rucksack and pulled out his next-to-last pair of socks sent from Knoxville. "Here, dry your feet and put these on before your feet freeze. How wet are your boots inside?"

"They're pretty bad," said Cohen.

"You're going to have a cold night," observed Frank, "but you have to put your boots back on. Always get as many pair of extra socks as you can before going into combat."

"Yes, sir," said Cohen beginning to look very apprehensive as the many dangers of his new location began to seep into his psyche.

Frank noticed Bieleck was putting on a second pair of socks. "After you get your feet tended to, call around to the posts in the company for a status check. Saint, work with Bieleck on getting the report." Frank pulled his daily log form from his rucksack and wrote with his gloved fingers holding a stubby pencil in the late afternoon light.

With daylight rapidly fading from the slate gray sky, the four ate their K-rations and piled the tin cans in the far corner of the foxhole lair. Down the center at the bottom of the hole was a deep trench where water collected; a shelf cut on either side of the trench permitted standing on reasonably dry ground. Above the standing shelf were individual seating notches carved from the earth. Above the seating notches, the foxhole walls tapered back toward the center of the hole to make the opening to the outside world as small as they dared. The digging of this type of foxhole was a delicate engineering job, balancing the likelihood of the earth giving way and collapsing on the occupants in unstable soil versus the earth having a high degree of structural stability that would support undermining of the surface. The goal was to make it as large and spacious as possible inside and as small as possible from the top side. Even with the best results from an hour of digging, two men could sleep in a horizontal position while the other two sat or stood. As dark settled in, a single candle was lit on one of the benches and a raincoat was stretched across half of the foxhole entry. With the passing of time, heat form the candle started to warm the foxhole's interior. The earthen enclosure was now more bearable during the growing cold.

"Since there are four of us, we will rotate a one-hour watch during the dark. Cohen you start," Frank said, "followed by the Saint, Bieleck, and me."

Cohen stood with the top of his helmeted head some ten inches above the top of the hole. The Saint said in an even, low voice, "Cohen, you're pretty tall. During the daylight you shouldn't stand that far above the top of the hole, but being as how it's almost dark, there's not much danger of you being seen now. Just remember to stay low in the daylight. And keep your rifle here in a horizontal position so you can swing it around on a moment's notice." The Saint motioned to a slight notch in the wall at the very top. "Remember in the dark you see with your ears more than you see with your eyes. If you think you detect a movement, look just to the side of the location and you may be able to see better. In the dark, your straight ahead vision is not as good as the ring around the center of your sight. Understand?"

"Yes, sir, I think so."

"How much training did you have with the M1?"

"Oh, I guess some. We got to the range several times." Cohen licked his lips as the Saint sat down. "I've had more training with the BAR. I'm a pretty good shot with it. This model has two firing rates, fully automatic and a slow automatic. Either one will tear up somebody pretty well, I guess."

"Yes," said the Saint, "I guess you're right."

*Cohen's scared to death,* thought Frank, *and he has every reason to be.*

At 2100, with Cohen standing in the watch position for the second time, they detected a whirring noise and then the whine became audible, as a Germen shell flew into their sector. "Heads down," said Frank in a sudden, harsh stabbing voice. The shell exploded somewhere to the left of the foxhole. "Bieleck, get C Platoon on the horn. Alcie, see how close that was to them." Frank stood to look out of the hole while the sergeant operated the radio. Frank hunched low.

The crackling radio confirmed the shot was in front and to their left. "Good," said Frank, "they're not sure where we are." Additional artillery shells continued to land in a random pattern in front of the company's position every few minutes; it was as if the Germans were determined to keep the American troops awake through the night. American artillery began to return fire during the noisy night. As the hours passed, the Americans did stay awake with the earth-shaking blasts splitting the night air. The pattern of landing shells was still sporadic, but occasionally they fell close to the company's position. One American shell was an obvious lucky shot as the initial explosion behind the Germen line was followed by a brief but rapid discharge of secondary blasts. "We must have hit a pile of ammo," said Bieleck. With the Saint now in the watch position, shells were much closer to the company's warren of underground hiding places.

After a pause in the German shelling, the Saint suddenly called out, "Heads down!" The shell fell very near their hole, and the four inhabitants grasped the earthen walls for stability amidst the wrenching of the ground and deafening roar. A shower of earth, snow, and rock pelted their heads and splashed in water at the bottom of trench.

Frank heard a slight murmur coming from one of the seats in the hole. "Cohen, why don't you say that aloud so we all can hear it," said Frank.

*"HaShem is my shepherd; I shall not want. He maketh me to lie down in green pastures; he leadeth me beside the still waters. He restoreth my soul; he guideth me in straight paths for His name's sake. Yea though I walk"*

A second shell was heard following the first, and it also struck the earth very close to their haven. The deafening blast was equally as loud as the last, although the earth shook less and none of the earthen shower fell on them.

Cohen gave an audible gasp for breath, then, *"through the valley of the shadow of death, I will fear no evil, for thou art with me; thy rod and thy staff, they comfort me. Thou preparest a table before me in the presence of mine enemies; thou hast anointed my head with oil; my cup runneth over. Surely goodness and mercy shall follow me all the days of my life; and I will dwell in the house of HaShem forever. Amen"*

Frank found that he and the Saint had joined the PFC's recitation of the Twenty-third Psalm in soft voices, reciting the words they could recall. "Thank you. I had forgotten that we Christians had borrowed the Psalms from the Jews." Frank's voice was soft and wistful, and he was not certain if he had said the words aloud or if he'd simply had that thought. During the pause in shelling, Frank realized he had not heard the frantic call for a medic. He took this as a good sign. Either all his men were still unhurt, or if a shell had found its mark, there were no survivors and no need to risk the lives of the medics running across open ground. And considering they were in the midst of a determined shelling, he held off on his radio check on the troop's status.

"Heads down," barked the Saint.

The deadly whirring and whine of the next shell grew with awe-inspiring speed and volume, and Frank suddenly gasped a last breath and reflexively slammed shut his eyes as the shell rammed into the earth adjacent to the foxhole forcing a section of earth to suddenly fly into the man-inhabited void . . . Then there was quiet. The unearthly quiet belied their feared expectations of the worst kind. Frank still held his breath . . . did he dare breathe? What had happened? He opened his eyes. Dust and snow particles flew in the air as he turned on a flashlight and pointed it toward the bottom of the hole. The sleeping bench where the candle had been placed had collapsed, burying their source of heat and light. He turned off the flashlight after seeing Cohen drawn up into a fetal position on his seating ledge, Bieleck with his head between his knees at the far end of the hole, and the Saint slouched over in a frozen pose after withdrawing his head from the watch position.

"My God, what happened?" mumbled Bieleck.

For the first time, Frank found words to express his sudden grasp of the situation. But the Saint spoke first, "It was a dud."

Words came softly from Cohen's lips, *"God is our refuge and strength, a very present help in trouble. Therefore we will not fear, though the earth do change, and though the mountains be moved into the heart of the sea. Though the waters thereof roar and foam . . ."*

The whirring whine of the next shell fell in front of the hole, exploding and jerking the four crouched soldiers. Earthen particles this time were shot violently in a horizontal trajectory striking the back wall of the hole and ricocheting off the top of the Saint's helmet. The raincoat covering the foxhole entrance was shredded and scattered in the snow. Alcie pulled his body down into a sitting position; there was no use watching now for German troops while they rained death on the company.

Another breath, *". . . though the mountains do shake at the swelling thereof. Selah. There is a river, the streams whereof make glad the city of God, the holiest dwelling place of the Most High. God is in the midst of her, she shall not be moved; God shall help her, at the approach of morning."* Cohen's voice increased in volume as he spoke in a normal conversation level.

*"Nations were in tumult, Kingdoms were moved; he uttered his voice, the earth melted. HaShem of hosts is with us; the God of Jacob is our high tower. Selah. Come behold the works of HaShem, who hath made desolation in the earth. He maketh wars to cease unto the end of the earth; He breaketh the bow, and cutteth the spear in sunder; He burneth the chariots in the fire. 'Let be, and know that I am God; I will be exalted among nations, I will be exalted on in the earth.'"*

There was quiet.

"Amen," the Saint's lips barley moved with his whisper.

They waited for the next shell . . . it did not come. The silence continued and still there were no more shells fired by the Germans although the American artillery kept firing for another fifteen minutes. A heavy fog settled over the troops, sealing them in another layer of nature's cold winter. The buried candle was not retrieved for fear of causing a greater collapse of earth. They now lacked a source of meager warmth. Frank marveled at the fog. He had the impression that fog only occurred in warmer temperatures, but that was not true in Belgium, as the fog seeped into their hole adding to the misery of the night. The men did not sleep nor did they talk of the shell that was intended to kill them but bore into the ground as a dud. They became aware of the life-robbing cold as they lost feeling in their feet and hands despite the repeated stomping and thrashing. They knew intuitively that it was cold, damp cold, damn cold, but they did not know that the thermometer dipped below zero degrees on the Fahrenheit scale. Hands stuck in their armpits had little effect on the numb fingers.

Change occurred in their confined world when the dim morning light appeared to chase the utter blackness from the sky. The reluctant but welcomed dawn slowly made its way from the east. The growing light cast an eerie gray glow through the persistent ground-hugging fog. As the sun rose above the horizon, it found openings in the clouds that allowed its rays to reach the top of the thin fog layer. The direct rays lit up the fog with an unearthly glow that permeated the soldier's world with warm, golden-orange hues. All the soldiers along the line of battle, both American and German alike, marveled at the glorious light cast across their confined nighttime habitats. When the occasional cloud blocked the sun's rays, the cold, ashen gray fog returned only to be relit by the next opening. Without recognizing it in these early morning moments, the American soldiers had ample reason to celebrate the sun's glow, and the men of the Third Reich had reason to dread the approaching day; the sunlight falling on the battlefield meant that American aircraft would soon be in the air attacking the German lines and dropping much-needed supplies into the besieged men of the 101st Airborne in Bastogne.

The four men in Frank's foxhole stamped their feet with greater vigor as they fought to restore feeling. After the hastily eaten breakfast of cold K-rations, Frank called around to the platoon leaders and learned of their overnight status. He ordered them to move out at 0800 after a two-hour bombardment by the artillery. With the growing light, the fog at the ground level thinned some, and they gained about two hundred yards of visibility along the horizontal line of sight.

The Saint crawled from their lair and looked for the shell that had not ended their lives. He could not see it in a mound of loosened earth next to the opening of their hole. He dared not probe for the shell lest he set it off by accident. They did mark the location and called the information to the engineers to handle it however they wished.

The Battalion supported by Sherman tanks did attack on the morning of the twenty-third into the face of fierce enemy fire. Soon American dive bombers were dropping their targeted payloads on supply lines, supply depots, and troop concentrations while the infantry was raking the enemy's lines with intense fire. American fighter aircraft were particularly effective against artillery positions and Panther and Tiger tanks. Djuric's battalion began to take ground with rays of the cold sun shining down on them. Men of the battalion spent another night in new foxholes two miles north of last night's position. Cohen, now assigned to a rifle squad and having survived for two days of combat, was considered a veteran.

By late afternoon of the twenty-fourth, Frank's company was withdrawn to get more replacement troops for the seventy-plus men who had died or who were no longer fit to fight. Those wounded who could still fight were not listed yet as casualties. It was cold and the snow was falling as the company entered the temporary camp at Fauvillers. It was as if they had been holding their breath for four days during the desperate struggle—their urgency was propelled by the impending fate of the 101st if the relief column did not fight their way through to Bastogne. At least now they had twelve hours to breathe and lick their wounds.

They ate their C-rations huddled in small village buildings as the dark of the night settled in, and it suddenly struck Frank that tonight was Christmas Eve. *I wonder what's happening in Knoxville tonight. Maybe Mom is getting them ready for church, or maybe they're having a quiet dinner. I know they have a tree up and decorated. Dad and Teddy probably went out to the country and cut down a cedar. We always had a cedar on the farm. There were spots where they grew like weeds along the streams. Dad said that was where the limestone was close to the surface and no other tree except the cedar could get a root system established.*

"Frank," the Saint's voice penetrated his reverie, "some of the men discovered that there will be a church service in the village and they, or we, want to go. OK?"

"Oh, yes . . . Can I tag along?"

The Saint smiled and extended a hand to pull Frank to a standing position. They walked from the building into the cold night.

Frank, the Saint, and seventeen men from the company entered the village church in Fauvillers that sat across the street from a triangular-shaped village square, or perhaps it was considered a park. No matter, it provided a picturesque setting for the church. The setting reminded Frank of pictures he had seen on Christmas cards that he always assumed had been inspired by a New England village. *Maybe those were French or Belgian villages.*

They climbed through the rubble that had been the church's bell tower before the 88mm shell was fired wildly by the retreating Tiger tank. Two candelabras with four candles each lit the entrance area and path into the church as they stepped over the last stones into the nave. The simple structure had suffered a serious blow to its front façade, but the back three quarters of the building were remarkably undamaged and had been swept clean of dust and debris.

More than a dozen candles illuminated the interior, casting dancing shadows on the stone walls and lighting the faces of the worshipers. The glow projected up to the underside of the timbered roof. Deep dark recesses hidden from the flames receded into the background as the altar and cross shone in the muted light. A group of village denizens sat on the undamaged benches; most were elderly women and men, but a few younger women and two children probably approaching ten years of age were also huddled together. There were no men of a "fighting age" present. The villagers watched the American troops line the outside aisles. One elderly woman beckoned to a young, baby-faced soldier to join her on the bench. He did so removing his steel helmet but keeping in place his wool cap. He placed the helmet out of sight on the floor at his feet. The woman clasped his left hand in both of hers as she claimed him for the remainder of the service. The rest of the soldiers removed their helmets and placed their weapons along the outside wall of the church.

The priest appeared from the black interior of the church behind the altar. He spread a cloth over the stone altar and carefully smoothed its folds onto the cold, solid, flat surface. The cloth with a lace fringe appeared to be a dusky yellow, the color coming from its age, the dim light, or a combination of both. A single, plain silver cross mounted on a tall staff stood in a stand at the side and above the altar. The cross was embellished by the small, sculpted figure of the crucified body of Christ hanging from the cross. The Americans remained in the side aisles against the outside wall, not wanting to take one of the few remaining seats from any villager who may yet come to the service.

The priest lit incense and began purifying the altar as he swung the censer hanging from the end of a silver chain and inscribed a tight circular pattern in the air on the four sides of the altar. The pungent odor filled the church before being pushed outside by the light breeze entering from the street through the structure's gaping wound. The priest then turned to the gathered faces and made a swirl of the censer to his right, left, and in the center of the nave for the ritualistic purification of the worshipers. His bushy mustache buried his upper lip below a tangle of gray bristles; a prominent, sharply pointed nose rose above the bushy-haired lip. The priest drew circles in the crisp air with the censer and recited Latin phrases that Frank could not hear and probably could not understand if he had heard. Nevertheless, Frank understood the meaning of the priest's actions and recognized it as the continuation of a timeless ritual in the Catholic Church.

The service proceeded with the priest reading, in Flemish, passages from a large bible on a stand beside the altar and again reciting Latin lines of worship as the story of the Christ child's birth was retold to the waiting congregants. At one point in the service the cleric paused and nodded to the worshipers, and an elderly village man dressed in ill-fitting, ragged clothes stepped into the aisle and walked to the side of the altar carrying a fiddle by its neck. Several fine, loose strings dangled from the end of his bow as he adjusted the pegs at the end of the instrument's neck and briefly drew his bow across the strings to test the notes. Satisfied, he touched the bow to the gut strings and began to play. The music was harsh and ragged but at the same time beautiful. Frank recognized the music without being able to place a name to it. As he played, the elderly man smoothed out his technique, and the music seemed now to float over and around the worshipers in the church and infuse them with memories of the way things had always been in the village until the last disastrous year, and the way they hoped things would soon become again. A profound silence enveloped the church as the violinist lowered his instrument at the conclusion of his playing. Corporal Collins, a radioman from the Second Platoon, stood and hesitantly stepped forward, leaned down, and said something to the old man. The two huddled together for a moment before the old man sat down, and Corporal Collins, holding the violin and bow, faced the altar, looked at the priest, and received a slight nod of the head. Collins drew the bow across the strings and began to play. Turning to face the worshipers, his eyes were rimmed with moisture as he completed the first verse of "Silent Night." The worshipers picked up the tune and sang the words in Flemish and English. Although most of the worshipers were uncertain of the exact words, they sang the phrases they recalled from previous holidays and sang on. During the second verse, Frank thought he heard a strange pronunciation of the word night, "nacht." He turned toward the back of the church and saw two Germen infantrymen standing amid the rubble of the bell tower, their faces lit by the glow of the candelabras. The enemy was guarded by an American soldier who cradled his M1 rifle in the crook of his arm. The Germans joined in singing the hymn; one had a deep baritone voice that was clearly audible in the chorus of village singers. With Frank staring at them, the taller of the Germans returned the stare and raised his hands, empty palms facing up, signifying his peaceful intent. Frank walked to the back. "Merry Christmas."

"Fröhliche Weihnachten," the German responded.

Amidst the singing, the muffled sound of a baby crying drifted through the church. Frank's first impression was that he must surely be mistaken, perhaps it was the wind blowing through the church's wreckage, but the faint sound of the child's voice persisted as the snowflakes started to fall through the damaged roof, coating the rubble with a light, new coat of white. He then thought the sound a unique part of this village's Christmas tradition to have a live baby at the worship service to commemorate the birth of baby Jesus. He was mistaken with both his explanations, as an elderly woman from the village stood and lifted a small bundle from the hands of a young woman who had been nursing the infant. The mother rearranged her clothing, pulled her coat over her shoulder, and smiled up at the older woman. The grandmotherly woman placed the bundle on her shoulder and gently patted the baby's back. Corporal Collins was now playing "Oh Little Town of Bethlehem," and the worshipers continued their three-language accompaniment. A second elderly woman stood and took the infant and kissed its brow, and then Sergeant Owens, standing in the aisle, did likewise. The child was thus passed from worshiper to worshiper, from Belgian to American to German to Belgian, each one bestowing dry, cool kisses to the now sleeping infant. Almost without exception as each person passed the infant's bundle on to the next waiting arms, the eyes of the reluctant person were ringed with tears. The baby's grandmother was the last to claim the bundled living gift to the service.

As Corporal Collins completed his playing, he returned the violin to its owner and leaned against the wall. The priest walked forward and kissed the infant's brow and made the sign of a cross on its forehead as he uttered an inaudible prayer for the child.

The priest then stood by the altar and began speaking in the local tongue. Was it Flemish? Frank believed so but was not certain. He knew the congregants understood the priest's every word, because two elderly women on the aisle moved their lips as they said inaudible words in response, or perhaps in unison, with the cleric. After a few minutes, the priest raised his hands, moving them in an all-encompassing gesture across the seated worshipers. He ended his message with a series of final phrases and then resumed in what Frank thought was a Germanic tongue, with guttural sounds and a new tone for the phrases, as he again raised his arms in a sweeping gesture. Then in English, "Even though we know that life always walks with death, we now know that the unspeakable and untimely spread of death always brings new life as well." Spreading his arms in the sweeping motion across the congregants and the destroyed portion of the church, he then looked kindly on the baby now back in her grandmother's embrace. "May you keep the Christ child always in your heart as the first step in God's promise of eternal life through our savior, Jesus Christ . . . Amen."

Following the brief homily, the priest set the altar with bread and wine, assisted by an elderly man of the village wearing a black cassock pulled over his bulky winter clothes. The villagers stood and moved toward the altar where they received the host, "the body of Christ," broken bread, and where some took a sip from the common cup, "the cup of salvation." As the villagers completed their celebration of communion, several of the Americans stepped forward to the altar to do the same. When they returned to their places in the side aisles, the two Germans walked forward to the altar, followed by the guard. A thought flashed across Frank's mind. *Were these enemies of the Belgians and Americans to be offered communion among the wreckage they had wrought? Would the gifts of the church be offered to the enemies of the state?* The priest stood facing the Germans, paused, and then smiled. *Yes.* The priest did not hesitate to place the host on their tongues as they made the sign of the cross on their foreheads and chests. Were they forgiven? Frank was confused by the meaning of the communion gesture, knowing the reality of what the German army had done over the past few years.

The priest then raised the plate of bread and beckoned to the remaining Americans, most of whom then stepped forward to receive the symbolic gifts. Frank was accustomed to an occasional celebration of communion in the Presbyterian church, with grape juice and a wafer, and believed the Catholic communion service was meant only for Catholics. Perhaps he was mistaken, or was it the gravity of the night that threw open the doors of the church to all men of good will? He didn't know.

For the first time Frank noticed PFC Cohen standing along the opposite wall of the church. He did not walk forward for communion, although Frank did. Frank was the last of the soldiers to receive the gifts, and he closed his eyes as a gust of cold air blew deep into the church, bringing a brief dash of snowflakes over the worshipers. As the priest placed the small piece of bread on his tongue, Frank experienced an unexpected and profound warm shudder that swept through him and released the tension in his shoulders and back. He visibly slumped and was now very tired. With the sip of wine from the chalice now held by the cleric, he opened his eyes and looked into small, dark smiling eyes. A soft voice said in English, "May God bless you and keep you and return you safely to your family."

"Thank you, Father."

Returning to his place, Frank leaned his back against the wall; eyes closed, and prayed, *God, help me understand all that's happening to me. Please. Please . . . Please keep Teddy and my parents and all my family safe through the war. You know I've not been very regular at this, but I need to talk with you. I'm so tired of the killing; take me from the war. Please, take me away, one way or the other. I can't go on killing. Didn't Jesus ask for the cup to be taken from his lips when he was on the cross? Well, take it from me if you can, if you will. I'm so tired.*

As Frank prayed, a deep wave of regret engulfed him. Although he fought it, his eyes dampened. *Am I crying for my part in this fucking war? Yes. My men, who I lead to their death? Yes. The Germans I killed . . . with my own hands? Yes, yes. Being away from Teddy? Yes. ... Didn't Jesus tell us to love and forgive? Isn't that the message of the Bible?* The tears increased, dampening his cheeks and the sides of his nose. *Lord, am I on the right path?*

The rest of the service passed in a blur as Frank continued to lean against the wall and recount with great sorrow what had happened in the last year. He opened his eyes and drew his coat sleeve across his face as he stared down at the floor with unseeing eyes; only memories flicked through his consciousness. The service ended with the priest pronouncing a benediction and then Merry Christmas in Flemish, repeated in English; the worshipers rose and hugged everyone within arm's reach and then shuffled to the street amid murmurs of "Merry Christmas" and "Blessed Christmas" exchanged with the American soldiers. The elderly woman who sat across the aisle from where Frank stood stepped to him and wrapped her short arms around him. The top of her head was still an inch below his chin, but she reached up and wiped his face with her handkerchief and whispered, "Blessed Christmas." Frank smiled, thanked her, and returned the hug.

Some of the other elderly worshipers were assisted in walking over the rubble by the extended hands of the young troops. The two German soldiers had been escorted earlier from the building and were now riding west in the back of an American troop truck headed for a prison camp for the duration of the war.

Frank and the Saint were two of the last to leave the church across the pile of rubble, and without a conscious thought they spontaneously embraced for the first time in their eight-month comradeship. They left the church, side by side, with the arm adjacent to their friend draped over the other's far shoulder.

Snowflakes continued to fall as the Americans made their way onto the street and started to walk toward their night's sleep in village buildings that would keep them out of the wind and snow but add little comfort to their rest.

# CHAPTER 33

## *Asleep*

### *January 1945*

THE AMERICANS DID reach Bastogne the day after Christmas, relieving the 101st Airborne troops, and continued pushing north. Hitler's daredevil thrust into the lightly defended American lines that produced this Battle of the Bulge had now been halted by the rapid response of the Americans, especially Generals Eisenhower and Patton and the resilient and adaptive American field commanders of companies, platoons, and squads. The fact that the German tanks ran out of gas also helped cut short the final grasp for victory by the dying, decaying Nazi regime. Their hopes of seizing American supply dumps and getting additional fuel saw only marginal success; the retreating American quartermasters either moved or destroyed most of their supplies in the path of the attacking Panzers.

Djuric's battalion was now pushing north, entering the southern limits of the Ourthe River valley about five miles southwest of Houffalize. The retreating Germans were, as usual, fighting a successful delaying campaign, with occasional counter strikes and the laying of mines.

Frank's company was not in the lead position in the offensive line on the first of January, 1945, and there was a relaxed mood that had infected all of the men, despite the presence of the enemy. They were sick of the war, wanted it to end and, most of all, wanted to go home. Anything in America was better than what they had experienced in Europe.

Frank found that PFC Cohen was walking to his right as they reached the crest of a hill overlooking the Ourthe on the cold, sunny day. "Pretty sight, isn't it?"

"Oh, yes, sir. It sure is," responded the stout young soldier, easily shifting the weight of the BAR from his right to left shoulder.

They paused briefly and gazed across the broad expanse of the shallow valley. "There's a little village over to our right; it's called Houffalize. We were trucked there in November and spent about twelve hours in a very cold rain. Then we got shipped south to France near the German border and then up here where you joined us. But Houffalize looked like a nice place to be if there wasn't a war going on." They continued walking down a slight grade across the snow-covered pasture, across a shallow rill, then back up the grade. The distant sounds might have been mistaken for thunder, but in a time of war everyone recognized the signature noise of battle.

"Yes, sir, I guess a whole lot of places would be nice over here if we didn't have to fight. My father brought my mother, brother, and me over in '35. We were planning to go to Germany to try and find some relatives, but with the Nazis in power, Poppa changed his mind and we stayed in Paris and Brussels. Of course, I was only a kid then, but the places we visited seemed nice."

"I don't know a lot about what's happening in Germany," Frank said, "but we were in a briefing, and Djuric said there was some very ugly talk coming down the pipe about what the Germans were doing with your people. They have been putting them in slave labor camps, and the Russians have found remains of what they call death camps. I hope your relatives make it through the war." Frank felt saddened to tell the boy a part of what he had heard.

"Oh, I know about that. Poppa has written with the news from the synagogue and some newspaper articles about what the Germans are doing. It's just unbelievable, sir," Cohen said with a faltering voice . . . After a pause, "My family has lived in Germany, well, it seems like forever, but I guess there was a time when they first came there. But as far back as my poppa knows, we've been there. Then for them to do this to us, it's just . . . ," he faltered. A second pause, then, "Poppa said when I left, don't get captured by the Nazis. But if you do, say you are a Unitarian and that the army mistyped your last name; tell them it's really Cahen. And if they check to see if you're circumcised, tell them that all boys born in hospitals in America are circumcised." Now Cohen uttered a dry chuckle. "Poppa was worried about me." Cohen smiled.

Knowledge of what the Allies were discovering about the German camps for Jews only added to the weight hanging on Frank's shoulders. Now he failed to see the stark beauty of the bright sun falling on the glistening snow and the sharp contrast of the distant forest's black tree trunks beneath the cold clear blue sky. With the snow and sun, the promise of the rebirth of spring was now not far in the future, but Frank was numb to the promise. The two walked on, climbing a slight rise and nearing the crest of a ridgeline. The sound of distant thumps punctuated their ears; they were getting ever nearer the battle line.

"I hope you didn't mind me going to the church service on Christmas Eve," Cohen suddenly offered.

"No . . . no, not at all." Frank was suddenly relieved the boy had changed the subject of their conversation. He could think of nothing to say in response to Cohen's news from Cleveland. "I was a little surprised to see you, however." Frank and Cohen started descending the slight grade through the lightly wooded hillside. By crossing over the ridge, the artillery sounds now were growing; the sound of exploding shells was added to the thumps of their launchings. Even the distant sound of machine-gun fire added a barely audible, chilling nuance to the growing, fearful noise.

"My mother plays flute and she always has a lot of music to play during the Christmas season. I used to go with her to some of the church services, and I really enjoyed the Christmas carols. I guess I know the words to most of them." Cohen smiled.

Frank chuckled "Yes, some of them are very beautiful, and

they never change; they're traditional. I especially like the calm, restful image of "Silent Night." It's so reassuring."

Cohen walked ahead and on Frank's right. "Yes, she knows by heart a lot of Christmas music. Besides the carols, there's Bach, Beethoven, Brahms—"

The sudden flash of light and concussion of the exploding shell blew the two men off their feet and threw them to the ground face first. They were unaware of the ear-splitting roar. Neither was the blast heard by most of the rifle squad who trailed behind them. They all were knocked from their feet and stunned. Half of those affected were immediately rendered unconscious, and three would die. The conscious men were aware that a shell blast had occurred; some had shrapnel wounds, others were only stunned by the concussion, the loss of hearing and the loud ringing in their ears.

Frank's world was dominated by a light as he regained a distorted semblance of semi-consciousness. The light before his eyes was about as bright as he had ever seen; it burned after the initial eruption and continued although his eyes were closed. It began to fade very slowly as he became more aware of the loud roar surging in his head. The roar began to diminish slightly, as well, and the light continued to fade into a hot pink red and a dark red hue. The sound ratcheted down from a loud roar to a loud hum and then a soft hum. The light and sound merged, turning darker and quieter and darker and quieter; then they were both gone into blackness, lacking light and sound, as Frank slipped deeper into the unconscious world.

The dimension of time did not exist as the blackness began to melt. Frank was now awake. Or was he? Consciousness joined time as abstract concepts that had no effect on him in his existence in a world that was suddenly very cold, chilling the core of his bones. He could no longer feel his legs below his knees. He crawled in snow, the feeling in his hands becoming more and more diminished. His struggle to move forward seemed endless, left hand past right hand already planted in the snow. Now anchoring the right hand and pulling forward continuing to move. Over a log buried in the snow, he did not care that a button was ripped off his long coat. His unconscious world seemed to be telling him, *Keep moving . . . no light anywhere . . . What happened to the sun? . . . Where's the light?* . . . Crawl. Pull. Crawl. Pull. After a seemingly endless time with the cold snuggling into his being, he started to accept the numbing chill as his friend, his companion. He had a feeling of accomplishment as he struggled on. *I'm feeling warmer . . . thank you, Lord . . . that's better . . . Maybe I'll rest before going on . . . just a bit . . . just res'* . . . The warm, friendly blackness swept over him again. He was comfortable at last; just as he had once welcomed sleep after a long day's labors of satisfying work, he now dropped into welcomed oblivion. The restful blackness enveloped him as the medics found him face down in the snow and turned him over, assessed his injuries, and quickly loaded him on a stretcher for transportation to the aid station.

Shades of light and black filtered into Frank's world. He was restless, wanting to move, run. Something was wrong. A rasping, grating sound echoed softly and then suddenly blared in full volume hurting his ears. Now he was running hard. He was in the midst of a large group of people all running in the same direction. The panic was contagious spreading among them; they all ran and shouted. What were they saying? What were they running from? What am I running from? Frank couldn't tell, but he knew that something was pursuing them, and now whatever it was, was after him, he was part of the crowd. He became aware that none of the people were clothed; he and everyone he saw were naked. It didn't matter; they were running for their lives. There in the distance was a large door. Frank understood that there was safety behind the door without anyone telling him. He ran on and on, and the door seemed to get no closer. People started stumbling and falling, dropping out of the life-saving race; he understood that as well. Old people, women, small children, healthy men all began dropping away. What would happen to them? Frank tried looking over his shoulder but could see nothing in the billowing blackness that followed—and was gaining—on the crowd. He was deathly afraid, more afraid than he had ever experienced. The door was now in clear view; there was a sign in large black letters on a yellow background. The people at the door started screaming, banging on the closed portal to safety. Frank pushed his way through the crowd; he was getting closer, now he read the sign, No Jews Allowed. Below the first line was a second, No Niggers Either. Frank crashed into the door and bounced to the ground. His head was dizzy; the cacophony of screaming continued as the people banged on the door. No one answered. There was silence. They were ignored.

The blackness—the mad hounds of war, the snapping, snarling, slashing—swept in on the throng of people. Frank gasped and thrashed his arms, then a deeper level of unconsciousness snatched him away. His body and the tangled hospital bed sheets were wet with his sweat.

Frank was unaware of the dimension of time as he emerged to a level of confused unconsciousness. He was in a dark, gray, dreary world. He became aware of a sound . . . the sound of feet . . . walking, many feet . . . there . . . there they were, soldiers emerging into his view. Bedraggled, spent men . . . four, sometimes five, abreast, marching through the grayness. They were surprisingly quiet as they trudged along, their faces staring forward into the distance, a few watching their feet. The rhythmic sound of the marching feet was very soft. They didn't march in step; this wasn't a formal assembly. They walked, snapping twigs and rustling leaves on the ground, these solemn and oh, so quiet men. Then Frank recognized the ashen faced, the stocky young private who had died north of Basse-Ham. There was another, a sergeant . . . He realized all these soldiers were his men. They were dead and they were marching. Where were they going? A cold chill shook his shoulders.

What if his commander asked him to recite the names of all his men who had died? He couldn't remember the names. There was . . . he couldn't remember the tall, red-haired soldier's name. Gripped by fear, he turned to look in the direction of their march, the line of soldiers disappeared into the misty, gray distance. It was such a long line—so long it seemed to have no end. Frank turned to look at the approaching marchers. There was that corporal, ah . . . he pissed his pants at Mortain . . . what was his name? Frank tried to speak but no sound was heard. Now he remembered his name. How could he forget Henson? . . . *Remember Henson,* Frank told himself. *You can tell them about Henson and how you helped him get mail from home.* There was Lieutenant Alfonse Rodgers who died near Basse-Ham. *Remember his name.* Rodgers handed Frank a photo as he passed. Frank looked at the picture of a pretty young woman whose face was blurred. He turned over the snapshot and read, "To my darling Alfonse, may God watch over you and bring you safely to me. I'll wait forever for you. Angeline." Frank froze . . . the girl in Paris. He turned the picture over again, and there she was now in sharp focus, smiling. Frank looked up and Rodgers was gone, marching into the distance. So many soldiers . . . Had he killed them? Was he responsible? What could he say about them? Had they been needlessly sacrificed? Had they? *Men, I'm sorry . . .* This time he spoke, "*I'm so sorry.*" He was crying.

Yes, he was sorry for their death and sorry for the part he had played in it . . . sorry . . . sorry. Frank understood the truth about soldiers: They didn't give their lives to protect freedom. They may have volunteered for service in a patriotic frenzy, but over here in battle, their lives were ripped from them in the agony of death. They weren't protecting liberty as much as they were scared of death and were first protecting themselves and their buddies. *I know what happened; I know the truth.* Now the soldiers looked different . . . yes they were different . . . They were Germans, all young men . . . No, some were boys, teenagers, just like the American soldiers. Then he saw the cold, blue eyes searching his face as the boy soldier passed. The eyes seemed animated wanting to tell him something. *What? What?*

His body jerked as he awakened in the soft light of the night, his heart racing and breaths coming in short gasps. His eyes flashed around taking in his location. He was in a room lying on his back. There were walls, a ceiling, and off to the right a closed door with an overhead transom through which a dim, filtered light entered the room. There were sounds, soft sounds of shuffling, of moving, of walking steps; someone was outside the room. His heart rate began to slow, and breathing calmed as he remained alert, looking, listening. Everything within his vision was at rest.

Had he been dreaming? There was the soft sound of footsteps again. Where was the person going, why? He became curious . . . *Where am I, what happened?* . . . He could not remember. He had been walking . . . Where was he walking, in Kentucky? No, not Kentucky. Was he in Tennessee? America? He couldn't recall, but . . . France, yes, France . . . No, not France. Where? Belgium, yes, Belgium. Was he in Belgium now? Was this a hospital? Was he injured? His head ached, but he couldn't tell if he had other injuries. If he was injured, it couldn't be too bad. He felt pretty good for being in a hospital . . . that is . . . if this was a hospital.

Frank raised his hand to his head and felt a bandage. There were no other bandages on his arms or torso. Then he strained to look at his feet and saw that his right leg was in a cast . . . or was it heavily bandaged? His left foot was also wrapped. He became very dizzy, lowered his head, and closed his eyes. He wondered where his troops were . . . what were they doing? were they fighting? were they on R and R? was the Saint all right? He thought of Henry . . . where was he, and was he all right? Where was Roger Cohen, the young psalmist? Now, why did Cohen come to mind? Was he walking with Roger? As he tried to recall events that had brought him to this place, his mind wandered. Then it suddenly struck him that Henry and Roger were very much alike; they both suffered from prejudice—prejudice by white people, not him, but other white people all the same.

*Now that's not very earthshaking. Prejudice happens, but why? Who gets picked to be a scapegoat?* His eyes opened. *It wasn't all white people, but there were enough to make the lives of "them" hard at times. Henry probably suffered more than Roger because of the color of his skin.* Then Frank realized he had an idea what Coloreds suffered through, but he didn't know what life was really like for Jews in America. Were there restrictions on what they did, where they lived? In fact, he tried to recall if he had ever known a Jew, he wasn't sure. There were probably Jews at Eastern Kentucky when he was in school, but he didn't know them, or at least didn't know they were Jewish. He had heard about country club restrictions on Jews, but that was not as bad as what Colored people suffered through every day. But if Cohen had lived in Germany, then he would know what prejudice was all about. *Now, that's prejudice . . . no that's hatred. Is prejudice in America the same as hatred?*

Frank's thoughts rambled in a confused tangle as he once again settled on white people as the source of prejudice, of hatred . . . He paused as he thought, *Yes, Jews and Coloreds are both victims.* He restated his revelation and tried to concentrate on it. *Prejudice in America is like the hatred directed toward the Jews in Germany, yes, that was true. Then there was hatred of the Jews in America, but maybe not to the same extreme as for Coloreds . . . Jews were white; why were they hated? Why were people like Gene Tulley and Mark Cooper so full of hate? It had to be hate. What else could account for their views? Yes,* he agreed with himself, *it was hatred, the need to feel superior to someone . . . Maybe that was the cause; then again, maybe it was hatred handed down from father to son. Would that make American society the culprit?'* He thought about his now incomplete newfound revelation; he was convinced he was right, but not sure why. Why? why did they hate? why? His thoughts became very confused as he closed his eyes and heard the soft, musical clock chimes strike three times from somewhere outside his room and, again, the sound of footsteps. He thought more of his life in Kentucky and Tennessee and the people he had known. Teddy and Ellen filtered into his memory and he relaxed . . . He was suddenly struck by an overwhelming, calming, sense of peace. He closed his eyes on the dimly lit room. This was one of several such visits he would make to the semi-awake world while he lay in a hospital bed. He would remember none of them.

Frank felt uneasy as he roused into his dream world . . . but why unease? What was gnawing at him, what had he done or not done? He was disappointed with himself, with Franklin Edward Warring. Disappointed with the way he had deceived his parents. Yes, that was it. . . . It was when he was growing up, still a teenager. Was his youth an excuse for his mistakes? It was Alice Fay Miller, the girl in Millersville. His friends laughed and called her a "real miller" from Millersville. Yes, he had denied being with the Miller girl, with Alice Fay. His friends had bragged about their sexual escapades with her, and he had joined in the lustful experience of youth. Another person had been created in her body. Was he the father of the baby? Her baby. He didn't know. Maybe all the boys she had been with were the father. As a teenager he didn't want to know; he was afraid. He didn't want to accept responsibility. She had been sent away by her parents, and when she returned, she attended another high school, the one in Paris where she lived with her aunt. She wound up as a hairdresser there, and her baby . . . What happened to him? He would be about eighteen or nineteen. Was he in the war, was he one of those killed? *Was he one of my men?* Frank had lied to his parents when they asked about Alice Fay . . . lied . . . Worst of all, he thought they knew he lied. He disappointed them . . . And, most of all he disappointed himself. As these thoughts rambled through his sleep world, he slipped back into a deeper level without dreams.

The timelessness of oblivion lifted, and Frank rose again to the level of unconsciousness that was now his existence, although he was unaware of that fact since he had no conscious thoughts. He was enveloped by the warm blackness. He couldn't tell if his eyes were open, there was nothing to see, or if his ears were working, there was nothing to hear. As he marveled at the nothingness, he became aware of a light—small at first that grew very bright, very fast to almost engulf him. There was a warm, red, filmy layer that surrounded the light. The light was so bright he couldn't see its source. Frank felt a warm presence next to him but he was unable to turn and see who was there. He now heard, without a voice being spoken, that the light was God. *My God, it's GOD!* Frank exclaimed, or did he just imagine saying it? *God, are you there*? he hoped he said aloud. Was he talking to himself? *God, are you there, can you talk to me?* . . . Silence . . . The intensity of the light grew even brighter, and his eyes opened as he woke. The blinding light shocked his senses as he jerked his head right and left, and he found that by going to the left, he moved his eyes from the ray of unfiltered sunlight streaming through a window. He was in a room. Although he faced the overhead ceiling, he could look down and see the window to the left that was a portal onto the bright day. He saw a deep blue sky with puffy clouds pushed by a stiff wind scudding across his view. With his head turned to the left, the sun's new angle fell across his lower face; his lips and right cheek were warmed by the sun's touch, as well as the right side of his body.

Did he just have a dream where he talked to God? He had trouble remembering. *God, did I just talk to you, see you?* . . . *A voice, do you have a voice?* Silence . . . *God, I've got a lot of questions. Can you help me?* He was aware of the growing, aching, empty feeling in his gut as he longed for assurance of a force mightier than himself, mightier than America, mightier than the world. The empty feeling had grown as he witnessed the bath of death in which he had been unwillingly washed—the blood, the terror, maimed bodies of young survivors. What was its purpose? Whose plan was being followed? Was there a plan? Was there a force? Why so many dead people? *why?* . . . *why?* . . . *why*? *God, I'm tired and empty* . . . *take me home* . . . *please, Lord, take me home* . . . *I'm so tired* . . . A yellow finch flew up to the window and landed on the sill, ruffling its feathers in the warming sun. Sticking its head under a raised wing, the bird then looked right and left and suddenly flew from sight as quickly as it had come. Frank gazed at the sky, closed his eyes, and slipped over the edge into a deep sleep.

After a time Frank was aware of the blackness that surrounded him, swirling, tumbling . . . *How could blackness move? How could that be?* He wasn't afraid of the moving emptiness; he was only an observer. He could touch the blackness, the emptiness, he could actually touch it . . . or could he? Did he have hands, arms, legs, feet? . . . he couldn't tell. *Isn't that odd, if there is nothing there how can it be touched? And how can I touch it if I have no hands?* Was he in one piece, was all of him there? . . . come to think of it, *where is there, where is here? Where am I? Am I standing, am I floating? I can't tell.* Something warm touched his hand. He started. He did have hands, or at least one hand. The touch was not threatening, it was soft and warm. *A small hand, my God, it's a hand . . . so comforting, so reassuring, so warm.* Could this be Teddy's hand? could it be Ellen's? yes it could be and he felt reassured, safe . . .

He was now a boy again, lying in his bed on an early summer morning with the window of his room open to the first, soft light of the dawn hour. Light had not yet reached the dark landscape of the farm, but it had begun to chase the night from the sky. He would soon have to rise and make his way to the barn to help Daddy with milking. He lay in his bed and heard the soft sounds of the mourning dove, the cooing, long and short coos. There was a long coo at first that started up in tone and then dropped slightly in pitch as it ended, followed by three short coos, each of those also dropped slightly in pitch at the end. Sometimes there were only two short follow-on coos. Did that difference in the number of coos represent a form of talking between doves? He wasn't sure, but he was certain that the dove's music was the most reassuring sound he could imagine. It matched the soft morning light and the cool breeze that rippled the open window's curtain. As he lived again in his memory he heard a dove's voice sing the familiar sound. Was he awake, was he dreaming? *There it is again.* He listened, soaking up the music of the morning and slept with his hand being caressed by the small, warm unknown hand.

The soft, swirling feeling of love lifted him to awareness in his dark world as the light of memory filled him with his love for Ellen. Ellen, Ellen . . . She had led him to the highest possible experience of love he had ever felt. She was love incarnate; she was love in flesh and blood. They wanted nothing but to please each other. Pleasing didn't depend on worldly goods—they lacked those—pleasing was based on the love of the other, their mutual acceptance and commitment. Then there was Teddy. He arrived and was wrapped in their mutual love-world. They were complete. They were one, a family sated by each other's affections.

Why had Ellen left? Why was her love ripped from him, from Teddy? . . . Now they had each other and that was still love, a fulfilling love, but . . . but, there was room for more, for another. Could Ellen be replaced? no . . . never replaced. But there was still room for love. Frank ached to love again, to experience again the love he had for Ellen. The aching melted away, a feeling of gratitude filled his thoughts, and he knew he had gained from Ellen's love and by it been taught how to love. The caressing, peaceful sound of the mourning dove began to register on Frank's auditory nerve . . . the one long . . . and three short coos entered into his understanding . . . a feeling of calmness . . . of peace prevailed, as he relaxed.

The swirling blackness was different now. Now it had form—swirling darkness with subtle highlights, shades of light, of color. As Frank rose to consciousness, he saw a dark purple, or was it a red black? It was hard to put a name to the world surrounding Frank. There . . . there it was again . . . the warm, soft hand touching his, holding his hand. The hand tightened its touch, now it was gone. *Oh, don't go, please come back.* His world now had a slightly brighter spot in the swirling blackness, a definite light there straight ahead. *There must be someone there. I'm not alone . . . if I knew where I was, I could soon find out if there were others near me. Where are my men? I nearly forgot my men! How careless of me.*

# CHAPTER 34

## *Bristol, England*

## *Spring 1945*

THE LIGHT WAS brighter now, beginning to glow, larger, so bright . . . there must be someone at the light . . . who could it be? *Could I be dead, actually dead? What if I am? Oh, God, give me strength, could I be in heaven? could I? no, really . . . could this be heaven? Are there angles here?* The light had a form . . . now a person . . . a person! He strained to see in the lightening darkness. *Oh, a woman . . . look at her.* The rolling lightness had taken form in the shape of a head. It was a woman, a person. *She's pretty, I think, and she has a cap on. Ha, ha, who would have ever thought that an angel would be wearing a cap. God, you must be a real kidder, angels wearing caps. Isn't that something? I thought angels had wings or halos. Say, I don't hear any harp music, I thought that was part of arriving in heaven. Pardon me for laughing, God, but angels with caps and no harps! Can you blame me for laughing?* There was no answer. *I guess you can't.*

The warm hand was back now, holding Frank's left hand. It felt wonderful, absolutely wonderful. There was a hand on his brow, a caressing touch. *That feels so good, don't stop, don't stop.* The angel with the cap was gone, there was a second angel now; this one seemed to have curly blond hair and no cap. *I guess the angels have some kind of rank order. The big-shot angels wear caps. and the newest angels don't until they earn their cap. Ha, ha, and everybody thought they had to earn their wings, well . . . now I know it's a cap.* He squeezed the hand holding his, and it returned the squeeze. The angel spoke but he couldn't understand her, did they speak a language known only in heaven? He had always assumed he could use English if and when he got here, but would he have to now learn a new language? He wondered if he would be expected to become an angel. *Now that's a stretch even for God. I just don't think I'm angel material.* The angel spoke again to the second angel. He could not see her capped head, but still felt her presence.

"Can you hear me now?"

*Thank you, God, you taught her English . . . that was fast.* "Yes," Frank's voice croaked his first audible words in heaven.

"I'm so glad. You've been asleep for a long time," said the curly haired angel. Frank saw that she was a girl—not a child and not quite a woman, but a girl-woman, maybe fifteen.

"It was a coma," said the capped angel.

"Coma," said Frank, "coma, what . . . ?" He realized his words were slurred but he spoke as well as he could.

A nurse with a bright white cap stuck her face into his sphere of vision. "You've been sleeping for a very long time, and the doctors believed you might not wake up, but I just knew you would. It's something that I feel deep inside when I take care of soldiers like you."

"Like me?" Frank mumbled.

"Yes, wounded soldiers like you."

"Where am I?" Frank croaked aloud.

"You're in a hospital in Bristol."

"Bristol . . . England?"

"Yes, Bristol, England. You were flown here a little over two weeks ago."

"Two weeks? What day is this?" he croaked again even less audibly than his earlier attempt to talk.

"January 22," said the nurse. "It took about a week to get you through the medical receiving station and the field hospital before you could be transported here. And you have been hooked up to these feeding tubes ever since."

"Hello there," came the bright, crisp friendly voice of the curly headed girl-woman who sat at the side of his bed holding his hand.

Frank recognized her face, that of the second angel. He tried to smile, but instead he lost hold of reality and slipped again into a sleep. Over the next week he would wake almost every day and then return to a deep sleep. Each time he woke, it was as if it was the first time. He would recall nothing of his previous waking experiences.

On the first of February, a bright sunny morning, Frank awoke again and looked around the hospital room. A young girl was holding his hand. "Good morning, Captain Warring. How do you feel this morning?" she asked as she squeezed his hand.

"Pretty good," mumbled Frank. "The sun is out, looks like a nice day. Who are you?"

"I'm Margaret Elizabeth Warren. My friends call me Kitty because of my initials," said the smiling, curly headed girl.

"Initials," mumbled Frank, *Margaret Elizabeth Warren*. "Oh, I see. Your initials are MEW, that's clever . . . Where am I?"

"You're in a hospital in Bristol, England, and you have been waking up almost every day since last Friday with the same questions." Margaret Elizabeth smiled at him and continued holding his hand.

"Really," mused Frank, "maybe I'll do a better job of remembering from now on. I just had the odd feeling that you were an angel."

"I know, you have asked me that before, as well, and I assured you that I am not, although I am glad you think I could be one." Margaret Elizabeth laughed.

"I seemed to have had the impression that I was in heaven with angels," he said with a chuckle that came out as a harsh growl. "I wondered why an angel had on a cap. But you don't wear a cap."

"No, no, I don't, but Lieutenant Adcock does, and she regularly attends you."

At that moment First Lieutenant Andrea Adcock entered the room. "Well, well, awake again, I see. How do you feel this morning?"

"As I told Miss . . . Kitty . . ."

"That's just Kitty, although I guess I could be Miss Kitty for you."

Frank smiled. "I told Miss What's-Her-Name that I felt good." Frank let out a muffled chuckle.

"Good, that's the best conversation we've had since you arrived. Maybe you'll stay with us now on a permanent basis. The doctor will be in to see you at ten o'clock. He'll be pleased to have the chance to talk to you, that is, if you stay awake for us."

"I'll do my best. Did you used to live in Knoxville or in Central Kentucky? You look familiar," Frank asked Nurse Adcock.

"No, I'm from Iowa. You probably have a vague recollection of seeing me during your earlier waking periods. Margaret Elizabeth is a volunteer here at the hospital. She's my aide."

"You've been one of my patients ever since you arrived," Kitty bubbled. "I visit you every day I come to the hospital, and I've seen you come around very slowly over the last week. Miss Adcock and I have been waiting very anxiously to hear from you. I hold your hand when I'm here."

"Thank you," Frank croaked. "Have there been mourning doves outside the window? I seem to recall hearing them recently."

"I don't think there are any doves out this time of the year, and besides if there were, we couldn't hear them with the closed window. In the last week, there were times when you seemed to almost waken. Your eyes would roll around behind your eyelids, and sometimes you mumbled something, quite unintelligible I would say. You did have tears in your eyes one day when you seemed to have a terrible dream. I felt so sorry for you then. A few times you opened your eyes, but you didn't talk much. and what you said didn't seem like words to me." Kitty almost giggled, before covering her mouth to hide her mirth.

"I've been accused of being unintelligible before," he mumbled and smiled.

"Oh, I wouldn't go so far as to say tha-at," she replied in her very British accent.

"I'll check back on you in a bit," said Nurse Adcock in her

measured Midwestern American accent. "You get some rest now, and I'll bring you some soup when you wake up and see how well you tolerate real food." She patted Frank's undamaged foot as she walked from the room.

"Miss Adcock is a wonderful nurse," said Kitty. "She knows so much about wounded soldiers; her knowledge is exquisite. When she first saw you she immediately said you were going to make it. She's really extraordinary."

"That's very reassuring that I didn't let her down by dying," Frank croaked and again smiled. He felt so good talking to a person, a pretty schoolgirl holding his hand. He realized she was reminding him that there was a life to lead after the war. The war . . . He had forgotten all about it. "How's the war going now?" he mumbled.

"Oh, we have the Jerrys on the run now for sure. Our forces are beating them up pretty bad on the Siegfried Line, and soon we will cross the Rhine. You Yanks have done a marvelous job in bashing their brains. The end's in sight. Soon we will have no more air raids. I'm so tired of sleeping on the floor in the cellar of our house; it's getting to be an awful bore."

All Frank could do was to smile at the girl, so full of life. There was a bright future for mankind yet. The Germans had not destroyed the spark of life, vital life, from the British, as hard as they had tried. *Thank you, God, for Kitty.*

"I better let you get to sleep. I'll see you tomorrow," said Kitty as she squeezed Frank's hand and walked from the room.

"I look forward to seeing you," he mumbled. *By God, it's great to be alive.* Frank could not account for the feeling of utter relief, well-being, and joy he felt surging through his body as he closed his eyes and drifted into a sleep from which he would awaken in two hours and remember all he had just heard.

On February 3, Lieutenant Adcock entered Frank's two-person room that he now shared with another soldier, Major John Jarvis Longstreet. The major was heavily sedated with severe burns to his lower body and a broken leg. Nurse Adcock told Frank that the major had been in a Jeep near the German border when his vehicle was hit by enemy fire, and like Frank, he had been flown to England for intensive medical care after being treated near the front in a field hospital.

"Well, you look chipper this morning; you've had breakfast already, I believe. Are you ready to do a little reading?" She handed Frank a stack of envelopes. "That's your mail that's been following you around the theater, and there's a package over on the small table. Somebody cares about what happens to you."

"Yes, I guess they do," he said taking the envelopes. Today, two days after awakening to life, Frank's voice was a little clearer.

"I put them in order by date so you can follow the time progression in which they were mailed." Nurse Adcock was well organized, Frank would have to admit.

He was beginning to develop a sense of equilibrium both in his ability to stand and to hobble around without putting pressure on his bad leg. He was also catching up on the war. Yesterday Adcock had brought him copies of *Stars and Stripes* plus copies of the Bristol newspaper, the *London Times*, and the Sunday edition of the Oxford paper. That was a lot of reading that he had started but not completed.

He thumbed through the pile of letters, looking forward to reading all of them and then opened first the oldest letter, one from Teddy.

*Dear Dad,* *November 21, 1944*

*It is Thanksgiving Day and we had a great feast today with a turkey and dressing, and sweet potatoes with marshmallows and green beans which I don't care for very much and other stuff and pumpkin pie. Granddad wanted a pecan pie but Granny said he gets that every Thanksgiving and this year she wants a pumpkin pie. So she said she would make the pecan pie for Christmas. Granddad said he could not wait that long and he would go door to door down the street to see if he could beg a piece of pecan pie from someone. Granny said he was a big old baby and he laughed, Ha ha. It is getting late in the day and he has not left yet to find his pie and he is asleep in his chair now so I guess the pie trip will wait.*

*I hope you had a good thanksgiving day wherever you are. Lily has gone to Nashville for two days to eat with her family. She has a sister June who talked to me on the phone and she seems to be real nice. She will be in high school so she is ahead of me by a lot.*

*My school is going swell. I got four A̲s on my report card so you are going to owe me some big money when you come home. I miss you and hope you beat the Germens and come home soon.*

*Love Ted*

*P.S. I will not mail this until Lily comes back and writes her letter to go with it.*

*Dad is still carrying on.* Frank smiled about Ted's description of the Thanksgiving pie episode. Frank continued to smile as he opened Lily's letter.

*November 24, 1944*

*Dear Frank,*

*I had a lovely trip over to Nashville for Thanksgiving with my family. The weather was beautiful and on Friday, June and I went to Shelby Park, not too far from our house, and played a round of golf. It was great fun. June has been playing for several years and plans to go out for the high school team, but I haven't played for four or five years. I'm explaining this because she beat me, and I'm trying to save face. She is maturing fast and is becoming quite a young lady. She is writing to the soldier whose name you gave me. She said this summer she plans to go up to Kentucky and visit the grave of the young soldier, Corporal Henson, I believe was his name. I told her he may be buried in France, so she is now writing the Army to see if she can find the location of his final resting place.*

*I have a girlfriend, a fellow teacher at Van Gilder, who got tickets for the Kentucky game this Saturday, so we will go down the hill to cheer on the mighty Vols. Go team. I bet if you were here you would cheer for the Big Blue.*

*I hope you were pleased with the election and Mr. Roosevelt serving another four years. The election this year was closer this time than his previous elections, but he won. He is beginning to show the strain of office in the lines on his face. I truly believe he would not have run had it not been for the war still going on. Well I am very confident he will not run again. His vice president is a fellow from Missouri, Harry Truman. Can you imagine a president named Harry? I can't. But with Roosevelt, the vice president seems to have very little to do but sit in the senate, so I guess we will not hear much from Harry over the next four years. Then he can go back to Missouri in 1948 when his term is up.*

*I do hope you and your company are keeping safe. We are all very proud of you and the way the American force is pushing the Germans back into Germany where they belong. They are losing ground now in all the countries that they invaded. The war in the Pacific is so very different than the one in Europe. We are starting to bomb Japan on a regular basis, and they are using their suicide planes with good effect against our big ships. I guess you have heard MacArthur has gone back into the Philippines at a place called Leyte Gulf. Everybody has their fingers crossed that he will succeed. Do you need more socks? Take care of yourself.*

*Your loyal epistolary friend,*

*With affection, Lily*

*No,* Frank thought, *I don't need socks.* For the first time in a long while in his waking memory, his feet were warm. He suspected the package on the table contained the latest edition of socks knitted by the ladies of Knoxville. He would have to send them on to the Saint. The Saint . . . He suddenly wondered what had happened to him north of Bastogne and whether the rest of the troops were

OK. He pulled the nurse call cord, which dropped a signal flag outside his door letting the nurse know he needed her.

After five minutes, "What's up?" said Lieutenant Adcock as she poked her head inside the door of his room.

"What happened to me? Why did they send me here, and what caused the coma?"

"My, my, you are just full of questions, aren't you? I guess you don't remember a thing." Frank shook his head from side to side. "Well your chart said you were the victim of standing too close to an exploding German shell, at least that's the way I interpret the description."

"Damn, what about the other men?"

"The chart doesn't say anything about that. But there is a young fellow here that was wounded in the same explosion, I believe."

"Really, who is that?"

"He's a PFC in the ward on this floor. His name is Cohen."

"No! No! Damn! . . . Cohen! How bad is he hurt?"

"He lost part of his lower left leg."

"Oh, no."

"Was he in your company?"

"Yes, he'd just joined us and had about three or four days of combat. I remember now, we were talking and that's the last thing I remember. I hadn't remembered till now. Damn, how is his attitude?"

"He seems very relaxed about the whole situation, maybe because he is heading back to the States soon."

"Can I see him?"

"I'll tell him you asked for him. He is in a wheelchair and goes all over the hospital. I bet he will make you a call."

"I would really appreciate that . . . That would be swell."

Both smiled as Adcock left the room.

After lunch Frank lay in bed with his eyes closed but not yet asleep. He opened his eyes at the sound of squeaking rubber tires on the polished wood floor. "Cohen, is that you?" he said as a figure disappeared from the door opening.

"Yes, sir," said the private as he reappeared bumping into the door frame with his wheelchair. "I was afraid you were asleep, and I didn't want to disturb you," his voice dropped in volume as he spoke.

"Please, come on in. I was just resting after lunch. Can you give that crank at the foot of the bed some turns and raise me up? I'm tired of being flat on my back." The squeaking hand crank did its job as Frank was better able to see the serious face of Cohen. "That's fine. Do you know what happened to us?"

"Yes, sir, an artillery shell exploded behind us and we went down. I didn't lose consciousness, but I guess you did. You may have shielded me from the blast, but I'm not sure. My leg was pretty bad, all bloody, and when the medics got to us they stopped my bleeding with a tourniquet and put me on a stretcher. I asked about you, and they said "where is he?" and I said "my God, maybe he was blown away," but they looked around and found you. You had crawled away into the woods. Then they got you on a stretcher and stopped your bleeding. You were out of your head, they said. There were several others hurt, but they stayed at the field hospital, so I guess they were not hit badly, but I don't know for sure . . . Sir, I didn't realize you were here until Lieutenant Adcock said I was to come visit you."

"Well that wasn't an order for you to come, but I'm awfully glad to see you and I'm so sorry about your leg."

"Oh, I was afraid something would happen to me over here." Cohen paused looking at his leg covered in an abundance of wrappings. "I'm just glad I can go home now. I hope I did all right for the short time I served."

"Roger, that's your first name, right?"

Cohen nodded.

"You did exactly the correct thing, and you have every reason to be proud of your service. You did exactly what your country called for you to do, and you did a good job. It was just your luck to be hit in that way. Maybe you were too close to me because my time must have been up."

"Oh no, sir, I wasn't too close; I was just enjoying the chance to talk. Thank you, sir," a relieved sound tinged the boy's voice. "I was just afraid maybe I hadn't done right, especially when I got scared and started reciting some of the Psalms during the shelling."

"You were very normal. We were all scared to death, and for some reason our lives were spared when that shell didn't explode. I've thought about that shell, that dud, and don't know if it was a fluke or if the Almighty had a hand in it. I guess we will never know. I especially appreciated you recalling the Psalms. It gave me courage. Thank you."

"I was remembering the years of Hebrew school that I attended. They just suddenly came back to me when the shells started hitting close. Don't worry about my leg. My poppa is an orthopedist in Cleveland, and he said he can't wait to get his hands on my stub and fit me with an artificial limb." Cohen laughed. "He takes pride in his work, and I think he really wants to treat me."

Frank smiled at the young man's attitude and realized he may have come to his room in anticipation of being reprimanded for an error that he was unaware he had committed. With that off his mind, the boy began to relax and show his spunk as a teenager.

"What are you going to do when you get home?" asked Frank.

A broad smile lit his face. "I guess I'll go to college this fall. I didn't expect to be there so soon, but now I guess I'm ready, especially if I can learn to walk again. I just graduated from high school last June."

"There are a lot of good schools in Ohio," Frank acknowledged.

"Yes, but I don't know where I'll go. I'll probably study pre-med, I guess. That's what my parents want me to do. I just don't know if I can be as good a doctor as Poppa. His patients in the hospital love to see him come in their room. He's always smiling and giving them confidence 'cause he said patient confidence is a good part of the cure."

"And I think you are well on your way to a cure." Frank smiled.

"How are you doing, sir?"

"The doc thinks I should make a complete recovery. I may have a limp, but time will tell about that. My brain seems to have been shaken up by the blast. I was in a coma for some time and my legs were injured, but the legs are healing nicely and my brain seems to be doing better. The nurse said it had stopped rattling inside my skull."

Cohen giggled at the comment.

"They're going to get me up in a wheelchair, like you, and then start me walking with a cane after I get more strength back."

"Hello, everyone," said Kitty as she walked in the door. Looking at Cohen, she extended her hand. "I'm Kitty, how do you do," with a big smile lighting her face.

"Hi, I'm Roger Cohen. I'm from Cleveland, Ohio."

"I've heard of Ohio. I'm from here in Bristol. You have a river, I believe, in Ohio."

"Ah, a river . . . oh yes, the Ohio River. Yes, it's at the other end of the state; Cleveland is on Lake Erie in the north of the state, and we have only a small river up there."

"And how is our captain today?" she said as she walked to the bed and took Frank's hand.

"Your captain is great today, Miss Kitty."

"I have to hold his hand every day as part of his recovery," she said to Roger.

"I'm sure that helps." Roger smiled. "Good medicine. I'm down in Three A, and I sure could use a dose of medicine," Cohen's voice dropped, and he blushed as he completed his invitation to Kitty. "Excuse me, captain, I'll stop in tomorrow morning and see you. I'll be leaving for the States in the afternoon."

"I look forward to seeing you then."

"Bye, Kitty." Roger disappeared down the hall.

"He's such a nice boy and rather good looking, I would say. I see he lost his lower leg."

"Yes, we were wounded at the same time by the same shell."

"Does that make you blood brothers or something?" asked Kitty with an impish grin. "I saw in an American movie once where an Indian and a settler cut their fingers and bound them together and became blood brothers, and I thought that might be a custom over there." Her smile broadened.

"Not in Kentucky, as far as I know, although I guess Cohen and I do share a bond now. He's a fine young man."

"All right, time for your shots," said Adcock as she bustled into the room. Bed down, roll over, and bare your derriere."

"Oops, time for me to leave," said Kitty, "I can't stand needles, and I hate to see you cry. See you tomorrow. I think I'll go see if I can find Roger in the ward. Bye."

"Here's your new mail," said Adcock as she handed Frank a letter from Knoxville dated January 5, 1945. "It's a month old. I guess it went to France first before they sent it here."

*January 4, 1945*

*Dear Frank,*

*Everyone is very upset at the news that you have been wounded. Mary's reaction may be better described as distraught. I am starting this letter, and I think everyone will write you a note. A telegram was received from the War Department, and Mary about fainted when she saw who it was from, but she recovered somewhat when she found out it was about a wounding and not the worst kind of news. She is just beside herself for you to come home. Ted was also very upset and cried when he got the news, but Will held him a long time and talked to him, and he is better today. He could not stand to go to school yesterday, the morning after we heard. We do not know anything about your injuries and hope they are not long lasting and that they are giving you good care. Please heal fast and come home.*

*Even though we haven't met I do feel I know you well enough to miss you along with your family. We all want you here in Knoxville. You have done your share in winning this awful war.*

*I remain your loyal epistolary friend, Lily*

*Dear Daddy,*
*I hope you are not hurt badly and can come home real soon. If you need help walking I can help because I have grown this last year and have passed Granny and am almost as tall as Lily. You can lean on my shoulder if you need to. Thank you for the Bobby Doerr glove for Christmas, it is swell. Granny said she got it for you to give to me. When you get home we can play catch and you can use my new glove and I'll use the old one. Lily gave me a new ball so we are all set.*
*I love you. Ted*

*Dear Frank,*

*I don't know where to start so I'll just say I love you and want you home where I can take good care of you and cook your favorite food. I was afraid something like this would happen but at least you are coming home. So many mothers are not as fortunate as me. Poor Mary Boudreau heard her middle son Harvey was killed in action when those crazy Jap suicide planes flew into his boat the Intrepid the day before Christmas. She says her oldest, your friend Henry, is still safe and they think he is in Germany now. That's a relief for her but she and all of us want this war to be over. Her youngest son is in San Diego and she's so afraid he will be shipped out soon to the Pacific. I read Lily's note and see she told you about when I got the telegram. I almost fainted but your Daddy held me up and then we found out you were only wounded. That instant when I saw the wire was sent by the War Department was the worst moment of my life. I pray to God and Jesus every night that they bring you home safe, and now I believe they have answered my prayers. Praise the Lord. Come home.*

*Your Loving Mother*

*Dear Son,*

*I am so very proud of you. You just happen to be in the generation that got called to serve your country and you and your fellows have done it so well, you are beating those bastards at their own game. It was such a relief to see that you were only wounded. Your mother and I cried tears of relief that it wasn't worse. Please come home as soon as you can and begin the rest of your life. You have finished your part in the war.*

*Dad*

Frank held the letters to his chest and wept as he rolled on his side. The tears washed away his lingering fear of death, erased loneliness that had built in him over the last eleven months, and tore down the wall that had contained his reservoir of love. He wrote the family a letter that afternoon, reassuring them that he was on the mend. Then he wrote a second letter to the Reeds in Carrolton, whitewashing his time spent in France and his hospital stay and assuring them that he and Ted would visit as soon as he returned home and could travel freely. He did want to visit the cemetery and bring Ellen up to date and show her he had made it through the war. He asked Adcock to drop the letters in the post before she left the hospital for the day.

# CHAPTER 35

## *Knoxville*

## *April 1945*

OVER THE NEXT six weeks, Frank got progressively stronger as he moved from the bed to the wheelchair, to the cane. His improved strength aided his prowling of the halls, and when the weather warmed, he moved outdoors to the grounds of the hospital. Kitty was often behind him pushing or by his side steadying his gait, especially during the first four weeks. As he improved, he often did not wait for Kitty's arrival but negotiated on his own the walks around flower beds by the hospital's front door.

Major Longstreet had a slower recovery, but he, too, made progress as he was brought to the waking world. He proposed marriage to Kitty, and she took the offer in the spirit that the grandfatherly appearing Major had intended and politely refused saying she preferred a husband without white hair. The Major countered that he was only forty and was prematurely gray, but forty to Kitty was still grandfatherly from her perspective at sixteen. The Major ended the marriage discussion when he confessed he would need permission from his wife to marry Kitty, and it might not be given. His next offer was to adopt her, but she said she had a very satisfactory father in England. The major also had second thoughts as he realized he could not stand to see young men come calling at his home in New Jersey to see her. If she were his daughter, he would have trouble sharing her with the men of the world.

During his period of healing, Frank asked the Red Cross

representative to get a report on the location of his men and whether the Saint was all right. At the end of March, he learned they were east of the Rhine near Darmstadt, Germany, south of Frankfurt. Frank smiled, realizing he had lived outside Frankfurt's namesake town in Kentucky. In a short note, the Saint reassured Frank that the worst of the fighting was over for his men. They were now being held in reserve as the line moved on toward central Germany through light resistance. The Saint also expressed relief that Frank was recovering well enough to be concerned for the men in the company. In a rare glimpse into the Saint's private world, he said Frank had been in his regular nighttime prayers, and he was relieved they had been answered after they had lost so many other men in action.

On the afternoon of April 2, as she left Kitty said, "May God send safety to be your companion on your travels," as she placed a kiss on his cheek and squeezed his hand.

On April 3, Adcock complained that she needed Frank's hospital bed and that they were kicking him out and that he would just have to go home, whether he wanted to or not. Frank boarded a troop ship late in the afternoon in the Bristol port on the fourth of April and arrived in the Port of Baltimore on the tenth. On the eleventh, travel arrangements were completed, and he boarded the C&O Railroad and headed to Union Station in Washington DC, where he found the George Washington waiting for its return trip to Cincinnati.

The afternoon and overnight ride carried him through Virginia, West Virginia, and Kentucky along the Ohio River and finally into Cincinnati's Union Terminal at seven in the morning. As Frank deboarded the train and entered the vast terminal, he was impressed by the scale of the rotunda, the row on row of passengers waiting seats, and the Art Deco murals decorating the room's lofty walls.

By ten o'clock he was on the southbound Louisville and Nashville Railroad heading for Knoxville. As the train passed over the Ohio River into Covington and then Newport, he said a prayer thanking God for bringing him home safely. He tried not to think about all the young men who had died in his command and were not returning. But when he couldn't forget them, he prayed a second time for them as he stared blankly at the passing countryside. He felt a little more relieved then, but still he couldn't forget, and he was certain he never would.

The L&N train wound through Campbell and Pendleton counties and then into the depot of the little town of Cynthiana. Frank knew that a few miles to the south, the train would be slightly west of Millersburg and the family's farm. As the train approached Paris, he recalled the many happy years of his childhood spent on the farm. *Maybe happy is not the right adjective,* thought Frank. *I don't know how many children rate their childhood years. Your childhood is your childhood. You have no frame of reference, so you are usually happy wherever you're raised.* But now as an adult he rated it as happy, *yes, happy*' There were times of great joy and some heartbreak, but the heartbreaks were few and far between the many times when life continued as usual on the farm where he learned to work hard just like his parents and grandparents before him and learned to enjoy being alive.

In the midst of Frank's rambling memories, the train rolled through the Bluegrass country and entered the outskirts of Lexington. The train sat in the Lexington station for about ten minutes; Frank watched passengers alighting from the train. Some were greeted warmly, probably by family members, and others were walking alone toward the terminal carrying their bags. There was an Asian looking young man standing on the platform straining to catch sight of someone in the milling crowd. That reminded him of his friend from college, George Ito. *I wonder if George's father and mother still work at the Chinese restaurant here, or if they went to an internment camp? I wonder where George is now. I know there were some Japanese Americans fighting as a unit in Europe, and Stars and Stripes said they did it very well. Was George one of those soldiers?* When he got settled back into life in Knoxville or wherever he landed, he would have to try and find George; he didn't want to lose contact with him.

As the train pulled out of the station, Frank walked to the dining car where a black waiter with a thin, Clark Gable-type moustache dappled with a few white hairs sat him against the window at a table for four. As Frank moved past the table, across the aisle toward his intended seat he heard a partial phrase of an ongoing conversation, ". . . she's such a namby pamby about such things."

A middle-aged woman and man already sat at Frank's table on the aisle. They were finishing soup and sandwiches for their lunch. The three tablemates introduced themselves and exchanged polite conversation until the couple from Danville finished their food, excused themselves, and prepared to walk to their seats in preparation for getting off the train at Richmond. As the man stood, he leaned into Frank's ear and whispered, "You'll get an earful from the old girl across the aisle. So far we know her daughter is a weak little dormouse and her son is a 'good for nothing' SOB and she wants to cut off Social Security payments from Washington to the poor people who haven't paid enough into the system. Good listening, and welcome home," he said patting Frank's shoulder.

Alone now at the table, Frank could clearly hear the vocal woman; in fact, it was difficult not to hear her. The woman seemed to be quite opinionated about many subjects, especially FDR who, according to the woman, was driving the country to ruin with "his" debt that he had run up for the country since 1940. She didn't know how he had done it, but she was certain he had stolen the last election. "No one, Simon, can win the presidential election four times in a row, no one. And that poor Dewey, to have the election taken like that. Now he's the real McCoy, being a governor of New York, not one of those politicians like Roosevelt."

Frank muffled a short chuckle as he recalled that in 1932 Roosevelt had also been a real McCoy and the governor of New York and not one of "those" politicians. *Simon must be her husband.*

"Yes, dear." The man nodded.

"And he's letting those labor unions get so strong that first thing they will want to run the companies they work for, and then who knows where they will stop or how high they will raise taxes."

"Yes, dear."

"Boy, I need more water." the woman spat out at the waiter as he passed with a tray of food.

The elderly Negro with graying hair nodded. "Yes, ma'am." His stony face made no sign of reacting to the degrading epithet. Frank cringed. The waiter retrieved Frank's written lunch order and the menu with his left hand and then poured the woman's water with his right hand.

Frank tried to concentrate on the passing scene from his window and ignore the annoying woman. The train was slowing. He now recognized the community they were entering, Richmond. *Over there,* looking west, *that's Eastern's campus.* Frank recalled the cold, sunny day four years ago when he and Teddy hitched a ride, or actually several rides, on their way from the Forks to Knoxville. *I'm ashamed of that trip. I was running away, I had failed. Everything was gone except Teddy. God, that was an awful feeling, an awful time. I just didn't know where to turn, what to do, so I went home like I'd always done when I was lost. Mom and Dad didn't judge me; they took us in like that was their place in life to do it, do it without question. But they're family. I guess that's what families do, or what it means to be a family, you take care of each other. I may have to take care of them soon . . . Yes, like Henry is planning to do with his mom and dad. Yes, I may have to do it sooner than I realized. They're what, sixty-four and sixty-six? I think that's right. Damn, they're getting on in years.*

"Here's your lunch, sir," said the waiter.

"Oh, thank you very much," said Frank as he caught the waiter's eye.

"You're very welcome, sir," a slight smile flicked across the otherwise stoic face. "Are you just coming home from the war, sir?"

"Yes, I've been in France and Belgium, and the Germans finally got me in the leg." Frank pointed at his cane.

"I'm so sorry, sir, but thank you for going over there."

Frank was stunned by the simple remark. "You're," his voice

caught, "you're very welcome."

"My boy was over there driving the Red Ball Express trucks that were supposed to be safe, but when that Bulge battle happened, the German plane blew up his truck, and he's not comin' home. He's buried in some town called Li-gee or something like that."

"Yes, that's Liege, I believe in Belgium. I'm so sorry about your son. Those trucks meant a lot to us; we wouldn't have had any supplies without them. In the end they were as important in beating the Germans as the soldiers shooting the guns; the trucks brought the ammo to use."

"Boy, I need more butter," the voice came from behind the waiter.

Ignoring the voice, "Yes, sir, that's what my boy said. He was real proud of his job, and so was I."

"You have every right to be very proud. I lost a lot of good young men and boys in my company, and I just can't stop thinking about them. My boy is growing up in Knoxville, and I don't want him to go to war."

"No, sir, no son should have to go to war. That's very hard on a father . . . and on a mother. It's very hard to give up your son, very hard." The elderly man's face fell, eyes looked at the floor, and the inability to speak closed his lips.

Frank rose and grasped his right hand and held it between his two hands as the waiter's eyes looked into his; moisture circled his slightly yellowed frames of the jet black irises. The waiter was now the old man that his years dictated, no longer a spry servant on a train. He squeezed Frank's hand and turned to get butter for the lady.

"Boy, if you can't find time for my butter with all your talking, maybe someone else can," the irritated voice jabbed in the air.

Frank glared at the woman. "He's a man who just lost his son in Belgium, ma'am; he's no boy." Frank placed a five dollar bill on the table and picked up his plate with his left hand while the right maneuvered the cane, and he walked down the aisle and out of the dining car.

The woman looked after him with a stunned, blank look on her now pasty face, no longer animated by the free-flowing criticisms of the world as she saw it. She had no idea why that soldier was so rude to her. "Maybe he's suffering from that battle fatigue." Her husband's face turned a bright red as he looked at his half-eaten hot roast beef sandwich.

The train was rolling south of Berea as Frank finished his lunch, and he felt a tap on his shoulder. "Here's your change, sir," said the waiter as he handed Frank three one-dollar bills and several coins. Frank's first thought was to say, keep the money as a tip, but then he didn't want to give credence to the idea that the man was a servant; the man was acting as an equal, and he was equal in Frank's eyes. "Thank you."

"Let me get that dirty plate for you." He retrieved the plate and fork from the empty seat next to Frank. "I hope you have a fine time meetin' your people in Knoxville or wherever they are."

"Thank you, they're going to meet me at the station in Knoxville, I hope." Frank chuckled knowing nothing could keep Teddy and his parents away.

"I'm sure they'll be there for you, sir. It was a pleasure serving you."

Frank extended his right hand, and they shook hands for a second and final time.

The train rolled into Corbin at two o'clock. Frank couldn't see the restaurant where he and Teddy had lunch that fateful travel day in '41. *It was Sanders Restaurant, I think.* That's where they heard the president announce on the radio the declaration of war with Japan and got a thunderous roar of approval from the senators, representatives, and the people in the restaurant. That declaration changed Frank's life, and in retrospect it was the beginning of his personal recovery, as well as the beginning of the nation's nightmare. Now when would the fighting and killing end? No one knew for sure, but in Europe it must be getting close. He couldn't tell about Japan. Unfortunately both Germany and Japan were run by maniacs who were leading their countries in a march to a certain suicide. *Maybe that's the only way to wipe the slate clean of their hatred and the leaders who preach their right to dominate others. Maybe.*

The allies were across the Rhine River now in several places, and it was just a matter of time. The Russians were coming from the east and Americans from the west; Hitler's Germany was doomed. Several more concentration camps had been liberated by the advancing troops, and the sights of what the Nazis had done to the Jews were unbelievable, virtually indescribable. *Ovens for burning human bodies, gas chambers for mass executions, who could possibly have dreamed up those atrocities, who?*

In the Pacific, that little island that no one had ever heard of before, Iwo Jima, had been taken by America, and Okinawa had been invaded. The air force was firebombing Japanese cities now on an almost daily basis. *Can you imagine firebombing civilians?* It occurred to him, *How different is that from gas chambers and furnaces?* Frank stared out the window as the train crossed the Rockcastle River; he rubbed his brow and closed his eyes as he recalled both English and German cities had also been the victims of incendiary bombs. Now it was the Japanese's turn.

Lieutenant Adcock said that he had mentioned when he awoke from the coma that he thought he was in heaven and had had a one-way conversation with God while unconscious. Maybe so, but he couldn't recall it now . . . or could he? Something seemed familiar about the idea of talking to God. *Maybe God answered me and then erased my memory, ha, maybe.* Frank gave a soft, ironic chuckle.

Something was also familiar about the idea of matching the similarity of feelings against Jews in Germany and with feelings against Negroes in America; at least he knew he'd had that thought before, but where, when, he wasn't certain. And now, if he made a list of atrocities, he would put Germany at the top of the list for its inhumane treatment of Jews and Japan for its treatment of Asians and failing to treat American prisoners as humans. But would he include America's firebombing of civilians along with Germany's furnaces for burning people? Would he put Americans on the list a second time for the treatment of Negroes? He shuddered.

Maybe we're all capable of atrocities at times. Maybe that's human nature to be willing to kill if we feel threatened enough. But we can't blame it on human nature; we all have the power to choose, don't we? Frank thought about guilt as it applied to him, what was my role in the war, am I responsible for it, for . . . death? He shuddered at the now-remembered feeling of his rifle butt caving in the skull of the German boy; could he ever forget that sensation in his hands, in his arms? And then there were the staring blue eyes. He hoped he could forget, but at the same time, deep down he doubted he could bury it with the war. It seems the more you want to forget something the more you remember.

As the train continued rolling south of Corbin, Frank recalled that Nazi sympathizer guy, the one who saw them in the restaurant and then gave them a lift to Williamsburg. Frank couldn't recall his name. *Started with a C, I think. What was his name? Something Caudill, Cooper. Yes that was it, Cooper. I wonder if he went to prison, and if he did, if he's out now. That son-of-a-bitch, he's the type capable of supporting atrocities. Maybe he couldn't actually pull the switch or whatever it took for the gas chambers to work, but he's the type to support the ideas, and in this world that makes him as guilty as the switch pullers.*

Frank's black frame of mind lasted until the train stopped for two minutes in Williamsburg. Then he recalled the gracious lady from Williamsburg, Belle Conley, who was a distant relative of that Nazi sympathizer guy. His mood improved as the train wound through the Cumberland Mountains. Sitting by the window and facing forward, he could see all of the train cars between his car and the engine whenever the tracks took a long turn to the right, and when they went left he could see no cars in front of his coach. The switching panorama occurred frequently on the twisting and turning track along the upper reaches of the Cumberland River. *Here is La Follette, sleepy little town,* as the town slipped behind them. Then came Lake City and Clinton before the engine slowed entering the outer edge of Knoxville. Frank was surprised at the nervous level of excitement that grew in his chest the closer he got to the Knoxville depot. He had made it. He was home. He would be with his family. He laid his head back against the seat, closed his eyes, and said, *Thank you, Lord, thank you for bringing me home.*

He stood with the help of the cane and pulled his large duffle bag from the luggage rack at the end of the car. He passed the ladies' and men's restrooms and stood in the narrow aisle of the swaying coach by the end door; the train lurched through the myriad of switches taking it through the small railroad yard on North Central Street and back and forth across Second Creek before pulling into the depot and finally rolling to a stop.

The conductor eased past Frank and the other passengers lining up to disembark. Steam billowed from underneath the car, and the conductor opened the outside door and placed the small stepping stool on the passenger platform. "Watch your step Ma'am," as the friendly, glistening black face extended a hand to the first woman to step off the train. Frank then received help when the conductor pulled Frank's bag onto the platform and extended his hand to help Frank negotiate the steps with his cane.

Once on the platform, he looked to his right and saw numerous passengers debarking from another train door and greeters milling along the platform, but no familiar faces. He then looked left, and there was Ted running as fast as he could to his father. Frank took two steps past the conductor before Ted hit him with his embrace that jarred him off balance for an instant before he could return the strong, clinging hug. Frank couldn't talk. His throat had suddenly tightened, but no words were necessary. Unlike at Frank's departures, Ted didn't cry; this was a time of joy for the son and father. Mary and Will soon arrived, and the family was together again hugging and with kisses shared by children and parents. Mary wiped her eyes as she released her grip on her son's waist and Frank noticed a very pretty face beaming at him over Mary's right shoulder. The late afternoon sun shone brightly behind Lily's head giving her hair an aura of highlights that she was unaware of. Frank's first impression was of an angel, a very pretty angel, whose bright smile held his attention. As Mary stepped back the angel stepped forward and kissed his cheek. "Hi, I'm Lily."

"Lands sakes, Lily! I forgot you haven't met Frank," Mary sputtered recovering from her understandable oversight.

"Well, well," said Frank, "so you are Lily my epistolary friend. I guess we have to change that title now that we have met."

"Yes, we can drop the epistolary part. It's so good to finally meet you," she said.

"I feel the same way . . . Yes, I really feel the same way." Frank laughed.

After a moment of adulatory comments about how well Frank looked despite his wounds, how thin he was and his need to be fattened up, how much Teddy had grown and how deep his voice had suddenly become, the family walked into the depot. As they opened the door, they heard a scream coming from a woman standing with a group of people; several were crying. The Warrings and Lily stopped, taken aback by the sudden turn of mood. "Wonder if they had a death in the family," Mary posed the rhetorical question. "Maybe it was a soldier who didn't come home."

A man and woman passed, heading for the platform, and Lily and Frank overheard the man say, ". . . just dropped dead." Still stationary in the middle of the waiting room trying to comprehend the scene, Lily took several fast steps to overtake the couple and talked to them in hushed tones. She then turned, and with an ashen face said to the Warrings, "It was just announced that the president died."

"Oh," Mary cried, a mixed cry and muffled shriek, "oh no, not now. He's so close to the end, oh no."

It was as if everyone had taken a blow to their body as their arms instinctively reached out, and they were soon in a tight circle that included Lily. Ted said in a frightened voice, "What'll happen now? He's always been our president." Mary and Lily cried softly as Frank and Will's eyes remained dry.

No one could answer Ted right away, then Will cleared his throat and said, "Ah . . . I'm sure it seems like it to you, and I guess he's been in office since before you were born, but the country will be all right. This has happened before, and we will be OK." Will gave Ted an extra hug.

Mary calmed her voice, closed her eyes, and said in a prayerful tone, "Please watch over the president, dear God. He's a good man and did so much for our country. And continue to watch over our country; it's a good place to live and be from. Amen."

"Amen," came the echo for the other four.

"Oh," added Mary, "and comfort Eleanor and their sons in this time of sorrow. Amen"

Again the echoing "Amen."

As they stood in the midst of the waiting room a sudden electronic shriek pierced their ears from the depot's speaker system followed by a sound of blowing into a microphone, *"Your attention please . . . is this on? OK, Ladies and Gentlemen, ah . . . Ladies and Gen . . . is that better? . . . OK, Ladies and Gentlemen, we have been informed this afternoon in a release from the White House in Washington that at 3:35 PM the thirty-second president of the United States of America, Franklin Delano . . . Roos"*—a choking sound, then a deep breath—*Roosevelt . . . died in Warm Springs, Georgia, ahem, ahem . . . and the thirty-third president, Harry S. Truman, was given the oath of office by Supreme Court Justice Harlan Stone . . . in the cabinet room of the White House . . . No further details are available at this time. My God, what wi—"* A sharp click signified that the public address system had been switched off.

A few of those in the waiting room who had yet to hear of the nations' disaster gasped, and new crying and muffled screams could be heard. Frank saw in the far corner of the waiting room two Negro Red Caps sitting on a luggage truck openly weeping as a tall white man emerged from a door with the sign, Office, neatly lettered on the frosted glass window pane. The man saw the Red Caps and went to them and joined them sitting on the luggage truck as he bent his head and grieved with his fellow workers.

After a few minutes, the Warrings relaxed their arms as they heard still other cries of disbelief from those in the depot. A second group of depot employees by the ticket window were openly weeping as if their best friend had died. Many in the country would have the same reaction over the next twenty-four hours as word of the president's death spread.

"This has been a real shock on such a special day for us," said Will. "We gain a son and father back home with us and lose a president. We'll always remember this day. I had planned to suggest that we go up to the S&W for an early supper . . . But I don't know if we should do that now."

After a pause, "I have an idea," said Lily, swallowing, and then with a clear voice, "I have bought food for the dinner we were going to have in my new apartment tomorrow night. Frank, we hadn't told you about it yet, but if you don't mind a little change in plan, I can cook dinner tonight. The apartment is on Clinch at Eighteenth, only four blocks from your house."

"That sounds like a good idea," said Frank.

"I agree," said Mary sealing the plan.

Ted had carried Frank's duffel bag from the platform, and now with some degree of growing difficulty, he continued to carry it forward as Lily took hold of the handle from the opposite side and shared the load with him. "Let's go," said Will. So Frank, Ted, and Lily walked through the main depot door followed by Mary and Will as the family exited to Gay Street and the trolley to Highland Avenue.

# ACKNOWLEDGMENTS

IN 2009, TWO years after my retirement, I enrolled in a writing class at Vanderbilt University's Osher Lifelong Learning Institute. The non-credit class, designed for mature adults, was led by Victor Judge. Victor is assistant dean for academic affairs Vanderbilt University Divinity School and a lecturer in literature and religion. The typical class course in the Osher program runs for six weeks in one of the three semesters between October and May. The writing course in which I enrolled was from the outset scheduled for the fall, winter, and spring semesters, or eighteen weeks in total. The course description for the class caught my attention, "Lead the Writer's Life," or something to that affect. That coincided with my newfound interest in writing, and prior to the first class I wrote a long, fictional short story. That story was handed to Victor during the first or second class, and in the following class after receiving the text, Victor praised the effort and said it was the beginning of a "coming of age," novel. Somewhat taken aback, I accepted the challenge and decided to pursue the story to its conclusion. The short story read by Victor in October 2009 turned out to be Part One of the whole story that eventually acquired the title *Warring* that coincided with the last name of the family about who the book is written. So, to a large extent, Victor is responsible for this longer story. After completing the writing effort, I do not believe it turned out to be a coming-of-age story; rather, it describes the life of a family and nation facing and overcoming devastating losses suffered at the end of 1941.

During the nine-month writing effort that stretched across 2009 and 2010, I completed the initial draft, which Victor continued to praise. What followed then was an eighteen-month period where a number of literary classmates and fellow writers read the draft and provided a variety of reactions, mostly favorable, and each citing different parts of the story as exemplary. The early draft underwent considerable change, primarily from comments relating to punctuation. The key contributors at this early stage were my wife, Tish, a dedicated supporter of my efforts, and two classmates with a far better grasp of punctuation rules for the written word than I: Dolores Nicholson, a retired school teacher, and Anne Lane, a trained journalist. As the draft took on a more finished appearance, others read and contributed comments: Gil Campbell, Alan Graber, Barry Jones, Lee Koehn, Jean Penrod, Ann Walsh, and Carroll Young.

Two of the first-draft readers—one, an unpublished amateur like me, Dr. Richard Stein, and the other an established writer who earned a living at the trade, John Egerton—encouraged me to continue with my goal of publishing the story. An eyewitness to and participant in the war in France, Sergeant Frank Neiswender, offered keen insights into the life of the infantry soldier. Frank enlisted in the army in Wichita, Kansas, as an eighteen-year-old high-school graduate, and was assigned to the Seventh Army, which landed at Marseille on August 15, 1944 and fought its way north along the Meuse River corridor in time to join in repelling the German thrust in the Battle of the Bulge.

With the final decision made to publish the volume, Susan Wilson took on the essential task of copy editing, a mysterious task (from my perspective) of placing the text in the correct form and asking pointed questions about the flow of words that appeared on paper. Susan's efforts were of enormous help. The design of the book's cover, type, and layout were handled by Peter Honsberger of Cold River Studio. Peter's contribution made the draft into a book, another invaluable service.

Local knowledge of the Forks of Elkhorn community were enhanced by my brother Wayne Womack, and knowledge of life in Knoxville during the war years was uncovered by Seaton Kaderly Bradford, my first cousin. My family lived in the "Forks" community for about four years during the Second World War, and my grandmother had raised her seven daughters, including my mother, to maturity in the home at 1702 Highland Avenue in Knoxville.

Finally, I would be remiss if I did not acknowledge the contribution of two volumes that gave vivid historic descriptions of the Second World War in France: *Citizen Soldier* by Stephen E. Ambrose and *World War II*, by H. P. Willmott, Robin Cross, and Charles Messenger. These volumes traced the flow of battle across France and included descriptions of the movement of military units, weaponry, and the deadly cost in manpower of the battling armies. Additional sources of information were provided by an indeterminate number of searches of the Internet and Wikipedia for historical facts, plus aerial photographs of today's countryside and towns in the parts of France featured in the book.

# ABOUT THE AUTHOR

WITH A FORMAL EDUCATION in architecture and urban planning Ed Womack worked as an educator, public servant and consultant in community development and urban transportation projects across the nation. Significant community planning services —land use planning, urban redevelopment, and new land development—occurred in Louisville, Dallas-Fort Worth, Nashville and numerous smaller communities. Key transportation projects included assignments on urban mass transit systems in Miami, Houston, Detroit, Seattle, Orlando, Raleigh, Washington DC, and Atlanta.

The gift of time provided by retirement from a forty-two year career provided Ed the opportunity to engage in a second career in painting, creative writing and preparing a family history from an extensive archive of inherited records. Ed and his wife Tish of fifty one-years enjoy keeping abreast of their far-flung family from their Nashville home.

CPSIA information can be obtained at www.ICGtesting.com
Printed in the USA
LVOW082226080513

332406LV00004BB/19/P